THANK YOU,
GOODNIGHT

A NOVEL

ANDY ABRAMOWITZ

Touchstone
New York   London   Toronto   Sydney   New Delhi

TOUCHSTONE
An Imprint of Simon & Schuster, Inc.
1230 Avenue of the Americas
New York, NY 10020

First Touchstone hardcover edition June 2015

TOUCHSTONE and colophon are registered trademarks of Simon & Schuster, Inc.

For information about special discounts for bulk purchases, please contact Simon & Schuster Special Sales at 1-866-506-1949 or business@simonandschuster.com.

The Simon & Schuster Speakers Bureau can bring authors to your live event. For more information or to book an event contact the Simon & Schuster Speakers Bureau at 1-866-248-3049 or visit our website at www.simonspeakers.com.

Interior design by Jill Putorti

Manufactured in the United States of America

10 9 8 7 6 5 4 3 2 1

Library of Congress Cataloging-in-Publication Data
Abramowitz, Andy, author.
  Thank you, goodnight : a novel / Andy Abramowitz.—First Touchstone hardcover edition.
     pages cm
  "A Touchstone Book."
  Summary: "Nick Hornby meets *Almost Famous* in this side-splittingly funny coming-of-middle-age debut novel about the lead singer of a one-hit wonder 90s band who tries for one more swing at the fences"—Provided by publisher.
  1. Singers—Fiction. 2. Musicians—Fiction. 3. Humorous stories. I. Title.
  PS3601.B7313T43 2015
  813'.6—dc23
         2014041615

ISBN 978-1-4767-9177-7
ISBN 978-1-4767-9179-1 (ebook)

For Caryn

You can outdistance that which is running after you,
but not what is running inside you.

RWANDAN PROVERB

It's later than it seems.

JACKSON BROWNE

THANK YOU, GOODNIGHT

PART ONE

THE VIEW FROM
THE DISCOUNT RACK

CHAPTER 1

You don't need eight words to set someone's life on fire. One seems like more than enough. But in my case, it was eight.

The cryptic text pinged from Sara's phone onto mine just as I was taking to the sky. The flight attendants, annoyed at us before we'd even taken off, had just commanded us through harsh smiles to neuter our electronic devices. Concealing my phone beneath a vomit bag, I reread the message.

"Your legacy is hanging in the Tate Modern."

Instantly irritated, I fired back a pageant of question marks. Sara's timing meant eight hours of me staring out at the blackness of the North Atlantic, ruminating on this distracting message from my girlfriend instead of the work that awaited me in Dublin. I could never sleep on planes, certainly not while sharing an armrest with some decrepit bag of bones who was either dead or sleeping with one eye open, and now here was something else to keep me awake. When I landed, it would still be the middle of the night back in Philadelphia, which meant more hours of waiting to find out what Sara meant.

My legacy was hanging in the Tate Modern. Jesus fucking Christ.

In my previous line of work, a lifetime ago if not longer, I'd found Dublin to be hospitable, even welcoming of the happy ruckus that always accompanied me. Back then everyone welcomed me. Those were different times. Now I was almost completely someone else. Better rested perhaps, although the mirror in the airplane bathroom reflected otherwise—a miserable ghost, with bags of defeat hanging under my eyes. If I was any whiter I'd have been Mexican folk art.

The labyrinthine highways of life had somehow made a lawyer out of me. I'd never been particularly happy about it. To add insult to injury, for my latest assignment, I'd been dispatched to Ireland to take the deposition of some credit manager for a bank. I didn't know what that meant other than that over the course of one interminable day, I was to sit in a conference room, a videographer's microphone clipped to my bourgeois Brooks Brothers tie, and quiz some poor knucklehead about securitized financing transactions that neither he nor I had the vaguest interest in. This required preparation. What I needed to do upon landing was hunker down and immerse myself in loan agreements, guarantees, credit default swaps, a rotting forest of e-mails, and other documents of financial audacity, and then gin up several hours' worth of questions to hurl at this paper pusher who, as far as I could tell, had committed the unpardonable sin of doing his job.

But here's the thing: preparing for a deposition is about as exciting as my washer's rinse cycle. After about a half hour in my hotel room, I slid into a sweater and headed out.

A comfortable chill hung in the Dublin air, fresh and restorative, good weather to lose myself in the dense blocks of timeworn Georgian buildings. I joined the midday flow of bodies coursing through the streets. I ate a salmon sandwich on a bridge arching over the Liffey. I sipped rich, black coffee outside the shops on Grafton Street. I bought Sara a book on Celtic mosaics that, despite being colorful—brightly colored art always feels like it's trying to meet me halfway, kind of like poetry that rhymes—didn't move me in the slightest. I waited to call her at just past dawn her time, hoping to catch her en route to her morning workout. "So, about that text," I told her prerecorded voice. "Call me. The dep isn't till tomorrow."

I wandered into the maze of tourists bobbing and weaving through Temple Bar and found myself outside a lively little pub that beckoned me in with the sound of Irish music just beyond its rugged wooden door. Having always considered business to be an incidental component of a business trip, I barely paused before heading in.

The bartender raised his eyebrows solicitously, and I pointed to the Toucan Guinness tap. Soon I was savoring the dry stout, its creamy head on my upper lip, while a flute, guitar, and violin stirred the room into an accelerating whirl. A buxom young woman got up and began to bounce in place to the music. She was wearing pink jeans, a tight white button-down shirt, and a sloppy-drunk grin. The clapping and foot stomping spiked to a crescendo, and I overheard two frat boys with backpacks loudly admiring the buoyant girl's "cans."

A man down the bar was eyeing me. This still happened on occasion. He had unshorn hair urging toward dreadlocks and he sported those smoothly intellectual black-rimmed frames that sniffed of *Clapton Unplugged*. I was soon to learn he was a software salesman from Los Angeles. He peered at me for ten minutes—it was a little creepy—before coming over and telling me I looked familiar. He knew me from somewhere, he claimed, wagging his finger. I shrugged.

In declarative bursts over the music, he bitched about the rigors of business travel and whined about missing his kids. Yet when I coughed up the politeness to ask the ages of the aforementioned children, he was all stammers. He forgot how old his kids were. I didn't think you did that. That said, there was a better-than-average chance that my own father could only offer an educated guess as to his boys' ages. "Whoa, you kind of caught me off guard here," the software salesman admitted with an embarrassed grimace. I couldn't help but smile and feel a little bit like a happy man trapped in a bitter man's body.

One day I'll die, I thought to myself, and this will be one of the things I did with my time.

The Angeleno cocked his head. "Why is it you look so familiar? I know you from somewhere and I just can't place it." Since he'd found it difficult to place key statistics regarding his children, maybe remembering stuff just wasn't his bag. "Are you in show business or something?" Show business. Like I'm waving jazz hands in a revival of *Guys and Dolls*.

The next thing I knew the conversation had careened off into all sorts of directions. He told me I should plan a trip to Polynesia. Why Polynesia? Because Tia Carrere—you know, that babe from *Wayne's World*—is from Polynesia and that's what all the women look like there. I asked him if he was really saying that every girl in this fabled land called Polynesia—which I don't think is even a country—looks like Tia Carrere, and he gave me an ardent nod and said yeah, that's right, that's what I'm telling you. American men are considered exotic over there, he insisted, and those Tia Carrere look-alikes eat guys like us up. I told him I knew for a fact there's no place in the world where they eat guys like us up. He sipped at his Bible-black beer, wiped his mouth, and said, "Trust me."

A few moments later, as I stood absorbed in the wild soloing of a redheaded violinist, my new friend snapped and pointed at me. "Eight and ten!"

I stepped out of the bar three pints later. Shadows draped the narrow streets and the late-afternoon air had grown aggressively chilly. This day had been a poor excuse for a bender. The benders I used to have would eat this bender for breakfast.

I glanced at my phone and noticed I'd missed Sara's call.

It looked quieter by the river, so I drifted through the stone alleys to the relative seclusion of a bridge. She answered in her office voice, soft and clandestine. It was close quarters at Bristol & Bristol Interior Design, which meant everyone could hear everything, and it was primarily populated with women, which meant everyone was listening.

"What's with the text?" I asked, my voice raised against the breeze.

"Is that like, 'Hey, I miss you, how are you?'"

"It's just like that. What's with the text?"

"There's my Teddy," she said. "So, you want to laugh?" The question was rhetorical—who doesn't want to laugh?—and yet it's usually a prelude to something manifestly unfunny. "Warren called."

"Warren who?"

"Warren Warren."

My eyebrows furrowed. I hadn't heard from the man in years.

"And he said—get this—you need to go to the Tate Modern so you can see *your legacy*."

"He what?"

"He said you should go to the Tate Modern. In London."

"I know where the Tate Modern is. I'm not following you."

"His exact words were that your legacy is hanging in the Tate Modern, second floor. If you're interested in your legacy, there's an exhibit you absolutely must see."

"An art exhibit?"

"Seems like a sensible guess, it being an art museum and all."

As I stood there with rigid confusion, I had a vision of Warren, my drummer once upon a time. He was watching me receive this information and cackling like a fool, his neck snapping back, his mouth open as if to drink the rain.

"Sara," I said, trying to remain calm, "did you happen to ask him what the fuck he was talking about?"

"I'm just telling you what he said." I imagined her hunched forward with both elbows on her desk, one hand holding the phone to her ear, the other toying with strands of her long black hair.

"What kind of exhibit? And in fucking London? He wants me to go to London? Did you tell him I was in Dublin?"

"I told him nothing. It was a short conversation and I'm simply relaying it to you, as I promised I would." I heard a slurp. Presumably coffee, though Malbec couldn't be ruled out.

Clearly, some celestial eclipse had shifted and blanketed my memory. There had to be a recent incident, inaccessible to me now, that had caused our paths to cross, Warren and me. I was blocking it out for some reason, but something had happened that made Warren's message make sense. Something that, since I was jet-lagged and buzzed on Guinness, was slipping my mind.

"So let me get this straight. Warren Warren calls me out of the fucking blue and tells me I have to go to London. He doesn't know that I'm already in Europe, but he tells me I have to get to London, to the Tate Modern, to see some fucking exhibit on the—what?— second floor. I have to do this if I give a fuck about my legacy."

A short, gray-haired tour guide in a green vest led a cluster of families past me on the bridge. "And then the Vikings come and run amok," I overheard him say. *Roon amook* through his thick Irish brogue.

Over the cellular airwaves and across the cold miles, Sara shipped me one of her patented sighs. "Teddy, you do know that using the word *fuck* six times in a single sentence makes you sound like an unhappy person."

"Fuck," I said thoughtfully. I lifted my hand through my windblown, airplane-oily hair and noticed I needed a shower. "You're sure that's all he said?"

"Yes," she replied flatly. "It was a quick call, there was a lot of noise in the background. It sounded like he was in a crowd. Maybe a crowded museum. Maybe—oh, I don't know—a crowded museum in London."

I was standing on the bridge trying to process this acid trip of a phone call. One of the three of us—Sara, Warren, or me—had lost it. At least one.

"I don't get it either," Sara offered, "but the thing is, Warren isn't God and you're not Noah. You can ignore him. You actually have a knack for ignoring people."

I didn't see how that was possible. Something was slung up onto a wall in a gallery just across the Irish Sea, something so extraordinary that it prompted Warren to do something he hadn't done in over a decade: make contact with me. I hadn't spoken to anyone from that period in my life in years. In most instances, space between people grows like mold, neglected just long enough to be noticed. You intend to wipe it clean, but the more of it there is, the more daunting a task it becomes to erase it. Not so with me and the band. I'd discontinued those people as if they were a premium cable channel that I'd finally realized was broadcasting nothing I wanted to watch. With all there was between us, things my bandmates knew about and things they didn't, it was better to just turn off the lights and lock myself out of that haunted house.

"I'll just call the idiot. Do you have his number?"

"He didn't leave it. I probably should've asked."

"Caller ID?"

"Blocked."

The pints of dark beer pooled with sleep deprivation made for a woozy goulash, and yet there was no time to rest. Even the bare minimum preparation for tomorrow's deposition entailed a time investment.

"Fuck that guy. I don't have time for this bullshit."

Through all the clatter in my head, Sara's weary goodbye barely registered.

I used to love record stores. Back when it was all undiscovered country, there was always the chance I might stumble upon Van Halen's *1984* or the Cure's *Pornography* and for a month or two I'd walk around on fire. These days, record stores were jungles of mockery and bad memories, given who I used to be. And now, fate—because fate is a bully—couldn't resist depositing a record store directly in my path on my walk back to the hotel. Another time I might not have even taken note, but the return of Warren had me drifting uneasily into the past, bothering me with emotions I'd long thought dead and buried. I went in.

Bristling with disdain, I perused the racks of chartbusters near the door. This was the safe area, the place where the storefront neon showcased the music that the kids were buying, the prefab radio-ready pop acts fronted by slinky, nearly naked twenty-two-year-olds or boy bands with youths of indeterminate gender. None of these people had ever held an instrument.

Past the bunny slopes and into the belly of the beast I went, submitting to the store's thumping electronica. I flipped through the *T* discs in Rock/Pop. Nothing. I wended my way over to Alternative, a section which used to house dark, unapproachable artists whose fans had scary tattoos and genital piercings but whose edges had eroded over time such that the moniker had evolved into a catchall of sorts. Basically, if you're an artist that gives a fuck and you're not jazz or country, you're alternative. Again I scrolled through *T*. Again nothing.

I found the cheapies bin way back at the rear of the store, territory unlikely to have been trodden even by the store's employees. The discount selection was downright offensive. Beck's *Odelay?* The Foo Fighters' debut? Billy Joel's *Turnstiles?* Surely, these albums deserved a more dignified resting place. I wanted to speak to the manager.

And there it was. One copy. Pristine, sullied by neither fingerprint nor weight of an eye. I stared despairingly at it, noting how cheesy and dated the cover art looked. *The Queen Kills the King.* A brief swell of fond memories sparred with the raw indignity of the discount rack. I suffered a flash fantasy about crushing the thing under my heel.

Then I fled. I stormed out and stomped my way up Grafton, feeling myself sliding into that familiar chasm of obsession. This time, it was Warren's oblique communiqué that took center stage. I wanted to know what his message was all about, but more than that, I wanted to waterboard the motherfucker for forcing himself back into my consciousness.

Streams of Guinness were still sailing through my veins when the hotel elevator door parted and I marched down the hall, past the ornate sconces, past the portraits of humorless men with monocles, every one of them looking a little bit like the Count from *Sesame*

Street. I could track down Warren's number and call him now, but I knew that would just be an even greater time suck. I needed to let this go for the time being, to calm myself, to put first things first. Work tomorrow, waterboard the day after.

And yet, in my sleekly decorated room, all burgundies and beiges, the smell of recently vacuumed carpet in the air, I neglected the manila folders and redwells that Metcalf, my sweaty associate, had dutifully prepared for me. Instead, I googled "Tate Modern." With the deep, dull haze that comes from thirty-six consecutive sleepless hours, I surfed the museum's web page, darting in and out of the links to permanent collections and featured exhibits. The hours vanished and brought me no closer to a clue.

If only he hadn't used that word.

Legacy.

I wondered how long that CD had been tucked away back there in the darkest corner of the record store. That's what they do with music nobody cares about anymore. They can't just throw it away—that would be bad for the environment or something. So it just sits there, fading further into irrelevance with every passing moment. Just like the lead singers of those bands. Guys like me. Guys who once had it all, but now have what everybody else has. Nothing.

The night stretched on. Sleep remained elusive, as though I were still crammed into the middle seat on that 777. It was with almost desperate relief that I finally watched the sun tickle the windows of my room.

I'd have to wing the deposition.

Probably would've done that anyway.

Some lawyers will say that, unlike being shelved in an office all day, staring at a computer screen and feeling your ass widen, depositions are "where the action is." This is only true if your idea of action is eight hours of watching ice melt in a water glass. The bank dweeb took an oath to tell the truth, but it was the most dry, monotonous truth you could imagine. His lawyer, an irritating little goober in his own right, sat next to him and did little more than look smug.

I was also never one for protocol, and what scant decorum I have tends to spoil in the oppressive pit of boredom.

"I'm handing you an exhibit—" I began, passing around a document I'd barely reviewed, when I noticed a short, squiggly hair dangling over the top page. "I'm handing you an exhibit that appears to have a pube on it."

Gags of horrified laughter filled the room. I blew a short breath at the hair. It sailed off in the direction of the witness, who gasped and shifted out of the way.

"Objection," said his lawyer.

That kind of thing might get someone else complained about or fired, but people at my shop tended to cut me a little slack, given who I am. Or who I was.

When my work with the witness was done, I handed him off to another lawyer with her own battery of questions. I could now sit back, zone out, mentally leave the building. I could scarf down twenty sugar cookies and fifteen cups of coffee.

I perused the *Irish Times*. There was a story about a member of the British Parliament charged with groping a young woman. A photo depicted him on the courthouse steps hand in hand with a sturdy, matronly lady. "Throughout all of this," the disgraced politician was quoted as saying, "my wife has been an absolute brick." What every woman yearns to be called.

The witness droned on about credit default swaps. I read the sticker on my banana.

He sermonized about political risk insurance. I tried to fantasize about the hottest person in the room. It was me. By a mile.

My thoughts kept returning to Warren's message like a tongue to a mouth ulcer. There was a time when I was accustomed to his good-natured shenanigans. This was, after all, a guy who used to amuse himself by pretending he was his own identical twin. But last I heard, he was now a teacher, a legitimate member of the community. If inciting me to drop everything and rush to an art exhibit on another continent was his idea of a practical joke after a decade of radio silence, it seemed out of proportion. Was he kidding? Was he drunk? Was he sending a coded message from a hostage situation?

I decided I'd try to call him at the end of the day, even though I suspected he would be disinclined to divulge details. He didn't seem to want to tell me about the Tate; he just wanted me to go there. And if he found out that I was actually in Dublin, a temptingly short trip from London, he'd be even less forthcoming. What a hilarious little caper he'd constructed.

The fact was, I could go. My firm was hardly holding its breath for the return of its favorite malcontent. Morris & Roberts would be there for me whenever I got back, with its bloated files and its nimrods down the hall, like Don Yoshida and his riveting tales of his dog's escapades.

Sara too would survive a few extra nights on her own. She'd trudge into the condo, splash some Spanish wine into a glass, and concoct an unnecessarily elaborate dinner. Langostinos in a red sauce, or a chickpea curry with spinach. Afterward, she'd drape herself in a T-shirt three sizes too large and sink into the couch for the guilty displeasure of reality TV—the selection of a wedding dress by someone too ugly to get married, the perusal of a new house by a couple who'd only end up divorcing and fighting over it. She'd eventually lose interest, her eyes would drift down to the book in her lap, and she'd fade into worlds puppeteered by Jhumpa Lahiri or Meg Wolitzer. She'd get through a dozen or so pages before passing out, waking up an hour later, and shuffling into the bedroom. If I were there with her, the scene would unfold almost exactly the same, except my legs might be crisscrossed with hers on the sofa or she'd talk me into a few rounds of Boggle or her sister in Sacramento would call and Sara would wave frantically at me while mouthing *I'm in the shower, I'm in the shower.*

Sara might actually applaud my absconding to London under the circumstances. For her, any day spent in the company of paintings, etchings, sculptures, or mundanely arranged soup cans was a good one. She bought in to the whole art racket with an uncharacteristic lack of cynicism. At how many galleries and museums had I watched her standing there, nodding in accord with the voice in the headset, her long, wispy limbs ideally suited for poses of artistic engagement?

Sara was more than an interested spectator in that word; she was something of a covert art hobbyist herself. For years now, she'd been scurrying up to her friend Josie's studio in Northern Liberties to let the hours float by in the service of her medium of choice: mosaic mirrors. This studio was a place where she and other mosaicists, both professional and aspiring, would—and this is just an outsider's perspective here—basically break shit up into little pieces and arrange them in weird patterns. Josie's commune was inhabited by a pack of breezy yet intimidating women who sipped wine, spoke caustically about everything, and set out to push the boundaries of expression. (If they failed at that, they at least succeeded at pushing the boundaries of fashion.) They accepted Sara as one of their own even though she's not gay, has the gumption to let her hair grow beyond her ears, and has a job that doesn't begin with the word *freelance*. But they took her in, Sara, their stray cat.

I, by loud contrast, had spent a lifetime nurturing a deep suspicion of art as an enterprise. An odd trait for a musician, I admit. I accompanied Sara to all the latest openings, but once there, I had a tendency to retch over the pontification about an artist's ability to transform the ordin'ry into the exquisite. Notice the eyelash. There's something slightly audacious, scandalous perhaps, about the way in which the paint is applied. In that one simple brushstroke, Akerblom subverts everything we know about contemporary portraiture. While Sara pursed her lips at a canvas smothered corner to corner in bronze paint and curiously titled *Three Trees*, I stared mistrustfully at it and thought to myself, I don't see trees, I don't feel trees, nothing about this painting is bringing a tree to my senses, much less three of them.

The point was this: I could go to London if I wanted. If I was stupidly obsessed, or let's say I just wanted to sleep again, I could scoot on over and settle this. And who wouldn't want to lay eyes on his legacy? Even when you knew your legacy had all the esteem of a cornflake smudge.

"I have nothing further," I heard the questioner say. He hunched over the table and peered all the way down to where I was sitting—in person, if not in spirit. "Mr. Tremble, do you rest?"

"Hardly." I snickered.

With a yawn, I stood and embraced the end of what I could've sworn was an endless day. But I'd used this period of immobility and repeated caffeination to its fullest meditative potential. All factors pointed in one direction. That direction was east.

CHAPTER 2

A cluster of young guys behind me at the Heathrow customs line were speaking, through wide Boston accents and with macho rowdiness, about the bachelor party they had flown in for. It suddenly struck me that every bachelor party I'd ever been to had been a disappointment. Warren's, for example, was both lame and disastrous. Which was precisely what we should've expected, seeing as how it had been masterminded by Jumbo Jett, our train wreck of a guitar player who himself was both lame and disastrous. He had a penchant for debauchery that made Keith Moon look like a *Downton Abbey* dandy, yet he was somehow a total drag. We'd been home for a stretch after the second record was completed, holed up with our jitters, awaiting the release of the album and the launch of the tour. A tour we had no business headlining. A tour I'd insisted upon against my better judgment and that of everyone within shouting distance of me. A tour I'd steered us toward pigheadedly out of ego, jealousy, and other unbecoming emotions. Somehow it had fallen to Jumbo to plan Warren's send-off into monogamy, even though Warren couldn't stand the sight of the guy. Jumbo may have had a hyperdeveloped instinct for partying, but he had no instinct whatsoever for organization. Hence, his elaborate plan consisted of tooling around our home base of Philadelphia all day and eventually staggering into some gentlemen's clubs. Not exactly the decadence and excess befitting a bunch of musicians in their twenties.

But with Jumbo at the helm, we could've easily ended up in a roadside motel with an emaciated hooker. So it went in the win column.

After navigating the maze of antiseptic airport corridors, collecting my bags at the luggage carousel, and hailing a cab, I was soon checking into the boutique hotel just off the Strand that Kathleen, my secretary, had booked last minute. The cold water I splashed on my face wasn't so much revitalizing as it was simply cold. Then I headed straight for the Tate Modern, ready as I'd ever be to confront my legacy.

Amid the swirling foot traffic at the museum entrance, I paused for a breath. There was a seemingly homeless Rastafarian on a vibraphone. I think he was banging out "9 to 5" by Dolly Parton.

Inside, the atmosphere was art-school vibrant and airplane-hangar reverberant. Swiping a floor map from the visitors' desk, I moved among the meandering appreciators, all the while fighting off a swell of anxiety. I wasn't so sure I wanted to see whatever it was Warren wanted me to see. On the escalator up to the second floor, I felt that adrenaline-fueled thump, a schizophrenic cross between This better be worth it and God, I hope it's a letdown.

The escalator deposited me in an open room with high ceilings, white walls, and artwork of varying species blooming in every direction. With a pit in my stomach, I started combing through the halls, detouring into the various chambers situated off the main room, a keen eye toward anything that could possibly shed light on what the hell I was doing there.

By the time I'd completed one revolution around the floor, anxiousness had given way to frustration. What if my legacy was gone, carted off to another gallery? What if I was looking right at it but just didn't get it? It occurred to me that I might very well walk out of there empty-handed. It also occurred to me that that might be the best possible scenario.

Then I noticed one wall at the end of the main room that I hadn't yet examined. I walked toward it and came upon a photography exhibit, pictures of seemingly random people printed on large canvases. They were candids of distantly familiar faces. The first shot was of a New York Yankee from the seventies or eighties—an outfielder, if memory served. He was aging and whalelike, besieged by pockmarks, lugging his big old self down a busy Manhattan avenue in a rumpled suit. The way he glared at the camera, Charles Manson daggers in his eyes, suggested that life after baseball had not been kind, albeit flush with hot dogs. I grunted in satisfaction; fuck the Yankees.

The next photo depicted a postcute woman in her midtwenties standing at a bus stop, an army-green duffel bag slung over her shoulder. She was wincing from the weight of the luggage and peering down the quiet road, impatient for the bus. Her features seemed awfully worn for someone in the flower of youth, and her hair seemed to be in a protracted estrangement from water and shampoo. I'd seen this woman before. She was the daughter of a right-wing senator who'd been excommunicated from the party upon revelations that he enjoyed parading around the house in his wife's lingerie. Either that or she was the former starlet who tipped one White Russian too many with Lindsay Lohan and ended up the target of a restraining order by that guy from *That '70s Show*. I hadn't thought about her in years, and the look in her eye suggested she knew it all too well.

The third photo was even sadder, a woman enshrouded in a raincoat on a rainless day, flanked by cops on a street corner. A high-end boutique clothing store stood in the background, and the way the officers loomed over the poor woman made the story all too clear. Thief! Her eyes were downcast to the concrete and her hands were stuffed dolefully in her jacket pockets, the very picture of humiliation. Although the hood of her raincoat snugly enveloped her head, one could still make out the woman who, fifteen or so years ago, had been the unflappable matriarch of a sitcom family, dishing out good-natured one-liners at her husband and children while carrying a basket of laundry. This actress-cum-shoplifter, like the bloated Yankee and disgraced starlet before her, had clearly seen better days.

Speaking of which: the next picture was of me.

It was a doozy. I was in a Mexican-themed cantina, the sort of place where the ceiling fans drone high overhead, the menus are laminated, and the heavily cheesed burritos stay with you for days. The photographer had snapped me unawares as I sat alone at the bar with a plate of mango salsa nachos and a mojito. At the precise moment that the shutter winked in my direction, I'd clumsily scooped an unbalanced heap of salsa onto a chip and the whole thing had fallen apart, leaving a bloodstain of sauce trailing down my shirt and a hailstorm of chopped onions, chicken squares, and jalapeños heading south for my lap. My chin was thrust forward buffoonishly and my lips were agape, a last-ditch attempt to steer the chip into my mouth before it lost its cargo. As a bonus, an unsightly sliver of cilantro was lodged between my two front teeth. You could see it perfectly.

Nobody in the history of our species had ever looked more foolish.

There was more. The title of the photo was printed on a little white card next to the canvas. Riffing cleverly on my band's number-one hit song, "It Feels like a Lie," the picture was called *It Feels like a Lie . . . and It Looks like a Mess*, which I guessed would seem funnier later. The photographer was someone named Heinz-Peter Zoot from someplace called Unterseen. Both sounded made-up.

This was my legacy. This was what the world now thought of the lead singer of Tremble, one of the most popular bands in the world a short decade ago. When they thought of him at all.

I struggled to suppress the stream of profanities boiling upward in my throat, and I came dangerously close to spending the night in a British jail for attacking a defenseless photography exhibit.

One final poster cemented my disgrace. It spelled out the title of this collection in bold black letters:

FADED GLORY:

WHERE DO THEY GO WHEN THEY HAVE NOWHERE TO GO?

A mug shot of the artist was conveniently located underneath, just in case the viewer was moved to spit, deface, or otherwise trash what he or she was looking at. This Heinz-Peter Zoot was a burly, shaven-headed, toothsome son of a bitch, some breed of carnival barbell slinger looking merrily proud in a white muscle shirt—fucker got all dressed up for his photo. I studied the features of this meathead, a man soon to die by my hand. To my immense horror, it dawned on me that I knew him.

I marched back to the picture of me and the nachos. Yes, goddamnit! I knew him! The memory of the encounter came roaring back. The cantina was in Amsterdam, where I'd traveled two years ago on firm business. All I'd wanted that night was a quiet dinner, but I kept noticing some jerk staring at me. I probably said something polite, like "Do you fucking mind?" and he apologized in heavily accented English—English dunked brusquely in the milk of Somewhere Else. Then he said he recognized me the moment he walked in and couldn't believe his luck. He was a big fan. I must've been in a good mood, because instead of swiveling my chair in the opposite direction, I invited him to pull up a stool. Which he did, and then proceeded to regale me with the extent of his fandom. He sang the praises not only of our first record, but also of our follow-up album—which exactly nobody owns—and even claimed to still listen to our music on a regular basis. I didn't dislike him. I bought the moron a drink. I smiled for his camera. I raised a Corona with him as another patron took our picture together. I was downright affable, and usually I am downright not.

And where did all that accessibility land me? In one of the world's most famous galleries, looking like the King of the Schlubs. In case the world was wondering where that loser from that nineties band was hanging out these days, he was sitting alone in a cheap Mexican tourist trap, a big fat salsa stain on his shirt and something gross in his teeth.

I glared at the act of betrayal hanging on the wall and plotted a riotous squall of violence. "I'm going to fucking kill him," I seethed.

A sudden flash of light burst onto the canvas. At first I thought the photo had somehow come alive. Then I turned my head. The flash went off again, this time searing into my eyeballs. Someone was now taking pictures of me, right there in the Tate. When I regained the use of my retinas, I saw the culprit. He looked like a rat. "Ha! It *is* him!" he crowed. Today was this scrawny little punk's lucky day. He'd watched the subject of a photo witnessing himself in that photo, and thought, Well golly, that itself should be a photo. How meta. How *Being John Malkovich*. There's something slightly audacious, scandalous perhaps, about the way in which the miserable slob observes himself being portrayed as a miserable slob.

I bared my teeth at the kid, but was somehow only able to point to the sign in the doorway. "No photos! Can't you fucking read?"

He hooted and darted off in a blaze of raw denim, leaving me to worry about which gallery *that* picture would end up in.

My exit from the music world was not graceful. We called the second record *Atomic Somersault*, but a more apt title would've been *Atomic Belly Flop*. No hit single, undetectable levels of airplay, and an unacceptably low draw on tour, all culminating in the inevitable blow of being dropped by our label. My agent, the otherwise indefatigable Alaina Farber, conveyed that particular news item at her chic New York office, rare vapors of surrender in her voice. Clad in a tight, hypnotically pink pantsuit—the color of teenage rebellion hair—she rocked back in her desk chair with a leg up on the table. While squeezing one of those hand grippers that make your forearms look like a relief map of Mexico—Who's the go-to person for opening jars now!—she informed me that she'd gotten a call from the record company.

"Game over, cupcake," she said. "Tremble is being released."

I'd seen it coming, but still it stung. "What are our options?"

"Well," she sighed. I'd never seen her sigh before. "We could always see if there's interest from an indie, something smaller but still with decent distribution. It's worked for other bands."

These suggestions were infused with exactly zero enthusiasm. Alaina had other clients, ones that actually sold records, ones whose concerts were a gathering of people, not empty seats, ones who could support her expensive perfume habit.

Lifting herself out of her leather chair, she strutted around the mahogany desk and leaned her slim figure against it. "Maybe now's the time to downsize, go small and less commercial. Free yourself of public expectations."

"I think the public expected us to make good music. Maybe we didn't do that on this record." My eyes remained downcast on Alaina's stiletto heels, which at that moment struck me as the ideal implement for puncturing a balloon. Or someone's dreams.

"Buck up, sugar packet." She playfully tousled my hair. "You hit the jackpot with that stupid song of yours. It's going to bankroll your kids' rehab stints. You'll be collecting royalty checks until you're wearing Depends."

I let out a weary breath and proceeded to look abused and dejected, mistreated by the industry and misunderstood by the vox populi. I didn't think *Atomic Somersault* was a bad album, just one that, as it turned out, had limited appeal. That wasn't really my fault, but record companies weren't concerned with the assignment of blame. A sense of accountability only came with the burden of a conscience.

"Listen, you know I'm not the kind of girl who says I told you so, but headlining a tour by yourselves instead of going on the road with the Junction? Head-scratcher, man. You shocked us all with that display of self-admiration. I say this with love, Teddy, but you were a dumbass of the highest order to turn down a tour with those guys. No one's saying they're not despicable human beings, but because they sell out everywhere they go without even trying, we overlook the occasional lapse in moral judgment. Six months of packed stadiums opening for the Junction would've set you guys on fire again. But no. You had to go it alone. Because you're Teddy Tremble and special and you had one hit like two years ago—an eternity in this business—and a new album that nobody cared about. You kind of fucked the dog. You fucked it hard."

"All of this you're saying with love."

"I'm just saying it was a missed opportunity, and I never really understood why."

I contemplated the carpet.

Two of her fingers, delicate as satin gloves, lifted my chin. "You're sulking, Theodore. You do know there's a fine line between tragic cowboy and wallowing drip."

"This is my life we're talking about. I don't get five minutes of self-pity?"

"Self-pity is a gateway drug. Look, we'll get a suite at the Paramount, we'll shoot back Jameson from the minibar. There's an awful lot I can help you forget."

The fact that Alaina's body couldn't distract me from my crumbling life only underscored how unfit I was for this industry. Besides, her stab at seduction was no more than the playing out of a familiar dynamic. She'd made a sport of offering herself to me, and I'd made a rule of declining. I'd already, on one occasion, mixed business with pleasure. It happened only once, it involved my wife, and nothing had been the same for me since.

Alaina shook her head with mock wonder at my mute rejection. "Do you seriously not see what a perfect crime we Asian Jews are?"

"Take care, Alaina," I said, and headed home to Philly.

I devoted the next several weeks to cultivating a full-bodied gloom. While my bandmates took the news in stride and moved on with their lives like adults, I sat on the edge of my bed at two thirty in the afternoon trying to visualize how I was going to make it through the dreariness of the next half century.

Then one day, my wallowing was interrupted by a call from my father.

"Ted, let's meet for dinner tonight," he said, more summons than proposal.

Lazing on my sofa with *A Fish Called Wanda* on pause, I sighed with great majesty. "I don't know, Dad. Tonight's not good."

"Come on. Get off your duff and meet your old man."

My duff and I had become quite close during those mopey days, and my father wasn't exactly the guy to coax me off it. "How about next week?" I said. "Let's shoot for next week."

"I'm in Charleston next week. Tonight. I'll make a seven o'clock reservation at Raymond's."

Raymond's was the stodgy steak place directly across from my father's law office that served as his personal dining room at least two lunches and one dinner per week. My dad was of that ilk, the ilk that went to steakhouses for lunch. A veggie burger was fine so long as you were wearing pantyhose.

I sat up. "Fine. I'll meet you. But I really don't want any shit, Dad. I'm not kidding."

"You're a gentleman and a scholar. See you at seven."

Whatever the fuck that meant.

Dad never hauled me in for a meal without an agenda, so I had to face the fact that I'd just booked myself an evening of unsolicited advice. This was a dinner meeting, and like all dinner meetings, it would be stiff and laborious, like the tough T-bone I would order.

Five o'clock found me slogging through town, a trucker's cap with the Harley-Davidson logo pulled tight over my eyes, intent on drowning my dread with a couple of predinner cocktails.

At the empty end of a bar, *SportsCenter* hanging overhead, I stared into my bourbon. Getting booted from my record label was a walk among the roses compared to dinner with Lou Tremble. The man had always dispensed wisdom like a pitching machine—hard, constant, sporadically accurate—wearing you down with dense sacks of bullshit packed into long stretches of uninterrupted speech until you surrendered. Surrender was good, because at least then you could get up and walk the hell away. The problem, of course, was that he wasn't all bad or all wrong, so you couldn't dismiss him outright. Yet as auteur of some ignoble deeds of his own, he left you with nagging doubts as to his credibility. He tried to instill in his two boys a strong conscience and a hardscrabble work ethic, and yet I always wondered how his practice of accepting blow jobs from perky little paralegals fit into that creed. Such behavior won't get you disbarred, but it turns out it can get you dismarried. Whatever. I'm not the first guy to be chewed up by the stunning humanity of a parent.

With ice cubes shrinking in my glass, I recalled the night I learned just what it was that made my old man tick. There was my mother, rinsing dinner plates and glasses, arranging them with tactical precision in the dishwasher. There was me, loitering at the table with my social studies textbook, learning about how Sam Adams incited a flock of bewigged colonists to dress up as Mohawks and spill some English tea in the name of the very freedom that my classmates and I so ungraciously took for granted. And there was my father, pacing about the kitchen with a phone to his ear, shouting at some underling about an important document that had to be sent out that night and had to be flawless. Swinging the coils of the phone cord like a jump rope while the remains of his fruit cocktail sat in a puddle of syrup, Dad barked at the young lawyer as if raising his voice would actually improve the quality of the work. (I have since learned that it sometimes does.) His dander was up particularly high that evening and he was firing off commands and insults at his dimwitted associate, half covering the receiver from time to time to share with the family just how dimwitted this guy was. *Can you believe this guy?*

Then, suddenly, midsentence, like a power outage silencing a stereo, he stopped yelling. My mother and I looked over at him with a mix of relief and concern. Had he suffered a stroke? Had the coagulated syrup from the fruit cocktail triggered a diabetic coma? He just stood there, holding the phone away from his face, marveling at the receiver.

Eventually, with a dumbfounded chuckle and a terrifying eye-of-the-hurricane calm, he said, "That kid just told me to fuck off."

I braced for a demonic bay of rage so mighty that it would echo over the Great Wall of China. Instead, he hung up the phone, sat down, and looked at me.

"That kid just told me to fuck off," he repeated. "Now, don't misunderstand. The little turd was way out of line and he's going to live to regret it. But there's a lesson here, Ted. What he did was healthy. A lot of times the world is going to crowd you. It's going to get in your face." He illustrated the point by leaning his mug right up to mine. "And there are two types of people out there. There are people who take mounds and mounds of shit and don't know how to stop the shit from piling up, and they just get buried deeper and deeper. And then there are people who, every so often, when it's absolutely necessary and called for, tell everyone to fuck off. Those people—mark my words—are happier."

Let's just say, I learned the hell out of that lesson. I tell an awful lot of people to fuck off, and the old bastard was right—it usually feels pretty good. I expected to need the full extension of that skill that night at dinner, so in what was fast developing into a pub crawl, I drained my bourbon, left the bar, and proceeded to shuffle down to Raymond's. Where I took a seat at the cougar-ravaged bar and sipped more bourbon.

When Dad blew into the restaurant, his tie strewn over his shoulder, I was already sporting a comfortable buzz. The host, whom my father greeted by name, showed us to Dad's special table, handed us menus, and said, with a rather excessive dash of corniness, how nice it was to have both Mr. Trembles here tonight. Dad thanked him; I ordered another bourbon.

"I read your review in *Rolling Stone*," he began.

"It's not my review. I didn't write it," I said through a bitter laugh. "And since when do you read *Rolling Stone*?"

"A kid at the office handed it to me. Sounds like they weren't all that enamored with the new album." He was grinning like we had one of those relationships where we could say anything we wanted to each other, no hard feelings. We didn't have one of those relationships. But since the review declared the album "equal parts catnap and faked orgasm," my dad's characterization was not altogether unfair.

"I don't read reviews," I lied. "But if I did, I certainly wouldn't read *Rolling Stone*."

Funny how my old man never invited me to dinner when the critics genuflected in praise.

Dad ordered a porterhouse, I a Delmonico, and then he tilted his head as might the diplomat of a first-world nation when preparing to educate his third-world counterpart. "Can I give you some free advice?"

"Why do I feel as though I'll somehow end up paying for it?"

"I promise it won't cost you anything."

"Let's just see what it's worth."

With a smile freighted with empathy, he said, "Ted, son, I think it's over."

I slurped loudly.

"I don't like seeing you like this."

"Like how?"

"Unhappy. It's a tough business, this music industry. You had a tremendous amount of success, you traveled the globe, you won a goddamn Oscar! Now go do something else, kiddo."

"Something else," I grunted. I wanted to go do something else right now.

"With your head held high," he added. "Look, you came, you saw, and you conquered, but let's be honest, your fifteen minutes are probably up. And let's be even more honest, none of you guys are heartthrob material. I don't mean to be harsh here, Ted. You've got a lot to be proud of. Lord knows I'm proud of you."

"Oh, well, that means a lot."

He paused and frowned. "Why do you always do this? Why do you always butt heads with me?"

"Why do I always butt heads with you when you tell me I suck at my job and I'm ugly?"

He held out his open hands, wrists up like a surrendering felon. "I'm just being your father here."

"That you are, Louis. That you are."

"I just want what's best for you. You know that."

I laughed too loud, took an ungainly sip of my drink, and had to wipe my chin with my sleeve. The whole maneuver struck me as very alcoholic. Not alcoholic like the half-naked bum swaying deliriously outside the liquor store, but like the tragic drunk, expensively falling apart while his family stages an intervention. "Just for fun, what, Dad, in your view, is best for me?"

"Something more stable," he replied. "Less time in hotels. You're a smart guy. You should see that this part of your life is over and now you have the luxury of doing something different, something with a better lifestyle. Look at Denny. He's a fine example."

Denny is my younger brother. (Real name Denny, not Dennis, an oddity my parents have never sufficiently explained.) He's smarter than I am, showy about it too. We never did much together, the five-year age wedge causing us to shift through childhood on only sporadically touching tectonic plates. The one thing I really ever did with him was take the mouthy little tyke to IHOP on weekends to split a pile of pancakes. To highlight an older brother's generosity, I'd point out that I'd given him the bigger half of the stack. To highlight his superior intelligence, he'd point out that there's no such thing as a bigger half, halves being defined as two equal parts. To highlight my irritation, I'd fork a couple of pancakes off his plate and back onto mine and tell him it looked like I had the bigger half now. Other than those IHOP trips, I have exactly one memory of him from childhood: at age seven, he caught our dad red-handed looting his Halloween candy and yelled, "You son of a bitch!" It took the old man ten minutes to catch his breath from laughter before scampering up the stairs after him with a rolled-up *Atlantic Monthly*.

These days I barely know the guy. I see him once a year at my father's office Christmas party. The two of us stand in the corner eating Swedish meatballs and ask each other if it's too early to split. Denny's business card reads Professor of English Literature at Ohio State University, but as far as I can tell, his job seems to be sitting in his office and downloading Grateful Dead bootlegs and/or napping. Despite the fact that he's a middling professor of who cares and I'm an Academy Award winner, my nerd younger brother manages to speak to me with this air of superiority on the rare occasions when our paths cross. It forces me to remind him that for an unacceptably lengthy period, his favorite band was Tears for Fears. That tends to shut him up.

"I'm not comparing you to your brother," my dad went on, having just unfavorably compared me to my brother, "but wouldn't it be nice to have a job that doesn't require you to wake up every day and pray that the magical forces that have made you successful don't capriciously vanish? You can get around to having a family. Listen, I'm not laying blame here, son, but wasn't it this crazy musician's life that caused things to go south between you and Lucy?"

"Uh, is this the part where I point out that you're no longer married to my mother?"

Dad consulted his place setting. "Mistakes were made. No one's denying that."

"A mistake? Like wearing socks with sandals? Showing up at the barber on Tuesday for a Wednesday appointment?"

"I don't blame your mother for leaving and I don't blame all of you for resenting me on some level. Lord knows I'm in no place to judge anyone else's relationship and I'm sure as hell not judging yours. Nevertheless, we are all adults and we should all learn to move on."

Suddenly, there it was, all coming into sharp focus. I was the musician whose marriage was undone by a wacky, unbound lifestyle. He was the high-powered lawyer whose marriage was undone by pathetic dalliances with women too young even for his sons to date.

"You know what, Dad? We're both clichés. We might as well drink to it."

A thick silence hung over our table, the kind of mutual discomfort you can only share with a parent. Eventually, the waiter brought our steaks. My dad thanked him; I ordered another bourbon.

Maybe he was right. Maybe after years in the music industry, the only place I was qualified to work was Moe's Copy Service or the Yankee Doodle Diner out on 611.

"Look, I didn't ask you to dinner to argue with you," he lied. "I came here with a suggestion." I pretended to concentrate on carving off a wedge of steak. I guess we hadn't gotten around to his free advice yet. "Want to hear it?"

"I'm not sure why you're bothering to ask."

"Law school." He said it with an air of majesty, as if revealing the answer to an astrophysical algorithm that had confounded all the world's best minds—Copernicus! Einstein! Hawking!—but him.

I dropped my fork and knife.

"Think about it," he continued. "You're a smart kid, you're well-spoken, you've got a creative eye, and you're argumentative as hell." He chuckled. That was how lawyers complimented each other. With insults.

"You're serious," I said.

"Of course I'm serious."

"Dad, every lawyer I've ever met is a complete ass." I looked at him. "No exceptions."

"All I'm saying is, it's a great way to support yourself, you'd be quite good at it, and obviously, you've already got inroads in the legal community. Look, Ted, if I had to reduce my little spiel tonight to one word—"

"And I really wish you would."

"—it would be *security*."

I resumed cutting the dead beast on my plate, this time with venom. "I promise to give it the consideration it deserves."

That night, as the meat sweats kept me awake and uncomfortable in my bed, I ruminated. I didn't completely dismiss the idea of law school, even if it had come from my father's mouth. It sat in the back of my mind like a safety date while I tried my best to come up with something better.

Crickets.

I decided to give music one last try. I devoted the next six months to writing and recording a solo album. I'd rock the cynics, rise above the legions of doubters. This would be my masterwork—intimate and personal, a gorgeous departure from anything the world had yet heard from me. Teddy Tremble's beautiful soul on display. That kind of thing.

I pursued inspiration all the way across the country. And inspiration, I decided, lay in a cabin on the Oregon coast that I rented for purposes of staring meaningfully at the sea, feeling the salty breeze tangle my hair, and eating fresh salmon. After a lot of introspection, it finally dawned on me that what the world needed was a concept album about a soldier's emotional journey as he walked from the bus station to his house upon returning from war. I didn't even pick a war. It was to be a serious and somber affair. The production would be almost entirely acoustic and I'd play all the instruments. I would call the album *st. agathe under low clouds*, which had no connection to the material, and it would be written just like that, poetically forsaking capital letters in a way sure to make e. e. cummings claw away at his coffin.

Away I composed in that A-frame cabin of knotty pine. Once birthed, I christened the songs with achingly enchanting titles like "Does Your House Have Seasons?" "A Milliner's Lament," and "He Asked Whose Sheep They Were and I Said I Watched Them for Lord Wren." Oh, how the critics would pant!

When it was complete, I decided I was too close to the project to render a fair critique. I needed someone else's ears. Ears I trusted. So I stalked Sonny Rivers, the legendary producer behind the two Tremble records, at his LA studio. He wasn't ecstatic to see me. I watched nervously as he listened, elegantly consuming cigarettes on his swivel chair for the full fifty-three minutes. When it was over, he said this:

"No, no, no. No. This is not you. I don't know who this jack-off is, but it is not you. The fact of the matter is, this shouldn't be anybody."

"All right. Okay. So you don't like it."

"No, man, I don't."

"You know, I recorded it in only four days."

"It sounds like it."

"Understood. Any ideas how to make it better?"

"Toss it. All of it. Start from scratch. Did I hear you sing something about the dogs of enlightenment running through the meadow of your mind?"

"You might have."

"That's a shame." He took an unhappy drag. "And shit—'She questioned my Aquarius'? Come on, man—what the hell does that mean? And what's with that Appalachian track you got in there? Just because you're playing banjo and singing about somebody's girl getting swept down the river, that doesn't make it bluegrass. And why are you singing bluegrass anyhow? You're better than this."

Perhaps I wasn't.

"I get it," I said, taking a breath. "It needs some work."

"And don't you know how much concept albums suck? They suck a lot. They're hokey, overly theatrical. They're like medicine—at best appreciated, never enjoyed. Tell me, Teddy Lloyd Webber, do you want to write rock songs or do you want to dance across a Broadway stage in a costume? This is *Cats*, man! Don't bring *Cats* into my house! Write a song. Don't give me a three-part miniseries. Just sing me a goddamn song."

"Okay, I hear you. I'm going to scale it back."

"You're *not* hearing me. I'm not saying scale it back. I'm saying get rid of it." His features contorted in pain. "And who's that lady singing soprano on that one track? No guest vocalists, man. You think you're Carlos Santana?"

Lady? He must have been referring to the English murder ballad that I decided to chirp out in falsetto. I guess it did sort of sound like Joan Baez getting shot in the kneecaps.

"And one last thing: white boys don't scat."

"You don't have to get racist about it."

"It's racist for you to scat. You enslave my people when you scat. You enslave them musically. It's a civil rights issue, starting now."

Sonny tapped out his cigarette into a dirty ashtray and got up. He gave me his signature bear hug and said, "I love you, motherfucker." Meeting adjourned.

Right then I made a decision. I didn't want to become a walking humiliation. I didn't want to release crap music that I knew would be panned before I even recorded it. I didn't want to get booked at Holiday Inn lounges where I shared the signage with "Happy Bar Mitzvah, Josh!" And I sure as hell didn't want to drift downward into those desperate, what-strain-of-crack-were-you-smoking? collaborations. Def Leppard and Juice Newton with the London Philharmonic. Alice Cooper Sings Gershwin and Bacharach.

So I walked away. I was done.

I probably should've just died. Dying would've been the right play, for oh how the cultural whorehouse doth moan, pant, and keep eternal vigil for the artist who flames out young. Heroes and legends are born from our tendency to mistake the brief life for the inspired one. I would've benefited from that phenomenon.

I should've OD'd in a Vegas suite while a pasty stripper pounded on my chest. My private jet should've torpedoed into a cornfield. Some wacko should've shot me, and as I lay there struggling through my final bloody breaths, I should've winked and wryly uttered some kickass last words—"My ride's here," or "I'll see you troublemakers downstream"—that would someday be silkscreened on T-shirts worn by disaffected youth.

None of that happened. I did not die. I'm still here. Reading memos about statutes of limitations. Arguing about the meaning of paragraph 41(b). Buying soy yogurt at Trader Joe's and carpet cleaner at Rite Aid.

And plotting revenge against the dirtbag who rubbed my nose in my legacy.

As early as it was back home, I knew Metcalf would pick up. For him, the true stress of the day was that apprehensive no-man's-land between waking up—the moment when it all came flooding back—and arriving at his desk, where the anxiety of all that lay before him was at least partially alleviated by the ability to begin chipping away at the load.

Metcalf answered halfway through the first ring. "Hey, Teddy. How'd the dep go?"

"Fine. Look—I need you to do me a favor." I spoke loudly as I walked back over the Millennium Bridge, the rush of the river wind colliding in noisy sibilance with the speaker of my phone.

"Sure."

"I need the phone number for a guy named Warren Warren somewhere in the Philadelphia area, possibly Jersey."

"Did you say Warren Warren?" Metcalf was a nerd, but he was no geek. The name might have rung a bell or two for a geek.

"Yes. You're going to have to hunt around a bit. It could be an unlisted number. I took a quick look and couldn't find it. I need this fast. It's an emergency."

"Sure. No problem." He drew out the words to accommodate his note-taking. "When do you need this by?"

"I just said it's an emergency."

"Okay. Well, I'm working on a brief for Yoshida today, but I suppose—"

I hung up.

Resting my forehead against the cold rail, I watched the Thames course by beneath the steel-latticed bridge. I had a vague notion that the years hadn't carried Warren too far from our hometown. Last I heard, he was puttering around some high school way the hell and gone near Allentown, teaching band or something. The way it came together in my head, he was probably here on vacation, sauntering through the Tate with his family when he came across his old friend looking like an unmentionable slob. "I know that guy!" he surely cackled. But then he probably started shaking his head, glad he no longer knew the guy in the photo. He was glad it wasn't his life. His legacy.

I considered two minutes a sufficient interval to wait before checking back in with Metcalf. "Any luck?"

"Not yet. Is this a name that came up in the dep? Did I miss something? He wasn't on one of the transaction documents, was he?"

"Calm down. It's nothing like that."

"Okay, good. I'm going to need a little more time. It's kind of tricky. You know, since his first name is the same as his surname."

"Just do it, Metcalf."

Surname. It was hard for Metcalf to suppress his fine Boston breeding and Harvard polish. He used to ask "How would you characterize the immediacy of this assignment?" when I gave him something to do, an annoying relic of upper-crust that would prompt me to bark, "You mean, how soon do I want it?" He used to have shrimp for lunch and play squash and get calls from friends named Devon and Lanier. That Metcalf was long buried under the new one, the one with perspiration and pudge. And yet the vestiges of a refined upbringing occasionally burped to the surface. *Surname.*

I headed off toward the hotel. By the time I'd reached my room, Metcalf had tracked down the string bean percussionist, and I immediately dialed the son of a bitch without any thought of the early hour. There was no answer.

By the next morning, I'd gradually realized that I didn't really have anything to say to Warren anyway. I'd found what he sent me here for. Had we actually connected, I probably would've just cussed up a storm and threatened to kill him. Which is what I was sure to do when we finally did catch up.

In the meantime, I had arrangements to make. I studied the geography of Switzerland on Google maps. There was someone in Unterseen I needed to have a word with.

CHAPTER 3

When Warren finally returned my call, I didn't even hear the phone ring. In the fluid jumble of the Zurich train station, I was tearing a bite out of a baguette stuffed with tomato and mozzarella. It was just as well. His voice mail was a half minute of unbroken laughter, full throttle, like he was finding the whole thing freshly hilarious. "How about that picture? Right?" he finally managed to say.

How about it.

There was an irony here. I was setting out to confront an artist about his art, to register my disapproval of someone else's creative expression, and in that act, I was changing sides. Maybe my songs had never inflamed violent passions in anyone or been sufficiently outrageous as to provoke a government ban somewhere, and maybe that rendered me an artistic failure. Perhaps it was the mark of a robust vision to piss a few people off along the way, and perhaps that made Heinz-Peter Zoot a superior artist. He could explain that to me while I was choking the life out of him.

I followed the river through the town and out past a row of gingerbread houses, soon arriving at a stone road that curved up a hill and through a light patch of trees. The road ended at a small, solitary triangle of a home set squarely in a clearing. The silence was smothering, as not a single voice echoed up from the town, not a single car hummed by. I couldn't even hear the river's peaceful babble. I was completely alone in Unterseen's pastoral innocence. Just me and my blistering anger.

There'd been ample time to let my rancor rise. Back in London, I was sure that every face that met mine was in on the joke, that every smirk was a masked sneer from someone who had seen the exhibit. The journey into a world of unmolested Swiss beauty did little to douse my bitterness. The train had weaved past cozy clusters of houses on green hills, around idyllic ice waters, all of which fueled the illusion that this country was a timeless fairy tale, a place of magnificent terrain toothed with fierce jagged mountains. It seemed a land accessible only by plane crash. And yet when I gazed out at a stream, I saw only the rush of mango salsa. A shrub on a mountain face was but a wedge of cilantro besmirching an incisor.

Finally, I stood facing a house that may or may not have belonged to my nemesis. If this was, in fact, Zoot's home, the seclusion could well work against me if things got out of hand. Fuck it. I once had Bret Michaels in a headlock. I could certainly handle some Swiss photographer. What was he going to do, yodel at me?

Slinging my Morris & Roberts travel bag over my shoulder like the tough guy that I was, I walked toward the house.

Five feet from the front step I stopped dead at the sound of a voice inside. It was a deep baritone calling out in German or maybe French or perhaps Dutch, some language I for sure didn't speak. Before I could decide whether I recognized the voice as belonging to the lug nut I'd met a few years ago in the Amsterdam cantina, a large man pushed open the screen door. He saw me and froze.

It was him all right. Burly, bald, cutoff jean shorts and the same decaying white tank top from the exhibit bio photo. He stood there searching my face, looming over me from the raised porch, looking puzzled. Seeing him up close forced the image of that goddamn photo right back into my head, and I instantly understood why my scuffed saddle-tan loafers had carried me all this way.

"Heinz-Peter," I said, dropping my bag onto the front walk.

His eyes lit with pleasant recognition.

I moved swiftly up the front steps. "Congratulations on the Tate, fuckbag!"

As I reached the top step, I swung hard and landed my fist on his chin. The punch knocked him into the screen door, which slapped against the side of the house under his crushing weight. Stunned, he touched his face, glared at me, and howled something foreign. He took one step in my direction—Christ, he was a bear of a man—and soon my field of vision was consumed by a meaty set of knuckles headed for the bridge of my nose. The blow sent me clear off the porch, and the next thing I knew, I was flat on my back looking up at the cloudless sky. It's pretty, I thought. They do nice skies here, wherever this is.

My nerve endings got up to speed on recent developments, and raw sensation kicked in. A warm liquid trickled down my throat and my mouth flooded with a screaming pain. No, make that my whole head. Just as I began to process my wounds, that lovely view of the sky was eclipsed by a hulking figure. Like some kind of giant, Heinz-Peter straddled me with his massive legs, and I believed with great certitude that my life would end there. I die in Switzerland, I thought. That's my deal.

He leaned down, his nose to mine, and with a roar that shook the sleepy countryside, bellowed, "Why you do dis?"

You started it, you fucking idiot, I wanted to shout, but I couldn't seem to form words.

I lifted my head off the ground. My skull weighed a ton and the liquid sliding down the back of my throat was now gurgling in a puddle around my tongue and dripping down my chin, not unlike the mango salsa in that infamous photo. Once again, life imitates art, I thought, as my head thumped back onto the cool grass like a dropped bowling ball.

Heinz-Peter was massaging his jaw. He seemed to be awaiting my response to a question I hadn't understood. An extraordinary wave of nausea washed over me, but I was too woozy even to sit up and puke. I got off one garbled "Fuck you, fucking mutant," before everything went dark.

When I came to, the hazy blur cleared onto a pair of Cadillac-blue eyes. They belonged to a pretty, blond teenager. I was stretched out on a sofa, the girl perched in a chair next to me, holding something cold to my lip and studying my battered face. My mouth throbbed and an ice pick of a headache seared through my skull.

"Don't worry," the girl chirped. "I stopped the bleeding and the ice should keep you from getting too much of a bump." She let out a giggle. Her English was crystal clear with perhaps a dollop of Germanic Eurospeak. She had pristinely smooth cheeks and eager eyes, a hint of a teen pout in the curve of her lips.

"I'm Tereza," she said.

"Teddy," I croaked.

She adjusted the ice pack. "I know who you are."

Heavy footsteps suddenly began to hammer up a flight of stairs, and it dawned on me for the first time that I was in the photographer's home. I righted myself and took in my surroundings. We were in a living room of sorts, rustically decorated, photographs of all sizes crowding the walls.

"I can't believe you tried to beat up my father," the girl said, amused. She nodded at the lower hemisphere of my face. "You lost a tooth, you know."

"What?" I dispatched my tongue to explore my dental landscape and met an unfamiliar gap just right of center. "Jesus Christ."

The thick bootsteps came to a stop and my enemy overtook the doorframe. He stood there with his arms folded, perfectly still and perfectly huge.

The girl rose. "I'll go get some medicine."

"That's okay. I'm fine. Really."

Ignoring me, she disappeared, leaving me alone with the Jolly Green Giant.

Heinz-Peter lumbered over to the couch and dropped himself into the chair vacated by his daughter, perilously close to me on the sofa.

I took in the monster. Yeah, he could kill me. Though it would've been a lot easier to finish me off while I was unconscious. Unless he planned on nursing me back to health and then killing me. It was really his call.

This, I realized, had been a monumental act of stupidity, a true breakdown of rational thought on my part. Why hadn't I thought to bring the other *Faded Glory* losers along with me? We could have come as a mob of salty has-beens intent on taking back our dignity. That would've been the stronger tactical move.

Heinz-Peter's moon face hung over me, grinning with an impenetrable blend of menace and pity. "You are comfortable?"

I nodded cautiously.

"Tereza get you medicines." Then his face twisted, as if he'd suddenly recalled how it came to be that I, a virtual stranger from thousands of miles away, was lying on his sofa one tooth shy of a full set. "Why you hit me?"

Before I had the opportunity to point out the obvious, Tereza glided back into the room and presented me with an oblong white capsule and a glass of water. I inspected the pill. It didn't look familiar, nor did it have any word printed on it, much less a reassuringly familiar one such as Tylenol, Advil, Aleve.

"What is this?" I asked.

"Medicines," Heinz-Peter replied.

"Aspirin," Tereza said.

It was significantly larger than any pill I'd ever seen, prescription or over-the-counter, and, in fact, resembled a small lightbulb. I considered asking to see the bottle.

"Is good," Heinz-Peter encouraged. "Eat."

The pain was nearly unbearable, an unacceptable alternative to death, so I popped the thing into my mouth and chased it with a swig of water. It hardly mattered at that point that it was probably cyanide.

"I'm sorry I beat you up," the photographer said. "It is big honor to have you in my house."

"It really is," Tereza echoed. "We're big fans." Then she pointed at my mouth and conferred with her father in their native tongue. Whatever information was passed, it clearly upset the man, for he issued some emphatic grunt of surprise—*Boonsk?!*—and looked at me with grave concern.

"Let me see mouth," he urged.

Feeling foolish, I opened wide—there's no unfoolish way to present your throat to total strangers—and after a brisk inspection, the man's arms shot up over his head in a cartoonish show of frustration. Then he stormed out the front door in a fit of yapping and baying.

"He went to look for your tooth," Tereza translated.

"Are you serious?" I noticed it was easier to sit up now, what with some alpine analgesic whipping through my bloodstream.

"Let him look," she said, sitting down and crossing her legs.

"Stop him, would you?"

Even if the mad photographer poked around in the boot-stomped mulch and somehow came bursting back in with a dirty dislodged bicuspid between his fingers, I wasn't likely to put the thing back in my mouth.

Tereza looked at me lying lamely on her sofa, and an apple of a smile absorbed every feature on her cherubic face. "I love your music. I really do."

My eyebrows dropped into a skeptical furrow. "That's nice."

"I'm a huge fan. Seriously. I know everything you've done."

"You're funny," I said, meaning *You're insane.*

"I'm not joking."

"How old are you?"

"Seventeen."

"You shouldn't even know who I am." I struggled to my feet and staggered toward the front door to call Heinz-Peter off the case. It now looked as if I had an outside shot at getting out of there alive and saw no reason to squander the miracle.

"I listen to all kinds of music," she went on.

"You should listen to *many* kinds of music. No need to listen to *all* kinds."

"What do you mean?" she asked, clearly amused.

"I mean, sometimes old music is just old music."

"Is there something wrong with listening to old music?"

"It depends," I said, readjusting to the sensation of walking. "If it's Led Zeppelin or Nick Drake, then no. If it's Missing Persons or the Osmonds, then quite possibly yes."

"I listen to Led Zeppelin and Pink Floyd and U2 and Black Sabbath. I also listen to Tremble."

"You should probably go easy on the Black Sabbath. As for Tremble, your time would be better spent with Boy George solo albums." I paused in my tracks to massage a boulder of pain out of my temples. "Look, you're young now, but trust me, that won't always be the case. Don't piss away your listening years on music that's just not good. My point is—do you know what the word *myopic* means?"

Tereza stared at me with scientific wonder. "You're not what I expected."

"Well, we're all having new experiences today."

She gave me a once-over that was just probing enough to be insulting. "You're shorter, more pale."

As I hobbled through the house, I took note of the photographs covering every wall. I was struck by their mastery, the thought and skill rendered in each composition—experiments in angle, distance, and color saturation. "Your old man has some talent," I mused. "Although obviously I wish he'd never been born."

Upon reaching the foyer, I peered through the screen and observed my tormentor crouched apelike as he scoured the grass for my lost tooth. It was a noisy exercise, with snorts and grumbles of disgust. I pushed the door open. "Uh, friend?"

"I will find," he called without looking up. His thick fingers brushed through the grass. "I knock out, I put back."

"I don't think it works that way."

The man suddenly bounded to his feet, pointed at my mouth, and, as if it had just occurred to him, declared, "You need dentist."

I spun toward Tereza. "There's a dentist around here?"

The offense she took at my surprise was a few paces from playful. "Where do you think you are?"

"Lost," I replied. "Hopelessly lost."

Heinz-Peter drove at the speed of a camera shutter on the burst setting, flinging us along slender streets and charmingly precarious bridges. I bounced around the passenger seat, ice held to my lip, suffering steep penance for picking the wrong fight. My driver grinned and patted my knee like I was his date. "Mr. Teddy Tremble in my car," he boasted, showing precious little interest in the road. "This is big thrill for me."

I pointed at the windshield. "Focus."

He steered at a nauseating clip over a hill that dropped into a small town center with narrow cobblestone streets, shops that had no doubt thrived for centuries. An old gray woman with a cane crept up the walkway of a stone house. Children in school uniforms strolled alongside the road with boisterous chatter. All these people looked busy and happy. We'd probably ride over some of them.

"You don't like picture in museum?" Heinz-Peter asked, resuming our conversation.

"No, I'm afraid I don't. But hey, my drummer loved it, so don't feel too bad."

"Why you don't like it?"

"Well, let's see. It makes me look like a dipshit—that's certainly a big part of it. And you hung it up alongside pictures of other dipshits and you called the exhibit *Let's Laugh at the Losers* or something. Those are probably the main reasons I didn't love it. Would you like to hear others?"

I watched him parse through my critique. "I don't trying to make fun of you. I think you are victim of fame. This is what exhibit is all about." He waved his arm expressively as he said this.

"Well, art usually goes right over my head," I said.

"You are one time very famous," he explained. "But then it go away and you are not happy. Yes?"

No. "You don't know the first thing about me. You met me one time in a stupid restaurant in Amsterdam. And in that restaurant, did we talk about that? Not that it would've been any of your fucking business, but did you say, 'Hey, Teddy, now that you're no longer a famous musician, does your life suck?' No. Instead, you pretended to be my friend, you snapped some pictures of me, and a few years later, you stabbed me in the fucking back. I even bought you a goddamn drink."

He turned his body in my direction as if we were in couple's therapy. "No, no. My exhibit is showing fame is very painful for famous peoples. If you are happy or sad for real life, this not matter."

"It matters to me. Hey, you know what? Maybe I'll write a song about some miserable oaf who lives in the mountains and takes pictures of people having dinner and pretends to understand them. And maybe I'll call that song 'Song about Heinz-Peter Zoot' and I'll post it on YouTube and play it in Times Square. What do you think?"

Heinz-Peter looked troubled. "What is this—miserable loaf?"

I leaned back and held the cold compress to my lip. Tires crunched gruesomely over either a thick branch or a crossing guard. A woman in a billowy dress hung clothes on a line outside a small red cottage while a young boy straddled a bicycle. They were going to have meat pie for dinner.

"I am very sorry, Teddy." The sentence was delivered cleanly—no accent, appropriate use of a linking verb. No doubt he could apologize proficiently in most of the world's languages. "I am big fan. I don't try making fun at you."

"Oh no? *Faded Glory? It Feels like a Lie and It Looks like a Mess?*"

He threw me a look of confusion.

"That was the name of your exhibit, remember? The name of the photograph."

"Oh, yes, yes. Marius, my assistant, he make names. I don't too good English."

"You don't say." I should've guessed that there was a coconspirator, someone with the necessary tools to slander and be cute about it.

"My pictures say only that you are human being like other peoples." Heinz-Peter continued to plead his case.

"Well, other peoples aren't hanging in the Tate, staining themselves with nachos."

Without any warning or the slightest decrease in speed, the car lurched off the road into a small, unpaved parking lot. "Here is dentist!" he announced.

At the far end of the lot sat an old stone hut. The front door was a thick slab of oak, reminiscent of that pub in Dublin. I noticed a chimney and thought it a curious feature for a dentist's office.

"Are we meeting him at a bar?"

Heinz-Peter got out and headed toward the door of the hut.

I had no choice but to shadow the big lug across the gravel parking lot, a hand on my battered jaw. "Faded glory," I muttered. "Faded fucking glory."

Inside, a prune of a man who seemed to be a casual if less than enthusiastic acquaintance of Heinz-Peter's led me back to a dim room with a reclining dental chair. A cigarette dangling from his lip, he peered into my mouth, then shook his head in discouragement. "I don't know," he mumbled in a thick accent. He frowned at a tray of sharp metal instruments. "I don't know."

He then proceeded to hack and claw at whatever remnants of

tooth were still wedged in my gum. He pulled and tugged, at one point practically kneeing my chest for leverage. After ten agonizing minutes, he dejectedly tossed his tool—Early Man's version of an X-ACTO knife—back into the pan and extinguished his cigarette right next to it. "I don't know," he grumbled again. "I don't know."

I asked this ray of fucking sunshine for some novocaine. Startlingly, the word was not within his lexicon. "Novocaine?" I repeated with growing alarm. I, of course, had no clue how to say "numbing agent" in any dialect but my own. How do you pantomime "local anesthesia"? I said ouch and ow and winced with great cinema until he got it and, looking annoyed, shuffled away to see if he had some lying around.

He returned a few minutes later and unceremoniously injected a gallon of colorless serum into the inside of my cheek, which hurt just as much as Heinz-Peter's uppercut. Within seconds I felt seriously stoned and indifferent to the clear fact of my imminent death. I felt myself slipping away, but my last thought before blacking out for the second time that hour was remarkably sensible: Are you supposed to lose consciousness during a routine dental visit?

Through a gathering fog, I watched as the dentist miserably poked an unlit cigarette between his lips and struck a match.

Here's where I note that Sara had strongly counseled against my coming here.

I called her from the London hotel, told her the whole story, how all these years I never knew that my legacy actually involved a little piece of cilantro staining my smile. She seemed to consider the tale a sort of dark comedy—until I mentioned how I'd decided to modify my travel itinerary.

"That's a very bad idea," she'd said. "It's dangerous, Teddy. You don't see that?"

"I can take care of myself."

"Look, I know you think you're a bit of a tough guy, but having a temper doesn't make you a badass."

I hooted. Sara never used words like *badass*—she'd gone to Dartmouth—and she could only hope to sell it by attaching it to a cute little sneer.

It was rather unlike her to interfere. We tended to stay out of each other's way. We shared an apartment and looked forward to the comfort of each other's company at the end of the day, but we could go for long stretches where we were little more than apparitions haunting the same apartment.

"I'll be fine," I assured her.

"This is foolish, Teddy," she charged, a siren of panic in her voice. "Traveling to some unfamiliar place to find some man you know nothing about? And then what?"

"Calm down, Sara."

"It's not me that needs to calm down. You're angry now, but your anger will subside, probably just as you're staring into this photographer's face. You can't stop people from saying things about you. You should have thicker skin."

"This is different. It's a cheap shot."

"You can't stop people from taking cheap shots at you either."

"Sara—you're making far too big a deal out of this."

"Me?"

"I'm going to Switzerland to have a little chat with an artist. I'm not going to Bolivia to take down a junta."

Having reached something akin to a crescendo, Sara sailed over the edge into a plane of helpless silence. Helpless silence was, in fact, her stock in trade. It greeted her first thing in the morning and planted its cold kiss on her each night. She had learned the hard way, maybe the hardest way, that life shouldn't be frittered away on vanity and caprice. I was a former rock star, however, so vanity and caprice were *my* stock in trade, with a warehouse that never ran low on inventory.

"I'm not going to disappear, Sara. I promise."

"Do whatever you want." And she hung up.

How idiotic to promise someone you won't disappear, as if vanishing were something you scheduled.

There was a degree of justice in my landing here in this dentist's chair. The universe had witnessed my clamoring rage, and for my trouble had awarded me a prosthetic denture. Surely a perverse contortion of biblical justice, this tooth for a tooth. For Sara, there was no concept as meaningless as justice. She'd learned from experience that there was no justice, would never again be justice. That was as plain as day. But some of us needed to be hit over the head.

Literally.

The scenery wore the refreshed, vital colors of early evening when Heinz-Peter steered us back up the stone driveway. The day had begun to end.

A dinner invitation had been repeatedly extended—if he now considered me a friend, he had a rather twisted concept of the word—and roundly rejected. I'd survived H-P's fist, his driving, and the handiwork of the village dentist. It seemed ungracious to push my luck. I waited in the car while the nutjob fetched my bag from inside his house.

Sensation was returning to my face. The anesthesia had worn off and yet the throbbing pain that I'd considered inevitable, given the crude dentistry practiced upon me, had not come. I climbed out of the car to breathe the sweet mountain air and consider the logistics of getting home.

And that was my last glimpse of Swiss serenity.

Just then, the front door of the house opened and a dozen or so teenagers poured out onto the lawn. I looked on dumbly at the collection of youths that had materialized out of nowhere, when Tereza appeared on the front step, hovering over all of us. Like the shepherd of the flock, she pointed directly at me. "There he is!"

Before I could grasp what was happening, this babbling little mob came swimming over to me and practically pinned me up against H-P's jalopy. They called out my name, they shook my hand, they smiled goofy smiles. They were loud and unruly and unacquainted with notions of personal space, and it was all so fucking weird that I was certain I was still conked out and drugged in the dentist's chair.

As Tereza stepped down onto the lawn, hands tucked deep in the pockets of her zippered hoodie, looking self-satisfied and casual, I caught her attention. What the fuck?

"I love your music," said one shabbily dressed girl who couldn't have been more than a kindergartener the last time any of my songs had played on the radio. A boy with a tepid, desperate growth of facial hair stood next to her and echoed the sentiment. "I grew up on your albums," he said through a mild accent. On came absurd rapid-fire declarations and inquiries that competed for my attention: "I know every lyric of every song you ever recorded!" (A dim accomplishment; we only had two albums.) "When is the band getting back together?" "Are there any plans to release rarities, outtakes, bonus tracks?" Even sadder, some of these bedraggled fools clutched Tremble memorabilia—copies of my CDs, album jackets, photos—and held them up to my face for me to sign. It was as if they were all part of a pathetically misguided cult, celebrating my guest appearance at their compound. I had no idea what was going on; I just knew I wasn't happy about it. Was the London exhibit not a sufficiently elaborate means of ridicule? Had Heinz-Peter hired a herd of young extras to pretend to adore me?

I reached into the crowd and grabbed Tereza's arm. "You want to tell me what's going on here?"

She pursed her lips. "What do you mean? I knew they'd want to meet you. How's your mouth?"

"Who are these people?" I pressed. "And what's wrong with them?"

She held out an open hand to the prattling sea of losers. "They're fans."

I was at a total loss. "Of what?"

The front door swung open again and Heinz-Peter stepped out to tower over the merriment. He raised up his arms and laughed with the showmanship of a mad carnival barker.

I turned to Tereza. "It's been a really long day. Can you give me a lift to the train station?"

It was then that I became aware of a deep grinding rumble behind me. It grew louder and louder, like a rusty chain saw, at last revealing itself as a weathered, puke-green van waggling up the driveway. It had barely stumbled to a stop when its doors burst open on all sides and a giddy throng of adolescents of all shapes, sizes, colors, and acne concentrations leapt out to join the commotion.

I surveyed this most motley crew. Everyone was of high school or college age and clad in attire I could only describe as densely European and weather-nonspecific. A brown suit here, a knit slouchy hat there. A plum-cheeked bleached blonde with vampish eye makeup and a *London Calling* T-shirt here, a bespectacled boy in a striped Izod with raised collar there. All of these boneheads wanted a word with me.

Then a lanky dude in an army jacket stumbled out from behind the wheel of the van, his gait unsteady. He instantly drew my attention because, for one thing, he seemed to be drunk, and for another, he'd been driving. Listing to the side as if he might collapse onto the grass, the guy locked me in the crosshairs of a finger gun and called out, "You know it, brother! You know it!" His relationship to the proceedings was unclear. As was mine.

I found Tereza in the mix and leveled a scowl at her. "Seriously— what the hell?"

She tossed me a careless little shrug and walked away, leaving me at the epicenter of a puzzling little blowout in the land that music forgot.

Somehow I ended up sitting on the front step, nursing a Belgian blond ale that six children had competed to stuff into my hand. Around me were three members of Tereza's posse—a boy of peach fuzz and cracking voice, and two breezily chatty girls.

"How did Tremble get acquainted with Cameron Crowe?" the boy wanted to know. For some worthless reason, he was desperate to learn the genesis of our involvement in *Ballad of the Fallen*, the Crowe-directed film that made a spectacular hit out of a song that had already appeared on our debut album. "Did you write 'It Feels like a Lie' specifically for the movie, or did Cameron Crowe just really like it on your album and ask to use it?"

"Tell me something," I replied. "What are all you people doing here?"

"Do you still hang out with famous rock stars?" the girl to my left inquired.

"I'm a lawyer, you understand?"

"What's going on with the rest of the band? What are Jumbo, Warren, and Mackenzie doing? For years I've been checking for solo albums, but I can never find any."

"Solo albums? They're all teachers or locksmiths or insurance brokers now."

Until Warren had recently come cackling back into my life, I hadn't spoken to or heard from any of those people since we split up. It was easier than I would've imagined to allow all that time and distance to wedge into the spaces between us. When things ended, not only was there no longer any reason for us to talk, much less travel en masse like a camp bunk, but we were all in need of some time apart. On top of all that, there was that ugly little secret I'd been shouldering, the one that was at least partially to blame for why we all ended up having to look for other work in the first place. It wasn't just my lame songwriting that did us in; it was my clouded judgment. It was just as well I didn't have to face them and constantly be reminded of it. Especially Mackenzie, whose sudden absence in my life made things both a little bit easier and a whole lot harder. Of all the people from those days, Mack was the one who required the most effort to forget.

None of these misguided youths had asked me the most obvious question of all: how had a god such as myself ended up in this tiny village nowhere near anywhere? Which was a shame, because that chain of events was far more entertaining than any war story I could've told about my life in the music business. Instead, this strange tribe simply accepted the miracle of my presence and proceeded to interrogate me on trivialities—like the inspiration for the girl described in "New Morning Azalea," a song I'd forgotten I'd written. A song everybody had forgotten I'd written.

"If I had to pick a favorite person in the band, I'd have to say Jumbo," one girl mused. "No offense."

"Why would you have to pick a favorite person in the band?" I asked. "How would that ever come up?"

"That guy could really rock out," she went on. "What was it like working with him?"

"Irksome."

Jumbo Jett was a monstrously talented guitar player and just about the biggest mess of a human being I'd ever known. Unkempt, unpredictable, and uncouth, the ox that stinks up the dinner party. Whereas the hedonistic rock scene was never really my thing, Jumbo cannonballed himself right into that pool. Surely he was a livelier subject for a photography exhibit than I. The pictures would title themselves. *Man Barfs Blue into Fake Plant at Morton's. Inappropriately Displayed Butt Cheeks at Airport Lounge. Band Rehearsing While Guitarist Sleeps It Off on a Barge Downriver (Guitarist Not Pictured).*

"So much has been written about his impact on music," the boy gushed. "Jack White of the White Stripes, James Mercer of the Shins, the guys from the Black Keys—they've all cited him as a major influence."

"Well, I can't stop people from saying stupid shit."

"Come on. Even with his wild reputation, he couldn't have made the music he did without being a true professional, right?"

The man was the very opposite of professional. The moron lacked even the faintest wisp of a work ethic, which, frankly, was understandable since he'd never held a real job. There was a brief stint at a small medical supply company after college, but he was quickly fired for tickling a coworker. There's no tickling at work; most people understand that without even having to sit through the training seminar.

"Maybe you're right," I allowed. "He's an accomplished guy. During the time I knew him, he gave up drinking alcohol at breakfast and having sex with strangers at truck stops. You can't not call that progress."

"How about Mackenzie?" the boy asked through a puppy-dog grin. "What is she doing now?"

The mere mention of her name could still release a tide of overwhelming thoughts. Thoughts that, even after all this time, tiptoed on the edges of my understanding.

"No idea," I said. "Go look for her yourself."

Around back, guests stood in clusters and slurped from longneck bottles or sat in chatty huddles at wooden picnic tables. Someone had brought out a portable stereo—a "boom box" to some of us—and, to pour salt on an already dangling scab, began blaring our second album, *Atomic Somersault*. I shook my head. The industry publications that had bothered to review it were at best dismissive, at worst cruel: "Dismal disappointment from a once promising band, the biggest miscalculation of producer Sonny Rivers's career." "I would sooner spend my hard-earned cash on their debut—which I already own—than on this waste of a follow-up." "A horn section? Really? Is this Teddy Tremble and the News? Teddy Tremble and the Range?"

And yet, as those forgotten songs echoed across the darkening yard, the memories were not all bad. I was transported back to those high-octane days and euphoric weeks when we were holed up in the studio, cruising on the thunderclap of our Oscar-winning hit. We knew what the expectations were, and we had every confidence that we'd exceed them. I could still visualize Mackenzie standing in the recording booth in a baby-blue tank top, her fingers gliding over her bass, hair tucked behind her ears to make way for the Princess Leia headphones. I heard a subtle drum fill and immediately saw Warren twirling his sticks, tossing them high in the air, goofing off between songs. All of it was just as vivid as yesterday, and just as gone.

I remembered a time when I actually felt protective of these songs, when I believed our follow-up to have been unfairly dismissed and derided. The critics piled on because they were sick of our faces, I used to argue, sick of the ubiquitous nuisance that was "It Feels like a Lie." So maybe it wasn't *Highway 61 Revisited*. It wasn't Milli Vanilli's *Remix Album* either.

Suddenly, a flashbulb exploded in my face. Once the blinding white fuzz dissipated, the big troll himself was standing before us, clutching his favorite weapon and pointing it at his guests.

"Teddy!" Heinz-Peter cried, throwing an arm around my neck. We were lost brothers now. "You are happy? Having good time, yes?" He waved a grand arm at the crowd of kids. "Tereza make party for you!"

"I'll have to find some way to thank her."

"All of these nice peoples at my home," he called out, hammering away at the darkness with his flashbulb. "Must to take pictures, Teddy. But this time I *tell* you I taking pictures, yes? No secret! Ha!" He beamed at his own cleverness, the Scooby-Doo smile too big even for that moon face of his.

"Tell me something," I said. "Everyone else around here speaks perfect English. Why does yours suck so bad?"

He let out an exuberant laugh, which I interpreted as incomprehension, and patting me hard on the back, started for the house. Then he froze, pivoted, and pointed to the sky in a stroke of excitement.

"Look!" he bellowed, presumably meaning *listen*.

The song wafting from the boom box was "Troubleshooter," a slushy puddle of a ballad I'd written in a fever of melodrama after the death of my English lit professor. I heard my double-tracked voice whining through the verse—"The old school walls fall down like rain / With ghosts of Shakespeare, Poe, and Twain." Why couldn't I have just rhymed *rain* with *pain* like a normal person?

"This song I love it!" H-P shouted, striding away and singing along. He couldn't form even the most grammatically basic sentence in English, but damned if he didn't know every last lyric.

"I'm not the only person ever to take a swing at that guy, am I?" I posed the question to a pair of boys shuffling skittishly on either side of me, bottles of local ale in their clutches.

"He's quite entertaining, but a good man," one said, his wire-rimmed glasses glimmering in the waning light. "And he really is a big fan of your music. A lot of people around here are."

"You people scare me," I said. "This place is like some kind of lost colony. You have no idea how alone in the world you are. There's real music out there. I can show it to you. You've got the Internet in Switzerland, right?"

The kid with the glasses grinned up at me. "So what did Heinz-Peter do to make you so angry that you came all this way to fight him?"

I snorted; it hadn't been much of a fight. Then a tiny itch of pride ripened inside me, and for some inexplicable reason I felt hesitant to elaborate.

"I don't know," I said. "I guess he captured a moment."

At some point, it fell to me to man the grill, to poke and prod sausages and burgers, nudge them off their charred bellies and onto their backs. The affair had quieted down from a raucous backyard party into a subdued evening picnic replete with the easy murmurs and cinder-like aromas of a campfire. Tereza, a cagey ally at best, kept me company, and together we allowed our lungs to fill with mesquite as the charcoal hissed under the gridirons.

"You're getting more comfortable with all of this, aren't you?" she said, smiling. "You're once more adjusting to your fame. I can see it."

"Why aren't you listening to Dr. Dog? Where's your Pernice Brothers? Your War on Drugs? There's all this good new music out there."

"Don't let all of this go to your head," Tereza teased. "We don't only listen to Tremble."

"You realize that some bands actually deserve to be forgotten," I went on, sliding a spatula under a sizzling mound of beef and hoisting it onto a paper plate. "Charles Darwin is alive and well in the arts."

"I don't think you really believe that your music deserves to be forgotten," she said. "If you do, then you're not the artist everyone here thinks you are. You're certainly not the artist that my father is."

Of course I wasn't the artist that all these delusional castoffs took me for. They had no idea how utterly bizarre it was to have moved on with your life, to have changed directions in everything you did, and then randomly discover a lunatic fringe on the other side of some lost mountain that was still grooving to your music years after the rest of civilization had wised up.

Maybe every band was awarded some little time-warp town that remained forever loyal, perennially committed to the notion that the group for which it pined would one day rise from the ashes. Perhaps there was a village in Tibet where everyone wore a Men Without Hats shirt and sang "The Safety Dance" all day. Maybe a town in Cameroon woke up every morning breathless with sunny hope that Katrina would round up the rest of the Waves and launch a tour.

"You seem like a nice group of mountain people, but being cut off from the rest of humanity has messed with your minds," I said.

Tereza's eyes bore into me, her face beset by a disturbed crinkle crawling its way across her nose. "Is this how all Americans say thank you, or just you?"

I watched her plate a sausage for a hungry guest. She delivered the food with a warm, hospitable smile and a gentle pat on his shoulder. It struck me as a nurturing gesture, maternal even, and I found myself asking where her mother was.

"She died."

"Oh."

"Two years ago."

"I'm sorry to hear that."

"We were boating on the river." She jerked her chin to the side, signaling that the river in question was a neighbor, a familiar friend. "We flipped over in the rapids and she hit her head on a rock. Drowned before my father and I could pull her to shore." I watched the light from the burning coals flickering across her face as she kept her distance from the memory. "It's amazing how quickly things happen, you know? One minute we were a family in a boat, the next minute we were in the water, and then we were on the riverbank and she was gone forever. She still had her life vest on."

"I'm sorry I brought that up."

"It's fine."

"That must've been really hard on you and your dad."

She gazed out at the lawn crackling with life, friends and relations fading into the falling night. "We've never been alone." She said it as though it were a mixed blessing.

The back door of the house suddenly flew open and Heinz-Peter came lurching out. "Teddy!" he called merrily. He was carrying a long wooden object—an oar? an ax?—and slinging it in the air as he giant-stepped his way across the dark yard.

I squinted at the implement that this madman was waving over his head. The remaining pockets of light finally revealed its identity.

"Oh Jesus," I groaned. "Is he fucking kidding me?"

"You don't get it," I yelled at the crowd. "You people have all lost your minds." They didn't seem to care that they'd lost their minds. Maybe that's the beauty of losing your mind. "It's out of the question. Go hassle Wang Chung."

At the sight of the guitar being wielded by their host, everyone untangled themselves from their conversations and joined Heinz-Peter in beseeching me to do an impromptu gig right there on the lawn. And no matter how forcefully I rejected their ludicrous invitation, no matter how much disdain and hostility I showered upon these hill-town hicks, still they egged me on. An intimate backyard concert, they argued, would be an ideal coda to an evening they would cherish for the remainder of their lives. I told them to get a grip. I couldn't remember the last time I'd picked up a guitar, and I'd long forgotten the chords and the words to all the Tremble songs. And anyway my mouth hurt like hell.

"I'd rather lick a train station toilet than play for you people," I declared.

"You are with friends, yes? Play for us!" H-P cried out, holding the instrument out to me with the rallying charisma of a medieval ogre.

"You are not my friends," I insisted.

"Play for us, Teddy Tremble!" he boomed.

"Listen to me carefully. You all need therapy. You're embarrassing yourselves."

The fucked-up chanting and screaming was growing louder and more fanatical. A real musician would've soaked up all this ego stroking, riled the crowd up louder like a shirtless stadium god, or bowed his head in a slushy sigh of false modesty. I, however, wanted only to take off down the driveway and never look back.

Tereza was now standing next to me, having managed to navigate her way through the crowd. Cupping one side of her mouth, she leaned into my ear and shouted above the fray. "Teddy, maybe you're not the same person you used to be."

"You're finally realizing that?" I yelled back.

"It's okay with me," she said. "But if it's not okay with you"—she turned an open palm to the crowd and offered up an innocent little shrug—"it looks like you've got a chance to go back, even for just one night."

Go back where? I wanted to shake her. It isn't there anymore!

"It doesn't work that way, Tereza," I shouted into the air between us.

She shook her head in bewilderment. "I don't understand. You're holding a guitar and there are people who want to hear a song. Are you really sure you don't want to play?"

As we stared at each other, speakers of different languages on the

Tower of Babel, something inside me suddenly began to shift. As I scanned this mad pack of misbegotten zombies, locked eyes with each and every one of them, it all became funny. They weren't putting me on. Their hearts were in exactly the wrong place, but their hearts were there, beating up a storm. A bunch of kids clamoring with everything they had to see their favorite musician perform just for them, and they would not be refused. I remembered what that was like. Who didn't?

A powerful silence reigned for a moment; they smelled surrender.

"Give me the goddamn guitar," I snapped.

If these fools wanted to hear the feeble warbling of a middle-aged has-been, then tonight was their night. They would recoil in disgust and never listen to or speak of Tremble again. It was high time they were acquainted with what we in the real world called reality.

So—fuck if I didn't find myself sitting on an aluminum folding chair, twisting the pegs until the strings were in tune. My fingers, uncallused and alien, moved sluggishly at first, without the speed or agility they once had. But then, as if from hardwired instinct, they placed themselves on the right strings, on the right frets, at the right time. The songs flooded back and I had the random sensation of being rocked on my grandmother's shoulder like a child, back to where I started after a lifetime of being away. The music came. Chord flowed logically to chord. I didn't need to go looking for them; they'd been there all this time.

My thoughts, however, were anything but harmonious. A disquiet gathered in my head, faint at first, like the distant rush of a car engine finding its way through the neighborhood. But then the car was outside, honking in the driveway, and the hinges of every closed door within me started to shake. My mind went wild and my thoughts became unbound and unstable, disobedient and carried by no current. Like jazz.

Then something completely unexpected happened, and it was like I never saw it coming.

PART TWO

EXCUSE ME, DID I ASK YOU TO BLOW ON MY FOOD?

CHAPTER 4

I came back weird. On that first morning after the trip, I awakened, showered, and dressed feeling slightly off and a little jittery. It was more than the routine anxiety of not wanting to return to work. I sensed an invisible force telling me I wasn't supposed to return to work.

On her way out to an early appointment, Sara poked her head into the bathroom and called to me above the steady teeming of water on tile. "I'm going. I left you some coffee."

"Thanks," I shouted back. Then I pushed open the glass door and stuck my head out like a wet terrier. "Thanks," I said again.

She smiled. "Bye."

My mind seemed to be circling above something I wanted to say to her; I just couldn't land on it.

Buttoning the sleeves of a light-blue oxford while avoiding eye contact with the bedroom mirror, I realized I was humming a tune. My mouth was forming words: "I could've sworn she'd gone missing, she was hiding in plain sight." Then it formed the words again, then again. I just couldn't place the song.

In the kitchen, I poured the remains of the coffeepot into a mug. But instead of taking a sip, I rested both hands on the countertop and stared at the stream of vapor rising out of the cup. By some mystery, I felt like I'd already chugged a two-liter bottle of Mountain Dew, so I upended the mug into the sink and headed out.

It was out in the hall, awaiting an elevator to begin my six-block commute, as the one-melody phrase kept repeating itself to me, ever clearer, that I had a perplexing thought: I'd never heard this song before. "I fucking made it up," I said out loud to the empty cream-toned walls.

At eight a.m., Metcalf was already popping Xanax like Flintstones vitamins. Before I could even set my briefcase down, he came bursting into my office with information, anecdotes, and tales of bad behavior that I'd missed during my European jaunt.

"I can't deal with you right now," I told him, waving him away. I faced the window and gazed out at the metropolis, surfing a sensation of coasting above the snarling zoo of buildings, as opposed to being lost within it.

I opted out of a practice group meeting, e-mailed my colleagues a succinct abstract of the Ireland deposition ("Went fine"), and fought off a progressively hysterical Metcalf, who kept returning to my door with a Big Gulp in his paw. I was used to these displays of Metcalf's ever-tense mental state, which had accelerated a physical deterioration that was getting harder to ignore. With the vitamin D–deficient complexion, the jowls of Silly Putty, and the taiga-like hairline, he appeared to be in perpetual treatment for a disease that beat the shit out of him but didn't have the decency to kill him dead. Several times a day, he would charge into my office, his shirt trying to untuck itself, and cry paralysis over a list of pressing issues he was unable to resolve without my input. My input was usually something along the lines of "You figure it out" or, if I was in a good mood, "Metcalf, you need a girlfriend." My reward for being taxed with a human being so overwrought and frazzled was the gift of an occasional gaffe. There was, for instance, the conference call a few weeks earlier, an hour-long shouting match involving a dozen or so lawyers. As it concluded, everyone throwing out parting shots and threats of running to the judge, Metcalf was so busy scribbling on his notepad that he barely noticed himself absently chirping "Love you" into the speakerphone. He would've heaved himself out a window if the fucking things opened.

Noon found me walking back to my condo. Once inside, I marched straight down the hall to the room we'd set up as an office. Hands in my pockets, I stared at the wall. My Martin D-28 acoustic stared back. She'd been in here all along, and while I'd always been aware of her, like the old picture frame hanging in the bedroom, I hadn't looked at her, really looked at her, in ages.

I allowed my eyes to settle on the sides carved of East Indian rosewood, the neck of mahogany, the ambertone top. I'd bought it in a guitar shop in the East Village in the midnineties figuring that if it was good enough for Jimmy Page and Hank Williams, it would probably suffice for a rhythm player who knew no more than two dozen chords. It had accompanied me into the studio and onto stages across the globe. It had been a patient accessory when I sat down in living rooms, hotels, and bus seats trying to follow the bread crumbs of a song that wanted to be written.

Slowly, I reached over and gripped the neck. The lower strings rang out in soft dissonance at the disturbance of being touched. I blew dust off the frets and held the body up to my face. This is weird, I said to myself. I should be at the office reviewing that discovery motion. It needs to be filed in a few hours.

With great care, I carried the guitar into the living room and, dropping a yellow pad beside me on the couch, I strummed. Although I'd been estranged from this instrument for longer than I cared to remember, we picked up right where we left off. I immediately began to pair chords with that unrelenting melody that had been looping through my brain since my shower. "I could've sworn she'd gone missing, she was hiding in plain sight."

An hour later, I stuffed one of Sara's caramel nut Luna bars into my jacket pocket and headed back to the office. Once there, I returned to my window and resumed my trancelike absorption in everything within view.

I felt isolated, on edge, out of my element, and unsure if there even was an element out there that would feel like my own. I didn't know whether these were growing pains or the pains of realizing your growing days were done, but either way, for a reason I couldn't place, it all hurt so good.

That evening, Sara scooped up her goblet, ambled lazily around the table, and planted her bony ass on my lap. Dinner often ended in this seating configuration. She tended to eat faster and drink more than I.

"Were you here today?" she asked.

The Martin, my tell-tale heart, was propped up against the sofa.

"I stopped back at lunch," I confessed.

Her jaw literally dropped in amazement. "You came home in the middle of the day to play guitar?"

"I had to pick up some work that I left here," I said, fumbling through a lie while stirring my penne in vodka sauce. "I grabbed a bite and just decided to strum for a few minutes."

Red wine stained the edges of her smirk like day-old lipstick. Her words were smeared together in something just shy of a slur, as if she were speaking in cursive. "I've never seen that thing come down off the wall. Play something for me."

"I don't think so. And your exceedingly bony cheeks are crushing my legs."

"Masculine to a fault," she muttered, turning around and straddling me as if readying a lap dance. At close range, I could see her bloodshot eyes, and I wondered how she'd found the time to drain a glass or two before I'd walked in the door.

"What did you do today?" I asked.

"Nothing. A couple of client meetings. The usual."

With a luxurious yawn, her head tumbled onto my shoulder and I caught the dying wisps of her lavender shampoo. It always reminded me of our trip to Provence years ago. It was the happiest I'd ever seen her, breezing from one medieval town to the next in our tiny white convertible two-seater, lunching on baguettes and cheese, lounging in cozy cafés under lamplight at the foot of a mountain. For that brief period, Sara seemed to have left herself and the dark weight of her past back home. One afternoon we picnicked on a rock in a secluded gorge by the Verdon River. As she leaned back on her hands, barefoot with her knees bent, she watched the current with a serenity that matched the river's constant flow. "I'd like to live by the water one day," she said. "The sea or a lake or a river, it doesn't matter." I didn't see myself ever moving out of the city, but since we were just talking, I said, "How about a summer home on the Riviera?" She smiled, still staring at the rush of cold water. "Or a little cottage in Maine or Cape Cod," I added. She turned to me and there was no denying the look on her face. She was holding me accountable for the peace she'd momentarily found. "Promise?" she asked.

Still draped over me like a wilted rose, Sara was now half-asleep. We stayed that way awhile, sandwiched together between chair and table, serenaded by Stan Getz's breathy sax atop a Jobim composition from the sixties. Sara often cooked to bossa nova, disappearing into the lush sway of its rhythms, the sandy scent of its melodies. Unless she was cooking for a crowd, in which case she went Jackson 5 for the energy boost.

"Go lie down," I said, patting her back. "I'll clean up."

She planted a delicate kiss on my neck. Then came another, and then a warm, wine-dipped whisper. "Come with me."

"You're sound asleep."

"I can rally." She lifted her head and tried to make her bleary eyes dance, but it was a dance that foretold swift collapse. I wasn't without sympathy: if I were in a relationship with me, I'd have to beer-goggle too.

Her eyes closed in a hazy flutter. I soothed her back with the tips of my fingers and surveyed the disturbance of plates, glasses, and utensils in front of me.

Sara let out another long hush of a breath. Just as she drifted off, she drizzled a sigh of words into my ear. "I've always hated this table."

*   *   *

Sara and I, classmates in high school, had reconnected during my band years. One afternoon, on the way to Warren's to go through some new material, Jumbo and I stopped into a strip mall deli to pick up sandwiches, and as we waited for our takeout, I ran into Marianne Sadler, a friend from the old neighborhood. After we'd exchanged pleasantries, Marianne gripped my shoulder. "Did you hear Sara Rome lost a kid?"

"What?" I remembered the girl from school, a stylish broomstick, quietly intelligent, someone you knew your whole life and noticed only in a certain, limited way.

"Her son, Drew. Just a few weeks ago. Totally unreal." Marianne had become friendly with Sara through mommy-and-me classes. She told me Sara was now an interior designer.

"Jesus. How old?"

"Two."

"Jesus."

I don't know what compelled me to call her the next day. Maybe it was the blade of tragedy cutting deep in the place where I'd grown up and into the people I'd grown up with. And why wouldn't I call? It was me. In those days, I owned the world.

"Is this Sara? Sara Rome?"

"Yes," answered a lifeless voice.

"It's Teddy Tremble. Do you remember me?"

"Of course, Teddy. Wow. How are you?"

"I'm okay. Listen—I just ran into Marianne Sadler. She told me some awful news. I'm so sorry . . ." As my voice trailed off, I heard only a quaking breath on the other end.

A half hour later, I was sitting on a black sofa in an immaculately decorated den, a mirror with a mosaic assemblage of pastel tiles hanging overhead. Our paths hadn't crossed since graduation, but Sara was still long and lean, with black hair and penetratingly Welsh blue eyes. Her face now seemed gaunt and lifeless, unnourished by food or sleep.

"You didn't have to come over," she said.

I looked around the room. Toys sat undisturbed in bins lined up along the wall, a jarring orderliness to the colorful games and playthings. The place was full of quiet, empty of mess. Her husband, Billy, had fled to the office for a few hours.

The accident had happened on the ride home from the Academy of Natural Sciences, where Billy and Drew had spent the morning marveling at dinosaur fossils, digging for bones at the mock archaeological site, and working up the nerve to touch turtles and snakes cradled by young staff members. On their way out of town, an SUV raced through a red light and rammed into the door where Drew was strapped into his car seat. Billy escaped with a few gashes and bruises. Drew died at the hospital before Sara could get there.

She seemed eager to shift the subject. How was it, she wanted to know, that a mediocre student of average popularity and unremarkable charisma could land himself in a world-famous band? She didn't quite put it like that. She told me I looked exactly the same as I did in high school, which was not in this case a compliment, since rock musicians do not aspire to the appearance of dishwater-dull teenagers.

A few years later, when Lucy and I were tunneling into divorce, I moved into my condo. My decorating vision being what it was, I thought it best to outsource all decor decisions and immediately thought of Sara. Really, it was an excuse to call her. I hadn't been able to shake her story, my connectedness to it all.

Sara made my condo up nice and swank, a place I could only pretend to fit into. My life was anything but normal in those days, so she'd be over at odd times trying to pin me down on blinds versus curtains, steel blue versus denim blue, my views on something called a sconce, and oh, how about an island in the kitchen? She always seemed to be working, combing through catalogs, holding swatches up to the light, and often swinging by my place deep into the evening so as to oblige my anarchic schedule. It never even occurred to me that the late hours helped keep her mind from wandering into other places, from going home, where her husband no longer lived. More than once, I asked her how she was doing, employing a tone that made my meaning clear, and each time she answered, without looking up, with a curt "I'm fine." I started offering her a late-night drink, and then found myself offering her an early-morning coffee.

It was not a romance born of romance. The rhythms of courtship unfolded over carpet patterns, tables, comforters. I did not wow her with limos to Broadway shows, introductions to Michael Stipe. I did not take her to a meadow with a picnic of chutneys and urge her to smell the eucalyptus in bloom, nor did I lead her out to a beach at midnight and enchant her with lines like "Do you know what the Mayans used to say about the moon?" I was an open door, that's all, and she walked through it.

I welcomed her into my condo and my life because she was beautiful in a real and natural way, and she seemed like a portal out of the world of the fickle and into the world of the sophisticatedly mundane. Where conversations concerned friends' upcoming birthdays, pesto sauce preferences, and the pitiful state of the school district. Where it was perfectly acceptable to pass an evening together holding lattes at Barnes & Noble.

There was nothing about her that brought the thorny end of Tremble to my nose. That's why I connected with Sara. Why she connected with me is a bit of a mystery. Maybe it was because I neither required nor offered depth of any kind; my waters were shallow, she could see the bottom. Maybe it was to escape the metastasizing poverty in her core; maybe it was because she had already succumbed to it. All I know is that by being with me, one day at a time she began to walk different blocks, speak of different things, and distance herself from who she was.

Compared to the heavy Wagnerian circumstances of Sara's separation from Billy, the dissolution of my marriage was easy listening. It wasn't the age-old story either: I didn't dump my minor-league wife for a piece of ass worthy of a rock star, although by all standards and clichés I had every right to do so. Lucy was my college girlfriend, cute and comfortable, like a Volkswagen Beetle. At the time we got together, I was no more than a political science major who happened to be in a band. After graduation, when our demo miraculously got some attention and things began to spiral, Lucy bravely bore the adjustment to being a band widow, despite her nagging suspicion that everyone in that industry was a closet heroin addict.

There were, however, little things—you could call them signs—that indicated my marriage was in trouble. We stopped going to movies together because we couldn't agree on one. Musicwise, we were totally incompatible, which might seem like no big deal—you play your albums, I'll play mine—but it reflected a more basic divide. Once, when *Bitches Brew* was on the stereo, she said that all jazz sounded the same. That stung. When she announced that her favorite song was "Against All Odds" by Phil Collins, I knew our days were numbered.

"Cliché?" she asked.

"Absurd," I said, with a mouth full of disdain. "That's like saying your favorite movie is *Revenge of the Nerds II*. It's just not appropriate. Phil Collins himself would slap you for saying that."

She looked defensive. "It's a matter of opinion."

"Not always."

Ask her what her favorite Beatles song was and she'd say "If I Were a Rich Man" from *Magical Mystery Tour*. But "If I Were a Rich Man" isn't on *Magical Mystery Tour*. It's on *Fiddler on the Roof*. Who cares if she meant "Baby, You're a Rich Man?" That's not the point. This is the greatest band in the history of the universe. Know the fucking song title.

On top of everything else, I sensed she was leading me down the path of sexual apathy. She acquiesced, rarely initiated, and during the act itself, her face registered never excitement or lust but rather impatience and frequently discomfort. The fact that I was hanging out with musicians who seemed to have far more adventurous partners only fueled my dissatisfaction. I deserved better. Didn't I?

The end finally came when she caught me at a Phoenix hotel with Mackenzie. My luck being what it was, I'd never touched the bass player before that day. Tremble had a show that evening, so the afternoon found me setting off on one of my get-lost drives. These were essentially the vehicular version of a get-lost hike: I'd borrow a car, steer it out onto the road, and discover America. It was the only time I had to myself.

On my get-lost drive that day, my head full of dark thoughts about what was shaping up to be a disappointing tour, three things happened that had never happened before. First, Mackenzie joined me. Totally spur of the moment. She'd hopped into the car when I caught her sitting on the parking lot curb with a copy of *Tess of the d'Urbervilles*, and I seduced her with my aim of finding the perfect southwestern sunset. Second, this particular get-lost drive somehow became a get-lost, run-out-of-gas drive, stranding us on the side of an Arizona highway like two characters in a John Denver song. We waited to be rescued on a gorgeous stretch of road with mountains and cacti and the buzzing of insects. I kissed her. I know it took her by surprise, but after an initial recoil, she had a change of heart and kissed me back. Extremely back. When the tow truck deposited us at the hotel, we went straight for my room.

And that's when the third thing that had never happened before happened: Lucy showed up unannounced. She'd decided to surprise me on tour. And surprise me she did. She knocked on the door hours before the show, and upon seeing I wasn't alone, she picked up her bag, fled the hotel, and didn't speak to me until a week or two later when a break in the tour allowed me a few days at home.

Then she flipped. Fucking attacked me. And it wasn't one of those chick-flick tantrums that starts with wild swatting and screaming and eventually collapses into a weepy embrace—I hate you! I hate you! I . . . love you!—and then there's sex on the ottoman. No sir. Shit got thrown—plates, not pillows. We trashed the place. Rather, she trashed it; I deflected flying candy dishes and ducked behind furniture. In retrospect, that mad scene was probably the closest I've ever felt to being a true rock star.

She left me practically the next day, and I remember respecting her for it. Over the years, mutual friends have told me that she's still bitter. You'd have thought she'd be over it by now. I'm nothing special. Ask anyone.

Something also shifted in Mackenzie after Phoenix, although less dramatically. No fights, tiffs, hostility, or even serious talks. She just became quietly inaccessible to me. Even when standing next to her on stage, I had the sensation of looking at her through a telescope, as if she were drifting farther and farther into the wings.

When Sara moved in with me, life couldn't have been more different than life with Lucy. We acted the part of a couple in many ways. We ate, we argued, we shared a bed. We hiked the Canadian Rockies together. We had friends with whom we took in the new Asian fusion restaurant or the new Wes Anderson movie. She tolerated my hypersensitivity to the smell of trash—I made trips to the chute nightly, no matter how full the bag—and I put up with her insistence that we remain in the movie theater until the very last of the credits had drifted up the screen. I personally didn't see any reason to hang around and catch the Dolby logo ten minutes after the movie had ended, but she enjoyed the dreamy blanket of the movie experience and was in no hurry for it to end. And apparently, assistants to the key grip are people too.

There was no imbalance of power in our home because she was neither impressed with nor affronted by my fleeting fame. As far as she was concerned, I was just an irritable, disagreeable lawyer, a little too arrogant for my station and possibly bitter about having thrown in the towel too soon. Her frighteningly precise memory prevented me from having to worry about her not remembering the correct name of a Beatles song. And while most days she was a Joni Mitchell kind of gal, she brought her own copy of *Bitches Brew* to the relationship, and her number-one favorite song of all time was actually by Mötley Crüe, a lovable gem of a detail that suggests we don't know everything we think we do about Sara Rome.

Our relationship did have more empty rooms than most, and

every so often, in the long quiet of a Sunday afternoon, they troubled me. We were not confidants. Sara was only sporadically curious about my previous life, and even then, only superficially. I got the sense that there was something about Mackenzie that made Sara uncomfortable. Maybe it was the fact that when I spoke of the band, I never spoke of Mack. That I seemed to keep her to myself like a secret of mixed quality. That unlike Jumbo and Warren, there was nothing to ridicule or deride about Mackenzie. That unlike Jumbo and Warren, I had slept with Mackenzie.

And we never talked about Drew. Not almost never; never. Sara had always acted as if the horrific experience was something she could just move away from, like a school district. It was as if she'd packed up all her stuff, moved it into my apartment, and closed the door on her past. Locked it out, simply and definitively, much like the returning GI who trembles in front of his house and forbids his nightmares from crossing over the doormat with him.

Though the time never seemed quite right to ask, I always wondered whether things like that were really capable of being left out on the lawn.

It is the lunch hour and once again I am shifting into my coat and moving hurriedly past the secretary station, past the confined cubbyholes where youthful lawyers are shelved away until they emerge old and rumpled three decades later.

Past conference room four, in which seven indistinguishable men (not a skirt among them today) sit and contort their faces into what they think true listening should look like, and at least two of them battle the undertow of bladder pressure because it is way too soon to get up and take yet another piss.

Past Barbara Mitnik (partner, late forties, stout) sipping water from that synagogue mug adorned with Hebrew lettering, smiling at her computer monitor, surely drafting another one of those insipid parenting columns for some suburban magazine. *I was at my Rachel's soccer game last weekend and found myself thinking, Cherish every moment, it really does go by so fast.* When she's not busy composing tripe, Barbara enjoys a preoccupation with her gluten allergy.

Past Spencer Kipling, who winks at me in the hall and for once doesn't mention Death Cab for Cutie. Eighteen months ago we shared an elevator ride during which I happened to have been listening to the one Death Cab song I have on my iPod. "Didn't take you for a Death Cab guy," he remarked. And I'm not—hence, only the one song—but since then, Spencer has been operating under the misimpression that we share a passion. Articles are forwarded to me, visits are made to my office. What do I think of the new album? How psyched am I that they're back in the studio? If only I'd had the presence of mind that day to tell him I was listening to Olivia Newton-John.

Past the empty office of recently dismissed junior partner Chas Rooney. Nice guy. He'll land somewhere that places a higher premium on his penchant for sharing his views on the best albums to "get busy" to.

Past Kelvin Kim, who is fidgeting with the miniature Stormtrooper on his desk and speaking in low tones into his cell phone. "But honey, I wasn't being defensive." At the moment, Kelvin is fit and reedy, but give him time. In a few short years, he'll look like everyone else: a thirty-eight-inch waist, simian posture, and cheeks flushed from the sugar rush of a late-afternoon cupcake that someone (doesn't matter who) abandoned in the kitchen.

The irony of law firms is that they're stocked with hypereducated drones whom you hire for zealous advocacy but who are only there because they didn't feel particularly strongly about doing anything else with their lives. They sit, they read, they argue with each other because they think that's their job, they squander the prime of their lives, and incrementally, over the empty rainbow of each day, they invisibly lose contact with what they love about themselves. Then, some grim morning, they awaken and, upon looking in the mirror, realize they've become a painting in the neo-Flemish style—all severe poses, intense expressions, hard lines.

Now I'm in a packed elevator, sharing the descent with a dozen men and women, all of whom have set out with the aim of grabbing something "reasonably healthy" for lunch, like a salad or a turkey sandwich with lite mayo, but will fuck the whole thing up with Thousand Island dressing or a bag of Fritos.

Then I'm out walking the city blocks among the legions of the despairing clock watchers, the pairs of lunching duos who exchange short, pointless utterances about last night's *American Idol* or how the weather may be gorgeous now but the weekend is supposed to be rainy and cold and doesn't that just figure.

And all these interactions are so vacuous that they are essentially transactional. They do no more than register receipt, like verbal invoices. I got your bland comment, here's mine.

But I know what all these people really want to say, what they are dying to scream from the deepest pockets of their souls. It is this: How did I end up here in this tiny little infinite universe, and what do I do now?

The next thing I know, I'm standing in the lobby of my condo building, my patience dwindling as I await an elevator. I feel the strange yet familiar hot volts of creativity surging within me. There's some self-loathing in there too; I'm on the doorstep of forty, for chrissakes. My eyes meet those of the doorman and I make an impatient gesture at the elevator. He shrugs. "It's been slow all day," he says. Like that helps me.

Finally, the door opens and I rush in. I feel like a sneakered secretary with a cigarette in one hand and a twitchy finger on the trigger of a lighter in the other: desperate. There's a melody in my head that I'm barely holding on to. I need to commit it to tape. I stab the door-close button with my finger, but the doors don't budge. The elevator wants to wait. I alone don't justify the trip. If this tune flies out of my head, it'll be gone forever. I viciously poke the door-close button again and again. The button is purely cosmetic. I pound the wall in frustration.

The last time I churned out four albums' worth of material with this kind of fever, I was a stupid kid with vast expanses of time to write but neither the experiences nor insights to guide my hand. I was nineteen, a busboy at a country club for the summer, vacuuming the lobby, parking guests' BMWs and Audis, lugging coolers of Coke and Heineken out to the golf course. I lit Sternos and slid them under chafing dishes. I dunked curly fries into simmering vats of hideous liquid. Occasionally I got my ass pinched by a miniskirted MILF whose posttennis lunch consisted of three Bloody Marys and a cantaloupe wedge. Through all those summer days, I went blissfully unsupervised, as my boss, a mangy fellow named Brad, disappeared each morning into his office to get stoned. Brad spoke to each employee exactly once a day, usually during his early-afternoon rounds. The exchange was brief. He'd cast his bloodshot eyes in our direction, bid us "Get your shit together," and then retreat to his office to change his bong water.

It was during that summer that I first learned to write a song. After checking in with Brad, I'd escape into the woods nearby and play the beat-up guitar that I'd stashed there just before my shift. I learned to find a melody in the groove of strummed chords. I learned to pair that melody with a stirring topography of words. It just came to me. I became so enamored with my newly found talent and wrote with such tireless energy that at summer's end, I went back to college a changed kid. I was a songwriter now. It became my new identity. From there, way led on to way, all the way up—and all the way back down again.

I was now reconnecting with that kid. That old exhilarating spark was duking it out with the part of me that should've known better.

CHAPTER 5

After all these years, Sonny Rivers still took my call, and he looked as unhappy about it as ever on the other end of our web conference.

He cleared his throat, his patience already vanishing. "You ready yet?"

"Hang on."

I strummed and toyed with some amplifier knobs. The telecaster needed more treble. I checked the mic—check, check, one, two—then returned to the computer and started fidgeting with the camera.

"Do you know how valuable my time is?" he complained.

I positioned myself on the stool and reached for the guitar. "Can you see me okay?"

"Come on, man."

"How's the sound?"

"Play the damn song."

I glanced at the screen and watched Sonny light up a cigarette in his Los Angeles home.

"You still smoke?" I said. "Who still smokes?"

He glared at me and shook the match dead.

I had set up this video conference in the living room, which I judged to have marginally better acoustics than the office or the bedroom. We used this software at work, but obviously never to broadcast something that required sonic quality.

I lowered my gaze onto him. "Remember. Total secrecy, Sonny. I feel stupid enough. If it sucks, you forget this ever happened."

"I'm not in the habit of repeating myself and I'm not going to start now," Sonny intoned. The man never lost his cool. Not after eighteen consecutive hours in the studio. Not when a session player couldn't nail a part in twenty takes. Not when he couldn't find just the right amount of snap for the snare. He got ornery and crabby and decidedly mean at times, but he never lost it.

I took a sip from a brown beer bottle perched on the amp. It was warm and nearly stale.

"See, the way it works is, I drink and then you sound better," Sonny said.

"You're fucking hilarious."

"Play something."

I breathed. "Okay. You ready?"

"Play something or I'm out."

So I just went for it. For the next three minutes, I played "Whereabouts," my first original song in ten years. It had a driving, midtempo groove that I could fall into, and a coastal-highway melody that forced me up to the gritty heights of my range.

My face reddened with self-consciousness at the very first vocal line, my voice sounding thin, characterless, old. The lyrics suddenly felt trite and empty. Did I really just mention train tracks and an airport runway in the first verse? I hid inside the song and plowed through, pouring myself into it, trying to lose myself the way I used to. It was an endless three minutes. Was that last verse and chorus necessary?

When it was over, I hazarded a glance at the monitor. Sonny was looking down, the cigarette secured on the side of his mouth. He might've been picking at his shoe.

"Did you get that?" I finally asked.

Without raising his eyes, he said, "Hang on a minute." Then he got up and disappeared off camera.

I reached for my beer, warmer now and increasingly tasting of discouragement. Sonny had always been an enigma. He coaxed staggering performances from the fingers and mouths of artists of all genres, from hip-hop to country, and all talent levels, from as high as Stevie Wonder to as low as me, and unquestionably had one of the most respected ears in the industry. But an open book he was not. All told, I'd spent about four months holed up with the man in the confining quarters of a recording studio doing two albums with him on major label dime, and I knew next to nothing about him personally. But for all his mercurial moods and methods, you trusted him. Which was why he was the only option when I finally summoned the gumption to share. He would be blunt, just as he was when I played him that hideously ill-conceived, underwritten concept album years ago. He would tell me if I was no longer qualified even to sing "Michael, Row Your Boat Ashore" at a day camp. Maybe this time I'd even listen.

I sat there on my amp, waiting, wondering where in sweet hell he'd gone. I allowed my fingers to skate over the two-day indigent stubble on my cheeks. My skin felt particularly saggy that night, especially my chin and that unseemly upper part of the neck, all making me acutely aware of my physical deterioration at a time when it would've been helpful to forget it.

I glanced at all the wires and connections around me, momentarily comforted by such old companions. I'd fretted over the sound quality of this contraption—despite Sonny's dismissive and perhaps telling assurances that it was "good enough for our purposes"—but webcam was my only option. The closest thing I had to recording equipment these days was a Dictaphone in my desk drawer at work.

I blew an impatient huff through pursed lips and checked the wall clock. Every passing moment edged me closer to an awkward rendezvous with Sara, who could walk in any second. There was, I'd noticed, something not quite right with her today. That morning, she'd mumbled something about a late night, dinner with a friend. But earlier this evening, as I was readying this makeshift teleconference, her office had called looking for her. Ravi Chatterjee and his prim subcontinental Queen's English accosted me from the other end. Ravi, who shared an office with Sara but still somehow considered himself her mentor, was an okay guy, despite his penchant for pumpkin orange sport coats and a website photo in which he actually held a glass of white wine. It was unusual for Ravi to call our home number, but, he explained, Sara hadn't answered her cell. Half listening, half plugging in cables, I absorbed Ravi's griping about Sara's having missed a meeting, and I promised to have her call when she surfaced. I'd been too busy to question why Sara would miss a work meeting for some dinner with a friend. And now that I thought about it, she hadn't specified which friend she was to dine with. Sara had a solid, nonfluctuating cadre of friends, none of whom were really friends with one another. There was no roving cluster of "the Girls" who met for happy hour or giggled together through the new Matthew McConaughey flick, which meant that I couldn't interrogate one of her gal pals about her whereabouts because, in all likelihood, the friend wouldn't know. Unless Sara was up in North Philly at that studio with Josie and the artisans, she was basically off the grid.

Sonny reappeared on the monitor, sliding himself into his desk chair.

"Where the fuck did you go?" I huffed.

"Play something else."

"Something else? Hold on—what did you think of the first one?"

He looked irritated. "What did I just say?"

I noticed that Sonny now had a laptop on his knee. This was the equivalent of making a phone call in the middle of a take, which, come to think of it, I'd seen him do.

"Are you surfing YouTube over there?" I asked.

"Never you mind what I'm doing. Concern yourself with what you're doing. You got another bullet in the chamber or not?"

Annoyed but compliant, I launched into a tune called "Painless Days," a fingerpicking lark of a song that beckoned a girl to come outside into a springtime afternoon. Tonally, it was a departure for me. Structurally, it had no chorus. But I'd never written a song before that made me want to build a tree house and sit in it all weekend, so there was that. I'd grown slightly more relaxed, but it was evening now and my voice wore the tatters and strains of a long day. Ten years of not singing a note will do that to you. The six-pack I'd gulped down to chase the nerves didn't help either.

As I floundered through my performance, I knew that Sonny was either getting this or he wasn't. It was that simple. There was nothing more I could do at this point. I'd been writing at a frantic clip for weeks, and it was time to wave a wet finger into the breeze and seek feedback from someone I trusted. I needed to know if there was anything to this recent shock of creativity or if it was just a death rattle.

When my fingers had plucked the last notes of the song, I looked directly into the unblinking red eye of the mini-camera perched atop the screen. On the far coast, Sonny was reclining casually, savoring his smoke, his eyes focused downward toward his laptop. A smirk schemed its way across his face as if he'd just read an amusing e-mail.

Sonny didn't seem to notice I'd stopped playing. I let a moment pass before clearing my throat. He looked up and took a drag of his cigarette. "What are the others like?"

"Jesus, man."

"I asked you a question."

My hand lurched plaintively into the air. "I don't know. The others are in the same vein, I suppose. 'Whereabouts' is probably the most commercial, I guess. I don't really fucking know what that means anymore, but yeah, I'd call it commercial. There are a few others that feel edgier to me. I hear most of these with very sparse production. Raw, stripped down, like what Rick Rubin did with Johnny Cash and Neil Diamond. Though Neil Diamond isn't at all what I'm shooting for. I'm rambling—I should just shut up now." I paused for a swig. "What are the others like? How do I answer that? They're awesome, they suck, I don't know. I guess there's one that kind of rocks out—it's called 'America Eats Warhol'; that one I really like. And there are some that are darker thematically, not in the sense that they tell a story or any of that shit, but the imagery is sort of austere. I'm not saying I've written *The Wall*, just stuff that feels foreboding, brooding, Bonnie Prince Billy. But at the same time, I feel like even the darker songs still pull the listener in." I'd descended into something beyond rambling. I was flat-out not making sense. "I don't know what the fuck I'm talking about, so I'm just going to shut up now. But one last thing—"

"Do me a favor," he interrupted. "Quit telling me you're going to shut up now. Just shut up now."

I reached again for the beer, which was now piss warm. When I looked at the monitor, Sonny wore a cruel grin.

"You having a good time over there, asshole?" I said.

Then he leaned forward and frowned. "Look, you got some serious work to do."

I let out a bruised snort. Then I shook my head with all the dejection I'd fully anticipated. Why had I even subjected myself to this in the first place? This was a bad idea. I should've been able to recognize bad ideas by now.

I lifted the guitar off my knee and slid it away across the carpet. "You know what? Fuck that. I'm not working on this anymore. I'm done. Fucking done, man."

"Go make a record, motherfucker."

I stopped and looked at him. "What?"

"Get it down and get it down right. You need to make a record."

"Are you serious?"

"I don't like it when people ask me if I'm serious. It undermines all the other words that come out of my mouth." Then he checked his watch. "I'm late."

He folded up his laptop and bore down into the camera, pointing the blistering end of his cigarette at me. "You be careful with these cunning plans of yours. You hearing me?" He returned the cigarette to his lips and added, "I love you, motherfucker."

The screen was overtaken by a hand reaching out at me, as if to cover my eyes, or tear off a blindfold. And then he was gone.

I stood next to my guitar, unable to move, the light sweat of terror staining my shirt. Sonny's directive had taken on a dreamlike quality, like something I was told to do a millennium ago.

You will never again feel the way you do at this moment.

That's what he told us on our first day in the studio. At the time, I took our producer's words as both a call to Zen and a call to battle, a maxim intended to rouse a band of tenderfeet into both savoring the promise of the moment and delivering on it. Over the years, I'd recalled those words with melancholy. Sonny was right. Never again did I feel the way I did at that moment, on the precipice of my life, awestruck by everything, including my own sense of limitlessness.

Sony Music had signed us on the strength of some hook-driven demos and a strong draw on the bar circuit all along the Mid-Atlantic. From the Bitter End in Greenwich Village to the Bottle & Cork in Dewey Beach, from the 9:30 Club in DC to the Chameleon in Lancaster, we packed the house. Our pitch for a record deal had been played tantalizingly by a brash agent trying to make a name for herself. Two meetings with the slicker-than-thou Alaina Farber—a woman who could imbue the act of picking up dry cleaning with a whiff of eroticism—and the Sony rep, a seasoned, affable, and prematurely gray chap named Colin Stone, was putty in her hands. He believed her when she informed him—*informed* him—that we were destined to make a brilliant album or, at the very least, a homogenous blockbuster. Our debut, *The Queen Kills the King*, ended up going multiplatinum.

At the first of those recording sessions, we were led through the chic Brooklyn studio a little before noon (first thing in the morning in musicians' hours). The bewitching instruments, sparkling microphones, and serpentine arrangement of boards, cords, and wires lay about us like an indoor state-of-the-art Garden of Eden.

Sonny immediately ordered us to take up our instruments and play through the songs we considered our strongest, the ones we felt defined us. As we obliged, he sat on a swivel chair in front of the board, staring at us through the glass with his legs crossed and an inscrutable expression on his face. He reacted to nothing; his eyebrows had gone on hiatus. When we were done, I arrogantly volunteered my views as to which songs were radio ready and which were the deep cuts and how each was necessary for a complete and whole record. I said this to the man who made Aerosmith's and Dave Matthews's bestselling albums.

While I went on about hit potential and the demographics of college radio and the mass-market pipelines of MTV and VH1, Sonny stared back at me through piercing eyes. When my mouth had finally emptied itself of nonsense, he pounded a pack of smokes into his palm and said, "You can make something that people will celebrate or you can make something that's worth being celebrated. You have until I finish this cigarette to decide." And he walked outside.

It was the band's unanimous conclusion that his question was rhetorical.

But now, all these years later, standing alone in my condo, there was only the memory of confidence, only the metallic taste of fear. And then I heard a key sliding into the door.

Something about the way Sara entered the room made me forget all about music for a moment. With eye contact that felt slippery and hasty, she paused at the curious arrangement of instruments and computers clunking up the living room, then turned to the closet, drawing her long, chestnut-brown jacket off her shoulders.

"Everything okay?" I asked.

"Yeah," she answered over the wind chime of coat hangers. Brushing the hair out of her eyes, she nodded at the mess. "And what exactly is going on here?"

"I was just screwing around," I said with a shrug. "Hey—Ravi called."

"Here?"

"Yeah. Something about a meeting."

"That's odd. He knew I wasn't going to be around. I specifically told him. I was with Josie and Wynne."

I waded back over the wires and proceeded to remove the mic from the clip and dismantle the boom stand.

Shifting her frown to me, Sara said, "Teddy, not once in all the years we've lived together have I come home to find you playing music. That is, until the past few weeks." She looked serious, unusually pensive. "Let's talk. Can we do that? Both of us?"

I'd shared very little of my recent musical reawakening with Sara. While she could plainly see I'd taken to strumming the guitar again, I'd told her nothing of my Switzerland hijinks, or of this unforeseen avalanche of music and words.

"You know Sonny Rivers, right?"

She nodded. "He produced your records."

I took a long breath. "He wants me to record again."

"He wants you to what?"

"I've been writing a little lately, and I played him some of my new songs tonight. He kind of liked them. He thinks I should record them."

"Like, with the band?"

"We didn't get that far, but I think so."

Her face was a blank slate.

"I don't get it either," I offered helplessly.

"That's great," she said, her voice tepid, her eyes beset.

Even if Sara had known I'd been writing songs again, it never would have occurred to her that I harbored any sort of plans. She would have assumed I was writing songs the way most people write poetry, or the way she did her mosaics with her friends—as an outlet, a tawdry little secret. You write your songs or your sonnets, and then you bury them in your dresser drawer where they gradually sink lower and lower under the cuff links and condoms.

"So what does this mean?" she asked.

"I don't really know."

"You must know. Why else would you have played him your songs in the first place?"

Standing in the living room of my apartment, a lawyer of generic looks and advancing age—hardly the moment to ramp up a career in pop music—there were simply no words.

"I'm not kidding, Sara. I don't know what this all means." I looked away from her. "I don't know what's going on."

Sara circumnavigated the gear and yanked on the sliding door that opened onto the balcony. The room had become stale and muggy, the strumming and singing and perspiring having stirred the air into a broth.

"I see somebody's having a hard time getting older," she ventured with a smirk.

"Maybe."

Sara eyed the disarray before her—the chairs, the amplifier, the computer, the snake pit of cables, all of which looked as if it had been swept into the room by a flood. She took ginger steps to the sofa, smoothed out her pant legs, and dropped onto a cushion. "Let's back up. You wrote some new songs and decided to play them for the guy who produced your band's albums fifteen years ago."

I nodded, continuing to wrap the microphone cable in large loops that extended from my hand down around my elbow.

"And you did this because . . ."

"Well. It's complicated."

She let out a dark laugh. "What isn't?"

For some reason, I had the inexplicable urge to tell her that I wished she and I were less complicated. I wanted her to hear me say that. But that would have been a clear violation of our tacit, long-standing agreement to allow all our angst, hope, dread, joy, grief, guilt, and panic to jumble around of their own kinetics, largely unexamined.

"You're a musician, Teddy. That was your life until your luck ran out. And then you evolved. I hope you haven't been unhappy all these years, but by the same token, it would be perfectly natural to fantasize about going back to that world, especially since you would've preferred not to have left it in the first place."

I tossed the microphone cable toward my trusted old bag of gear. It was blue and faded and the fabric was unraveling on the sides where the boxlike tuners and guitar pedals pressed against it. It was the same bag I'd lugged around to gigs in college. It used to smell of stale beer. Now it smelled like the back of my shoe closet.

I took a seat next to her on the sofa. "Have you ever wanted to do something different?" I asked her, exploring the weary curve of her spine. "Have you ever felt the itch to change?"

She tilted her head downward, peering at me over a pair of invisible spectacles. "I'm not restless like you. When I feel the urge to change, I explore a new design style or I buy myself a new outfit, or we plan a trip and disappear off the face of the earth for a week. That's probably as much redefinition as I've got in me at this point."

I didn't say anything. As she stared at me, I knew she wanted to ask me if she was one of the things I wanted to change. She had to be wondering what it was in my life, or absent from it, that was leading me down this path.

"Speaking of change." She slapped a hand on each of her thighs, something people tended to do before standing. But she didn't move. "Sometimes it comes looking for *you*, not the other way around."

I had the notion she was speaking of present tenses, and I felt the air in the room thicken.

"There's something I want to tell you," she said.

"Okay."

I waited in the pregnant silence as she gathered herself.

"Billy called me."

"Billy. Your Billy?"

"Yeah." She looked away. "He wants a divorce."

That, I did not see coming. But somebody should have. Sara and

Billy didn't last very long after the accident, the marriage falling into a slow, methodical disintegration. One detail left unattended in their mutual flight, however, was their marital status. Over the years I'd wondered just how accidental that was, if maybe, on a subconscious level, a divorce would've been the final hammer swing on the life they once shared, and neither of them had it in them to do it.

Her being married never factored into our relationship because I never threatened to make Sara a bigamist (my starter marriage having been an event I wasn't keen on replicating) and Sara, for her part, seemed preoccupied with just making it through the day. It was a perverse sort of equilibrium, mutually assured purgatory.

Sara and I spoke of marriage exactly once. It was on a Sunday morning, a year after she'd moved in. As I pounded a ketchup bottle over an omelet, I offhandedly asked if she thought we'd ever get married. It wasn't a proposal; it was for discussion purposes only. I merely wanted to know where her head was on the issue, like if she thought we'd ever sail the Strait of Magellan or if she reckoned Puerto Rico might one day become a state. She looked out the window for a long moment. Then she asked if that was something I really wanted to discuss. I took it as a rebuke, but have since wondered if she was truly posing a question. I honestly can't remember it ever coming up again.

"Why now?" I asked her.

"I don't know. He may be involved with someone and . . . I don't know." The thought dissolved into the air between us.

"Is he getting remarried?"

She shook her head slowly. "I don't think that's what's driving this."

"Wow, Sara." I stared at her, weighing the many questions I could've asked. "So, what was it like, speaking to him after all these years?" I assumed it had been years, although there really was so much about Sara Rome I didn't know.

"It was strange. Needless to say, his call caught me off guard. Just hearing the sound of his voice knocked me a little. We kept it superficial—our jobs, our families, things like that. Then he said he thinks we need to, you know, make it official because of how long it's been. And one day one of us might want to get married again."

She didn't personalize it. The remarrying didn't necessarily involve me.

"How are you with all that?"

She shrugged with a woman's natural pragmatism. "It makes sense."

"Yeah," I agreed softly. "I suppose it does."

Sara never talked about Billy and I never inquired, assuming any thought of him would carry her to thoughts of Drew, a topic strictly off-limits. But now that I thought about it, there had been one instance. Late one night, soon after she'd moved in, I sensed an emptiness in the bed and, half-asleep, went looking for her in the predawn chill. I found her crumpled on the kitchen floor, the phone to her ear, sobbing to Billy. When her wet, puffy eyes flickered my way, it was only to convey that I wasn't part of this. This didn't involve me.

"So, what do we do now?" I said to her. "Drink to our mutual upheaval?"

"A drink is a good idea." She got up and dewrinkled those invisible creases in her pants. "But this divorce thing is not upheaval. It's the opposite. It's a settling down."

She carried herself heavily into the kitchen. I continued to disassemble the room to the sound of a wine bottle being smoothly violated by a corkscrew.

As leisurely paced as this divorce might have been, it was sure to change things between us. It was a step in the direction of finality, of bringing to a close a chapter in her life. And endings tended to deposit you at the doorstep of some other beginning. What would Sara want to begin? This was something I'd never before needed to consider. I didn't want Sara's situation to push her away from me, but at the moment, given the left turn my life was potentially about to take, I wasn't so sure I wanted it to nudge her much closer either.

This divorce *was* upheaval. It was upheaval precisely because it was a settling down.

She returned to the room cupping two stemless glasses, and held one out to me.

"Are you sure you're okay?" I asked her.

"I'm fine." She looked battered. "I don't want to talk about this anymore."

"Okay." I reached out to tap my wineglass to hers.

"We're drinking to you tonight, Teddy," she said.

I wasn't so sure. "I think we're just drinking."

CHAPTER 6

I stood outside the house and pondered the consequences. There would be many. A blizzard of them, most of them unwelcome. Suddenly, a simple knock seemed a dire, drastic step. I'd come this far, I told myself, though really it hadn't been very far at all.

Screw it.

I rapped twice on the door and a symphony of muted noises erupted behind it. Kitchen chairs skidded, skirmishing children trampled down carpeted steps. Finally, the door blew open and there I was, staring at Jumbo Jett.

We looked at each other, and his face, puffier than I'd remembered it, ballooned into a bulky smile. "Mingus."

"Hello, Jumbo."

He glanced over his shoulder, then scooted furtively out onto the porch, pulling the door closed behind him. Throwing an arm over my shoulder, he began guiding me back down the walk toward the street.

"Man, it's so great to see you," he said, even as he seemed to be escorting me off the property. Then he produced a white envelope out of the front pocket of his jeans. "Dude, would you mind keeping this in your car for a little while?"

"What?" I looked at the little package. "What is that?"

"It's nothing."

"What sort of nothing?"

"It's just some pot. No big deal. Sandy and Israel caught me smoking again. Personally, I don't see the problem. The kids were at school. They know I'd never do it with them around. But they can be real tightasses—you know how it is. And it is their basement, after all. So, if you could just hang on to it for a little bit until this all blows over."

I stopped walking. "Hold on a second. What the hell are you talking about?"

He looked at me as if everything that had just come pouring out of his mouth made perfect sense. Like this was an eminently reasonable way to greet each other after ten years.

"Start over," I demanded. "Sandy and . . .'"

"Israel."

"Sandy and Israel. And who the fuck are these people?"

"Sandy's my ex."

"Ex what?"

"Ex-wife. Israel's her husband. They're not real big into the whole marijuana scene, even for medicinal needs—and I've got plenty of those—and moving out of the house isn't really the best move for me right now, you know, financially. So, I gotta bite the bullet on this one. Their way or the highway. You know how it is."

He stole a peek back at the house and continued ushering me down the driveway.

"I have a lot of questions," I said. "But let's start with this one: You live with your ex-wife and her husband?"

"And their two kids."

"I see."

"They're good kids." Somehow that was relevant. "They really like me."

I was already sorry I'd come. "Jumbo, I don't mean to be rude, but what the fuck?"

"I recognize it's not all that common of an arrangement."

We'd reached the end of the driveway and were standing next to my aging Lexus coupe. "Dude, unlock it. Nice car, by the way. Gray totally works for you. Mysterious."

"It's silver," I said, clicking the doors unlocked.

I watched uncomfortably as Jumbo slid into the passenger seat and began rifling through my glove compartment. He removed a stack of CDs to make room for his envelope, which he concealed like a master spy inside the vehicle owner's manual. We'd been together thirty seconds and Jumbo had already made me an accessory to a felony.

Slamming the glove box shut, he started flipping through the discs. "The new Oasis. Nice." He turned it over and studied the track listing. "How is it?"

"Come out of there."

He shimmied his ungainly frame out of the car and closed the door behind him. "Thanks, Mingus," he said through an exhale of relief. "I owe you."

"Don't forget that that's in there," I said. Lecturing Jumbo was like riding a bike. "I'm not driving home with that in my car." We were not off to a good start, Jumbo Jett and I.

Then, for the first time, I had a moment to take him in—the faded daddy jeans, the doughy physique, the lawless hair one frizz away from electric socket bedlam. There was something strangely heartening about Jumbo in chaos. He was just as I'd left him.

"It's been a long time," he said. "I'm super glad you called."

Then, with an abrupt lurch forward, he locked a suffocating hug around my torso. It was like being absorbed into one of Maurice Sendak's wild things. He held on for a while, too long actually, and when I detected a subtle rocking, I patted him twice on the back to indicate it was time for the hug to be over.

"I've missed you, man," he said.

"Yeah. Listen, I was hoping there'd be somewhere we could talk, but I guess it's not going to be the house."

Jumbo frowned at the Pepsi-blue split-level perched atop the driveway in all its aluminum siding glory.

"Screw that," Jumbo said defiantly. "I pay rent."

* * *

The way Jumbo smuggled me into the basement made me feel like a truant twelve-year-old sneaking over for an afternoon of PlayStation. Unfinished and gloomy, the cellar was a dank, low-lit space with exposed cinder block everywhere except for the places where Jumbo had seen fit to hang a tapestry, a photograph, or a Tremble album jacket. There was a bed, in a way—two mattresses stacked on the cement floor. An ancient tan sofa with decomposing upholstery lined one of the walls, a generic wooden chair sat stranded in the middle of the room, and that about did it for furniture. Clothes hung like battle corpses over the sides of plastic college dorm crates, and a few cardboard boxes were put to work as nightstands. It smelled like basement down there, a mix of new car and wet dog. The most uplifting aspect of the place was the pounding of footsteps overhead, which signaled life of a mainstream variety somewhere close by.

"What do you think of my pad?"

How does one sugarcoat cinder block and cement? "It's fine. Maybe a little too 'It puts the lotion in the basket.'"

After warning me that the sofa was missing a leg, Jumbo lit a stick of incense on one of the highly flammable cardboard night tables and offered me a beer. I declined, it being ten o'clock on a Saturday morning.

Jumbo settled onto the bed and fixed me with an outsized smile. "Jeez, Mingus, look at us, together again."

Jumbo always called me Mingus. I guess at one point I knew why.

"You and I were buddies, man," he went on. "Since we were little kids. I never thought we'd go ten years without talking."

It was the raw truth that, with the exception of the last decade—a respite I'd earned many times over—I'd been along for the whole bumpy ride that was Jumbo Jett's life. I'd witnessed the good stuff: his ascent to revered yet volatile guitar god, the affable ruffian who chewed up the scenery onstage and who made for an entertaining if not always comprehensible interview. But I'd also had a front-row seat to a mélange

of horrors I would've loved to unremember. The runny nose he sported
K through 12. His unfortunate hobby of shaking people's hands with a
buzzer. His unbecoming sports illiteracy (the year the band was invited
to the Super Bowl, he nagged me to leave at "intermission").

"As you can see, I'm still playing." He gestured proudly toward a
squadron of guitars up against the wall.

That information was the first positive thing about my visit.

Whereas Warren, Mack, and I opted not to outstay our welcome in
an industry that didn't seem to want us anymore, Jumbo had pressed
on, instrument in hand, albeit on a slightly smaller scale. Scaring up
a few weekend warriors from the neighborhood and a shaggy high
school student or two, he formed Jumbo Jett and His Ragtag Honeysuckle Band, which had since endured countless Menudo-like per-
sonnel changes but still loitered around the Mid-Atlantic, looking for
love. Recent venues included the parking lot of Whole Foods, a har-
vest festival at a pumpkin patch, and an eight-year-old's birthday party.

As for why he was doing all of this in Baltimore, he told me he'd
relocated for Sandy, a social worker he met on a plane and to whom
he gave permission to eat him should they happen to crash in the
Andes. (Unlikely, as the flight was Philly to Atlanta.) "I fell head over
heels, man," he said wistfully. "She scratched me right where I itched."
But the love affair had clearly turned sour at some point, seeing as
how Sandy was now scratching some other guy where he itched.

"As passionate as I am about my music, the band is actually more
of a sideline at this point," he explained bravely.

"Oh?"

"I went back to school, Mingus. Got my degree. I'm a midwife."

"A midwife? But you're a man."

"It's a same-sex term."

"You mean unisex?"

"Yeah, that one."

It didn't sound unisex.

"All practitioners of midwifery are known as midwives," he informed me with the inflection of someone who'd memorized the manual. "We're respected independent contractors in the health care profession."

"Huh."

"We help women have healthy pregnancies and then, when it's showtime, we guide them through a natural childbirth."

Jumbo's presence at an actual baby delivery seemed as discordant an image as there could be. "You don't have to go to med school or something for that?"

"Nope," he said. "I don't think so."

"Well. Good for you, James."

"Yeah. Just don't eat lunch before a childbirth." Then he fake retched.

That seemed as good a time as any to cut to the chase. "So Jumbo, there's something I want to talk to you about."

"Oh yeah?"

"I'm not just passing through."

We were then interrupted by the sound of the door opening at the top of the stairs. "Jim? You down there?" a man's voice called.

"Yes indeedy."

Plodding footsteps advanced down the stairs, and soon a severely thin man, midforties and balding, stood at the base of the steps, a red rugby shirt hanging off his scrawny frame. He was carrying a little girl who instantly leapt out of his arms and bolted for a Fender acoustic propped up against an amp. Jumbo looked on with a smile as the toddler started scraping her fingers across the strings, chiming out an open chord over and over.

"Sounds great, Ingrid. Your practice is really paying off," Jumbo said. "Israel, meet Teddy. Teddy, Israel."

I shook his bony hand. The man was fucking emaciated.

"Tremble, right?" Israel said with a point and a squint.

I nodded.

"Great to meet you. We're obviously all big fans in this house."

There was nothing obvious about it, considering that the band's guitarist used to be married to this man's wife and had taken up residence under his stairs.

"And this little princess," Jumbo said, scooping up the girl and tickling her tummy, "is Ingrid. Ingrid, can you say hi to Teddy?"

I said, "Hi, Ingrid."

The kid said nothing.

Then Israel turned serious. "So, Jim, I just got a call and it looks like I've got to run into the office for a couple of hours. Sandy took Zed to the movies and I don't know if you guys are busy or were just going to be hanging out here . . . You know I hate to ask."

"We don't mind, right, Mingus? Ingrid can tag along." Jumbo had now inverted the two-year-old so that she was dangling upside down and squealing with laughter.

"You sure? I can always take her with me," Israel said, staring uneasily at his kid, whose head was swinging mere inches above the concrete floor. Jumbo was now shaking her like a can of spray paint. This Israel fellow must have been completely out of options to leave his toddler with a repeat offender of his "no dope in the house" policy.

"No biggie, man," Jumbo said.

"I really appreciate it, Jim. And please, just be extra careful and—"

"Don't worry, Is. We'll be fine. Teddy and I were just going to catch up a little. Maybe we'll take her down to the Inner Harbor. What do you think, Mingus? It's a nice day out there. We'll pack sandwiches."

"Sure." I smiled tight as a lash. "I love boats."

"He looks like he's being treated for something, that's all I meant," I said, as I buckled myself into the passenger seat of the great sandstone minivan. The sticky garage air smelled of mulch, motor oil, and bicycle tires.

"I suppose he is thin," Jumbo allowed.

"He's rickety."

"I know he's a big cabbage guy," Jumbo said thoughtfully. "That might have something to do with it." He was leaning through the open door, struggling with the straps of Ingrid's car seat. "Sorry about having to take the whaler. My Chevelle isn't great for kids."

It may have, at one point, been charmingly quirky that Jumbo drove a Chevelle, a car out of print since the seventies. But now, it couldn't have been more than a rusty, protective covering for a disgruntled muffler.

Jumbo slid behind the wheel and started rifling through a disorganized flock of keys. As he coiled his burly frame toward the rear and started backing the van down the driveway, wild giggling erupted from the backseat. "She cracks up every time I do that," he said bemusedly. "All I have to do is turn my head around to back up and she thinks it's hysterical."

"Well, reverse is the funniest of all gears," I said.

We'd barely reached the bottom of the driveway when Jumbo slammed on the brake.

"Christ!" he yelled, squinting into the rearview mirror. "I almost killed him!"

He checked on Ingrid, but the abrupt stop had barely registered, so engaged was she with a frayed picture book illustrated with golden-locked princesses.

Jumbo opened his door and began ambling down the driveway. "I didn't even see you, Dad," I heard him say.

Dad? I unlatched my door and stuck out my head. At the foot of the driveway, standing next to an antediluvian Oldsmobile, was a senior citizen in a drab-green jacket.

"It's not your weekend, Dad," I thought I heard Jumbo explain. "Did you forget?"

The man at the end of the driveway was stooped over with his arms wrist-deep in the pockets of his trousers—there's no other word for that variety of pants; it's just trousers—periodically lifting his expectant eyes toward his son. Jumbo laid a gentle hand on his back as the old man contemplated the curb. A miscommunication was being sorted out.

Then Jumbo pointed at me. "Hey, Dad, look. There's Teddy Tremble. Mingus, you remember my old man."

A brittle smile raised the edges of Elmer Jett's unkempt gray mustache, and we exchanged waves.

Jumbo's parents were divorced by the time we'd reached our early teens, but his father refused to be a stranger. Aside from sharing a roof with his son every other weekend and for two months over the summer, the old man attended all school events, including the close call that was Jumbo's graduation. He showed up at his son's Little League games to watch him sway dreamily in right field with his glove on the wrong hand. And for the entire month of July, they rented a Winnebago and embarked on a road trip dotted with Americana's greatest hits—Mount Rushmore, the Grand Canyon, Route 66. July was the only time I ever felt envious of Jumbo.

When the father-son confab reached its natural conclusion, Jumbo gave his dad an affectionate pat on the shoulder, and the geezer sloped back toward his beat-up ride.

"What was that all about?" I asked once Jumbo was back in the van, slinging the seat belt across his drooped chest.

"Oh, he's just a little confused, that's all. He thought it was his weekend."

"His weekend for what?"

"To hang out," he replied, pulling out of the driveway and waving one final toodle-oo at his father. "He still honors the custody arrangement. You gotta give him credit. It's been, like, thirty years and still, every other weekend."

I combed Jumbo's face for even a speck of irony.

"Hasn't anyone told him his obligations ended about twenty years ago?"

"Don't go all lawyer on me, Mingus."

"No one has custody of a thirty-eight-year-old, Jumbo. You have custody of yourself. I'm not saying a little parental guidance would hurt in your case, but you no longer need a court order. You can sleep over at your dad's any time you want. Concepts of custody don't apply anymore."

Jumbo flashed me a tolerant grin. "They do to him."

He then jerked some knobs on the dash and the AC roared to life like the afterburners on an F-14 Tomcat. Arctic wind huffed into the Monster Truck Show–vehicle. Within seconds I was shivering, positioning my body to avoid the streams of frigid air.

"What are we doing here, transporting a liver?"

"I'm kind of a worrier when it comes to temperature and kids," said the father of none. "You can suffocate on hot air much quicker than on cold air. Bet you didn't know that."

I didn't. Because it's ridiculous.

In the fish-tanged air of the Baltimore harbor, I watched Ingrid spin about on a merry-go-round, clutching the reins of a plastic horse as my once and future guitar player held her steady. I didn't imagine that any band had ever been launched under these conditions, and in that respect, I suppose we'd already made rock history.

As far as I was concerned, small children were pretty useless unless you wanted to preboard a plane. Parents always looked so miserable. I pitied them when I ran headlong into the interminable drudgery of their weekend grocery outings. They all looked like if you offered them immediate legal dissolution of the family, each member being handed a hobo stick and fifty bucks—"Good luck to you, son." "Same to you, Dad."—they'd go for it without a second thought. Young mothers seem to find catastrophe everywhere, even in the lunch tray that their husbands dared to bring over. *You got Connor a hot dog? Connor doesn't eat hot dogs!* And the husband stares back at her with a mountain of desolation, thinking, I took this girl to one fraternity formal twenty years ago. How did things go so horribly wrong?

"So, about that thing I wanted to discuss," I said when my companions had disembarked the ride. Jumbo had begun to tear off easily digestible quantities of turkey and bread and was handing them to Ingrid.

"Yeah, man, talk to me."

"Well." I searched for the right words; they didn't exist. "There's no other way to put this. I'm considering reviving the band."

He stopped cold. "No shit?" His eyes shot to Ingrid. "I mean, no shoot?"

"I've written some new songs. I want to record an album. Sonny Rivers may produce, schedule permitting."

"Sonny Rivers! Holy shit, man! That's awesome! I mean, holy shoot!"

Fortunately, the little girl was too preoccupied for the naughty word to register. Some fur-suited characters were gathering at a make-shift stage, and Ingrid was trying to decide if they were terrifying or the most wonderful things she'd ever seen.

"I never thought I'd be doing this again, but some things have happened to me over the past few months. I'll explain everything when we sit down and talk, but for the first time in a long time—"

Jumbo interrupted my backstory with unequivocal support. "Dude, I'm in. Definitely. Count me in."

"Hold on. I want you to think about it."

"Don't need to."

"Yes, you do. I'm talking about a commitment here. Taking risks, possibly leaving jobs. I'm not asking if you want an oatmeal cookie."

"Mingus, you don't have to tell me what's what. I was in the biz, remember?"

All too well. "I don't want issues, James. I've had enough of your issues."

"I'm a lot more responsible than I used to be. Hello? Exhibit A?" He gestured proudly to Ingrid. As if keeping a toddler alive for a few hours erased decades of waywardness and debauchery.

"You're a great musician, Jumbo. I wish you weren't, but you are, and that's why I'm here. But we're not twenty-three anymore. I want to do this the right way, like adults. Do you hear what I'm saying?"

"Of course."

"Well, just in case you don't, I'm saying that I need to be able to count on you."

"You can, dude."

Just as it dawned on me that I was being told what I wanted to hear and that it was unfair to extract a promise that Jumbo was ill-equipped to deliver, our two-year-old companion suddenly shrieked and bolted in the direction of the costumed furballs. A bargain brand Big Bird had begun to juggle bowling pins before a mass of bewitched kids, and Ingrid would be damned if she was going to miss it.

"Ingrid!" Jumbo yelled. "Stay! Shit!"

As he pulled up anchor and gave chase, I almost had to look away. I don't think I'd ever seen Jumbo run before, and there was something jarringly unnatural about it. It was like when they showed Kermit the Frog on a bike. It just didn't look right. Who knew he had legs?

I followed my companions, shaking my head, my steps heavy with ambivalence.

Minutes later, we were all seated on abrasive concrete while a collection of teamless mascots and characters without a network—not-quite-Eeyore, Smokey the Bear's inbred cousin—danced, cart-wheeled, and wobbled on unicycles before captivated children and their wrist-checking parents.

I stared out into the harbor, watching sailboats make for the bay in slow motion. I had to do this, I reassured myself. This was necessary. Without Jumbo, more than anyone else, we were a different band, a lesser band. I needed him. I hated that I did, but I did.

I'd filled Sara in on this sorry road trip the night before. Armed with a bottle of Chianti, we'd walked three blocks to the Mediterranean BYO owned by clients of hers, expats from Cairo whose restaurant had been around forever despite never hosting more than a smattering of diners at any given time. The hostess led us to a table by the window, uncorked our wine, and allowed a stream of deep burgundy to tumble into our glasses, all the while recounting the chorus of compliments she and her husband had received about Sara's decorating handiwork in their home. Soon afterward, a complimentary mezze platter of hummus, tzatziki, kalamata olives, and little cheese cubes surrounded by fallen dominos of grilled pita arrived at our table via a lovely olive-skinned young woman, the owners' daughter. As we smiled her away from the table, I said to Sara, "So, I'm going down to Baltimore tomorrow to see Jumbo." The night of my webcast with Sonny a week earlier had been the last we'd spoken of my musical fits and starts.

"Jumbo? Why?" She surfed a pita wedge through the tzatziki, then bent down beneath the table to retrieve her napkin. It was an endearing idiosyncrasy of hers that her lap seemed ill-fitted to accommodate a folded napkin, and at least twice every meal she had to blindly grope the floor.

"I'm going to ask him to help me. I think he could contribute to the recordings."

"Isn't he . . . kind of a moron?"

"He is."

She smiled weakly. "But not enough of a moron."

"He's plenty a moron. Let's put it this way: on the day of our record-company audition, he wore a tattered T-shirt that read 'I Got Sand in My Pants at the Sig Ep Beach Party,' and all I remember thinking was, Thank God he's wearing a shirt."

Sara gave me a mild smile behind which she was surely imagining the changes to come in the unlikely event anything actually happened with these songs. Where might this downward path end for the man with whom she cohabitated? Joblessness, the keeping of strange hours, shady characters crashing on our couch for weeks at a time, and then inevitably, tantrums, bitterness, alcoholism. It wasn't money that concerned her. We were fine. She made enough to live on, and I'd amassed a respectable savings. The true source of distress had to have been that she lived with someone who, in the middle of his life, was capable of casting off everything for something completely asinine.

"And after Jumbo?" she asked.

"He may be the only one who takes my call, but after him, Warren, then Mackenzie. That would be the plan."

At the mention of Mack's name, Sara's eyes skipped down to her glass. She changed the subject. "How'd it go with Marty Kushman today?"

Marty was the managing partner at my firm, which meant he faced a daily diet of tattletales, gossip, and all interoffice squabbles that required the services of a referee. He was also the guy you talked to when you wanted out.

"It went okay. I told him I was leaving but not quitting. A leave of absence, nothing permanent. Marty was cool about it."

"He didn't laugh in your face?" It was a cruel and entirely reasonable question.

"I didn't tell him why I was leaving. People leave law firms all the time. He didn't ask a lot of questions."

"Here's a question: Does your father know?"

"I'll tell him when I tell him," I said, irked at the very thought of his knee-jerk disapproval, how upon learning of my latest attempt to disgrace the family, he'd slam down his *Legal Intelligencer* and howl, "Goddamn that kid!" Had I forgotten all those scathing reviews, the hollow venues, the laughable royalty checks?

Sara swigged her wine as if she needed it. How rudderless she must've felt, one man in her life heaving himself into a midlife tempest that was guaranteed to put distances between them, and another man returning from the past only to discuss goodbyes. I knew the prospect of revisiting that old minefield of memories with Billy was weighing heavily on her.

"Sara, I know this is all very abrupt and very weird, but I don't want you to worry. About us."

"I'm not worried about us," she said a little too pointedly.

I cocked my head. "What does that mean?"

She swirled her glass and picked up a cheese cube, and for a moment, Sara seemed to drift up into the restaurant's Middle Eastern music. A plucked guitar and the taut rapping of a goatskin drum coasted gently over our heads. At last she returned to me.

"Teddy, I think you came back from Switzerland a different person. But . . ."

"But . . ."

"But that's probably not the worst thing in the world."

I leaned across the table, unhitched her hand from her glass, and took her long, spindly fingers in mine. "I'm going to be there for you as you go through all this divorce stuff. You know that, right?"

She gave my hand a dismissive pat. "You don't have to go all serious on me. I'm not afraid of what you want."

It was those words that had stayed with me. Why wasn't she afraid of what I wanted? I was terrified of what I wanted.

As I sat there facing the Baltimore harbor with Jumbo and the daughter of his ex-wife, I realized I'd crossed the Rubicon. The simple act of approaching a former band member and inviting him into my world of delusion had brought this folly outside the safe confines of my head. It would be harder now to turn back.

When the performance ended, Ingrid shot out of her seat and made for one of the fuzzy characters, some sort of moose. Jumbo tore after her.

It amazed me that this little girl felt comfortable in Jumbo's charge—Oh Jumbo, tell me the story about how Curious George went to Marseille and got the clap—but it amazed me all the more that this Israel fellow felt comfortable leaving his child alone with him. Jumbo was not reliable and he was not smart, and for most of his career, he'd been out of work. Nor was he overeducated. He'd attended Guttenberg University, which might have a stately collegiate ring to it, like some liberal arts school for trust-funders or an ancient, woodsy institution in Bavaria. It was, in fact, a correspondence course outfit in the Cherry Hill Mall. The minute you even considered enrolling, you were in the running for valedictorian.

But as I watched him hawk over this child, there was no mistaking that this family had, in its own deeply peculiar way, come to accept him. And whatever complications existed between him, Sandy, and Israel, they no doubt sensed the clunky genuineness of his affection for their kids. Perhaps I was grasping at straws here, but was that evidence of growth? Maybe in his own microscopic, stunted way, Jumbo was evolving.

On the walk back to the car, an exhausted Ingrid slung over Jumbo's shoulder with her thumb in her mouth, we passed a string of bars. Their doors were wide open on this pleasant Saturday afternoon, each one dark and empty of patrons, a scattering of bartenders and waitstaff lounging about. A chalkboard outside one establishment advertised the evening's live entertainment. The Naked Mannequins were headlining, Pete Sake was opening. Open mic from six to eight. Dollar drafts from five to six.

I stopped in my tracks. "I have an idea. Let's come back down here later."

"Oh, hell yeah! Celebration is in order!"

"No. It's an open mic. I want to play you a few of the new songs tonight, right here in this bar."

The impulse was a protective one, for my songs, and for Jumbo's first impressions of them. A maiden voyage through a song is like a first date, painting it with sensation and imagery that becomes forever inseparable from the music. It was asking an awful lot of my new songs to make themselves arresting when first heard in a dank basement, a single naked voice fighting its warbled chirp over a dampened guitar. A stage would serve the music better, kindle the flames of inspiration for Jumbo such that he would be moved to contribute to them, to make them better.

Jumbo grinned eagerly at my suggestion. "I like the way you think, Mingus."

As we approached the family minivan, I took hold of Jumbo's arm. "Look, this time around, if this actually ends up happening—and it's a long shot if there ever was one—I need you to be better. Do you understand? I'm too old to deal. You're going to go easy on the booze."

"No worries, man. My tolerance is much better than it used to be."

"You're going to sleep when it's nighttime, like everyone else. You'll show up for things. You won't tell anybody they look pregnant. You'll wear clothes, all the time. We're going to go about this very differently. You're going to go about this very differently."

Jumbo either said "I'm in" or "Amen."

"Another thing. No makeup." I was referencing his regrettable period of wearing heavy eyeliner and mascara on stage. It was garish and weird and made him look like the Phantom of the Opera.

Jumbo smirked in fond remembrance as he nestled the sleeping child into the car seat. "I'd forgotten all about that."

"You're lucky."

CHAPTER 7

So Sandy was a surprise. Older and frumpy, with kind eyes jailed behind outsized eyewear, she looked like a new grandmother, down to the flaking rouge. Once upon a time, Jumbo considered it his right to work his crass charm over pretty little things in bars, sauntering up to them and saying things like "Why don't you just tell me your safe word now?" Damned if it didn't work every time. None of those women looked like Sandy. Though maybe their mothers did.

When we returned to the house after the bar later that night, gripping guitar cases like decaying versions of our former selves, Sandy greeted us in the foyer. In low tones suggesting sleeping children in earshot, she invited us to deposit our instruments in the basement and join her and Israel for a drink in the den.

"So, I see you married Mrs. Doubtfire," I remarked once we'd descended to the seclusion of Jumbo's subterranean living quarters.

Jumbo didn't assume it was an insult. "Doubtfire was a handsome older woman, wasn't she?"

"You do know that was Robin Williams."

"Sandy's a saint, Mingus," Jumbo said, prying open a green army trunk. "Probably the best thing that's ever happened to me. I loved her. Frankly, I miss making love to her."

"Would you do me a favor and never say that again?"

People stopped "making love" when it became unfashionable to cry softly during sex. The very expression conjured up images of *Magnum, P.I.* mustaches and women in shoulder pads. Shasta fizzing on the night table. Roberta Flack.

I asked, "How is it that you got demoted to her basement and she brought in another husband? How did that go down?"

Jumbo looked uncharacteristically bruised. "I'm not the easiest guy in the world to live with, you know."

"If you say so."

As I returned the acoustic guitars to their stands, Jumbo fished around in the army trunk that doubled as a liquor cabinet. "You still a Southern Comfort man?" he asked.

"No, I'm not." The question pissed me off, freighted as it was with bad history. "Why don't you just have a nice civilized glass of wine with the rest of us, or a beer? *A* beer."

"Chill, Mingus. I'm a mellow guy these days," said the man who had stuffed a bag of weed into my glove compartment just hours earlier. "Do I have the occasional martini? Sure, but that's just for the antioxidants. You don't have to go acting like a wiener just because I offered you some SoCo. Sue me for wanting to celebrate with the good stuff."

"I already told you—there's nothing to celebrate. We're keeping this quiet for now, James. Do you understand?"

When we reached the den, Israel was setting down a tray on which our hosts had arranged a cascading pile of sliced gouda wedges encircled by a neat ring of melba toast. Jumbo said "Sweet!" and immediately plopped a hunk of cheese between two pieces of toast. With a loud, pulverizing bite, he instantly turned the crackers into a heap of crumbs on the rug. Israel's smile tightened. Jumbo proceeded to assemble another gouda sandwich.

Sandy entered the room carrying two glasses of red wine. Handing one to Israel, she smiled at me and said, "I've got red, white, beer, anything you'd like."

"Red wine is fine, thank you. I can't stay long."

I had a busy night ahead of me. I needed to drive home and grab a few hours of sleep so that I could wake up at 4:03 and stare into the darkness until it was time to get up.

Sandy returned with a glass of red for me, then watched worriedly as her ex-husband splashed a generous dose of SoCo over a glass filled with ice. At that point, the four of us took seats on the sectional like one big, happy dysfunctional family.

"So, what were you old rockers up to tonight?" Israel asked. "I saw guitars."

Jumbo thumbed in my direction. "You should've seen this guy. He hasn't lost it. Got up and did a few songs at the Muddy. Blew the place away."

Sandy looked at me. "I didn't know you were still playing. I'm sorry—was that insulting?"

I shook my head. "People said that to me throughout my career."

"Jim always said you'd gotten out of the music industry."

"I did. This was just for fun. Old times' sake."

That's when Jumbo made an august announcement: "Teddy and I are getting back together! Wait—how gay was that? Let me try that again. Tremble is getting back together."

I shot him a look that said Shut the fuck up.

Sandy's eyes volleyed uncertainly between Jumbo and me. "Really?"

"Yeah, that's why Teddy came down today," Jumbo explained, beaming.

I stared into my wine, wishing I could dive in and dissolve into the scarlet.

"Mingus here has decided that the time is right to bring Tremble back to the world. He's written a bunch of new songs—awesome fucking tunes—and he played them for me at an open mic tonight. They frickin' rock! I've always said this guy is like the reincarnation of Bob Dylan."

"Well, Bob Dylan is still alive," Israel pointed out, "so technically, Jim—"

"This is him, right here! Bob Dylan reincarnated. In the flesh!"

I shook my head at Israel. "Don't bother."

"I'm telling you guys, we are so back," Jumbo blathered on, unheeded. "We'll round up Warren and Mackenzie, head back into the studio, and cut a record worthy of the Tremble name." He grinned like he'd just won the lottery.

I gave my hosts a feeble wince. "We really don't know what we're doing just yet. It's all very preliminary. Jumbo is overstating it. Talking out of turn. Like he tends to do."

The clod took a loud slurp of SoCo and refueled his mouth with things he shouldn't say. "After a decade, Mingus here has had this amazing creative storm. Trust me, I have an ear for these things." He touched his ear, showing us where his ears were. "And I've obviously still got it, so, you know, sky's the limit!"

A speechless Sandy gazed out from behind her dated eyewear.

Israel pointed to me with a confused look. "Why does he keep calling you Mingus?"

I shrugged. I didn't know.

"Well," Sandy said, crossing her legs with aristocratic reserve, "that certainly sounds very exciting. Jim, maybe this will give you that boost you've needed, the direction you've been looking for."

"Fuck yeah!" Jumbo said, erecting another double-decker gouda-and-melba sandwich. "I always knew we had more left in the tank. If you ask me, we gave up way too quickly."

We gave up when we delivered a record that didn't sell and I compounded the sin by insisting we promote it all alone, instead of, say, sharing the stage with a band people actually wanted to see. We gave up when the world had given up on us.

As Jumbo applied a disintegrating chomp to his cracker concoction—a spot-on metaphor for the day—my head shook with paroxysms of doubt. He'd gotten worse. There had to be thousands of desperate guitar players out there. All I needed was one. What was I doing here in this house with these people?

"What about your job?" Israel asked his housemate-slash-wife's-ex-husband. "The midwife thing?"

"Music has always been my first love. You know that, Is."

Sandy, sensing many a devil in the details, retreated to generalized benediction. "Well, I, for one, wish you two the best of luck. Jim, you know you're always welcome in our house, but I know this isn't what you want."

"Things are changing for me," he said, frothing with cockiness and sporting a bumptious grin. "I can feel it."

With that, he threw his arm around my shoulder and shook me, forcing a swirl of red wine out of my glass and onto my slacks. And the rug.

"Nice, Jumbo," I said, frowning at the fresh stains.

"Oh, did I get you?"

It looked like I'd been shot. Felt that way too. "Yeah, you did."

"Oh, don't worry, that'll come right out," he assured everyone, as Sandy scampered off in search of a rag.

One day I'll die, I thought to myself, and this will be one of the things I did with my time.

I set my glass down on the table and thanked everyone for a lovely evening. The creeping bloodred blotch on my pants served as a reminder that Jumbo was a lot harder to appreciate when he didn't have a musical instrument in his hands. I shook hands with his landlords and made for the exit.

"What are you so pissy about?" he called after me as I evaded his attempt to escort me down the driveway.

"You're a fucking embarrassment. How could I have forgotten that?" I spun around and faced him, my finger brandished in anger. "What did I just say to you before we came upstairs?"

"I don't know. You gave up SoCo? Sandy looks like Tootsie?"

"I told you to keep your mouth shut. It's way too early to let people know what we're up to. At this point, we'll just look like a couple of delusional dimwits. I'm sure the hard liquor and ganja have killed your memory, but we did not exactly leave the business on our own terms."

"What are you talking about?"

"We got dropped by our label."

"Sales don't mean anything."

"Attendance at our shows was paltry."

"What do you mean? Like there were chickens there?"

"We have to handle this delicately. Don't you get that? How could you go and announce that we're back in business? We're still a punch line on VH1."

"I don't care what people think, Mingus. You know that about me."

"I hate that about you. I always have." I was suddenly aware that I was yelling. We were two guys in their late thirties bickering on a suburban driveway. "I'm out of here, man. I'll be in touch."

He followed me to the curb. "Dude, I got news for you. The whole point of making music is to get people to pay attention. If they don't pay attention, they can't very well listen, can they? Think about that."

"There's nothing to pay attention to. We haven't made any music yet. Think about *that*."

I reached for the car door. I needed to be away from this mess—a mess I'd made, unmade, and then moronically remade ten years later.

"So, what next?" Jumbo asked.

"Here's what's next," I said, struggling for composure. "I'm going to think about whether I still want to go through with this after being reacquainted with your unshuttable mouth. But assuming a cooler head prevails, I'm going to get in touch with Warren and Mack and . . . continue the process of eating my pride."

"Mack, huh?" Jumbo was grinning now.

"Yeah, Mack."

Jumbo just stood there with a stupid smile on his mug.

I glared at him. "Is there something you want to say?"

"Nope. Just that I wouldn't mind being a fly on the wall at that meeting."

"Frankly, James, I would've preferred it if you'd been a fly on the wall at this meeting."

I gave the door a fervent yank and enclosed myself in the pleasant hollow of a vacuum. Jumbo leaned down and tapped the glass. The big meatball wasn't quite done with me.

I rolled down the window. "What?"

With a guilty glance up and down the street, he said, "Want to drive out to the beach and shroom?"

"My answer to that question is the same as when you asked it in 1995." I raised the window and let out a towering sigh. Idiot. And what beach was he even talking about?

I sped away, forgetting that Jumbo's envelope of weed was still squirreled in my glove compartment.

I could barely keep myself conscious. The huge yawns that swelled forth must have looked like silent, anguished screams to the night owls driving past me on the highway. Leaning against the cold frame of my car, I stared vacantly at the gasoline nozzle. It was getting late and I'd decided against another ration of caffeine. After the day I'd had, you're either awake or you're not, and more coffee just meant more time staring into a rest stop urinal.

The deep growl of a bus overtook the station, and the enormous vehicle hissed to a stop at the next fueling island. The door cleaved open and a man and woman staggered down the steps toward the mini-mart. He wore a mugger's skullcap, boots, and a jacket of oily leather. She was a leggy platinum blonde in a skintight tube top, click-clacking precariously in hooker's heels. Given the glam cargo, it was not out of the realm of possibility that this was some type of tour bus making its way up the Eastern Seaboard. I remembered how those coaches were like living rooms and motels to us. There would be rowdy chatter and self-congratulation as we pulled away from the venue. Soon, the mostly empty bus would become a mobile pew of peaceful seclusion. Warren would crossword puzzle his way over the miles, his tray table down, his hand snooping automatically around his family-size bag of trail mix. Mackenzie would curl up against the window with a paperback, her canvas sneakers jutting into the aisle. Jumbo would be conked out somewhere, invisible until we arrived at wherever the tour was taking us next, at which point he'd pop up from the back, disoriented and parched, reminding us all of his existence. I might stretch my legs and park myself across the aisle from Mack, coaxing her into a game of backgammon or enticing her to put on a movie with me. We'd watch *Airplane!* and laugh—too loud, because of the headphones—at every stupidly hilarious gag we'd seen a thousand times, or *The Deer Hunter*, which, according to Mack, was back when Christopher Walken was "pretty." Sometimes, late at night, she'd pass out on my shoulder.

If she could be talked back onto the bus, talked down from all the resentment that she may well have been hauling through the years, I would enjoy more travels with Mackenzie Highsider.

With the steady rush of gasoline flooding into my car's tank, I texted Sara. "On my way. Be home in an hour or so."

She immediately wrote me back. "I'm still up. How'd it go?"

I decided to call. The highway was a lonely place, lonelier still at this refueling oasis. I found myself wanting to hear Sara's voice.

"What are you doing up?" I asked.

"I'm not tired," she complained with soft frustration. She wasn't lacking for things to invade her sleep.

"You okay?" I asked.

"Fine. How'd it go today?"

"It went. Jumbo hasn't changed a lick."

"I guess that's good in some ways and bad in others?"

"It's bad in every conceivable way. But he's on board."

"You weren't really concerned about that though."

"No," I said. "I have a great many concerns about Jumbo, but his availability for harebrained schemes on a moment's notice is not one of them."

Instead of laughing in allegiance, Sara went quiet. "I saw Billy today," she said.

I swallowed. "You saw him?"

"Yeah. We met for coffee. On a bench in Rittenhouse Square."

"Oh."

Though Billy had shown up from the past, he hadn't actually shown up yet—to my knowledge anyway. Until now, he'd been a voice on the phone.

"How was it seeing him?"

I heard the crackle of a slow breath being blown through pursed lips. "Difficult. It's been a long time. He's not a kid anymore, and I'm clearly not either. We've lived a quarter of our lives since we last saw each other."

As she said it, the thought seemed to mystify her, as if she was wondering, How could so much time have passed? Shouldn't I be getting better? Is this what better feels like?

"I don't know what to say, Sara. That must have been hard. You should've told me."

"I guess I didn't want to talk about it."

This wasn't how I'd imagined the reunion. I'd envisioned the inevitable meeting between Sara and Billy taking place in some lawyer's narcoleptically sleek conference room. They'd be separated by a table, a safe expanse of antique cherry or Madagascar rosewood. They'd meet at the head of the table, embrace in a way that felt so familiar and so weird that it would send them each back to their respective chairs.

"Did you talk about the divorce?"

"Yeah," Sara said. "We talked about a lot of things."

A lot of things could've meant a lot of things, and a protective impulse surged upward in me, a visceral reaction to my girlfriend of ten years meeting up with her estranged husband without so much as a heads-up. And yet this wasn't some ex-boyfriend or office crush; it was the man she'd taken vows with, gotten pregnant with, shared the worst kind of tragedy with. I couldn't be so selfish and petty as to take issue with a heart-to-heart so many years in the making. Especially when I was busy exhuming my own ancient history.

The echoing tap of heels on asphalt hooked my attention as the blonde in the tight elastic shirt came teetering out of the mini-mart with her companion's arm cradled possessively over her neck. For a passing instant, I fantasized about dropping the phone where I stood and scrambling onto that bus with them.

"What can I do, Sara?" I asked.

"Do? Nothing. There's nothing to do."

She was right.

"I can come home," I finally said.

She let out a long, lilting release of a laugh that soared high, then tumbled in descending rungs back down to her pillow. "Yes, Teddy. You can come home."

I replaced the nozzle and screwed on the gas cap. Behind me, the bus doors squeaked closed and the huge monstrosity rumbled away. I stared after it, watching the red taillights glide down the highway, carrying some other poor fucker's demons on its rude haunches.

CHAPTER 8

From the last row of a high school auditorium, I listened to labored cacophony, the hummable melody of "Morning Mood" just barely discernible through the clamor of lawless instruments. At long last, this composition, Suite 1 from Edvard Grieg's *Peer Gynt*, a melody of pacific beauty, the official soundtrack to a rising sun, made me smile.

The piece had appeared in one of my early piano books, and my mangled interpretation of it would cause my teacher, poor old Mr. Green, to cower in the chair next to the piano, cursing me under his breath. My parents had suggested I take up an instrument, but they couldn't have been heartened by my lack of progress or by the checks they wrote week after futile week, which Old Man Green sourly accepted before he made for the door. In the wake of each dispiriting lesson, my dad would appear at the top of the steps and offer his own brand of encouragement: "You don't have to do this anymore if you don't want to." I wasn't very good back in those days, so when I became a professional musician, the joke was on everyone who'd doubted me. When the band went to hell because, frankly, we weren't very good, the joke was back on me again. Where it has remained for a good long while.

Since those demeaning hours on my parents' piano bench, the

seasons have spun around and the years have turned over and over, but it turned out that kids were still butchering the very same music.

At first, all I could see of him were arms waving in the flow of the sound, imploring the players to respect pitch and tempo. As the piece wore on, the limbs betrayed just the faintest touches of frustration, then resignation, and finally failure. When the noise stopped, there came the voice.

"Well, it needs some work, guys. Right? Julie, you've got to play the right notes. It's not like just any notes will do. You've got to play the ones on the sheet. And Kenny, your timing today is a huge improvement over last time, so good for you, but it's still terrible. Tap your foot, count under your breath, do something. Friends, we've all got to play the same song and we've all got to play it at the same speed. This is not a hard piece. You're making it sound like 'Giant Steps,' but trust me, this is an easy one . . . I'm seeing blank stares. Don't tell me you don't know 'Giant Steps.' Nobody here knows 'Giant Steps' by John Coltrane? How am I supposed to work under these conditions? Go home tonight and tell your parents they have failed you!

"Back to Grieg. So—we're going to practice and practice and it's going to get better and better. It just has to. Do any of you practice, by the way? I'll take your word for it, but . . ." Then I heard the laugh, an injection of levity into the criticism. "All right, my friends. Let's call it a day."

The stage burst into a symphony of squeaking chairs, rustling papers, and chattering teenagers.

"Go on home," he bade them. "Practice your instruments. Get 'Giant Steps' from wherever it is you steal music these days."

Collecting themselves and their gear, the students emptied the stage and staggered past me out the back of the auditorium. A plucky, pint-sized, ponytailed blonde, whom Warren had addressed as Julie and who'd Sweeney Todded the hell out of *Peer Gynt* with her violin, was the last to leave, loitering by the stage. I began a slow shuffle down the aisle. Plucky, pint-sized, ponytailed blondes were always the last to leave the classroom. Class itself was never enough. It was too diluted, not sufficiently tailored to their own individualized needs. It was after class that the real schooling happened. I made my way toward them undetected.

"But Mr. Warren"—the panic was spurting forth like a mortal wound—"I've been practicing for, like, three hours every night. I'm really nervous that I'm never going to get it right and the concert is only a few weeks away and I'm going to blow it for everybody. Do you think maybe I should get a tutor?"

"A tutor? For concert band?" He laughed wearily as he gathered up his papers, his sloped shoulders speaking volumes about the tiresome frequency of Julie's visits. "You've got to not let yourself get all whipped up into a tizzy. You're very tense when you're playing. We've discussed that. You can't be tense when you're playing 'Morning Mood.' That's about as chill a piece of music as there is. Have you actually listened to the piece? Grieg is taking you somewhere very calm, very peaceful. It's early morning. There's a sunrise, maybe some butterflies. Nothing has come along yet to stress you out. Can you access that?"

"But Mr. Warren, I'm just worried that everybody else is getting better and even though I've been practicing like crazy, I'm still messing it up."

"I wouldn't say everyone else is getting better. No, I wouldn't say that at all." He was stuffing papers into his satchel, probably contemplating dinner.

By this point, I had almost joined their conversation. I stood just outside the spotlight ring that encircled teacher and student. His eyes flashed briefly in my direction, but he kept at it with the squeaky violinist.

"Julie, I'm going to give you the same advice I gave you yester—" He stopped dead. Then he turned and looked at me. "You've got to be kidding me."

I stepped out of the darkness. "Hello, Mr. Warren."

"Teddy Tremble, in the flesh," Warren marveled. "What are you doing here?"

I smiled. "My dog ate my homework."

We hugged. A sinewy network of muscles under his button-down shirt brushed up against my middle-age spread. Bastard was still in shape, even if the avuncular chin-curtain beard put a few years on him.

Warren turned to Julie. "Can we continue this tomorrow? Seems I have an unexpected visitor."

"I guess so," she chirped tentatively, her features bucking in distress.

Warren and I stared at each other, grins advancing across our faces as Julie strode out of the auditorium, the anxious echo of her footsteps trailing behind.

"So let me guess," Warren said. "You think I'm the one who hung that picture in the Tate, and you've come to kick my ass."

"I've recently learned that my ass-kicking days might be behind me. It's really good to see you, even under all that facial hair."

He caressed the tightly coiled curls on his chin. "Had it for years, but every day there seems to be more salt and less pepper."

Warren was a kid during the band years, a spasmodic axis of pep and punch riding bareback on a constant beat. He'd aged, but not in the weathered, deteriorating, line-carving sense. His was the seasoned, fortifying type of growing older.

"What the hell are you doing here?" he asked.

"Can we go somewhere and talk?"

"Look, if this has something to do with that stupid photo, I'm telling you, I didn't snap it and I didn't hang it up."

I looked around the auditorium and felt the energy of a stage rising up before expectantly positioned seats. My eyes lifted to the row of intense spotlights hovering above us like an alien spacecraft.

"I can assure you this visit is not about retribution," I told him. "It's about the opposite of retribution."

"Hmm," he mused. "The opposite of retribution is forgiveness, Teddy. What have you done that begs my pardon?"

*   *   *

We strolled through the abandoned hallways, past the regiments of lockers. Scruffy kids sloped by slinging backpacks, each of them lurking beneath a hapless misfire of a haircut. A brunette with phosphorescent green mascara and an outfit conducive to stuffing small dollar bills flashed Warren a wave of twittering fingers.

"Do the people here know who you are?" I asked as Warren fumbled for keys outside an office door.

"Who am I?" he replied, chuckling.

"Someone who used to be someone else."

"Some of the teachers know, the older ones, but nobody cares." He pushed open the door to what was little more than a closet with a desk and a chair. "Lauren and I have lived over the bridge in Lambertville pretty much since the band split, and, trust me, there's no royal treatment. I'm just the guy who teaches band and art appreciation. Every now and again, the owner of the coffee shop near my house will talk music with me, ask me if I ever met so-and-so, ever jammed with such-and-such. They don't realize how far removed I am from that world. I don't know jack about the music scene now. Somebody asked me the other day what I think of Ray LaMontagne. I was like, Ray LaMontagne? Sounds like someone who sang with Sinatra. But hey, I'm happy to shoot the shit. It's not like I went all Eddie and the Cruisers." His bag of papers landed with an exhausted thud on the floor, and Warren sat down at his desk. "I'm just living my life."

If Jumbo's basement home was a dismal shrine to a ship that had long ago sailed over the horizon, Warren's office was the witness protection program. The walls were lined with bookshelves packed with scholarly texts—*The Elements of Music, The Annotated El Greco, Botticelli Explored, An Integrated Approach to Harmonic Progression*—as opposed to self-aggrandizing memorabilia.

A single picture frame angled toward Warren's chair. I picked it up and took in the family photo. Lauren still looked magnetic, standing on the front step of a row house in a purple Lycra cat suit, two feline ears protruding from her hair. She had her arm around a young boy dressed in a Phillies uniform.

I turned the photo toward Warren. "I thought women stopped slutting themselves up for Halloween after they had kids."

"Not the right woman."

"And this gentleman?"

"That's Patrick. He's seven." He smiled at the picture he'd seen a million times.

I listened to my old friend wax tranquil about his blissful domesticity, which I'd come to upend. Warren, unlike Jumbo, had something to be stolen away from.

He slid open a desk drawer and took out a sandwich mummified in plastic wrap. "PB and J," he said. "I'll split it with you."

I shook my head, and he proceeded to unwind the layers of plastic and bite off at least a quarter of the sandwich. Warren had always subscribed to the view that physical health was maximized by having not three meals a days but five. The guy ate constantly. To have a conversation with him, you had to factor in time for him to chew.

I leaned forward. "Look, I need your help."

"What's up?"

I let out a breath on which my last shred of dignity escaped. "I want you to play music with me."

He stopped chewing. "What do you mean?"

"I want you to make an album with me, a Tremble album."

The words dropped like an anvil onto the desk between us. "Get out of here."

I stared seriously at him.

He stared back. "You want to regroup the band?"

"I'm doing it and I want you to be part of it."

He laughed heartily, then reached out and patted my knee. "Teddy, my old, dear friend, don't you have anyone in your life to tell you what a ridiculous idea that is?"

"I add two or three every day."

"Well, let me say from the bottom of my heart, I thank you for inviting me to join your band, but unfortunately, I am an adult now, so I'm going to have to say no."

"You need some time to warm up to the idea."

Laughter. "Can I ask you something?"

"Sure."

"Are you joking?"

"No."

"Okay, then can I ask you something else?"

"Sure."

"Are you crazy?"

"That's not a question I can answer."

He looked at me sadly. "Teddy, I don't even want to know the whys and wherefores, the sorry circumstances that made you wake up one morning and think, Doggone it, it's time to play rock star again. Count me out. Good luck."

"You'll give it some thought."

"I will not. This may be hard for you to comprehend, but I'm a member of a community. I teach kids about the wonders of music and art. I coach Patrick's Little League team. I'm on the board of my neighborhood association. Do you think I'd give all of that up for the privilege of sweating like a beast behind a drum kit in some empty bar well past my bedtime? I did that before. I'm glad I did it, but I won't be doing it again."

"Stop being practical and hear me out. This isn't a whim. It's been in the works for months. I've written a bunch of new songs—"

"I'll bet they're very good. You are a talented songwriter, but—and please don't take this the wrong way—I don't really care all that much."

I sat back and folded my arms.

"Come on, man," he went on. "You're out of your mind. What chance does a guy like you have? It's overcrowded out there now. I have no idea how the game is played these days, but I do know the rules are a lot different. You know that Internet thing, something they didn't have in our day? It's an enormously effective tool for forcing you to confront your own mediocrity. We have access to music now like never before, and there's an awful lot of it out there, most of it better than ours ever was. You're a middle-aged lawyer, Teddy. Look in the mirror and that's what you'll see."

"There's no reason to be cruel."

"Have you been sitting in your basement all these years with a guitar in your lap, weeping over old photo albums, mumbling to yourself about getting back on top?"

I snickered; his description of Jumbo was uncanny.

Warren began to fatten his leather satchel with various papers. "What about your law partners? They must think you've had a break with reality." He paused and stared at me hard. "Have you had a break with reality?"

"I've had a break with my firm."

"What does that mean?"

"It means I took a leave of absence."

"What does *that* mean? I'm not coming in for a while? Don't give me any work to do? Don't order me anything off the lunch cart?"

"I don't know." I hadn't thought that far. "Maybe it means I quit."

"You want my advice? Go and unquit. You've lost your crackers."

"I need you, Square," I told him. "I'd really rather not take the stage with musicians so young they look like I fathered them."

Warren flicked out the lights and we started down the hall.

"Why now?" he asked. "What's so special about right now? So somebody hung a bad picture of you in an art gallery. Big deal. Live with it. We put ourselves out there to be ridiculed if people so choose, to say we sucked, to laugh at us years after the fact. But we got paid a lot of money for that. Put on your big-boy pants and shake it off."

"I admit that seeing that photo pissed me off. But there's more to it." Somehow, a retelling of my escapades in Switzerland seemed unlikely to convince him I was of sound mind. "If it makes any difference, I happen to know we're still popular in Europe. Small, grotesque parts of Europe."

He grunted. "My royalty checks don't reflect that. Maybe you and the rest of the gang negotiated better deals. Speaking of which, what's up with the other misfit toys? You talk to them?"

"I haven't spoken to Mackenzie in years."

"Well, that stands to reason."

"What does that mean?"

He laid a knowing gaze on me. "Teddy. Come on, man."

"So I slept with her. Big deal. People in bands sleep with each other all the time. I'm surprised you and I never hooked up."

"You're talking about sex, and that's a convenient oversimplification," Warren said.

"Give me a break."

"Teddy, please. When you're in a band with the same people for many years, you get to know them. You see how they interact with one another, whether they like or hate or are annoyed by one another. Like right now. Can't you tell that I'm annoyed with you? You can tell whether they have private feelings that they keep under wraps because maybe they're married or they're chickenshit or some other reason."

"I loved Mack, but not like that. She was like a little sister to me."

"The little sister you slept with."

I huffed with vast exasperation.

"Listen, man, I don't care," he said. "You can remember it however you choose. I'm not going to argue with you."

"Thank you. As for Jumbo, yes, I've been in touch with him."

Warren was offended. "You didn't come to me first?"

"No, but I did come to you second."

"That hurts. What did he say?"

"He's in. I knew he would be, and that's why I started with him."

"Well, that seals it. You know I've had way more than my share of Dumbo for one lifetime."

"And so have we all, but—"

"Let me guess. He's changed, he's reformed, he's a disciplined guy now. Spin it for me. Jumbo's a totally different person."

"Jumbo is exactly the same."

"Of course he is. You go play rock star with that clown. Leave me out of your midlife crisis."

Silently we twisted down the dark, empty corridors toward the lobby. I hadn't been inside a high school since I graduated from one, and I felt the unsteady teenager I used to be urging toward the surface, fighting for breath. I'd worked hard to bury him under layers of artificiality that, over time, cemented; I'd become what I pretended to be, as the saying goes. I didn't want to be that seventeen-year-old kid anymore, just as lost and lonely as everyone else, though perhaps a little more deft at concealing it. I'd had a group of friends I spent a lot of time with but never felt truly a part of. I'd pile into the car with them in search of a party on a Saturday night, but I was the one secretly hoping we wouldn't find it.

They don't tell you that about high school. How a place can leave you just as suddenly as you leave it. Just when that itch on your skin finally gives, when the mud hardens, that's when it kicks you out. The place that made you who you are closes its doors to you forever, and the rest of your life is lived in exile.

"When's the big performance?" I asked, as Warren and I passed the auditorium double doors.

"Two weeks from yesterday."

"You're fucked."

"Oh, I'm fucked all right. But it doesn't matter. That Julie girl will make her fiddle sound like a dying animal, and her mommy and daddy will still give her a standing O like she's Itzhak Perlman. But here's the thing. I guarantee you that in every class there's one kid who gets jazzed about what we're doing. A circuit breaker flips in that kid's head and—boom!—that's it. He or she is one of us for life."

"Listen to yourself. One of us. For life. That's why you can't say no. That's why you have to accept my proposition."

"Wrong," he sighed. "That's why I'm here, Teddy, and it's why I'm not going to leave."

We pushed open the doors and ambled out into the chilled evening air, our heels tapping out an echo under the high canopy of the front walkway.

When we reached the flagpole, I pointed to the student lot and said, "Well, I'm over there."

He dipped his head toward the teachers' lot. "And I'm over there."

The symbolism was not lost on me.

"I'm sorry you came all this way for nothing."

"It wasn't nothing to me."

He started to walk away, then stopped. "I'm glad you sought me out. Look, maybe you're going through something strange in your life or maybe you're still trying to find your way. I don't know. We've all been there. Whatever it is, we're still buddies. You know that."

Through the darkness, I watched his form blend into the dim shadows. Goddamn you, Square. Goddamn you for pitying me.

Soon, I was rolling swiftly down 95. The lanes of the highway were thick with cars, each one driven by some poor son of a bitch doing very little other than growing older. I jacked up the stereo and sought cover in a college radio station. It was playing a song I'd never heard before, a melody high, earthy, and sad. There was something about the night, the air, the music, the high-speed forward motion, the recent reconnections with lost things and lost people. Tonight it hung around my neck like a judge's decree.

CHAPTER 9

"I want to talk to you." It was my dad on the phone.

"You do, huh. What about?"

"Meet me at the gym. We'll talk there." The gym was shorthand for the posh Sporting Club, an aristocratic spa where the well-bred of Philadelphia overpaid to perspire—certainly not sweat—in their Lululemon and Under Armour.

"What do you want to talk to me about?" I hate surprises. After college, there are very few good surprises.

"We'll talk there."

I didn't relish being summoned like a lapdog, but my day was rather open and a little exercise wouldn't kill me. On top of that, it is an axiom of magical thinking that the one day a son declines his father's invitation is the day the old man up and dies. Like I needed that.

With the tart taste of passive obedience in my mouth and the dread of an impending lecture, I tossed on my most threadbare T-shirt and walked across town.

At the club's front desk, a synthetically buff guy with feathered hair and spandex shorts told me to sign the guest book. Behind him, stacks of vitamin-enriched bottled water, Gatorade of all hues, amino shakes, and powdered whey towered over us. He handed me a towel and said, "Enjoy your workout." An oxymoronic benediction, if ever there was one.

Through the glistening crowd of midday workout fanatics, I saw Lou Tremble climbing off a treadmill. He spotted me and pulled the earphones out of his ears, winding the little wire as he walked in my direction. I wondered what type of music got my father pumped up for a workout. Growing up, I would comb through his record collection and imagine a hipper past for the man. I'd finger through the cardboard sleeves with the psychedelic designs of Stevie Wonder, Cream, Spyro Gyra, and think, When exactly was this man cool? Somewhere along the line he must've gotten lost, his eight-tracks and cassettes sprouting overnight the names Manilow, Sedaka, Anne fucking Murray. Old, edgeless music seemed to pursue people throughout their lives, finally catching up with them when they were too slow and tired to outrun it. You grew up on Smokey Robinson and Dizzy Gillespie. Through your daughter's bedroom door you overheard Springsteen, his voice filling you with a forgotten wildness. Somewhere in the nineties you hummed "Unskinny Bop" on your way to the office. And then you woke up at age sixty-five and found yourself singing "Ding ding ding goes the trolley." The house always wins.

My father approached me in a shiny blue tank top. He regarded my shirt, which bore the Chicago Cubs logo.

"You still have that?" he said, smiling. "I bought that for you when I was out there for a meeting with the Wrigley Company. You must've been in high school."

"Actually, you got this on a trip to Vancouver. You had a layover at O'Hare on the return. Thanks for thinking of me."

I have never been a Cubs fan.

Dad wiped a modest sheen of perspiration from his brow and flashed a frothy grin at a young woman on a shoulder press machine.

"So, what are we doing, Rocky?" I asked him.

"I just finished up with cardio, so let's do some weights. Easier to talk that way."

I didn't mind that my old man still hit the gym with the optimistic verve of the skinny kid on the wrestling team. Nothing wrong with a guy raging against the dying of the light with forty-five minutes on the treadmill. But this business of weight lifting, of snarling at the mirror while urging his sun-spotted skin to rise up into biceps: just fucking inane. It was fueled not by the quest to stay alive or even by a healthy modicum of responsibility, but by this pathetic fantasy that he was hot, that he could inspire impure thoughts. You're north of seventy, Lou. You're only hot when you step out of the condo in Delray that you should be wintering in.

To be fair, my father was not the only member of the family clinging to an obsolete self-image.

He led me over to the free weights and slid a forty-five pounder onto each side of a bench press bar. Then he said, "I ran into Marty Kushman the other day."

Fuck. The Philadelphia legal community was quaintly incestuous, and I should've anticipated that the news would reach my father in nanoseconds. Plus, my old man had known the managing partner of Morris & Roberts for centuries.

"Know what he said to me?" he went on.

"I can probably guess."

He rested his foot on the bench and squinted like a cowboy. "You're leaving the firm?"

"I left the firm."

"And you didn't think to mention this to me?"

"Did I hurt your feelings?"

"Why didn't you tell me, Ted?"

"Go," I said, nudging him toward the bench press.

He lay down and blew through a set of ten reps. He might have been the oldest guy in America who owned weight lifting gloves.

"You're looking huge, man," I said. "Huge."

He leapt to his feet. "So, what's all this about?"

"It's not about anything. I've just decided to try something else for a while."

I added a twenty-five pound plate to each side of the bar before sliding onto the bench. I do have my pride.

"Another firm? Why didn't you come to me? You know I have very good relationships with all the major players in town."

"I know," I said, gripping the bar. "You're adored throughout the community."

With quick, shallow puffs, I bounced the bar off my chest, hoping to outpace the fatigue, to reach ten reps before my arms caught wind of what was going on. They grew wobbly after about four. The last time I did any hard-core weight lifting was college. Because I'm an adult.

As soon as I'd dropped the bar back onto the supports, he continued his cross-examination. "Where are you going?"

"I haven't decided yet, but it's not going to be a firm."

Someone took a fishing wire and yanked up his eyebrows. "You're going in-house?"

There was no good place to have this discussion with my father, but perhaps a gym was preferable to a dinner table, where Lou was liable to end up with a salad fork in his neck.

"All right, look—I've been talking to some people about cutting another record. I'm going to try to get back into the music business."

"What in the hell are you talking about?"

I didn't blink.

"You're serious."

"I am."

"Did something happen at the firm?"

"People leave law firms all the time. There's no need to get a booger up your nose about it."

"So let me see if I've got this straight. At the age of—what are you now?—forty-one, you're giving up the law to try to be a rock star again?"

"I'm thirty-eight, Dad, but don't feel bad. It's a pointless detail. I'll just go ahead and refer to you as eightyish."

"Ted," he said darkly. "Why in the world would you do this? Why throw away all your hard work, your stellar reputation?"

"Save it, Lou."

I lay down on the bench and labored through ten angry reps. Lactic acid was already swamping my arms. I would soon be bench-pressing a bar with no plates on it.

"If you're feeling burned out, take some time off. Hell, we all feel burned out every now and then. Go to the Bahamas."

A powerful-looking woman in yoga pants asked if we were still using the bench.

"Oh, we're done here," I said pointedly, scooping my towel off the floor and crossing the room to an array of intensely individualized weight machines. I leaned against an ab contraption and stared out the window.

All too soon, my dad was standing next to me again.

"Ted, am I not allowed to ask you about your major life decisions?"

"You can ask about them," I said. "Politely."

"Fair enough. I apologize for my tone. I'd just like to know why you're doing this."

I resisted a surge of fluster. That's how you lose with my dad, by letting him get to you. The son of a bitch has an answer for everything.

"Can't we just agree that you and I are very different people?" I asked.

"So?"

"So—we won't always understand each other. I can make my own fucking decisions. I am, after all, forty-one or thereabouts."

"Oh, cut the bullshit." His arms were now crossed over his chest in civilized battle stance. "All I want to know is what makes you think you can go back to your teenage fantasy of being Elvis."

Something about his invocation of the King triggered a loud guffaw from my throat. Suddenly I was fat and sideburned, combing the gaudy halls of Graceland in a jacket with an oversized collar.

"You know, it's an interesting thing, getting schooled on age appropriateness by a granddad in a muscle shirt. How many protein bars did you chow before you came here? I mean, look at you. Haven't you ever heard of golf?"

"Don't change the subject," he lectured. "I've obviously struck a raw nerve, but I assure you that was not my intention. Look, Ted, if I had to sum up my spiel today in one word—"

"I really wish you would."

"—it would be *practicality. Judiciousness. Common sense.*"

"That's more than one."

It had been a huge miscalculation to come here. Actually, it hadn't—my calculations hadn't yielded any other outcome than this. When all your uncertainties were swirling around in a windstorm, the last person who would understand was a man for whom there were no uncertainties. He didn't tolerate them. For my father, confusion was like sickness, a light mist that you could barrel through with backbone and denial. He never understood what it meant to be in a band. To him, when you had a son who was a musician, you simply had to wait around for him to outgrow it. And yet here I was, groping for reasons that he might deem worthy. He made me feel foolish and small in a way that only a parent can.

Then my head drifted to the flurry of music I'd written over these past weeks, the spikes of inspiration charging through every avenue of my life. The most revered producer in the business telling *this* motherfucker not to ignore it. I couldn't remember the last time the sky had seemed so high.

I made a show of checking the time, an expedient gesture for facilitating departure. Then I looked at my father. Why did I give a rat's ass if this made any sense to him—or, for that matter, to anyone else? Facing him now, I realized that this would've been the perfect occasion to follow the advice he himself had recommended so many years ago: Fuck off, old bastard, I'd say. It would've been healthy. Fuck off, you ridiculous geriatric Schwarzenegger wannabe. You gotta do it sometimes. It's good for your blood pressure. I yanked one out of the quiver, brought it up to the bow, and tensed the string.

Then I made for the high road. It was out there somewhere, and the sooner I found it, the sooner I'd be free. I was going to be the bigger guy—if not the one with more defined delts.

"It's been a pleasure as always, Dad, but I really must go. But listen, if you're going to max out on squats, make sure you get one of those kids over there to spot you."

CHAPTER 10

I wasn't done with Warren Warren. Again I stalked him from the deep reaches of the auditorium. Again I hid in the cheap seats, waiting for rehearsal to end while the conductor did his best to cajole something akin to music out of his students. When I finally emerged like Nosferatu from the shadows, Warren shook his head and gathered up the leaves of sheet music from his music stand.

"Another ten years go by already?" he said grimly.

The novelty of having me back in his life had lasted precisely one day. Just about my lifetime average.

"Relax. I just came back to buy you a drink," I told him.

"Bullshit."

"No, I felt bad for blindsiding you with the band thing. And it was good to see you. I just wanted to hang."

"You want to have a beer with me, you call me up and ask me proper. Then we'll pick a mutually convenient date. That's how it's done. You don't just show up at somebody's job. What, you think I'm stupid? You didn't like the answer you got the other day, so you're back here asking again." He made a show of looking weary. "I've got a life, man. A wife, a kid, papers to grade. I don't have time to sit in a bar and get badgered. Go sell crazy somewhere else."

He started up the aisle toward the auditorium doors.

"What about me?" I said, trailing him. "You think I was sitting on my ass eating Ho Hos, looking for something to do, when you called and told me to go to London? Fucking London, man."

"I didn't think you'd go, fool."

We paraded through the doors and entered the school lobby. It was deserted save for a nervous-looking boy, backpack straps over both shoulders, texting with his phone held up to his face. Warren asked him if he had a ride home, and with a pubescent fidget, he said he did.

Once we were alone in a dim corridor, I grabbed Warren's arm and pulled him to a stop. "One drink, man. Just one drink."

"Hell no. I am not going to sit down and get pestered for an hour about what has to be the most asinine, most juvenile, and the most downright stupid idea I've ever heard in my entire life. And take note of where I work. I hear stupid ideas all day." He paused. "Teddy, listen to me. I'm not trying to step on your dreams. If you think playing music again will make you happy, you should go and do it, one hundred percent. I support your rebellious spirit and I promise I will be rooting for you. But because Teddy has always been all about Teddy, you're confusing what you want with what I want. I don't want to be a musician again."

"That's a big fat lie. You're a goddamn music teacher."

"Do you know what I do when a student is giving me grief and I just can't take it anymore? I walk away." Warren's voice lowered, and his eyes drooped sorrowfully. "Teddy, please don't make me walk away from you."

"Just let me buy you a drink. One drink. We can go somewhere close." A mischievous grin pushed its way through. "Real close."

He looked on warily as my hand disappeared into my jacket pocket and extracted a long-necked bottle. His head swiveled left and right, film noir style, checking if there was anyone else to witness this atrocity. "Did you bring wine into my school?"

"I wouldn't dream of it."

The bottle that emerged from my jacket contained a red-brown liquid, the color that a desperate actress might dye her hair in a stab at self-reinvention.

"Bourbon." He was aghast. "You brought bourbon into a high school."

"Doesn't it just sicken you as an educator?"

What I'd smuggled in was not your run-of-the-mill piss in a bottle where one sip makes you want to chug a homeless man's vomit just to get the taste out of your mouth. My agent of seduction was Eagle Rare Kentucky bourbon, Warren's favorite. Not the ten-year swill either; the Antique Collection. Ninety-proof, aged in charred oak barrels for seventeen years. You feel a little more hillbilly just taking its narcotic embers into your nostrils.

He gave a deep sigh, faltering in the presence of kryptonite. "You didn't."

"I did. And I didn't even bring glasses."

I used to inhabit a universe without rules. For an unhealthily long spell, speed limits, closing times, that thing about not going into the clubhouse to meet the players—none of that applied to me. The Super Bowl was never sold out. Restaurants were never booked. Even the concept of a clock had a looser application to me. I was encouraged to show up to places at specified times, but if I was ten, fifteen, ninety minutes late, people smiled and did their best not to look inconvenienced. Such echelons of deference will go to someone's head, and despite all the humbling experiences I've had since, I couldn't help but continue to carry some of that entitlement around with me. Still, it seemed well over the line to be dribbling a basketball and sipping whiskey in a high school gym long after dark. I felt under imminent threat of *getting in trouble*, even if I'd probably aged out of the jurisdiction of the principal. (Are we ever beyond the jurisdiction of the principal?)

"Aren't we going to get busted?" I asked, as Warren sank a foul shot.

"Who's we? You're not a student and you're not a teacher, so you're not getting sent to the office and you're not getting fired."

"You're not really a teacher though," I posited, as he snatched the bottle from my hand. "You teach band and art. Aren't you sort of expected to treat rules with contempt?"

Teachers are not one-size-fits-all. They're pigeonholed, fairly or not but mostly fairly, depending on what they teach. You stared up at those dreary souls in class and pictured their weekends, trying not to feel sorry for them. On Saturday nights, science teachers sat at home and read magazines in an easy chair with public radio on in the background. English teachers had other English teachers over to play Boggle and trade salty barbs speckled with Joseph Conrad allusions. Gym teachers got shitfaced on Bud Light at a friend's corner bar. Math teachers cooked for, and spoke to, their cats.

But the music teacher—he was a man of mojo. You and your friends would occasionally run into him out on the town. You'd catch him on the street with his groovy wife and hipper-than-thou friends, and they'd all have excellent names. Meet my wife, Ocean. And these are my friends, Silas and Boo. He wouldn't say goodbye either. He'd say Onward! or Peace on you. Then you and your buddies would spend an hour debating whether or not he was stoned. Did you see his eyes, man?

"I don't know what you're talking about," Warren said, wiping a wet slurp onto his rolled-up sleeve. "My band teacher was a five-foot tightass who wore bow ties. And my art teacher was a semisenile battle-ax who went to school with my grandmother."

For quite some time, we alternated taking shots and doing shots, dribbling the ball in and around the paint, our jumpers getting wilder, our layups increasingly off the mark as the smooth Eagle Rare glided through our bloodstreams and did its thing.

"How did you find that Tate exhibit anyway?" I asked him.

It had been on the field trip he chaperoned each year, he explained. A family that owned art galleries in New Hope had started a foundation that annually sent five students who possessed a "highly developed appreciation for art" to visit museums out of the country, where the art is obviously better. Kids had jetted to Paris to appreciate the Louvre and the Musée d'Orsay, to Amsterdam for the Rijksmuseum and the Van Gogh Museum, to Florence, Rome, Berlin. This year was London.

"Must be nice," I said. "None of my field trips had ever required a passport."

"Nor mine. If we couldn't get there in twenty minutes on a yellow bus, we weren't going. But I gotta admit, when I saw that picture of you in the Tate, I was sorry I hadn't taken it myself." Warren cackled with callous joy. "*Faded Glory*. Classic."

"Like you could pull that off," I said. Warren's harmless and mostly good-natured pranks were rarely executed with the necessary deft.

He bristled at the affront. "Are you kidding? Candid photos of you looking like an idiot? That's shooting fish in a barrel."

"You mean like Clark, your identical twin? Was that shooting fish in a barrel?"

Warren laughed. The man had once decided, for reasons that eluded all of us, to pretend he was his own identical twin. Groupies, waitresses, autograph seekers—to each and every one he would deny that he was the drummer for Tremble. Nah, I'm his brother, Clark, he'd say with a smirk.

"That was an awfully complicated way to have fun," he allowed.

"Or when you decided to change the pronunciation of your last name?" One day he decreed that, effective immediately, his last name should be said with the accent on the second syllable. War-*ren*.

"That was a French thing. I still think I might be a little bit French."

"Like your name isn't enough of a joke."

"What it lacks in creativity, it makes up in emphasis," he stated.

He gave the basketball a serious bounce. It thwacked off the hardwood, surged high up toward the banners, and sailed down through the net with a breathy swish.

"Damn, Square!" I exclaimed.

He affected nonchalance. "Why does everybody always forget I'm black?"

Joining me on the bleachers, Warren snatched the bottle from my grasp. "Can't say I'm surprised that a photo like that sent you careening into a midlife crisis. It's like a switchblade right across this legacy of yours. Right? It leaves you no choice but to get back out there and rewrite history."

"So you understand then?"

"Sure I understand. I just think it's stupid. What have you got to be ashamed of? You went where just about every kid with a guitar dreams of going. You're not allowed to get older? You're not allowed to sit in a restaurant and eat a goddamn taco? You're even part Tex-Mex, aren't you?"

"That's a cuisine, not a nationality."

"Whatever. Leave me alone."

We sat in the gymnasium, polished in sweat and hazy from the booze. It didn't seem like twenty years since I'd banged around the walls of a high school gym. Memory does that sometimes, jumbles things up, messes with your sense of chronology. Some moments linger in sharp focus, reminding us that they happened, reluctant to drift away because they suspect we need them.

Warren asked, "How's Sara?"

"She's good."

Even if that was true, I wasn't in much of a position to know for sure. We'd both been rather preoccupied lately.

"She's been hanging out with her ex-husband," I said.

"Really?"

"Yeah. He came out of the woodwork and asked for a divorce."

"Well, that's probably a good thing, right? Closure for them, closure for you two."

The fact was, it hadn't felt like anything was closing. It was more of a rattling of hinges. "I don't know. I haven't been around much. And she tends toward tight lips anyway."

"That's gotta be hard for her though," Warren said.

"Sometimes it feels like I live with a ghost," I said. "She's like this presence I observe through dishes in the sink or impressions on a pillow. I won't see her, but I'll know she was there because of a blouse slung over a chair."

"Maybe she'd say the same about you. Except for the blouse. Or maybe not except for the blouse."

"I hate to say it, but she may just be happy to have me out of the house."

"Well, it sounds like you're being the supportive fellow I would've expected," he said, slapping my back.

I forced myself to my feet. The dizzying disconnect between my senses and my brain's processing of them was now fully pronounced.

I staggered toward a red rubber dodge ball sitting in a far corner of the gym. It took forever to get there, what with the whiskey pushing the wall further and further away. When I'd finally retrieved it, I trudged back toward Warren and stood over him. Then I pulled the ball back behind my shoulder, poised to release it into his face.

"Whoa! Whoa! Whoa!" he yelled, holding up his hands defensively.

"Join the band or you get it in the nose!"

"You throw that at me and I will kick your ass!"

"Warren War-*ren*!" I stood firm, ready to heave the ball at point-blank range. "I need you, damnit! We can do this!"

"Screw you, man! I have a goddamn life. Go get one yourself."

My throwing arm quivered. "Don't make me bring the heat."

"I promise I will kill you. You will die."

"Join me, young Skywalker. Together we can rule the galaxy!"

"You need therapy."

"And that stupid strip of a beard makes your chin look like it's swinging in a hammock. You have a fucking hammock on your face."

In a sudden blast of motion, he sprang up from the bench and hurtled himself at me like a linebacker. With a wallop not dissimilar to the one delivered by Heinz-Peter back in Shangri-La, Warren tackled the shit out of me. As I came down on my back under his weight, I learned why they call it hardwood. I didn't come close to getting off a throw.

"Get the fuck off!" I yelled, struggling against his lean network of muscles. The tussle only ended when he finally rolled over and writhed in inebriated laughter. The alcohol did little to cushion the cracking of my spine against the floor, and for a few searing seconds I thought I might need a stretcher. But soon we were both lying there, catching our breath, staring up at the artificial incandescence of the ceiling.

And then Warren started singing. In a low register and an unrelenting operatic vibrato, he began to belt out "It Feels like a Lie."

"Shut up," I whispered, as his gratingly tremulous baritone boomed up to the pennants.

The sound of that song was pure mockery, a symbol of my years of creative bankruptcy, a sonic taunt that practically dared me back into the ring. But on he sang in this new and intolerable vibrato. He sounded like a goat.

As I gazed up into the fuzzy gymnasium lights, it was all starting to seem familiar. I was flat on my back, I was drunk, the room was spinning, and I'd had some sort of physical altercation.

"You know what I think?" I began, once the last echo of Warren's voice had faded. "I think that on the day you die, you regret all the things you wanted to do but didn't try hard enough at." I sat up and looked at him. "Do you know what I mean?"

Warren grunted without so much as lifting his head. "I think on the day you die, you regret all the homeless people you walked past and didn't buy a sandwich for." He frowned at me sideways. "Self-centered dickhead."

Moments or hours later, we were sitting in my car. We'd staggered out of the building to fill our lungs with fresh air, and I'd shepherded us toward the visitors' parking lot. My car was the only one around, yet it still seemed like a minor miracle that we found it.

Like zombies, we sat in the front seat with the windows down, the stereo casting my rough demos out into the sleeping world. Warren rubbed his beard and looked faintly troubled but substantially drunk. After three songs, I shut off the radio. Just when I thought Warren might've passed out, he up and spoke, his voice a slow, drained grumble. "You're putting me in a difficult spot, Teddy."

"Yeah? How so?"

"Well, for one thing, those might be the best three songs you've ever written. They blow everything else away, even the hit."

"I never liked 'It Feels like a Lie,'" I admitted. "The song itself felt like a lie. It wasn't me at all. I would've flat-out refused to play it, but I had a band to feed."

He pointed at the dashboard radio. "If you'd written songs like this ten years ago, I wouldn't be teaching music to the tone-deaf way the hell and gone in Bucks County, Pennsylvania. It wouldn't have mattered that you told the Junction to go fuck themselves, that you sent us out on tour on our own, headlining with about a quarter hour's worth of decent material. But hey, that's the smoke of a distant fire."

"I know," I said. "I know."

"But . . ." He breathed deeply. "But I'm thirty-five now and . . . Look, it just doesn't matter how good the songs are. You have to know that. We weren't an act that absolutely demanded to be heard. We were just a good little rock band that rode the wave of one irritating four-minute jangle that you just know they're gonna play at your funeral. Come on, man, look at us. We're well beyond our sell-by date. The industry won't take us seriously."

"Why are you so obsessed with age? There's plenty of music being made by people who look like absolute shit. You tell me when Ric Ocasek was ever cute. Sonic Youth—everybody in that band looks like a Microsoft employee. Nobody really cares about the ages of these people."

Warren shifted in his seat. "I'm not obsessed with age. If anybody's obsessed with anything, it's you—about the past. You know, man, you talk like there's this place you've got to climb back up to. But it isn't so. Shame on you if you've got a chip on your shoulder, especially after all this time."

I let my hand drop out the window and land with a smack on the side panel. We sat for a languid spell under the dim interior car light, the one sign of life in the whole ink-black parking lot.

"Teddy, when I come home at night, I like what's waiting for me."

I said, "I'm not here to sweep you out of your life and away from Lauren and your kid. But come on, Warren, I know you. You love everything about making music. You may say you have no interest in doing a record with me, but whatever you decide, however this ends, we both know that's not true."

He let that claim hang unanswered as we continued our silent contemplation of the night. Out past a line of trees, I was just barely able to make out the lonely risers of the football field. Given our condition, it was entirely possible that we'd still be sitting here when dawn broke over those bleachers. And that would be just fine. I'd enjoy watching the window of morning slowly push open the sky.

"You play these songs for anyone else?" came Warren's low voice. "Other than that dipshit?"

"I played them for Sonny."

Warren turned. "Sonny Rivers? He still talks to you?"

"Reluctantly."

"What did he say?"

"He told me to go make a record. If you want to get technical about it, he said 'Go make a record, motherfucker.'"

Warren humphed.

"And if you can believe this, he wants to produce and he wants to help shop it around."

My passenger was shaking his head now, staring out into the darkness as his fingers explored his facial hair. There had to be an answer to all this out there somewhere—or somewhere deep in that beard.

"I'll tell you what," he said. "You get Mackenzie on board and I'll think about it. That's not a commitment. You understand me, you annoying pain in the ass?"

"Okay," I said, containing the edges of my grin.

"Don't smile, you bane of my existence. You haven't reeled me in. I am merely agreeing to give it further thought. That's it. And believe me, I'm not doing anything that takes me away from my family. Get that through that tiny, irritating, narcissistic, desperate, delusional head of yours."

"Message received," I said, somehow smug about this now. That was all the mistake I needed him to make. Just one measly error in judgment. From the barest flame abounds the all-consuming blaze.

Warren sighed a deep, defeated breath and reclined into the seat back. His eyes folded closed and he seemed on the verge of sleep. "If you'd mentioned Sonny two hours ago, you could've saved us both a bitch of a hangover."

"Look at it this way. If this all works out, you can resurrect Clark, the brother you never had." I slapped him on the chest. "I know you loved doing that twins thing."

He let out a listless grunt. "You do know that to normal guys that means something completely different."

I regained consciousness under a blanket smelling of cedar. It was like awakening in the woods among the oaks, pines, and Rocky Mountain Douglas firs, the scent of a fire wafting from a nearby cabin. The rustic peace was soon obliterated by the pounding on my skull. I had a vague recollection of Lauren pulling into the school parking lot and glowering at me as her husband and I slumped into the backseat of her car. Someone had left a glass of water and two maroon ibuprofen tablets on the table. Being served painkillers in strange houses was developing into a pastime of mine.

I slipped out before anyone else had stirred, but not before finding a pen and a stray piece of paper. "Thanks—and sorry in advance," I scribbled.

Squinting into the early-morning light, I took in the Warrens' row house on this quiet tree-lined street on the outskirts of Lambertville. The neighborhood seemed very aware of itself as a choice for a specific type of living, a town for people who'd gone looking for simplicity in the form of food fairs and antique shops.

Hoping to be reunited with my car, I set out in the direction that I guessed the high school to be. In town, I bought a cup of coffee in a little corner bakery, the kindly graying woman asking if I needed a nice lemon muffin to accompany it. I croaked out a thanks but no thanks, the first words of the day sounding as if they were spoken by me plus fifty years, and shouldered on.

I left Sara a voice mail as I sailed down the highway toward home. She hadn't responded to the text I sent letting her know I wasn't going to make it home last night. Nor did I hear from her as I sloped from one room of the condo to the next during the balance of the morning, dragging my headache with me into the afternoon.

Ravi Chatterjee had left another message on our home line, yet again trying to locate Sara without sounding threatening or overly concerned. It hardly comforted me that I wasn't the only one trying to track her down. She could've been up at Josie's studio, ducking the universe, or she could've been with Billy, sifting through the particles of an old universe. Something could have set her off in some other direction. It could've been the estranged husband who'd reappeared out of auld lang syne, or the longtime boyfriend who'd dematerialized into a fantasy of his own creation, or something else I didn't know about. What else, I wondered, did I not know about Sara Rome?

Worry mounted as the afternoon limped by. When evening descended, there was still no trace of her.

To distract myself, I considered the next order of business in my own jigsaw—that being the making contact with and recruitment of Mackenzie. Mackenzie Highsider. There was nothing about that name that didn't rattle my nerves.

For years I'd been playing out the scene where we met again, older and wiser. Seasons upon seasons of pondering the abstraction of our reunion had only allowed the fantasy to flower. I pictured her catching sight of me across the street or in a restaurant, and with a double take, her jaw would drop and she'd pause with hands on hips. We'd hug and she'd tell me I looked the same. She'd tell me she'd missed me and that she hated the way things ended between us, that she'd finally let go of her anger.

But the truth was, I was terrified. I could only assume that one inglorious deed of ours in that Phoenix hotel had stayed with her over the years. What I didn't know was whether she'd spent all this time thinking of me the way she did in the minutes just before we were discovered in that hotel room, or the way she did in the minutes just after.

I switched on the table lamps to illuminate what was feeling like a grippingly empty apartment. For further distraction—one that involved less dread and queasiness—I revisited some unfinished songs. I picked up my guitar and positioned myself on the sofa, pages of quatrains fanned out in front of me on yellow legal paper. But my eyes kept gravitating toward my phone. My ears kept hallucinating the sound of a key in the door.

I recalled a manila folder of abandoned lyrics that still sat buried in a closet. Maybe it would provide inspiration. I had no compunction about stealing outright from my younger, more vital self, so I walked down the hall to the office, opened the closet door, and rifled behind a curtain of Sara's dresses, outfits only invited out of the house on the rare formal occasion. Also hidden away against the closet wall, behind the veil of hanging clothes, was a collection of Sara's mosaics. I'd seen some of them before, but only accidentally, when they were being transported from Josie's studio. Their life cycle was concise and uneventful: they were created, they were carried home, and they were sent directly to storage.

I allowed my eyes to wander over these heavy decorative mirrors of Sara's creation. The broken glass and colored stones were arranged in impressionistic fashion, elusive and abstract. You weren't quite sure what you were seeing in the disjointed tiles, but they spooled you into a swirl of motion until you had to turn away. As a mirror of their creator, they were beautiful, absorbing, unsettling.

Then I made another discovery. Urged deep into the back corner of the closet was a globe constructed of a crinkly material that sounded like tissue paper. Gripping a string at one of its poles, I hoisted it out into the light. It was a paper lantern, a purple sphere with green and yellow flowers pasted onto it like continents. I hadn't known Sara to venture outside the genre of mosaics, and I pondered whether her indulgence in the cabal of paper lanterns was a onetime thing, an outlier, some wild experiment that had erupted in the hot chaos of Josie's studio, or if it signaled a transition. She'd perhaps entered her paper lantern period. I twirled the string between my thumb and index finger and watched the globe spin smoothly and efficiently, the tight tissue paper making the faint rustle of an April breeze.

A sharp voice behind me pierced the air. "What are you doing?"

I turned. "Sara. Jesus."

"What are you doing?" She looked horrified, as if snooping through my own closet was a violation of her privacy.

"Where the hell have you been all day?" I demanded.

"What?"

"I've been calling you, Ravi's been calling, everybody's been trying to track you down."

She marched at me and snatched the lantern string from my hand, then set about carefully returning the globe to the closet.

I proceeded to lecture the back of her head. "You can't just fall off the face of the earth, Sara. I didn't know where you were. I was worried. Look, if you're going to go hide out at Josie's, you've gotta let somebody know, for chrissakes. And if you were with Billy again, all I can say is—"

It came out of nowhere. She turned abruptly and her open hand slapped hard against my cheek. Her ring landed on my upper lip, stinging my tooth and snapping my head to the side. Before I could react to the shock of violence delivered by someone who'd never shown the slightest capacity for it, her voice came at me through gritted teeth—low, seething, desolate.

"Where am I every year on my son's birthday? Sitting in a field of tombstones, you selfish piece of shit."

She left me there, holding my battered cheek, her words stinging just as harshly as the blow, my face reddening in a rush of shame. I hadn't budged when she returned a few minutes later with a napkin wrapped around two pieces of ice.

"Come on," she whispered, and I followed her out of the room.

We sat on the couch for a long while, she holding the ice pack to my face and I too stunned and guilt-ridden even to apologize.

Then she said, "You should probably know that Billy did come with me this year."

I looked at her.

"He'd never gone out there before," she added.

"You and Billy went out there together?"

She nodded. "We've been talking, with the divorce and all, and it came up. His birthday." It seemed to require considerable effort for Sara to bring the words out of her mouth. "I told him I go there every year. At first, he said he didn't think he could do it, but then he said he wanted to, and he thought it might be easier with me there."

I stared at her sullen profile, her sagged shoulders. "And?"

"There's just nothing easy about it."

I sat there and processed the thought of the two of them at the cemetery, standing together side by side. Did they hold each other? Did they hold hands? Did they collapse under the exponential grief of two parents standing over their child's grave? Grieving because everything had fallen apart? Everything.

Outside, the sun withered behind the skyline, sucking the blue into pink.

"I'm sorry, Sara."

She turned to me. "Teddy, do you really think that while you're out there putting together your grand plans, I'm just sitting home waiting to hear about them?"

It wasn't even an insult; it was a question posed in good faith. She truly wanted to know.

I studied the worn creases of her skirt. The earthy smell of grass still clung to her clothes and hair. Why the hell didn't I know where she was today? How could I not know how she faced this anniversary after all the years we'd spent together?

And yet, it wasn't as if Sara had been talking and I hadn't been listening. Drew was a closed subject. Her accusations of self-centered bastardhood were hard to dispute, but at the same time, there'd been precious little for me to have ignored. I didn't know how she marked her son's birthday every year, but it wasn't because I wasn't paying attention. It was because in our relationship, we had a litter of sleeping dogs that we simply let lie.

But Sara had slugged me because I'd fallen short of expectations. What had never really dawned on me was that Sara had expectations of me.

"I'm sorry," I repeated in barely a whisper.

She got up to carry the damp napkin into the kitchen.

"Sara."

She stopped. "What?"

"That lantern. It's really pretty."

She cast the final sigh of the day and continued into the kitchen. As the dissolving cubes clanked into the sink, I wondered how long that globe had been lying in the closet. If, at one point, it had been a beacon, a signal to her lost son, her lost husband, or her lost self, then there was no denying that she'd long ago given up and buried it, having surrendered the dream that it could ever help anyone find their way home.

CHAPTER 11

Alaina Farber strode into the reception area looking every bit as slim, tight, and animated by innate elegance as ever. When she marched up to me in her sin-scarlet suit, I could do nothing but drop a dispirited little frown. "You know, I used to be younger than you," I said with a sigh.

"My Theodore has come for me at last," she proclaimed, planting the business end of a peck on my lips and throwing her arms over my shoulders. Her taste in high-end perfume smelled intoxicatingly familiar, like my brilliant, unreachable past. Her hand dropped down my back and cupped my right butt cheek. "You've kept yourself in shape," she observed. Then, with a raised eyebrow, "Is that a roll of Smarties in your pocket or are you just happy to see me?"

"I see somebody still needs her sexual harassment training."

"Nonsense. I'm an expert."

She led me through a glass door and down a corridor of offices, each one populated by a chattering, pacing agent. It felt like millennia since I'd set foot in the agency, and the faces I used to know had been replaced by successive generations of burnouts in the making.

"New digs?" I asked, pausing in the door frame of her office. "Or did you just have the walls pushed back?"

She sank into her chair and started reading something on her phone. "I moved ages ago," she said absently.

I scoped out the room, the walls crammed with photos of Alaina with her famous clients, a roster of A-list actors and musicians. There were those I recognized and those that bore the wild, world-owning shine of people I should've recognized. This documentation of Alaina Farber's rise to the top only magnified my drumming sense of irrelevance.

"You're up there." Though intended for me, the remark was addressed to her phone. As she thumbed out a text, I scanned the jumble of frames, surprised that any photo of me hadn't long ago been stuffed into a box and hidden away in a closet, maybe somewhere down the hall where they kept the mop bucket.

Then I discovered it, an eight-by-ten of a frozen moment in the prime of the band. My ruddy mug was centered between my agent, whose arm was slung insouciantly around my neck, and Colin Stone, the perennially upbeat label executive who'd shrewdly shepherded us along the road to stardom. Jumbo lounged behind us in an outfit of black and white stripes that made him look like the Hamburglar or the least convincing salesman at Foot Locker. I couldn't specifically recall when the photo had been taken—all those days now had all the focus of a smear—but it was snapped at the East Village Italian restaurant that doubled as our hangout, the place we congregated for dinners and cocktails. As one of Alaina's premier clients, Tremble enjoyed all her oily affections and zealous indulgences. She'd cozy up to me in the booth and take slurps of Warren's whiskey. Jumbo would pound beers or, when feeling superior, a classy glass of Southern Comfort. Mackenzie would lose herself in the specials insert.

"What was the name of that place?" I asked.

Alaina finally looked up from her device. "You've forgotten the fucking Mirabelle Plum?"

It had distant recognition for me. I never needed to know the name. I always got a ride.

"It's still there and the gnocchi still kicks ass. And I think your ban has been lifted."

"Right. The ban."

We'd just turned in the tracks for our sophomore release, and the label was grumbling—presciently, as it turned out—because too many of the songs were in need of "reworking" for radio-friendliness. The gist of their complaint was, Where was "It Feels like a Lie, Part Two"? As if corporate intrusion into the sacred realm of the artist wasn't galling enough, they compounded the treachery by dispatching some cocksure newbie to convey the message. We didn't take well to the criticism, rendered as it was for so mean and castrating a purpose as airplay. Nor did we appreciate its being delivered by this arrogant little twerp. We were nine fucking months removed from a number-one hit and an Academy Award. A testy exchange between the label kid and me spiraled into a bona fide donnybrook when Jumbo lunged at the guy. After the predictable upending of a table and the pitching of a glass against a wall, we all ended up locked in a rugby scrum that stumbled out the front door. Only Mackenzie escaped the fracas, standing to the side guarding her wine. A paparazzo was on hand to record the badly behaving musicians, and Jumbo's side of the story was printed in all its eloquence in the *New York Post* the following morning: "This is just [bad]! You get some [jerk] who doesn't know [anything] about this business coming in here talking [nonsense] to us. I mean, [rats]! Don't come into our [darn] hang in SoHo [sic] and give us [grief]. That's just [unfortunate]! Really [very] [unfortunate]! We won a Golden Globe [sic], for Christ's sake!" The restaurant owner didn't see the humor in a trashed dining room: ban imposed. A short while later, Alaina sauntered into the Plum with a tight skirt and heels and apologized as only she could: ban lifted. But by that point, it hardly mattered: band defunct.

I had spoken to my former agent only once in advance of this visit, and even then, very briefly. I'd simply called to ask if we could meet. She wanted to know if this was just a social call from a long-lost friend. I admitted that there was a little more to it but saved the full embarrassing truth for when I saw her in person. She asked if I'd finally come to my senses and if the "little more to it" involved the two of us "mauling" each other in a Jacuzzi at the Paramount. I told her it probably didn't but that I was impressed with her ability to make the word *mauling* sound seductive.

"So." Alaina dropped her phone onto her desk. "It took you ten years to pay me a visit, Theodore."

"I never saw the point in bothering you."

"Humility. Cute. I guess better late than never. But if you start kissing my ass, I'm going to think you want to kiss my ass."

I gave her my best unassuming shrug. "I left the business. I honestly didn't think you had room in your life for a client whose only value to you was sentimental."

"Ten years," she said, shaking her head and clicking like a scold. "Without so much as lunch."

"The phone lines run both ways."

"I'm me, okay? You know I'm not going to call. It was your job."

"I became a lawyer, Alaina. I started hanging out with fucking lawyers. Meanwhile, there's a picture of you and Adele. There's you and Robert Downey, Jr. You and—holy shit, is that Demi Lovato?"

"Okay, so, the mere fact that you know who she is makes you a perv. And listen to yourself. You're the pathetic little supplicant and I'm the castle bitch who's finally deigned to allow you past the guards? That hurts my feelings."

"I apologize. I didn't really know you had feelings."

"That's more like it!" She pounded the desk. "There's my salty little misanthrope." Then she picked up a pen and twittered it between her fingers. "I do have emotions, you know. Would you like to hear about some of them?"

"Guile is not an emotion," I told her. "Neither is unscrupulousness."

"I was actually going to tell you about my grandfather."

"Oh. What about him?"

"Well, he kicked it recently."

"I'm sorry."

"I accept your apology. He was, however, one million years old. I never told you about him?"

I shook my head. "Alaina's pop-pop isn't ringing any bells."

"Well, I'm going to tell you about him now." She swiveled philosophically in her chair. "When I was a little girl in Shanghai, he and I used to listen to music together on a beat-up piece-of-shit record player."

"Wait—you lived in China?"

She fluttered her fingers over her face like a magician bewitching a deck of cards. "Um, hello?"

"I always assumed you were adopted by some Manhattan Hebrews or something."

"Mutha, Chinee. Fatha, Upper Rest Side."

"Huh. How could I not have known that?"

"Don't feel bad. Demi Lovato doesn't know a thing about me either."

I crossed my legs and settled in for story hour.

"So, believe it or not, my folks hooked up when my dad was studying to be a chef in Shanghai. This was the late sixties, mind you, when you could neither waltz into nor out of the People's Republic whenever you fucking felt like it. Chairman Mao was not an easygoing cat. But my dad, resourceful Manhattanite that he was, somehow managed to smuggle his pasty Jew ass in, learn how to cook a noodle or two, and stay there long enough to meet, marry, and knock up my mom.

"I was but a young whippersnapper, but I do have some wonderful memories of Shanghai and all of us living together in my grandparents' puny apartment. Every evening, my grandfather and I would sit and listen to music, just the two of us. He'd put on records of old Chinese folk songs and we'd park ourselves on the floor, side by side. I remember the dusty vinyl smell of the speakers, the claw scratch of the needle dipping on the grooves. I can still picture the way the old man would soak up that ancient music, his eyes closed, a contented smile on his face. Looking back on it now, I know he was trying to pass these songs on to me because he feared that his round-eyed son-in-law would one day drag his beloved daughter and granddaughter back to the States—shanghai us away, if you will—and I would live my whole life estranged from my native culture. Which is exactly what happened. And thank the good Lord for that.

"Then one day my dad came home with a Beatles album. *Rubber Soul*. Imagine, Teddy darling, what a coup that was. This was China in the early seventies. You couldn't exactly flip on Casey Kasem's *American Top 40*. I have no clue how he got his hands on it or how it even got into the country, but it wouldn't be totally outlandish to suggest that my family was the only one on the entire mainland to be rocking out to the Fab Four.

"Now, I'm sure my dad expected his old-world Chinese father-in-law to recoil in horror at this brash, obnoxious Western music. You know, like, Dude, where's my lute? But he fucking ate it up! Couldn't understand a single lyric, mind you, but the guy went bananas for 'Norwegian Wood,' 'Michelle,' and 'In My Life' like an American schoolgirl in heat. So now my grandfather would come home in the evenings and instead of putting on creaky recordings of a bamboo flute from the Ming Dynasty, we'd sit together and spin *Revolver*, *Magical Mystery Tour*, and *Sgt. Pepper*, because my wily old man somehow got hold of the whole freakin' catalog."

I found myself transfixed, amazed by how much I hadn't known about Alaina. I guess I'd assumed she'd just materialized on the planet one day in her current feline form, accessorized and pissy.

She snapped her fingers at the air. "Pay attention. I am going somewhere with this. So, when I was seven, my dad finally came to his senses and said enough of this shit. He got a job at a restaurant here in the city and moved my mom and me to New York. My grandparents, of course, stayed behind in the old country like the good little Commies that they were. Now, I know it's been decades upon decades, but God, Theodore, I have a clear memory of that last night together, the night before we left China. My grandfather and I sat down on the floor like we always did, but on our final night under his roof he didn't put any records on. He was too sad. He just sat there with this dark look on his face. He looked like he was losing everything. I still see it, Teddy, I really do. I didn't know what to say to him. I was just a stupid, albeit uncommonly beautiful, kid. I didn't understand distances, separation, missing somebody while you grow older, any of that.

"Finally, after sitting there quietly for a long time, I got up and put on a record. It was 'Let It Be.' I told him not to be sad. One day I would move back to China and we'd be together again, but until then, he could play his Beatles records over here in Shanghai and I'd play them in New York, and we could each imagine that we were sitting in the same room, listening side by side like we always did."

I stared at her, hoping she wasn't going to come apart. I wasn't good with that.

"See? I was kind of a nice kid," she said.

"We're talking about forty years ago," I reminded her.

"Anyhoo, I obviously never moved back to Shanghai and I only saw my grandfather a handful of times after that. But when he died a few months ago, my mother and I flew over there to go through his things. We were cleaning out the apartment—that same little place I knew as a kid—sorting through all the random shit you accumulate over the course of a lifetime. And do you know what I found?"

I shook my head.

"The albums of one stupid, insignificant, boring little band. A collection of nobodies that named itself after its marginally talented, bland-faced front man. The same marginal talent that's sitting in front of me now. None of the other acts I've worked with over the years were to be found, and need I remind you, there have been some big ones. Real big. A lot bigger and a lot better than you."

"I think you've made your point."

"The only records in his collection that had anything to do with his precious granddaughter's career were yours. You were my first client to make it big, and I imagine that made him a whole mess of proud."

I blinked at her, unsure how to respond.

Alaina suddenly turned dark and serious. "It's a terrible thing, Teddy, to die while missing someone. Don't you think? It seems like something too brutal for the universe to tolerate."

Then she rose and walked around her desk, positioning herself directly in front of my chair. It was a simultaneous act of intimacy and control.

"So, my little rhubarb," she said, folding her arms. "Are you catching my drift?"

"Did you really just say 'a whole mess of proud'? We're Eudora Welty now, are we?"

She kicked me on the shin. "Are you getting my point?"

I looked up at her. "I think you're trying to tell me that you have an overdeveloped sense of loyalty. Either that or your grandfather lost interest in your career very early on."

"I have an overdeveloped everything." She smiled warmly. "It's good to see you again, Teddy Tremble. And in the name of my grandfather, I forgive you for ignoring my existence for the past ten years."

I rolled my eyes. Then, heavily, I reached into my jacket pocket and removed a CD. "I'm actually not here to talk about the past."

Alaina's eyes turned devilish at the sight of the CD, and she accepted it with a quizzical twitch of the nose. "What is this? Do you have a son or some grandnephew in a band?"

"You can go fuck yourself, you know that?"

"Oh, believe me, I know."

"It's me," I confessed lamely.

"You?" she gasped. "But . . . but . . . I'm confused. You're not a musician. You're a lawyer. You gave all this up years ago. You left it behind, turned the page—"

"Will you give it a rest?"

She regarded the jewel case dubiously. "This is really you? I'm speechless."

"That's not what speechless sounds like."

"So, go ahead. Tell me your story. There's obviously a story behind this, probably sadder than the one I just recounted about my dead grandfather, but you're clearly dying to tell it to me."

"Why do you say that?"

"Because FedEx still costs less than a train ticket."

"You got me there," I said.

"Beautiful does not seem stupid." Leaning her slender body over the credenza, she inserted the disc into a glistening piece of stereo equipment that had a CD tray, a USB port, an MP3 dock, and anachronistically, a tape deck. "Is this new music you've brought me or swing versions of your oldies? Extended dance mixes with Moby? Tremble for Babies?"

"It's new stuff."

"Hmm. Delusions of relevance. I've seen this movie before."

"Maybe I'll exceed your expectations."

"That'll be easy." She snickered. "So before I subject my delicate ears to your cacophony, tell me where you think this fits in."

This was the familiar Alaina, the one constantly aquiver with a marketing angle. Everybody had to fit in somewhere. The Pet Shop Boys were still at it because the musical tastes of Eurofags hadn't evolved in the past quarter century. The few members of Lynyrd Skynyrd who hadn't ridden over themselves with their own motorcycles could still do "Gimme Three Steps" to a crowded barbecue because somebody had to make music for dirtballs. So where did that leave me?

I said, "Do I look like I fit in anywhere?"

"Well, that is the question, my little yogurt parfait."

A soft knock interrupted us. A young woman pushed the door ajar and poked her nervous face into the room. She was a slight girl in her early twenties with punky blond hair blanketing her head.

"What is it, Marin?" Alaina snapped. "We're working."

"Dave Chenier is on the phone. And he's really mad."

"Why?"

"He's not happy with the way the movie is going. And also, Vernon transferred him to me because you were in a meeting and, um, he didn't like that."

Dave Chenier was a well-known actor and pompous prima donna who'd made an appearance in nearly every art-house film of the past fifteen years. The warmest thing I'd ever heard anyone say about him was "No comment."

Alaina groaned. "Transfer the little vaj to the conference room. I'll take him in there."

Marin slunk out, and suddenly I felt just as small and meek as she. My history with Alaina and whatever wells of loyalty still pooled in her backyard might have earned me a meeting, and apparently even a nail on her office wall, but it didn't get her pissing away valuable time that could've been devoted to the service of clients with a name and a future. Maybe Warren was right. Even if the songs were pouring out of me as if some artery had swung free inside, there were just too many other variables to factor in.

I stood. "I should go."

"Go? Sit your ass down."

Ignoring her, I walked to the door. "Look, I would appreciate it if you listened and told me what you think, but I'll understand if you don't want to get involved." Before reaching for the handle, I paused and smiled. "It was good to see you too, Alaina."

She caught me as I waited for an elevator, marching up to me, a hot breath of chic scarlet carving up the lobby. "We don't walk out on me, Theodore," she said, clearing her throat. "You may have forgotten the rules."

"I feel silly being here." I pressed the elevator button. "Listen to the music if you want, but either way, no hard feelings."

Her head jerked like I'd just jabbed her on the chin. "What the fuck is that? No hard feelings?" Behind the reception desk, a young man with spiked hair and a pastel-green tie pretended to busy himself by fussing with papers. "Who do you think you're talking to?"

"Relax." I was already growing weary of this world I was so intent on charging back into. "I'm just letting you know that I understand all the angles. God, you are so much work."

"I know what my job is. I don't need you to tell me how to do it," she snapped. "But don't give me your girly little no-hard-feelings routine. It's a huge turnoff."

I became conscious of the smattering of people milling about in the waiting area, all quietly enjoying our altercation. I wondered if I looked familiar to them, if they were trying to place me, if they were doing the math in their heads and judging me.

"I have a train to catch," I said. "We'll talk later."

Elevator doors parted, I boarded, and then it somehow occurred to me to flash my trump card, if for no other reason than to gauge its power.

"For what it's worth, Sonny Rivers loves my new stuff. He wants to make a record."

As the doors glided smoothly toward each other, Alaina's bejeweled hand chopped the air between them. The doors cowered back.

"Come off, Triscuit," she commanded.

I complied.

"Sonny Rivers has heard this?"

I nodded. I really should start leading with that one.

"How did that happen?"

"I played it for him."

"Hmm. And he liked?"

"Well, as I mentioned in my previous sentence, he wants to make a record."

Her eyes narrowed in devious deliberation.

"Why are you squinting?" I asked.

"I'm not squinting. I'm Asian, asshole."

I could literally see the wheels spinning behind her eyes, work-shopping the moves she'd need to make in order to organize the world in sync with her vision.

"Jumbo's in," I added. "So is Warren. Sort of."

"Well, butter my buns and call me a biscuit. Somebody's been busy. The whole motley fucking crew."

"Getting there."

"Jumbo's still alive, huh? You really want to work with that neb-bish again?"

"You were the one who always talked me out of firing him."

"I considered it an erratic move to ax the only person in the band with talent. What about the chick?"

"I haven't spoken to Mackenzie yet."

"Of course you haven't. Fraidy cat."

"I'm not afraid. I'm apprehensive. And Dave Chenier is still on hold."

A courtly ding signaled the arrival of another elevator. "I'm actu-ally going to ride down in this one, so give me a call if you want to talk." I held up the bunny ears of a peace sign. Which I'd never done before in my entire life.

Later, while rumbling home on Amtrak, I got a text from Alaina: "putting your demo on now. will try to stay awake. zzzzz."

I wrote back, "you owe me. i stayed awake while you went all amy tan on me. zzzzz."

Her: "eat me. and don't think i don't know this is all a ploy to get me back in your life. i still know u better than u know yerself."

Me: "there's not that much to know."

A few moments passed, then she wrote: "can we try not to bang the bass player this time?"

CHAPTER 12

I shook the fine grounds of a Costa Rica blend into a filter and watched the drips as they fell into the coffeepot below, each hiss a whispered admonition. I'd awakened with a knot in my stomach, knowing I couldn't put off the next part of my journey any longer.

I still remembered when Mackenzie, then a sophomore, showed up for her audition (yeah, we made her audition) after the bass player we'd been jamming with, a senior like me, failed out and was summoned back to the family garden-gnome business. The rest of us had already been playing together for a while. I'd known Jumbo since childhood, and I'd met Warren through a college friend. "His name is Warren Warren," the friend warned. "I don't know if that's a black thing or not, but he's a really good kid."

I knew Mackenzie as the breezy, sporty geek whom I'd seen on campus benches holding shabby copies of Günter Grass and Saul Bellow, always looking like she was clued in to a secret that the rest of us wouldn't learn for another five, ten, fifty years. Something about her sense of self-containment drew me in, and even though I knew I'd never have the ability, or really the interest, to converse with her about Grass or Bellow, I knew she was the one. I knew it before she'd even plugged in and followed us through "Free Fallin'" and "Take the Money and Run," before I'd seen her easy sway, her bottled warning of a grin, the organic cool of an instrument in her hands. On that first afternoon, she handled the Petty and the Steve Miller effortlessly, then knocked my socks off with "Houses of the Holy" and "Sunshine of Your Love."

"You're going to need to learn originals," I informed her with obnoxious self-seriousness.

"I can do that."

"You should know going in that this is going to be a commitment. We have plans. Being a college band may be fine for some people, but we're more than that."

My delusions of grandeur were met with a chuckle. "Okay," she said through one of those smiles where she sort of stuck out her tongue and looped it up to the bottom of her front teeth. "But I should mention that I'm the vice president of the Ultimate Frisbee team. We meet two afternoons a week on the quad and we're usually done by six. I'm also in the Student English Association. That hasn't met yet but I expect it will at some point."

Jumbo snorted. "You'll have to quit both of those."

Mackenzie, to her credit, ignored him.

"You'll definitely need a car," I told her. "That's a necessity. Do you have one?"

"No."

"It doesn't matter," I said. "Warren's Camry has a lot of trunk space."

"It's my dad's Camry," Warren was quick to correct in defense of his pride.

"It holds most of his kit," I went on, "and the rest of us don't have a lot of gear anyway. Our PA system is pretty puny, although once we make some money, we'll upgrade. I'm thinking we'll mic up your bass amp instead of running it directly through the board. You okay with that?"

"Yeah," she said, not really paying all that much attention.

Jumbo pointed a stern finger at her. "There may be drugs. Can you handle drugs?"

Again, Mackenzie ignored him. She was a quick study.

Our very first show together was a fraternity basement, and even though it was the only venue that would even consider booking us— and by booking, I don't mean to suggest that any money changed hands—I'd accepted it with an air of condescension. My grandest musical accomplishment up to that point had been in high school when my aggrieved rendition of Richard Marx's "Right Here Waiting" separated Debbie Devereaux from her bra right there on my parents' piano bench, and yet somehow I still felt that the ZBT house was beneath me.

The gig was not uneventful. Around midnight, the room mobbed and sweltering, we were in the middle of "Nevada Blue Sky" when Jumbo's guitar simply cut out. That happened with college bands. Technical difficulties bedeviled many a gig, as equipment would burst into an ear-splitting buzz or hum or simply make no sound at all for no apparent reason. Fortunately, "Nevada" was one of my least imaginative compositions, with one groove that you could ride from intro to coda. So while Jumbo fiddled with and pounded madly upon his moody amp, I waited for the song to fall apart one instrument at a time. Mack, meanwhile, played on unfazed. She and Warren kept the pulse of the song alive, pressing on with the beat and the bass line through a colloquy of foxy smirks, improvising a stream of flourishes, runs, and fills that stewed up so natural a jam that we sounded like we did this every night. I was dazzled by her poise and mesmerized by her low-key sense of showmanship, though very much relieved when Jumbo's Strat rejoined the proceedings.

After the show, as we hauled our gear across campus, I said to Mackenzie, "Nice going. You handled that curveball like a pro." As if I would have any insight whatsoever into how a pro behaves.

A few weeks later, she appeared at my door on a Sunday afternoon, her guitar case and mini-amp weighing her down.

"Sorry I'm late," she panted.

"You're not. You're two hours early."

"Shit. Really? I thought we said four thirty."

"Six thirty. But come on in."

She dropped her gear on my floor and ruffled her hair with a hand that bore the indentations of her guitar case grip. "I hate to ask, but how busy are you right now?"

Minutes later, we were in my hand-me-down Saab en route to the Center City row house that her boyfriend, a Wharton student named AJ, shared with three roommates and where she'd left her bag of schoolbooks. Mack was under the impression that AJ had some departmental dinner, so she wasn't surprised when nobody answered. But she desperately needed her schoolwork for the next morning and was reasonably certain a back window was unlocked and accessible to anyone equipped with a modicum of derring-do, and who wasn't skeeved out by inner-city shrubbery and the untold varieties of rodentia therein.

I followed as she vaulted a waist-high fence and crept down an overgrown alley that ended at a small patio at the rear of the house. There was a back door that looked militarily reinforced, kitchen windows covered over with wrought iron bars.

"Your boyfriend lives in Rikers Island," I observed.

"That's his room," she said, pointing up at a second-floor window. She scoured the patio for implements of elevation; there was nothing but a sagging bag of charcoal and a rake. "If you can somehow lift me up to the windowsill, I can pry it open and slip inside."

I dropped to a knee and Mack placed one sneakered foot in my hand. Then, leaning against the mossy bricks to offset her weight, she planted her other shoe in my free hand, and I hoisted her up the side of the wall.

"Sorry I'm not anorexic," she quipped. She was light and taut, like carrying an empty bookcase.

With Mack's small feet in my hands—sleek Pumas with pink stripes on the sides—I was eye level with the back of her immaculately toned legs, still deepened with the trace of a summer tan. I tried not to stare too long at the hovering hemline of her olive cargo shorts.

"Are you high enough?" I called out, shifting my head to the side. I thought it untoward to speak directly into the space between her legs.

"I'm at the ledge," she replied. "If you can boost me a little higher, I think I can lift the window. Can you give me a few more inches?"

I chuckled.

"Okay, that was gross," she allowed.

Simulating a barbell curl, I raised Mack higher until she said, "That should do it."

At the sound of wood sliding in a frame, I hazarded a glance upward, just in time to watch her legs sail out of my hands and through the window.

I was already in the car when she came bounding out the front door, one strap of a backpack over her shoulder. Something clicked in me at that exact moment. I guess you could say I fell in love with her, although there was so much to love about what was happening in those days and the many tomorrows that followed that it would be hard to parse out the particulars. I would come to think of that time as the best days of my life, and, on more than one occasion, I have wondered if she was the reason.

There was a lot about being the bassist in a successful band that she had to look past. She didn't luxuriate in the fatuous dissection of the songs, the laboring over macro aspects of music. ("Suppose we introduce a low pump organ to really bring out the angst in the second verse"; "You can't have two thematically similar songs, both in E minor. Are you insane?") Nor was she in it for the camaraderie. To her, Jumbo, Warren, and I were like irritating brothers with whom she was trapped in the family sedan for a summer road trip. On a good day, and when she was so inclined, we rose in the ranks and became two-bit drug dealers who could connect her to the occasional joint. Although she was the most articulate of all of us, she had little tolerance for verbalizing what was best left said by the music. At band meetings, she was typically silent, eyeing us secretively from under her short shag haircut, finally offering input that didn't sound like input at all: "If you guys are done talking, can we just play the damn thing?"

With a glance at the clock on my condo wall, I realized time was getting tight. It was a five-hour trip out to Pittsburgh and I'd reserved for myself the last appointment of the day at the sex therapy offices of Mackenzie Highsider. Under the stream of a nervous shower, I allowed the conversation—the one that I'd been preparing for for years and that was now going to happen this afternoon—to unfold in my head.

I knew that Mack felt some complicity in the destruction of my marriage, a detail she seemed to struggle with until Tremble went on permanent hiatus and she didn't have to face me every day. I fully expected that she'd nurtured a keen bitterness and resentment toward me, perhaps made all the worse by the gradual realization that maybe we were each other's missed opportunities. If we hadn't been caught that evening under such cheap and trashy circumstances, if we hadn't been busted, who knows? Maybe we would've had a chance.

Mack was the least likely to join us on this second adventure, the least likely to speak to me, but I owed it to all of them to try to lasso her back into the fold. I'd misled them and screwed them over by guiding the band off track in ways they didn't even know about. It was time I faced the music.

I was still wet when a visitor buzzed up from the lobby. A towel wrapped around my waist, I led a trail of footprints into the foyer and pressed the intercom. "Hello?"

"Mingus?" came the voice through metal static.

"Jumbo?"

"Mingus."

"Jesus."

There were good reasons underlying my policy of never answering unexpected calls, and there were consequences for violating it.

Soon Jumbo was standing in my living room in a Members Only windbreaker, nodding approvingly at my apartment and scratching his balls.

"Nice digs," he said.

"Thanks. Say, James, what exactly the fuck are you doing here?"

He pulled a CD from his jacket pocket and held it out to me as if it were a million-dollar bill. "Some seriously cool shit on here, man. You've got to hear it."

Partially due to his monomania, but mostly due to a really open calendar, Jumbo had crawled out of his meth lab of a living arrangement to share with me in person the fruits of his creative energies. He'd overdubbed some guitar parts on the demos I'd given him, and evidently didn't think twice about hopping in the car for two hours to show up at my house unannounced to deliver them.

"Put it on," he bade me. "Tell me what you think. I got some guitars in my trunk. We can jam out a bit. You want a beer?"

My jaw tightened. "Did you just offer me a beer in my own house? At nine thirty in the morning?"

He checked his Walgreens digital watch and frowned. "It feels later."

At least he hadn't come all this way to retrieve his pot stash, which, it just then occurred to me, was still buried beneath an Oasis disc in my glove compartment.

"Is your chickie around?" he asked.

"No, she's at work. People work on Fridays. Everybody but us, apparently. Listen, Jumbo, it's not a good day. I've got an appointment."

"Oh yeah? Who with?"

"That really isn't any of your business, is it?"

Distracted momentarily by our mint dish, he sloped over to the coffee table and began to unwrap a Life Saver. He then plopped himself down on the couch and unzipped his jacket, thereby revealing a Cheech and Chong *Up in Smoke* tee that cradled his spare tire. Then, to my horror but not to my surprise, he started clawing fiercely at his scrotum, gritting his teeth and squeezing his eyes shut in frantic pursuit of some blistering itch. When the attack subsided, he looked up at me as if nothing had happened.

"You can't just show up here, Jumbo. You should've called, like a normal person."

"This appointment you've got today, is it medical?"

"It's none of your goddamn—" There was no point in trying to wear each other down. He would hound me all day. "I'm going to see Mackenzie," I blurted out.

"Well, that's perfect! I'll join you. We can talk to her together."

"We could, except that you're not coming, so we'll have to talk to her separately."

"How awesome is my timing?" he mused, unwrapping another mint. "So, where is Mack these days?"

I sighed. "Pittsburgh."

"What's she doing there?"

"She's a sex therapist."

His face lit up. "Get out!"

"No, you get out. Seriously. I'd like you to get out."

Jumbo pitched backward into the sofa cushion. "So Mackenzie Highsider became a sex therapist. How about that."

"We can't all be midwives."

Hands bulked into the pockets of his Wham!-era windbreaker, Jumbo hoisted himself off the sofa and pursued me as I dug an overnight bag out of the hall closet and stuffed it with a pair of jeans, a couple of shirts, underwear, and socks.

The sound of a grown man whining drifted over my shoulder. "Come on, man, let me come with you."

"Absolutely not."

"We'll double-team her." He winked. "Get it? That's a sex therapy joke."

"No, it isn't."

"I know what's going on here, Mingus. You're embarrassed to be seen with me."

"Isn't everybody? You never say the right thing, you look like Ronald McDonald . . ."

"I got news for you: How can you be ashamed of me if you asked me to join your band? We're partners."

"We're not partners. We're loosely affiliated. That's how I like to think of it."

I combed around the bathroom for toiletries amid Sara's bathing products and facial creams. When I emerged, Jumbo was standing there looking pitiful and arguably homeless. "I came all this way."

"Uninvited."

"I've worked really hard on the songs, man. Really hard. Don't you want to hear them?"

"Isn't that what the disc is for?"

"But there's a ton of shit I want to talk to you about. You know how I work. We need to listen to these songs together. My process is important."

I heaved another grievous sigh. "Christ, Jumbo."

The very thought of being caged up in a car with this man for five hours was reason enough to bag the whole thing and beg Marty Kushman for my job back. But Jumbo did have a point. There was a benefit to gliding across the state together, our music flooding out of the stereo. Insights could be shared. Ideas exchanged. Would a new Tremble album have an acoustic feel? Would there be the pounding piano or the swell of a Doorsy organ? Did a certain song cry out for a cello?

And while the very sight of Jumbo sent my blood pressure into the stroke zone, I couldn't help but feel a twinge of pity for the man. I'd be sending him home to his troll-like existence beneath his ex-wife's stairs. No wonder this bonehead was up for anything—a road trip across Pennsylvania, a career change.

The other truth was that the prospect of being in the same room with Mackenzie was eating me alive. If Jumbo was nothing else, he was a distraction. (He was often nothing else.) His presence in the car would keep my head occupied—with musical banter, with his bound-less inventory of inanities and things in need of fixing. Was I really so far gone that I was considering Jumbo Jett to be a source of moral support as I ground away on that endless treadmill of the Pennsylva-nia Turnpike?

I marched back to the closet, retrieved a frayed duffel bag, and threw it at him. "You can borrow a T-shirt and sweatshirt or some-thing, but you're on your own for a toothbrush."

He pumped his fist. "Awesome! I love you, Mingus. I really do love you."

"Please don't ever say that to me again. Especially alone in my condo."

"You're making the right call here, man. I think we're going to look back on this little trip as a defining moment for this band!"

"That's wonderful. Just meet me downstairs."

"You got it." He bolted out of the room. Over his shoulder, he yelled, "Just gotta get my dad out of the car."

"Fine, whatever. Wait! What?" I charged into the foyer. He was already halfway out the door. "What did you just say?"

He stood there, blinking at me, lacking the wherewithal even to look sheepish.

"James. Is your father here?"

"Sorry, dude," he said with a shrug. "It's his weekend."

CHAPTER 13

Jumbo stuffed himself into the passenger seat, cranked the volume on the stereo up to deaf, and announced that he'd be on the lookout for a Waffle House. His father, by karmic contrast, seemed perfectly content to sit in the back and stare mildly out the window like an eroding stone.

At the first rest stop outside Philly, I got out to fill the tank while Jumbo bounded into the convenience store in search of whatever it was he considered breakfast. Before I had the chance to drive away and leave him there—had his old man objected, I doubt I would've heard him anyway—Alaina called. The sight of her name on the caller ID only added to my mounting collection of anxieties, as I assumed she was calling about the demos.

"Hello?" I said.

There was silence on the other end.

"Hello?" I repeated, louder this time. "Alaina?"

After another moment of dead air, she finally spoke. "That was me being speechless."

"Ah," I said.

"I admit, when you wandered into my office the other day with a CD in your hand, I thought early senility. I didn't want to represent you; I wanted to make sure you got home without getting hit by a car.

I would've let you down easy, I really would've. I would've suggested the senior tour, told you to pack your guitar and pointed you in the direction of a nice friendly resort in the Caribbean. Nobody enjoys a washed-up musician like island tourists with faces full of shrimp and pineapple. I was already picturing you in your Tommy Bahamas and khaki shorts, strumming 'Margaritaville' in a tiki lounge."

"Those places aren't me. The drinks are all watered down."

"But Teddy, my little macaroon, we don't need the tropics just yet. These songs knocked me out cold. I don't know where you found this material. I've never considered you particularly poetic or deep or even terribly deft with a melody. But this is some serious booty here. You treat these songs right in the studio and I'll get people interested in this—and that's without my having to remove a single article of clothing."

"I'm glad you like it," I said.

"What's the one where you sing 'hiding in plain sight' over and over?"

" 'Hiding in Plain Sight.' "

"Interesting. I've been humming that one so much, I thought it was a real song."

"It's not."

"You'll do a record, we'll explore some licensing opportunities with the networks, maybe get you on an HBO soundtrack or something. I'm going to make shit happen. In the meantime, a gym membership wouldn't kill you."

"You don't think you're jumping the gun here?" I asked. "You've got a lot of ideas for having heard only a couple of tunes."

"That's kind of my job, Fruity Pebble, and I've kind of been doing it awhile. I didn't take time off to ravage the justice system like someone else I know."

She would send over a contract. She took more points than she used to, she warned me, but she was worth it. Then she'd get on the phone with Sonny to ink him up for producing. In the meantime, I was to go get my little band together.

It couldn't have been as easy as my agent was making it sound. "Alaina, you really think this has potential?"

"Other than the potential for self-embarrassment? Yes, though it's almost a medical miracle at your age. Seriously—it's really strong work, Teddy. I'll just go ahead and say it because I know it turns you on: I'm a whole mess of proud of you."

I laughed. "Okay, but just in case, I'll keep that Caribbean resort idea in mind. I still know all the chords to Buffett. All two of them."

Jumbo emerged from the mini-mart, a stack of dripping coffees three stories high balanced in one hand, a bag of Funyuns and a Chipwich in the other. "Some kind of world we're living in when they put the Nicorette gum right next to the Newports," he complained, placing the coffees on the roof of the car. "That's just not playing fair."

"Alaina just called," I told him.

When I relayed her meows of optimism, Jumbo reacted with a spastic pump of his fist—a newly acquired tic, I'd noticed. "I knew it! I goddamn knew it! I got news for you, Mingus, these demos are going to change the course of music history." He celebrated with more fist pumps, goofy dancing, and even possibly a jumping jack. By the time he calmed down and distributed the coffees into the various cup holders, he'd accidentally taken a sip from all of them.

Once I pulled us back onto the road, Jumbo shared the good news with his father, and though Elmer uttered not a single word, his many wrinkles, spots, and yellowish discolorations did curve upward in what I presumed was a smile. Then he went back to mute contemplation of the scenery.

"Is he okay back there?" I whispered.

"Of course. He's psyched."

He didn't look psyched. He looked cadaverous.

"He's one of our biggest fans, always has been. Check this out." Jumbo twisted his fleshy self around. "Hey, Dad, which one do you have on today?"

I watched in the rearview mirror as the old man unzipped his jacket and revealed an aged rust-red concert T-shirt with the Tremble logo.

"How much does my dad rule?" Jumbo said, grinning beatifically. With that, he flipped down the sun visor and examined his ungovernable locks in the mirror.

(A word or two about Jumbo's hair. While it generally defied description, it was an unruly mess of curls and frizzes that incorporated the worst elements of nearly every hairstyle of the past quarter century, though it was not technically a hairstyle in and of itself. It was the color of a particularly viscous motor oil or a brown sauce served at a Chinese restaurant, something they put broccoli and water chestnuts in. It looked better uncombed, which was fortunate because he so rarely subjected it to the rectitude of a brush. On the rare instances when he did comb it, he looked like a harmless mental patient out for the day with an uncle. Sometimes his hair wanted to be a perm, other times a mullet, and occasionally it smacked of a bob.)

Equipped now with fuel and sustenance, we could get down to the business of listening to the music. Through the magic of a simple software program that any eight-year-old could master but I'd assumed to be well beyond Jumbo's technological grasp, he'd recorded guitar parts on top of my demos so that it sounded like we'd played them in the same room. Foaming with excitement, his cheeks and chin already glistening from an inorganic pie whose flavor was cautiously described on the wrapper as "fruit," he slid the disc into the stereo.

Instantaneously, I suffered the forgotten thrill of hearing the sound of a new Tremble song. I was amazed. It was all still there. In some places, Jumbo's guitar was restrained and textural, adorning the song with subtle flourishes. In others, the playing was caustic and volatile, chewing up the scenery. But through and through, it was Jumbo's guitar in all its masterful dramatic voicing. Sure, the words that came out of his mouth filled you with the urge to stuff a pack of gauze into his windpipe, but put a six-string in his hands and he was somehow . . . exquisite. Before I worked with Jumbo, I thought a banjo had no place in rock music. Before I worked with Jumbo, I didn't think a pink double-neck guitar could be applied with class. Before I worked with Jumbo, I didn't think you could tastefully use stompbox effects pedals without fetishizing Joy Division. But Jumbo, damn him, understood what worked and he understood how to get there. Filtered through him, the music undeniably sounded better. It was the only reason anybody put up with him. To witness his talents was to wonder why he never latched onto another band after Tremble; to witness his decision making was to understand why he ended up a cellar-dwelling midwife.

"This is good stuff, Jumbo. Very good stuff."

"See, Mingus? I know what I'm doing. We play this for Mack, there's no way she can refuse us."

I muttered to myself, imagining the many ways she was likely to refuse us.

"You got a game plan?" he asked. "How are we going to break this to her?"

"Who's we? I said you could come to Pittsburgh with me. I didn't say you could join me in Mackenzie's office."

He looked mortally wounded.

"James, don't even argue. I'm not talking about this anymore."

"Dude, be honest with yourself. Someone like me is far more likely to walk into a sex therapist's office than you. Maybe you're not remembering the glory days, my friend, but it was with me that things got messy. It was in my hotel room that someone got defiled or maybe drizzled with—"

"So, I'm going to say this again, more slowly this time. Our visit has nothing to do with sex therapy. If you think you should write that down, by all means do so. I'm not going in there for sex therapy. I'm not going to pretend to have a sexual problem. Sex is not going to come up at all. She could be a goddamn auto mechanic for all I care. Is what I'm saying beginning to make any sense at all to you?"

Suddenly a maelstrom of coughing and gagging erupted in the

backseat. Elmer lurched forward in a fit of hacking so intense and relentless that his face instantaneously went from its resting shade of ashen gray to ketchup red, and I was sure that the old man was going to die right there in my car. Either that or some dark, gelatinous organ—a lung, a liver, a segment of small intestine—would be disgorged from his gullet and sail clear over the seat back.

As this violent whooping went on for a truly alarming length of time, I pulled over onto the shoulder and shot Jumbo a worried look.

"He just needs some air, is all," my passenger said.

Jumbo got out, opened the rear door, and extracted his father, who was still convulsing in barks and gags. With the calm facility of a health care professional, which he claimed he was but could not possibly have been, Jumbo slowly guided his old man toward the edge of the trees lining the turnpike.

I watched them standing together beyond the shoulder of the road, the father hunched over, hands on his knees like a marathon runner at the finish line, struggling to regain the normal patterns of inhaling and exhaling, and the son hovering over him, patting his back and cool-headedly coaching him to relax and wait it out, telling him he was going to be fine. Sure enough, the seizure subsided and the horrendous noises coming from Elmer's lungs gave way to the gentle wind of passing cars. For someone who could rightly claim to be the root cause of so many crises, Jumbo could responsibly quell this one, and it was fascinating to witness.

"Does he need medical attention?" I asked once Jumbo had deposited his father back into the car.

He waved dismissively—don't be silly—and reached for his coffee. If it had been up to me, I would've driven straight to a hospital or at least a frickin' Rite Aid. At a minimum, the guy needed a cough drop.

"Is he sick?" I whispered.

"No more so than the rest of us, Mingus. Don't you have any older relatives with ailments?"

I had a grandmother who'd lost it—she sent me birthday checks four times a year—but I wasn't exactly trotting her out on road trips.

"So, he doesn't have, like, tuberculosis or anything?" I asked.

Jumbo shook his head. "I doubt it."

Feeling somewhat like an ambulance driver now, I merged us back into traffic.

At some point, I needed to check in with Sara. She couldn't have been terribly high on the idea of my coming out here, now that my recruitment efforts had shifted to Mackenzie, and I probably should have offered her some reassurance. I should have told her that whatever had gone on between Mack and me way back when, it was a dead issue. Mack didn't like me anymore; she couldn't have. I'd made her an accessory to adultery. Most people could shake off such a thing—me, for example, who didn't give it a second thought—but not the honest and true soul that Mack was. In all likelihood, the years had allowed all those bad feelings to calcify into something stronger, a bitterness unlikely to taper off. I suppose Sara sensed how much I hoped Mack didn't loathe me. I felt it in the way she looked at me, a world of unspoken words behind her eyes.

But other things were pulling Sara away too. This husband of hers had returned, compelling Sara to face her past, to look it in the eye, to speak to it, to bid it goodbye. Changes had come for Sara, changes that no one but Billy had the power to exact. But Sara couldn't change without my life changing in either minor or possibly monstrously major ways. Things were happening for me—finally. I had plans. I wanted my changes, not hers.

As I gazed out through the windshield, I knew I had to live with wherever this galloping highway was leading me. Just as I had to live with wherever Sara's highway was leading her.

Both of my passengers were now silent. Jumbo was squinting out at the scenery. Elmer was reclining in the backseat, his jacket zipper at half-mast, his head turned to the side. He looked small and tired.

"So what is all this about?" I said to Jumbo. "Is your old man try-ing to make up for lost time after he and your mother split?"

"Not at all. It was me who went missing, Mingus. Dad was always around. The band kept me away a lot. He missed the hell out of me."

I wondered what that was like. My old man never missed me for a second. I'd come back from a tour and he wouldn't even know I'd been gone. He'd occasionally ask about a trip, but only as a spring-board for tales of his own travels. You played Hong Kong, did you, Ted? The last time I was there, I was taken to the most outstanding French restaurant. It was over on the Kowloon side . . . And never in a million years would Lou Tremble tag along on an excursion such as this just to spend time with me, what with all those clients to service and associates to terrorize. Perish the fucking thought. If he were in the car today, he'd be leaning over the seat, chinking the shit out of my armor with all the reasons why this whole trip was a joke. And he would've had zero patience for the likes of Elmer and his roadside display of infirmity. For him, all sickness was in your head, conquer-able merely by attitude adjustment. Unless you had *cancer the size of a Big Mac* or something that required *extended hospitalization*, chances were it didn't exist. That's how I was raised. If you took the day off to lie around in bed and moan, you were either faking or not trying hard enough to ignore it. I heard the mantra countless times grow-ing up: "You just say to yourself"—there was a lot of saying stuff to yourself in my father's code of health maintenance—"You just say to yourself, 'I'm not going to let this get me down.' It's usually just as simple as that, Ted. If you want to let it beat you, well, I guess that's up to you." In other words, the world could present no problem for which there wasn't some overly simplistic and absurdly useless solu-tion. Yeah, sure, I'll get up and walk it off. Can I have my fucking antibiotic first?

I stabbed the stereo knob and twisted up the volume, the music giving me the fortitude to barrel through. Outside, the farms had given way to a steep barricade of mountains to the right.

A few songs in, Jumbo piped up. "I got news for you: When do you want to stop for lunch?"

"You need to work on your usage of that phrase. If you say you've got news for me, news should follow."

Jumbo sat there, unruffled.

"Do you understand? Don't tell me you have news for me and then ask a question."

"Tomato, tomahto, my friend."

"No. It isn't like that at all. It's like when you say *irregardless*. That's not a word. It's just *regardless*."

"Both are accepted."

"But one is wrong."

I felt him staring at me, studying the person he'd known in some form or other his entire life. "How does it feel to be right all the time?" he asked.

"It's an enormous responsibility."

He laughed tolerantly. "I love you to pieces, Mingus, but you're a little mean. You were never like that before."

"Yes, I was."

"Well, it's okay. Music will cure you." He patted my knee.

"Get off," I said, swatting his hand away.

Jumbo twisted his fleshy neck toward the backseat. "Hey Daddy-O, you hungry?"

In the rearview, I watched the old man muster up a nod.

"We'll stop at the next exit," I muttered.

As we proceeded to tunnel through the Alleghenies, I was treated to another vicious ball scratching by my front-seat passenger, the sixth or seventh of the day.

"Fuck." Jumbo was growing concerned. "Do you think you can get lice in your pubic hair?"

I rolled down the window and took shelter in a wallop of fresh air. "You can do anything you want, Jumbo."

CHAPTER 14

It's easier than you might imagine to ruin everything.

We were in New York for the sessions that would become our second record, *Atomic Somersault*. Expectations were hefty. Our hit had propelled our debut album to platinum status, and within the past year we'd stood on a stage in LA and been handed a little gold statue before the eyes of the world.

The strange thing was, I actually believed these new songs were stronger. They say you spend your whole life writing your first album and only a year writing your second, but I didn't think I needed a second quarter century to pen a follow-up. Maybe we didn't have a chart-topping single this time around, but I didn't care. I actually preferred it that way. There was more to these songs, more places to lead the listener. This album would earn us fans who cared about music, not just kids who needed an anthem to belt out the window at their horrible, autocratic parents.

At the end of a long day of recording, my bandmates and I were clustered at the hotel bar, nursing drinks almost like civilized human beings, when a blustery voice slashed the tranquility.

"Teddy fucking Tremble!"

I turned and saw Simon Weathers, lead singer of the Junction, sauntering over. His hair was cut in jagged spikes, and he was clad in a black leather jacket with black leather pants and black leather shoes, as the world had seen him countless times on the cover of *People*, and in a mug shot or two for some drunk and disorderlies.

Simon strode up to us and pumped my hand. "What in the fuck are you guys doing here?"

"Hey, Simon." I'd met God's gift once or twice before, having shared the stage at a music festival. We also shared a record label at the time. "We're just in town finishing our new record."

"Good for you, man, good for you."

I reacquainted him with my cohorts, and he nodded at each of them, sizing them up one at a time.

"What brings you here?" I asked.

He scratched his head with practiced weariness. "We're doing a couple shows at the Garden starting tomorrow night." The Junction purveyed a sixties-inflected form of brash Brit rock, despite being a quartet of Ohioans.

"Nice," I said.

"You like playing MSG?" Jumbo jumped in with a critical lean. "See, I'm not a big fan. I get this weird vibration on the stage there. *Wah! Wah! Wah!* It's very distracting. I've complained. You ever get that? *Wah! Wah!*"

"Anyway," Simon said, turning to Mackenzie, "what are you playing these days? I remember seeing you with a Fender jazz bass at South by Southwest. Do I have that right?"

"The sunburst one," Mack said, smiling coquettishly.

Simon nodded in approval. "A Geddy Lee special. Rocked my world, baby. I remember wondering what in the fuck the bassist for Tremble was doing with an instrument like that. You know what I mean? You don't do jazz, you don't do prog—like, what do you need that for? But you made it work, baby. You dug a deep-ass groove with that thing."

"Thank you." Mack blushed. For all her glorious ascension in the world, the woman still blushed.

"Next round's on me," Simon declared with a wink.

"I have to pass," Mack said. "I'm wiped. I'm going to call it a night."

"Boo!" Simon heckled. "Really? The night is so young."

"Not for some of us," Mack said, and with a wave, she bid us all goodnight. "Nice seeing you, Simon."

"Likewise. Likewise indeed."

Simon summoned the bartender with an open-handed smack on the bar. "Ketel One, rocks for me"—he drew circles in the air with his index finger, a cowboy closing in on a steer—"and another round of whatever my friends are drinking."

Simon then proceeded to ponder the vacant doorway through which Mack had just exited. "What is it about her?"

I shrugged. "What do you mean?"

"She's fantastic."

"Mack? Yeah, she's great."

"There's something about her. Every time I run into her, she lingers in my mind for days. I can't explain it. There's something very real, very tangible about her." He was impressed with himself for using the word *tangible*. He turned his head to me. "You ever hit that?"

"No, Simon, I have not hit that." I raised the finger with my wedding band (though I wanted to raise the one next to it).

He grinned. "Ah. Gotcha."

Could it be that Simon Weathers was tiring of the dull parade of starlets and Victoria's Secret models? That as he lay awake in bed, a Brazilian goddess in angelic repose six inches to his left, he pined for something more, something meaningful, for someone with whom he could trade erudite barbs, with whom he could pass a slow Sunday morning on the veranda with coffee and the *New York Times*? Please.

He suddenly gave my shoulder an epiphanic pounding. "Here's what I'm going to do: I'm going to bring Tremble on tour with us."

"What?"

"It's perfect! We've both got new music on the way. We'll hit the road together. It'll be huge. Six months ought to be enough time for Mackenzie to develop, shall we say, an appreciation for me, right?" He snickered in a way that everyone else in the world must have thought was magnetic.

I stared at him. "You want to do a Junction/Tremble tour so that you can seduce my bass player?"

"Isn't that the whole point of everything, man? Seduction. It's the reason we write songs and the reason we sing them out loud. Disagree with me. I dare you."

"I disagree with you."

"You're full of shit," he said, laughing. "And anyway, who fucking cares? Do you have any idea the kind of scratch you make playing to sold-out stadiums?"

"I have some idea," I said tightly. "We did eighteen months of them."

He took three gulps of his vodka in rapid succession while I glared at him, a lean fury flaring up inside me. Did this lout actually think we needed his charity? Did he really expect that we'd allow ourselves to get hauled from one city to the next as his opening act, diluting our brand, warming up the stage for him?

And did he really think Mack was up for grabs?

"Maybe you should come open for us," I suggested, grinning without joy.

"You never know. Stranger things have happened." Then he emptied the glass down his craned gullet.

I was confident his proposal would be forgotten in the brine of Ketel Ones. Oh, but I was wrong. A few months later, Alaina called and relayed what she considered the best news in the history of news.

"I'm not going on tour with the Junction," I told her, indignant and a little whiny.

"I'm sorry—what did you just say?"

"It's a terrible idea, Alaina."

"Theodore. Are you baked?"

"Weathers is insufferable. They break up twice a year. It's fucking toxic."

"Maybe I'm not being clear. They don't want you to join their band. They're just going to let you play in front of their infinite crowds."

"We can't go from headliner to opening act just like that. Don't you think it cheapens us?"

"It would cheapen you to open for Scritti Politti. It would cheapen you to open for Lisa Lisa and Cult Jam."

"It doesn't sit well with me," I said. "It's not what we're all about."

"Let me break this down for you. You've had one hit. A strong, well-received album, but one hit. One hit doth not a career make. Do you want a career? Do you want lifelong fans? Because that's what you build on tour, the kind of fans who keep coming back, who wet themselves when you release a new album because they know that it means you're coming to town. The kind of fans who will pay a babysitter fifteen bucks an hour for the privilege of paying a hundred bucks a ticket, who will see you play twenty years from now when you look like shit, sound like shit, and can't write for shit."

"I'm not worried," I countered to her Allen Ginsbergesque parataxis. "We may never hit the jackpot like we did with 'Lie,' but I think we'll stick around. You've heard the new album."

Alaina laughed like an ice-covered sidewalk. "I thought you were different, Teddy. I really did. I knew you had an ego, but to turn down an opportunity to share billing with the Junction—to benefit from that vast promotional machine—all because you think you deserve more? That is a rare level of ego indeed."

It wasn't a concert tour; it was a charade in the name of bagging Mackenzie.

"Call it what you want, Alaina. I'm not hitting the road with Simon Weathers. That's not who we are."

"Fine," Alaina said. "You can explain that to your bandmates when they're ringing up your fries at the truck stop two years from now."

All these years later, it still shamed me to think about the selfishness, the myopia, the dictatorial disregard for the livelihoods of people who counted on me. The possessiveness over things that didn't belong to me. As Simon Weathers might've said, Who in the fuck did I think I was?

CHAPTER 15

The receptionist was fussy, dumpy, and bumbershooted in a floral muumuu, and I almost laughed in her face when she asked if I had insurance, never imagining that the unseemly afflictions that sent one to a sex therapist could be covered by a health plan.

She smiled me over to the lobby, which was a sea of royal blue from the upholstery on the chairs down to the carpeting. I stood under the constellation of floodlights and peered out the windows into the parking lot. Mack's office was located in a squat three-story building set back a ways from a busily commercial avenue outside the city. I'd turned the car over to my traveling companions and dispatched them to a bookstore, coffee shop, pet mart, anywhere, to get them out of sight. I would've tasked Jumbo with finding us a hotel but he and I held widely differing views on what constituted acceptable lodging.

Here I stood, ablaze with nerves, even more so than on the night I played for Sonny in my apartment living room. Right here was where I would make it right again. This was where Mack accepted my apology, so long in the making, and we moved into the future together, which is to say that we could go back. We could stand next to each other again, night after night, our instruments alive in our hands, doing what we were meant to do with our time on earth. We had no business sequestering ourselves away in offices, disguising ourselves as professionals, going through the motions of ordinary relationships when our significant others knew, had always known, we belonged somewhere else. Mackenzie knew this; she just needed to be reminded. Then everything would be right, my sin of pride and greed with the Junction finally wiped clean.

"Teddy." I turned my head and there she was.

"Mackenzie." Seeing her after all these years sent volts of electricity down my suddenly unsteady legs.

We stepped toward each other with a measure of cautiousness. I crossed my arms over her back, pulling her into me. It was a sensation of wonderful familiarity. She'd had the decency to stay the same height, to inhabit the same proportions, to keep her hair and skin an ambrosia of Arcadian scents, as if all for the benefit of my homesickness.

She wasn't really hugging me back. She administered a few obligatory pats on my shoulder blade as if I were an unpleasant distant cousin she'd run into at a wedding.

"You look great, Mack. You really do."

She issued a half smile. "I don't know about that."

Then she led me down the hall in this familiar ritual where I played the role of intruder into the lives of people I used to know. I was the corruptive Sunday school troublemaker inciting my assiduous classmates to abscond through the bathroom window.

Her office was spacious and airy. It had a seating area with a sofa and love seat of reddish-brown leather and an espresso-finished trunk coffee table between them. The room seemed to be draped in a muted autumn of soft greens, yellows, and browns, all of it coaxing comfort, assuring you that this environment could do you no harm. Even the fresh soapy scent in the air—was that bubble bath?—conveyed the message that this was a place where you could divulge your dirtiest secrets free of threat and judgment. Be calm, said the arrangement of the furniture. Be at ease, said the air.

Alone together in her office, I could finally take Mack in. She was still beautiful, all the more so by not having struggled against time's advancement. The short shag haircut and boyish outfits had been supplanted by butter-yellow pants and a brown sweater, longer sandy-highlighted locks that framed a warm, earthy face behind 1950s cat-eyed frames. She'd become more womanly, the mom you suddenly noticed after a year of carpool, but seemed to have held on to that athletic ease of motion, her genetic bounty. Her father had been a power-hitting centerfielder up and down the minor leagues before becoming a scout in the Cincinnati Reds organization. Her mother owned every swimming record at her high school. Naturally, the child of those two parents would pursue a vampiric career playing bass in the stale-beer air of dingy bars, swathed in blue light. But Mack had always resisted the physical drag of our lifestyle. She constantly sought out opportunities to move, exploring on foot the blocks of each new town, rising early for a dip in the hotel pool, even once saving a man who'd bumped his head while doing laps.

Before offering me a seat, she shut the door and turned to me. "So. To what do I owe this unexpected pleasure?"

"I was in the area and decided a visit was long overdue," I said.

She tilted her head. "Do you have an issue you want to discuss?"

I stared blankly.

"A sexual problem?"

"Uh, no."

"Well, you made an appointment, so I didn't know what to think."

"Well, don't think that."

"Hmm." She was looking at me, nodding without warmth.

"I'm out here for work and just thought I'd stop by." The repetition of my lie sounded to my own ears like a stammer, like protesting too much.

Mack folded her arms.

"It's just a visit, Mack. Sue me. Aren't you glad to see me?"

"Yes. Of course." She continued assaulting me with a keenly inhospitable smile, a smile that erected walls.

"Can we sit down?" I finally suggested, tugging at my collar. "I'm getting a bit of an Abu Ghraib vibe here."

She gestured to the couch and lowered herself onto the love seat opposite me, at which point I was reminded of my one brief sojourn on a psychologist's couch. It was during the band years. The pressures were walling up around me and my moods were vacillating between combative and withdrawn. (I know, poor me.) The day Alaina observed a preconcert tantrum—something about my shirt looking like a woman's "top"—she connected me with a flaky "shrink to the stars" who, at my first visit, made the mistake of encouraging me to lie down on his sofa, a heavenly velvet recliner. At first, I was worried that this was going to go *Ordinary People* or, worse, *What About Bob?* (The doctor did have a passing resemblance to Richard Dreyfuss.) But lying snug in the stillness of that office, lulled by the watercolor of a tomato patch and the pastoral enchantment of a wooden owl, I started thinking that a fair percentage of patients must fall asleep. Next thing I knew, the minute hand had completed a lap around the clock and my cheek was stained with drool. As for the psychiatrist, he was lights out in his chair, notepad and pen resting on his turtleneck. I quietly let myself out and declared myself cured.

I looked at Mack. "How have you been?"

"Fine." Then she added, "How are you?"

"I'm okay. But since you asked, I guess I'm a little curious as to why you hate my guts."

"I don't hate your guts."

"So, then what? You're just kind of a bitch now?"

Her jaw tightened, then slowly came an uncomfortable chuckle. I remembered this habit of hers, laughing lightly during moments of confrontation. "I'm not a bitch, Teddy. And I'd rather you didn't speak to me like that in my own office."

I stared deep into her. "You'd rather I didn't speak to you like that in your own office? Jesus, Mack, who are you? It's me. Remember?"

This Mackenzie was so unlike the Mackenzie I'd known that I was almost worried. Where was the Mack who traded paperbacks and rewatched eighties movies with me on those endless bus rides? The one who sat and talked mindlessly with me at the bar for hours on end while our drummer and guitar player drank down aquariums of crude whisky? The one who got up at a reasonable hour and met me in the hotel lobby for scones?

It didn't take a person of great perceptiveness to see that this woman was not going to join my band. She wanted nothing to do with me.

"Is this about Arizona?" I asked, seeing no reason not to cut to the heart of it.

"Is what about Arizona?"

"This!"

"I don't understand," she said.

I felt a sudden need to tell her now what I'd never gotten a chance to say. That I understood the bitterness. That nothing was her fault. That I didn't handle things well with her because it was *her*. Things got weird because *I* got weird. We should've talked.

"All these years, Mack. You've carried around bad feelings about me all these years because of one night? The glory days, the music, the world travels, everything we did together—all of that means nothing to you because of one unfortunate incident?"

"Teddy, you're showing up out of the blue and putting a lot of words into my mouth."

I shook my head slowly. "I see the way you're looking at me."

She fell silent.

"I cared about you, Mackenzie. I always have."

"I didn't think it would be this strange to look you in the eye," she said. "Looking at you is like looking through a keyhole into a house I used to live in."

She stared into her lap. The air in the room grew heavy.

"I know things got complicated between us, but surely you don't hate me," I said softly. "Do you?"

"Of course I don't hate you." She sighed. "Things just ended on a down note and—"

"No," I interrupted. "Let's try it again. *Surely*, you don't hate me."

She squinted quizzically at me for a moment, then a smile bloomed. "I don't hate you. And don't call me Shirley."

"Thank you. That's all I was looking for. You can't hate someone with whom you've watched *Airplane!* a thousand times."

At last she graced me with that easy laugh, the one I'd been waiting a lifetime to hear, all the tension in the room drained away.

"I'm sorry," she said. "I've got a lot on my mind at the moment."

"You don't owe me any apologies."

"I didn't know what you were up to in coming here, especially this stunt of trying to surprise me at my office. I mean, why didn't you just call and talk to me?"

"I was scared. You're scary."

"Maybe this *is* all because of Arizona. I've always wondered if somehow our episode there brought everything to an end. Your marriage, the band. It's irrational, I know, but the whole operation did seem to fall apart after that."

If only she knew what it really was. It was the handy truth that *Atomic Somersault* was thirteen tracks of who cares because it conveniently explained the empty auditoriums, the universal deterioration of interest in our music, and ultimately, the decision to walk away. It also cloaked the other truth: that we might've been rescued from our middling, pedestrian album if I hadn't steered us away from a prime opportunity.

But that was why I was here. To make all of it right.

"Mack, the band didn't end because you and I slept together. You should know that because you're a sex therapist. The band ended because our luck ran out. You should know *that* because you're a musician."

We then dove into small talk, compressing into bullet points the notable events, or nonevents, of our lives since Tremble's fizzle. She told me she was happy. She had neither a spouse nor kids and offered no good explanation for how she found herself in this line of work. "Nothing else appealed to me," she said, still mystified by her own choice. "Maybe it was that heavy diet of Jane Austen and the whole scandalousness of sexual repression."

As for me, I told her that, all in all, I had little to complain about and that I was more or less the same son of a bitch I was ten years ago.

"Are you still with Sara?" she asked.

"I am."

"That's terrific, Teddy." She seemed genuinely pleased. "Did you guys get married?"

"No. Not married."

"What's wrong with you? Sara's a catch. You should marry that girl."

"What kind of therapist says, 'What's wrong with you?'"

"You're not my patient."

Then I made a crude two-handed air bass and asked if she still played. She nodded. Late at night, weekend afternoons with the windows open—those were her favorite times to jam. "I still know all our songs," she bragged. "And I haven't lost a step with *Disraeli Gears* and *Physical Graffiti*."

I grinned inwardly. At least that puzzle piece was wedged into place.

"How about you?" she asked. "Are you still at it?"

"For a long time, no," I replied, averting my eyes. "I decided the healthier course of action was to move on."

"That's surprising. Maybe you shouldn't have given up so easily. Maybe none of us should have."

There was such promise in that sentiment. Maybe she too had regrets, unfinished business ripe for revisiting. Yet at the same time, I hoped she hadn't spent the years pining for a past that I'd single-handedly derailed. There was an elephant in the room, and as usual, it was me. I always seemed to be the elephant these days. I would've so much preferred to have been a giraffe. The elephant remembers; the giraffe lifts his head and forgets.

Mack regarded the clock on the wall and said, "How long are you in town for?" Before I could formulate a response consistent with this ruse of a visit, she added, "Maybe we can have dinner tonight. It'd be nice to catch up a little more. I'm unexpectedly not nauseated by the sight of you."

"I doubt I'll get a better dinner invitation than that one."

I stood. "It's so good to see you, Mack, and I'm relieved that your memories of our adventures together, that your memories of me, aren't totally unpleasant."

She rocked her head in contemplation. "Look, maybe you've been a bit of a sore subject in my mind all this time, but the band never has been. I wish what happened between us hadn't happened. We shouldn't have done that to each other, and to your wife. But you did invite me into your spectacularly successful rock band. You were a little self-important and you took rock 'n' roll a tad too seriously for my taste, but what kind of a brat would I be if I didn't look back at that time as being pretty special? I got lucky and I know it."

"I invited you into a band that was playing fraternity formals. We went nowhere until we were a foursome. We all got lucky."

Mack said she had some work to finish up, but would make a dinner reservation and text me the particulars. I was practically out the door when I remembered I hadn't come alone.

"By the way," I said, pivoting. "Just as a warning, I might have a surprise with me later on." And the surprise's father.

She eyed me warily. "I hate surprises."

"Yeah. So do I. You'll hate this one too."

"How'd it go?" Jumbo asked.

I was in the passenger seat, catching my breath and taming my temper over the fact that Jumbo had just nearly run me over with my own car. They were late coming back—they'd stopped into a drugstore for some antifungal cream to quell the itchy business in Jumbo's

nether regions, then purportedly had a celebrity sighting at Dunkin'
Donuts (I lacked the energy to explain how unlikely it was that they'd
seen the actor who played Captain Kangaroo, he being dead and
all)—and came howling through the parking lot right at me. Only a
last-second swerve saved me from being swallowed by the front tire.

"It went fine," I said.

"Is she in?"

"We didn't get that far. Let's just focus on the task at hand."

That being the dispiriting process of hotel hunting amid deserts of
drab commercial sprawl.

"So, what's the plan, Mingus? How are we going to land her?"

"We're having dinner tonight. I'll raise it then. But honestly, I'm not
optimistic. It doesn't seem like the kind of thing she's going to go for."

"What did you tell her?"

"About the band? Nothing yet. It's kind of a delicate subject."

"But you told her about me."

"Not exactly."

"You didn't tell her I'm out here with you?"

"Exactly."

I'd come to Pittsburgh on business, so went the lie. Why would I
have brought along the guitar player from my long-defunct band? Or
his father, who had jumped in the car to honor a custody arrangement
that had expired sometime in the eighties?

"That hurts, man. You've got your biggest selling point eating
doughnuts just down the street, and you don't even tell her."

"It was a judgment call," I said, though it was nothing of the sort.

Jumbo maneuvered through the late-afternoon traffic, grunting
with approval or rejection and sometimes fascination at the Five Guys
and the Famous Dave's, at the Outback, Hooters, and Pei Wei that
lined the road like crooked teeth.

"Where are we all going for dinner?" he asked.

I looked over at him. "I assumed you guys were heading back to
Dunkin' Donuts, hoping to run into Mr. Rogers."

"You're not letting us come to dinner?"

"Don't start, James. I told you back in Philly that you could ride out here with me if you wanted, but a seat in my car didn't get you an invite to every item on the itinerary."

Jumbo and his old man could unwrap chimichangas in front of the TV, for all I cared.

"You know, you don't own Mackenzie," Jumbo stated with reflection. "She was my friend too."

"Well, I'll tell you what. When you drive out here to talk her into joining Jumbo Jett and His Ragamuffin Daffodil Band or whatever the hell you call yourselves—"

"It's Ragtag Honeysuckle. Get it right."

"—then I'll stay out of it."

If, by some miracle, Mack did not walk out on me when I revealed my grand plans, then maybe—maybe—Jumbo would get the nod to come out and say a brief hello. It would be like the dinner party hosts who allow their pajama-clad children to flurry down the steps to greet their guests and steal a spring roll before scampering back up to watch another video.

But we weren't going to get that far. Mackenzie was not going to think re-forming the band was a good idea. It certainly didn't sound like a good idea. She was going to stare across the table at me tonight like a guidance counselor weary of the sixth-year senior. Is this really what you want to be doing at this stage of your life? her pitying look would say. And my answer would be the same one I was once accustomed to dispensing, the answer with which people like me must always be equipped.

Let's not talk. Let me just show you.

CHAPTER 16

As the evening sky splashed out all kinds of blues and pinks, Elmer celebrated the splendor of it all with another coughing fit, this one of greater intensity than the first. Jumbo seemed to have the matter in hand, so I left them in the Best Western parking lot and lugged my overnight bag inside to see about rooms.

There wasn't much to the lobby. A reception counter to the right, a pair of functional chairs to the left, all lit by the unforgiving kind of fluorescence that makes every zit and every wagging nose hair visible from twenty yards out. The fraying chairs were occupied by two guys who stared dumbly into the distance, as if awaiting a ride to anywhere.

Dropping my bag onto the linoleum tile, I requested two rooms. The girl behind the counter typed and clicked and every so often emitted a soft, drawn-out "Ooooo-kay." She was cute but in a way that tended not to last. She should bask in the bounty of her youth, for the lustrous hair and flawless complexion would soon lose interest in her and move on to another canvas, leaving her to run out the clock with a chips-with-lunch type of body.

Nonsmoking rooms ran $109 each, a price that hardly foretold opulence and luxury. I handed her a credit card.

"Dad's fine," Jumbo announced, parading through the automatic sliding front doors. "Just catching his breath."

"One oh nine plus tax," I told him.

He bellied up to the desk and proceeded to rifle through a fistful of fives and tens. I shook my head at my companion's piggybank payment method, anticipating all the new hotel memories Jumbo would manufacture to go with my old ones. The trash can urinations. The complaints about the "broken" shower that was not broken at all but merely beyond his technical grasp. The insistent sliding of his key into room 2270 at the Marriott when his things were down the street in room 2270 at the Westin.

The young woman accepted payment and returned to typing and clicking. A dot matrix printer somewhere behind her sprang to life with a robotic buzz.

"So, what's her deal? Is she married?" Jumbo asked.

"Who? Her?" I pointed to the young hotel employee, who looked up skittishly.

"Mack," Jumbo clarified.

"No, she's not."

"That's interesting," Jumbo mused.

"Why? You're not married. I'm not married."

"True, true. But Mack was different. I always pictured her with a husband and a bunch of kids." Somehow that lifestyle earned Jumbo's designation as "different."

"I don't know what to tell you, Jumbo. For all I know, she could be a lesbian now."

He mulled the point. "She'd make a good one."

The girl slid two mini-envelopes across the counter, told us we were all set—a hellaciously off-the-mark summation of our position in the world—and pointed us toward the elevators. As I handed one of the envelopes to Jumbo, I heard a voice over my shoulder.

"Holy shit, it *is* them!"

The two guys sitting in the lobby chairs were no longer looking bored. They were looking at us.

"Tremble," declared one of them. He was in his late twenties with an impotent beard, adorned in loose jeans and a sweatshirt that read Penn State. "Aren't you the guys from that band from, like, forever ago?"

Jumbo grinned with false modesty. "That's right, fellas. Guilty as charged."

The bearded guy looked at his friend, whose sweatshirt bore the name Ursinus, which I assumed was a college but could've just as easily been a glandular problem. "You remember these guys?" Then, to us, "I didn't know you were still together. I just saw a VH1 *Behind the Music* about you."

"Well, gentlemen, it's all true," Jumbo boasted, impervious to the guy's tone of mockery.

"What the hell are you doing in a Best Western?" asked Ursinus.

"What the hell are *you* doing in a Best Western?" I shot back. I was in no fucking mood for this.

At that point, Penn State jumped up and began belting out "It Feels like a Lie." He made a real big deal of it, with flair and flamboyance, raising his voice, getting most of the words wrong, waving his arms grandly like this sad little lobby was a Broadway stage. The counter girl looked uncomfortable. It was becoming a memorable shift.

"All right, all right, well done," Jumbo cut in. "Glad they're still grooving out to us in Pittsburgh."

"Yeah, right," the guy cackled. "Just like they're still *grooving* to Dishwalla and A-ha."

I was going to let it go. Run-ins like this went with the territory. At a mediation in New York a few years ago, a smug piece-of-shit lawyer looked across the conference table at me and said, "I'll bet you never expected to find yourself here." In line at Nathan's Hot Dogs in the Orlando airport, I heard someone mutter, "Oh, how the mighty have fallen." People occasionally whispered and pointed. I can't say I've never lost my temper in those situations (I "accidentally" jostled the Nathan's guy's soda arm), but it was best not to escalate. You suffered the negative attention, maybe shot back with a simple insult—hair was always a safe target, so were clothes and weight—and that usually shut them up. You moved on.

"Well, it was a real pleasure meeting you guys," I said, tossing my bag over my shoulder.

"So, what—are you still together? Still sharing hotel rooms?" Penn State heckled.

"Let's just say you haven't heard the last of Tremble," Jumbo announced, yet again misreading the room.

"How will I ever contain my excitement?" Ursinus piped up. "Where's the show tonight, guys? The Days Inn?"

"That's really fucking funny," I said sharply. "How many gold records do you have, dipshit?"

The dipshit's grin vanished. Both gentlemen glared at me, pocketknives in their eyes. "Mouthy for a fruity little singer, aren't you?"

Jumbo stepped between me and our two fans. "Okay now, fellas."

The dipshit gave me a slow, menacing smile, a common antecedent to violence, I have learned.

"Back off," Jumbo said mildly. "Let's not have an incident, shall we?"

Jumbo was moderately burly but about as intimidating as Fozzie Bear. These clowns weren't exactly in top physical shape either, but they were thick and meaty, considerably younger and less removed from their brawling days. The good money was on them.

The one with the fragmentary goatee—the amateur vocalist out of Penn State—took a step toward Jumbo, getting nose to nose with him. "Why don't *you* back off, you big fucking zero?" As his taunting intensified, he opened his eyes wider and wider, and I wondered if maybe one of us should hold an open palm under his chin to catch his eyeballs when they popped out of their sockets. "I'm hearing some tough talk, but you know what I think? I think you've got nothing to back it up. I think you're just a couple of little girls."

"Now, friend, there's no reason to get sexist," Jumbo said, placing a fatherly hand on the guy's shoulder.

It was a miscalculation, if it was a calculation at all, to initiate physical contact. In a frightfully swift motion, Penn State shifted his weight onto his back leg, then exploded forward and clocked Jumbo in the cheek.

"Ow! That fucking hurt!" Jumbo shrieked, staggering backward. He smacked into the reception desk, knocked a stack of brochures to the floor, and somehow nicked the ring-for-service bell.

In a flash, I was on top of Jumbo's assailant—nobody hits him but me—ready to plant my knuckles in the guy's beard. Turns out though, what seemed like a flash to me was more than enough time for the guy to duck and allow my fist to sail lamely past his face. Before I could blink, a mighty blow was delivered to my gut from Ursinus, who, last I checked, was on the other side of the room. The wind was knocked clean out of me and I crumpled to the floor.

Down on the cold linoleum, I braced for further beating—a shoe to the head, a hard kick to the kidneys, additional gusts of violence to solidify my mortification and disgrace. One man's cautionary tale is another man's war story, and I knew these punks would go back home and tell all their sorry punk friends how they delivered a beat-down to a couple of aging rock stars. As for me, I was tiring of getting punched—by dirtballs in Central Pennsylvania, photographers in Switzerland, interior decorators who shared my bed.

Then it was as if a thick blanket was draped over the room. Nobody moved, nobody spoke, nobody screamed in agony. I raised my eyes and beheld our two fans up against the wall, an elderly man clutching their throats. Their eyes were wide with fright and they gasped for breath as old Elmer Jett secured their windpipes with his gnarled fingers.

"Which one of you took a swing at my boy?" The sound that came out of the asthmatic-cum-military-chokeholder's mouth was as ominous a tone as I'd ever heard. Neither punk could summon the air to respond.

"I showed up late to this party," Elmer went on, his voice somewhere between a murmur and a snarl. "But I think maybe someone here has forgotten his manners." He looked at each of his captives with a threatening scowl. "Now, which one of you hit my boy?"

While Jumbo nursed his jaw by the reception counter and I struggled to my feet and tried not to vomit, Jumbo's dad, who hadn't so much as moved or spoken all day except to have a seizure, had finally piped up to animate the cliché of old-man strength and Eastwoodian menace.

He leaned in as close as he could, his Depression-era wrinkles mere inches from the faces of these distinguished graduates. "I am an exceedingly violent man and I hold a bitch of a grudge," he growled, low and gritty. "You better hope to hell I never see either of you again. I won't be nearly so amiable."

With that, he released his grip on the two throats, and the castrated duo crumbled into sputters of panting and huffing. (Seems wherever Elmer went, someone was short of breath.) They grabbed their overnight bags and hightailed it out into the evening.

Jumbo rushed over to his father. "You okay, Dad?"

Elmer simply nodded, the crusty geezer apparently restored to his default setting of mute.

The gut thumping I had taken was beginning to wear off, so once again, the only lasting injury was to my pride. My gratitude toward Elmer for his timely intercession was somewhat diluted by the revelation that we now required the services of a seventy-nine-year-old tubercular bodyguard. Go us.

"I'm heading up to the room," I muttered miserably. "I'll call when I know what's up."

"We'll be ready, Mingus," Jumbo enthused. He'd already shaken off the most recent disaster; every moment was lived in a vacuum. "We'll conquer Mackenzie and then we'll head back west!" He pumped his fist.

"We live east," I grunted, starting for the elevator bank.

"Ha! True enough. Don't know what's with me today. Jet-lagged, I guess."

We had driven—and hadn't changed time zones.

Jumbo turned to the receptionist and rested both elbows on the counter. "I got news for you. Where would I find a vending machine?"

My room greeted me with a burned-out bulb. After some blind patting on the walls, I happened upon a light switch in the bathroom. Now I could see, but breathing was becoming a problem, as my lungs clenched from the fog-like stench of cigarettes. A nonsmoking room apparently meant that no one was smoking in it right now. I could practically hear myself getting emphysema. When a complaint to the front desk proved discouraging—"All the nonsmoking rooms smell the same, sir"—I cracked a window, took in the breathtaking view of a buckling roof, and set out on a stroll while the room ventilated. I don't know what more I could've expected from a hotel whose most lavish amenity was that it accepted credit cards.

After visiting the soda machine on the first floor, I carried a Diet Coke down the long, underilluminated hall toward the side exit. The journey brought me past a set of glass double doors through which I viewed an indoor pool encircled by balconied rooms. That never made sense to me, those indoor balconies. This was not a resort. What breed of guest was going to plant himself in a plastic chair with a Sue Grafton mystery and bask in the chlorinated air to the echo-heavy sound of splashing? If you were staying in this hotel, it was because you were in town for a funeral or for a cheap affair, or you were hustling your brand of mayo to the TGI Fridays across the street.

I pushed through the door at the end of the corridor and found myself in a remote area of the parking lot with a Dumpster. The huge green bin was abuzz with insects—tiny, rancorous voices celebrating the dropping of the sun like a throng of spring breakers. The insects and I weren't alone. A woman with stringy, copper-hued hair was standing by the Dumpster, clad in a brown-red shirt and black vest onto which a Best Western logo was stitched. The woman's lips were curled in a frown of monumental gloom. At least you're not me, her empty eyes seemed to be saying. She raised a cigarette to her lips, sucked the life out of it, and flicked it over her shoulder into the bayou of wet diapers and warm tuna. "It's like fucking Maui here, no?" she said, and headed inside.

Tremble's second tour had, in fact, brought us to Hawaii. We took the stage in Honolulu as the headliners I declared us to be, belting out the songs for which we were famous and the songs that would soon render us unfamous, while the Junction ravaged the mainland with a rambling cyclone of sold-out shows. If my cohorts harbored the same concerns I did, they hid it well. They seemed to be having a blast on the road, on the planes, and in the bars and bistros of America, and when the house lights went down, we actually sounded better than ever. It was just that not that many people were around to hear.

Before long, I realized I'd made a grievous miscalculation with our collective musical futures. I would return to my hotel room each night feeling as lost and adrift as a tiny island in the Pacific.

Sipping cocktails on a breezy beach one night on Oahu, Jumbo removed a joint from his breast pocket and got up to light it in the bamboo tiki torch next to us.

"What the fuck are you doing?" I demanded of him, looking nervously around our table.

"What? I thought it's legal here."

"In the United States? Put that away."

He returned the blunt to his pocket and sat back down. "I just thought it would chill you out a little," he explained. "You've got to be the most uptight guy in all of Hawaii."

I'm certain that at that moment my mind formulated some nauseatingly pompous response, like "Heavy is the head that wears the crown." Something that paid tribute to both my overtaxed leadership and my unappreciated intellect.

"We sound awesome!" the guitarist enthused. "So what if the crowds are a little thinner than we're used to? Look where we are, man!"

He waved grandly at the star-peppered sky, at the surf that slumbered just out past the beach lights. "Last week we rocked the Fillmore in San Francisco. The week before that, the Showbox in Seattle. We're living the dream, Mingus."

Perhaps, but the dream was slowly dying—and I'd sort of killed it.

"Look around you," Jumbo went on. "Pick out the hottest girl in this whole bar. No—you know what? Pick out the hottest girl on this whole island! You can sleep with her just like that." He snapped his fingers. "You could do anything you want to her, and so could I. You know why? Because you're Teddy fucking Tremble and I'm Jumbo fucking Jett."

"You're getting carried away."

"Am I? You want me to prove it? You want me to prove it with that little slice of Lord-have-mercy over there?" I didn't even bother turning my head to whomever he was pointing at and now waving and pirouetting his eyebrows. "The point is that you, me, Mack, and the Square are all on the best paid vacation anyone could dream up, and you're the only one who doesn't seem to realize it."

Our server materialized with a tray of cocktails. "Gentlemen," he said. "A Kona brown ale for you, Mr. Tremble, and a Southern Comfort on the rocks for you, Mr. Jett."

Jumbo beamed grandly at his refill and said, "Mauna Loa."

"Is there anything else I can get for you gentlemen at the moment?"

"I think we're good," I said.

"Please don't hesitate."

"Mauna Loa," Jumbo repeated to the waiter, who smiled back and moved on.

I looked at my bandmate. "James, the Hawaiian word for thank you is *mahalo*. We've only heard it five thousand times in the past two days. Is that what you're trying to say, or have you decided to recite the name of the world's largest volcano to every person who hands you a drink or opens the door for you?" I dipped my lips into my auburn beer. "You could also simply say thanks. They understand English here in the US."

The stench of roadside hotel Dumpster jarred me out of my old mistakes and back into my new ones. I pulled my phone out of my back pocket and called Sara.

"How's the trip?" she asked.

"Okay so far. Jumbo ended up coming with me."

"God—why?"

"Because it would've been weird if it was just me and his dad."

In explaining how it came to pass that I set out on a trans-Pennsylvania road trip with that father and son duo, it dawned on me that their reasons for driving out here were no less credible than my own.

Sara was still at the office, having just returned from the home of fabulously well-to-do clients on Delancey Street. A redecorating project was bleeding from one room to the next, as this genteel couple sought to address the discord of a house in which the Provençal lavenders of French country abutted the sleek blues and oranges of midcentury.

"It's just as well you're out of town," Sara commented. "It's probably going to be a late night for me too."

"What's going on?"

"It's Michel's last day, so there's a dinner party."

"Oh. That should be fun, right?"

"There's been a lot of talk of sangria," she said.

"Sure."

"It seems to flow through Michel's veins. But I guess that stands to reason."

"Right," I agreed vacantly.

There was a pause. "You don't know who Michel is, do you?"

"Yes, I do."

"Christ, Teddy, I've introduced you a dozen times."

"Of course I know Michel. I just didn't know she was Spanish."

"He's not," she said curtly.

I sighed in defeat.

"Is it nice being oblivious?" Sara asked, her tone dry.

"That's kind of a loaded question, but no, I don't think it's terribly nice."

She was chuckling on the other end; I had no idea at what, but it was usually me.

"You keep a lot of secrets." I pled my case through her laughter. "I don't get a ton of information from you."

"Well, I can't imagine you'd pay much attention if you did."

"That's not fair, Sara. I mean, come on, you get together with your ex-husband and you tell me about it after the fact."

"He's not my ex-husband—that's the point."

"No, that's not the point."

"Why does that bother you?" she asked.

"I'm not saying it bothers me."

"Teddy." She took a hefty breath. "There are things Billy understands about me that you just never will."

Her words were perfectly valid and perfectly true, which probably explained why they stung so much. The sentiment had been framed in the present tense too. Billy *understands*. That ran contrary to my understanding of divorce, which I'd always viewed as a parting of the ways.

"I didn't mean for that to sound so harsh," she said.

"It's okay."

"Aren't there things that Mackenzie understands about you that I never will?"

She was being deliberately provocative. Billy and Mackenzie were hardly equivalents and she knew it. I gave it fair reflection anyway.

"I'm not so sure. Maybe."

I buttressed myself against the functional architecture of the Dumpster. "Look," I said. "I don't know how much longer I can go on arguing with you."

"And what does that mean?"

"It means I'm standing next to the most foul Dumpster in all of Pennsylvania. I'm asphyxiating. I'm actually surprised you don't smell it through the phone."

"I do, actually. I just thought you hadn't showered."

Then she said, "Want to call me in the morning?"

"Yeah. Have a good night."

"I'll send Michel your regards."

"Yeah, tell her I wish her well."

"He'll appreciate that."

The hotel side door had the clunky weight of the hatch of a sub. As I passed the game room—and I do not mean games room; the tiny space housed exactly one amusement, a seventies-era pinball machine featuring the image of a mustachioed race car driver grinning with seductive machismo—I became aware of two silhouettes shuffling down the hall. One of the silhouettes was slight and frail, the other large and oafish. The oafish one carried a duffel bag.

"Jumbo?" I called, walking toward them.

"There you are. I've been calling you." He interrupted himself. "Where'd you get that soda?"

"From the soda machine."

"Interesting." Our voices sounded blunt and boxlike in the narrow corridor. "Listen, we have to leave."

"Leave? What do you mean you have to leave?"

"One of my patients is having contractions. I have to get back to Baltimore. Pronto."

"Are you kidding me? One of your patients?"

"She's going earlier than I thought."

"Jesus, Jumbo, you're not an ob-gyn. Whatever it is you do at those births will happen just fine without you."

"I'm sorry, Mingus. Nobody is more committed to this band than me, but today I'm still a midwife. People are counting on me."

Hopefully, that wasn't true.

"So, I'm supposed to just blow Mack off?" I said. "We drove across the fucking state."

"Calm down. I got the front desk to have a rental car dropped off. You stay and work Mack over." He paused to snicker meaningfully. "Dad and I have to go and we have to go now. Mrs. Winchester can't go into labor without me."

Only Jumbo could manage to be practical and impractical simultaneously. It was a horrendously inconvenient time for him to develop a sense of responsibility.

"Besides, you and Mackenzie seem to do just fine on your own." He winked and gave me a jocular elbow to the ribs. "Dad, I'm going to grab us a couple of Cokes and meet you in the lobby. We'll jam the new Tremble tunes the whole way back! And Mingus, no more dust-ups. My old man won't be there to save your sorry ass!"

CHAPTER 17

On the other side of the glass, a gathering of diners filled the bistro. Simple wooden tables stretched back in long, narrow lines under pendant lighting as stylish, well-groomed patrons sipped wine in happy profile.

Mackenzie materialized from the shadows. She had slid herself into a pair of jeans but had not abandoned those voguish glasses, which bridged the thick flows of blond hair cascading down both sides of her face.

"How's your hotel?" she asked.

"No better place to stay if you're a chain smoker."

I couldn't stop looking at her. I was utterly disarmed by the sight of the person who for so long had inhabited my dreams, who'd haunted me, guided me here without ever knowing it. When she reached for the restaurant's door, I was suddenly overcome by the need to confess, an unexpected urge toward forthrightness. It would be unfair of me to conceal the reason for my visit and allow the charade of a dinner between old friends to unfold as I lay in wait for just the right moment to pounce.

"Look, Mack, before we go in, I need to be honest with you about something."

She eyed me suspiciously. "Okay."

"I'm not out here for work."

"What do you mean?"

I tried to breathe normally. "I came out here to see you. I drove out here with Jumbo. Jumbo was going to be the surprise I mentioned earlier. So was his father, actually, but that's a whole other fucked-up story."

She looked instantly traumatized, like I was one of her freak patients. "Wait. Jumbo is here with you?"

"No. Not anymore. He left."

That didn't seem to help. "Teddy, you're scaring me."

"You're going to think I've completely lost my mind."

"What's going on?" But the mortal astonishment in her eyes conveyed the beginnings of understanding, and I felt that familiar shamefaced look creep over me.

With a grimace, I said, "We won't make you audition this time. Promise."

"You're kidding."

I shrugged.

"You want to get the band back together."

I nodded.

"Is this a joke?"

"Depends how you look at it."

"You're insane."

"I keep hearing that."

"You drove to Pittsburgh to show up at my office unannounced and ask me to walk out of my practice and play music again. You actually did that."

"It wasn't unannounced. I had an appointment."

Her stunned silence afforded me the opportunity to relay the whole sorry saga, beginning with my public flogging courtesy of Heinz-Peter Zoot, right up through Sonny, then Alaina.

"It's happening, Mack. We've got all the old players back. We need you."

Mackenzie was shaking her head at this pitiful little horror movie. Faces and names were popping up out of the past like zombies undead and stammering, with designs on dragging her away.

A pack of young women, coworkers I would've guessed, breezed up and maneuvered around us to enter the restaurant, looking at us as if witnessing the genesis of a domestic dispute.

Mackenzie fumbled for words and fidgeted with the buttons on her overcoat. "Your timing is not ideal, I'll say that much."

"Come on, Mack. You were the one in the band that I could most relate to. You had to have known that."

"And yet you came to me last."

"You also happen to be the only one in the band who terrifies me. For obvious reasons."

She started to laugh. "So, you're going around foisting your midlife crisis on people you haven't seen in years? That's what Teddy Tremble has come to?"

"Why does everybody keep calling this a midlife crisis? I'm thirty-eight."

"You know, it's funny. Every day, people come into my office to deal with issues in their relationships. They come in, they sit down, and say things like 'My wife isn't interested anymore' or 'Once a week just isn't doing it for me.' That's what the majority come to me for. Not sex addiction, not curing them of some shame-inducing practice that appalls their partner, but improving the connection with the man or woman in their lives. For most of these people, helping them involves little more than a recalibration of their expectations. 'Your wife isn't twenty-five anymore, she's fifty, so no, the mere sight of her naked body may not bring you to your knees.' Or 'Wouldn't once a week be okay if it knocked your socks off?' More often than not, I'm just slowly helping people accept reality."

"So the key to happiness is low expectations?"

"No, but the key to unhappiness is definitely unreasonable expectations."

"I'm not unhappy. That's not why I'm doing this. And to be honest, my expectations feel more reasonable the deeper I go."

"The hallmark of a delusional mind." She rocked forward onto her toes. "I can't help you, my friend. I'm a sex therapist, not an everything therapist. You need an everything therapist."

"You're a bass player, Mackenzie. That's what you are."

In a better world, that remark would've awakened something inside her and she would've started to nod slowly, the momentum building within, her thoughts racing, an inner voice thumping *Fuck yeah! That's exactly what I am! A bass player!* and she'd be swept away into the current of the bold, burnished future. Instead, she was peering at me over her glasses with a look that rendered me utterly defenseless.

"Before you say no, do me a favor. Don't say no," I pleaded.

With hands stuffed into the pockets of her jacket and her mouth agape, she looked everywhere for help—the passing cars, the row of restaurants and closed shops up and down the block, the night sky circling above. Her toe tapped the asphalt.

Then I remembered my glove compartment. It was the path to a place where the memories could flood like the falls, where I could turn her mind's camera back to the glory days and seduce her with the ecstatic shiver of those times returning.

I heard myself say, "Look, I have a bag of weed in my car. It's not mine and I can't vouch for the quality."

She froze, horror flowering amid bewilderment. I'd just compounded all my other offenses by proposing we do some drugs. Music and pot. How old was I?

"Bad idea," I said, retreating. It was my second in as many minutes. "Forget I mentioned it."

She sighed, already wearying of me. Then she tilted her head down the block. "Come on. Let's get your stash. I live around the corner."

*   *   *

Mackenzie must've considered herself dirtier than most people, or maybe her profession inspired the desire to come home and get clean, for at every turn in her old red Victorian, which loomed munificently over the hushed street, a carefully arranged dish displayed some type of designer bathing product. Soap blocks, soap shells, soap bombs, soap flowers, even little containers of body butter lay about the place in every direction. Their names swept you away into a tranquil land of exotica: bonsai deodorant, buttermilk bath bomb, citrus sage shampoo bar, French chocolate bath melt.

Mack took genuine delight in my misadventures in Europe. The tale inspired convulsions of silent laughter, her torso swaying back and forth but never quite toppling as a densely packed joint was passed between our pinched fingers. We were sitting on the living room rug, our backs against the sofa in a room illuminated only by a Tiffany dragonfly lamp.

"We really have a lost legion of fans in Switzerland?" she asked, bemused and incredulous.

"And not even casual fans," I said. "They wanted to know where your solo albums were. They asked where they could find bootlegs of our shows. I was signing ticket stubs!"

"That must have been a blast."

"I was too busy trying to escape to enjoy it."

"Why am I not surprised?" she said. "The rest of us would've eaten it up, you know."

Mack placed the joint, now a shrunken stub, in a soap dish that she'd brought onto the floor, and remarked, "I have to say, I think it's pretty cool that one little photograph could get you writing songs again."

"I had no choice. That picture reduced me to a joke. I couldn't go to my grave as an object of ridicule."

"A photograph catches one moment, Teddy, and you have had plenty of good ones."

"And yet when I die, people will think of me and laugh."

"Who cares? You'll be dead."

"I wouldn't have given my legacy a second thought were it not for Warren calling me about that exhibit. Ignorance would've been such bliss."

Mack looked doubtful. "Other than Abe Lincoln, Martin Luther King Jr., and Hitler, I really don't know what a legacy is or who has one. I'm just saying that if you're really lucky, you get one miracle in this life. Seems awfully presumptuous to be asking for seconds."

"All I want is to go out on my own terms, to not see a chump every morning in the mirror. You may think that our band's legacy doesn't matter, but it's different for me. I was the one up there, front and center."

"So, the bass player doesn't get a legacy."

"The band bore my name, Mack."

"You're breaking my heart."

"The point is, nobody took a picture of you drooling over Doritos."

Dizzy and mellow from the smoky haze and soapy aromas wafting together, I let my head drop backward onto the womb of the carpet.

"I've got to do this now. If I don't, this thing will follow me into old age and I'll spend the next forty years pining for something that will continue to move further and further out of reach. Time flies, Mack, and the next thing you know, you're eighty-two and you don't have much more of it left. We get old in a hurry, and pretty soon the music is too loud, the winter too cold, and we're using words like 'gorgeous' to describe a salad instead of a woman. I need to act before the whole thing moves beyond my grasp."

Mackenzie groaned. "Well done—pretentious *and* corny. But good luck organizing the world the way you want it. Stories tend to tell themselves."

"Come on, Mack. How much fun would it be to play again?"

"Fun? This is the first I'm hearing of fun. This whole thing sounds like a grudge match. Teddy Tremble getting back at the world for premature neglect."

I sat up and studied her, searching for traces of longing behind the scaffold of her features, for empty spaces in need of filling. "It'd be fun if you were there. That would be fun for me."

I watched her tilt her head to the ceiling, her eyes fluttering closed.

"Don't you miss it?" I asked.

"Clearly not as much as you have."

"There are things I miss, but that's not why I'm doing this. If this were just about reliving fond memories, I could probably move on. I certainly wouldn't have gone to the trouble of scaring up Jumbo. I'm doing this because there are some things I want to change, things I want to make right."

"I think what we did the first time around was right enough."

I shifted on the rug like a drunken snow angel, and for a time, I may have drifted off. When I opened my eyes, she was standing over me, holding out her hand. "Let me show you something."

She led me up the stairs, past a museum of bathing products on display, our stoned legs teetering beneath the unfamiliar weight of our sluggish bodies. Stopping at a dark room, she gave a tug at the string of another dragonfly lamp, which cast a warm orange halo over what soon revealed itself to be the music room. This was the space in which the Mackenzie of old dwelled: bass guitars upright in stands, an old Peavey amplifier in the center of the room, six-strings (electrics and acoustics) against the wall, an electric piano off to the side. It had the retro charm of a Haight/Ashbury recording studio circa 1967. I stood at the threshold and marveled.

Mack flipped a switch and the amp buzzed to life, its tubes shimmying at the fresh current of electricity. She grabbed a bass, sat down on the amp, turned the volume knob, and allowed her fingers to wade over the frets. The low notes glided up into the rafters, graceful yet commanding, smoothly rupturing the night.

She looked up at me. "Plug in. Let's see what we remember."

*   *   *

There are some of us who never had a choice. It was always going to be this way. Whether graced with talent or not, we were going to spend our lives in this often turbulent but always embracing sea. If we can make music, we make it and there's no hope of turning off the spigot. And if we can't, we listen and obsess. It becomes the Dewey decimal system by which our world is organized. We see a cheerleader in pigtails and think, Isn't that skirt a little too Oh-Mickey-you're-so-fine? We see a guy in a blazer with his sleeves rolled up and realize we've been neglecting that Mike + the Mechanics cassette boxed up in the attic all these years. Every unheard song out there is like the last page of a book: it has the answer. We know that this new album we just shelled out ten bucks for will somehow make us more complete, that it will plant one more post in the architecture of our selves.

People like us become someone different for a while when we fall in love with new music. The transformative qualities are real, even if they are imagined. In my Simon & Garfunkel mode, I was a little more cerebral and poetic in a Carl Sandburgian way; I cut back on the cursing in favor of actual words. When I was into Bob Marley's *Exodus*, I was a more laid-back me. When listening to *Misfits* by the Kinks, I spoke with a bit of a sneer. I felt a little tougher during my enchantment with Public Enemy. I channeled a haughty impenetrability during the weeks when I thought *OK Computer* was God's gift. I was a jittery little fuck in my Police phase, what with all that nervous reggae crammed into those albums, and in my Jackson Browne period I grew a beard. (I don't know why. He didn't have one.) It's a junkie's hunger and it springs forth from your subcellular components—organelles, I think they called them in biology class; maybe nuclei, mitochondria, Golgi apparatus. Occasionally, it feels like a prisoner's existence because we don't always choose the object of our obsession. An intense interest in the Muzak of Sven Libaek and the Carpenters has never landed panties on any guy's floor. But in certain very limited circumstances, being yourself has.

The point is, we are happy to be powerless to resist the thrill of a new sound. You can leave the cell door unlocked. Nobody's making a run for it.

That's some of us.

Others aren't nearly so afflicted. There is no pain, no suffering, no Sandburg, no sneering. There is just the angelic simplicity of being absorbed in your song. That was Mackenzie. And what a thing to hear. What a thing to watch. The way that the bass roots a song, gives it its steady footing and its ability to move—that's what Mackenzie always lent to the Tremble machinery. As we strummed and plucked in the meek orange light of her upstairs room, the years melted away. I watched her falling into herself, into that unshakable peace, mellow and confident, following herself out of somewhere and into somewhere else.

When we finished playing and set down our instruments, she dropped her hands into her lap. "I don't mean to bring the discussion back to my body, but I should probably tell you that I have breast cancer." She winced apologetically. "I hate saying it that way, but there really are so few euphemisms."

I looked at her, thunderstruck. "What?"

"I'm not sure why I just told you that," she said. "Because really, I'm totally fine. They got it early. Nobody's telling me not to buy green bananas or to stay away from the collected works of Dumas."

"Holy shit. Why didn't you tell me this earlier?"

"When was earlier?"

Four months ago, while applying deodorant after a shower, she noticed a lump in her armpit. She would've ignored it, constitutionally hardwired as she was with an inability to panic, but having lost her mother six years ago to Hodgkin's, she read the genetic writing on the wall. Within ten days, she'd undergone a mastectomy. Her most recent round of chemo had been earlier that week.

"I just assumed you had access to my medical records, showing up here with a stash of antinausea," she said with a coy twinkle.

"Jesus, Mack." I felt ashamed, prattling on all night about the need to be taken seriously as an artist, bitching about bad photographs of me eating Mexican food. "You must've wanted to slap me all night."

She didn't speak up to say otherwise.

"Are you okay? Who's taking care of you?"

"I'm no recluse, Teddy. I've got friends. Really good ones, it turns out."

There was, she assured me, no shortage of people populating her fridge with Tupperwared meals she was too nauseated to eat, soothing her with six-packs of Canada Dry ginger ale. For the time being, she was still tethered to the treatments every few weeks, but the end of that vicious battery was approaching, and her doctors were optimistic that she would soon have her forehead stamped with the words In Remission, that sought-after designation that somehow still sounded ominous.

For a long moment, the only sound was the high constant hum of the amp.

"I also have an ex-husband checking in on me," she volunteered.

I flinched in surprise.

"Remember Colin Stone?"

"The Sony rep? Sure. The Dire Wolf. What about him?"

"He's at MCA now, but . . ."

My jaw went slack. "You married Colin fucking Stone?"

And who wouldn't? Colin was a lifer in the music business, a gregarious, distinguished-looking record exec with dense hedges of gray hair and an enveloping grin. He had a really enthusiastic handshake—he swung you a bit, he was so damn happy to see you, he might just pull you right into his suit jacket—and was always either on his way to a leisurely, lubricated meal or just returning from one. He was our main point of contact when Sony signed us, and he brimmed with encouragement at every meeting, even later on when we couldn't catch a cold. Colin was a good bit older than us, so it often felt as though someone had brought a dad to our Mirabelle Plum marathons, but a dad who went out more nights a week than we did and who drank all of us under the table in passing.

As a member of the band, Mack had never viewed him in a romantic light. But a few years later, she told me, when she was in her graduate program in New York, they ran into each other on an elevator and realized they lived in the same building. Right then and there, he invited her to tag along at a dinner with the Flaming Lips (regular people have dinner; Colin always had *a* dinner), and in an aberrant move, she accepted. Another invitation followed, and soon she was accompanying him to record release parties and on visits to his ailing mother (an impossibly ancient Czech woman who made a mean mushroom soup). They even got into a rather delightful minor car accident together.

The marriage lasted just over two years, and it didn't take nearly that long for Mack to realize she'd made a mistake. She wanted to be done with the music business, and that included not being the child bride of one of its most enduring characters. The inevitable end brought relief and friendship. She decided to start over in a new city, and Pittsburgh had felt like home ever since.

"Colin and I were never right for each other," Mack concluded. "I think we both knew that all along. He's a sweet guy and the life of every party, but I'm not really one for parties."

"I thought I was going to be the one with all the surprises," I said. "But you've got me beat. You married Colin Stone, you got breast cancer, you dined with the Flaming Lips. I'm dealing with a lot of stuff here."

She playfully knocked my shoulder with hers. "I find this proposition of yours rather fascinating. Outlandish, fraught with the potential to backfire and visit upon you even more embarrassment than you've already been through. That's just irresistible. Besides, if you're really willing to risk your reputation and dive back into the fray, these new songs of yours must be pretty damn good."

"You overestimate me."

"A mistake we've all made before."

She buried her head in her hands and made weird little noises while kneading the flesh of her face. Then she popped up. "Screw it. I'm in."

I eyed her like I hadn't quite heard correctly.

"It was the bridge of 'New Morning Azalea' that sold me," she said. "I always loved that song."

"What are you talking about?"

"Just now, when we were playing 'Azalea,' it hit me. This is fun. I miss this."

"Are you fucking with me? Are you just really high?"

"My practice can wait. There will always be sex and there will always be people all twisted up about it."

"You're coming to this too quickly." No pun was intended. "Just to be clear, you have cancer."

"But the goal is to not have it for very long. You kick it out or it kicks you out."

Assuming things progressed as expected, she had to endure only a handful more chemo treatments. She'd managed to keep her office open throughout this ordeal, although she admitted that there were occasional midsession sprints to the bathroom that she hoped didn't leave her patients with the impression that their sexual messiness made her sick. So, except for the days when she had to be available for the IV, and the few days thereafter when she had to be available to puke at a moment's notice, she could probably swing a stint in a band.

"Let's be honest—in any given week, Jumbo barfs more times than I do anyway," she posited.

I stared at her, floored. "Mackenzie Highsider, how is it that, as long as I've known you, your next move is always a mystery to me?"

"You know my deal," she cautioned. "You know who I am now, what I'm going through. You know my reasons; they're not the same as yours. If you still want me, I'm in."

In the end, that was the root of it for her. Mackenzie's bass line. She didn't care about any of the untidy complexity. She just wanted to play music like it didn't matter what came next. So what if we all needed to dab on some antiwrinkle cream before bedtime? So what if we should all go a little easier on the carbs? So what? Fuck the label and the agent. Fuck the street team and the tour manager. Fuck the Nielsen SoundScan numbers and the whores at the radio stations and the creatively bankrupt sellouts in A&R. Fuck them all. This wasn't a space shuttle launch. Let's just play the damn thing.

I curled her hand beneath mine. "For the record, we both know you've already read the collected works of Dumas."

We strolled across her dew-drizzled lawn toward my car. The cool night air felt good against my face, reviving me with the desire to move. I knew that sleep would remain at bay for hours, so I decided I'd drive home now and arrive before morning.

Mack offered to speak with Colin and get him high on these mad plans of ours. Colin was not only still an A&R muckety-muck at MCA, but he was still tight with Sonny Rivers and, like everyone else on the planet, accepted Sonny's word as gospel. With Sonny and Alaina having boarded the Tremble train, Colin didn't stand a chance. This beat-up old gaggle of has-beens just might get a hard look from a major record company. We hadn't even all been in the same room yet.

I unlocked the car and faced Mackenzie, and as I stared into the eyes in which I knew lay my rescue, I thought of the night so long ago in New York, our fateful collision with that lout from the Junction.

"Did you know Simon Weathers had a thing for you?" I said.

"What?"

"Simon Weathers. He totally dug you."

"He did not."

"He said so himself. Think of it, Mack. If I'd let him anywhere near you, you could be leading a totally different life now, a kept woman in the LA party scene, and doing much better drugs than the sad stash I plucked from my glove compartment."

There was a pause. Then, "What do you mean, if you'd let him near me?"

"My band was not for the pillaging," I told her. "You date him, the next thing you know, you're playing bass for him."

She yawned, shivered, and pocketed her hands. "I wouldn't have touched that guy with a ten-foot pole. And you know I hate parties."

"That's something I never really got about you," I said. "You could've had a different guy every night."

She scoffed. "You're projecting your own stereotypical male fantasy. A different guy every night doesn't sound interesting to me. It sounds like an awful lot of work."

"You know what I mean."

What I meant was, I was right there all along. Could it possibly have been that she'd passed up a parade of rich and famous musicians because of secret, uncomfortable feelings for the guy standing two microphones over on the same stage? Was that anywhere near the truth?"

"That just wasn't my thing," she said. "For a guy, the coolest thing about being in a rock band is scoring with women. For me, the coolest thing about being in a rock band was being in a rock band. I loved my instrument and the wonderful sounds that came out of it when we all played together. I loved your songs and I loved how people gave up their evenings and their money to hear us play them. I loved seeing our records in stores. I loved hearing us on the radio. I loved going to Hamburg. I loved waking up in a strange town with the rhythms of life beating all around me while I looked on as an outsider, like a bird on a wire." Her mouth curved knowingly. "That's what it was for me. I was happy I did it, and I was fine when it was over. I wasn't going to run off with Simon Weathers. I wasn't going to run off with anybody."

My eyes dropped to the wet blades of grass encircling my shoes. The realization hit me: Mack was not homesick for the Tremble years. She regarded her past with a pleasant nostalgia, an attic of memories best kept as such. She knew what the past was and what it wasn't.

But worse, Mack wasn't homesick for me, and that discovery filled me with a horrible emptiness. The torture, the regret, the reverie that I'd lugged with me from year to year because of what happened with this band, because of what happened with Mack—she, wherever in the world she'd been, had never felt it.

I'd seen one flower and invented a jungle.

As I guided my car out of the sleeping neighborhood, past the rows of dark windows and the angular jungle of rooftops, I thought of that afternoon in Arizona, still as fresh to me as if it had happened a week ago. I remembered the two of us waiting for the tow truck, how she sat cross-legged on the hood while I leaned next to her with my arms folded, both of us gazing out at the pink wallpaper sky, a dusty desert wind breathing sand against our clothes. When I turned and placed a hand on each of her legs, gently pulling her toward me by the bend in her knees—and I will never know what fortified me with the courage to do it—there was the briefest resistance, a jolt of surprise in the buckling of her eyebrows. But then her mouth fell into mine. She tilted her head to kiss me, cupping my face in her hands as my arms snaked under her shirt to feel the skin of her hips.

The ride in the tow truck cab was quiet, each of us squinting through the open car window. At the hotel, we stole through a side entrance, making quickly for my room. I remembered the confident way she pulled me across the suite and onto the bed. I remembered the jagged slant of light slicing her midsection as she straddled me and pulled her shirt over her head. I remembered how neither one of us spoke a word. I remembered the rhythmic pulse of her body, how her eyes seemed full of stars.

And I remembered the knock on the door.

Everything changed that night. Distances mushroomed between us and remained there straight on to the end. In losing her in just that way, I gained a fantasy, a delusion that had been my troublesome companion ever since.

I swung by the Best Western to gather my bag and check out. Grabbing a coffee from the burner in the lobby and a pile of shrink-wrapped empty calories from the vending machine, I took to the turnpike feeling like a darkening sky.

With the city lights drifting behind, the land around me became a blindfold, a ribbon of nothingness upon which stark, weather-beaten truths projected themselves. You never know where things are headed, where the veering road will ferry you, the things and people that slip through your fingers when you're not looking, sometimes even when you are. One minute you're a young, stupid kid with nothing but time, everything within your control. You have a girlfriend, a beautiful one with Pacific-blue eyes and a glistening mouth. You kiss her on the train platform as she leaves for home. You hold her close and absorb the smell of her cheek, and you watch her waving to you through the window as the train pulls away. But you don't think to hold on to that moment, to capture the juicy sweetness of her lips and keep it inside you forever, even though she's leaving for a four-week study program in France. Because you don't contemplate the guy from San Francisco who takes the seat next to her on the first day of class. They'll get to talking, he'll tell her of his plans to explore some cozy town in Brittany with ruins and a winery, and he'll invite her along. And then, just a brisk four weeks later, she'll tell you she doesn't think it's such a good idea for you to pick her up at the airport.

The next thing you know, you're calling a strange city your home and you're calling a grad student your fiancée. You occasionally reflect on the winter weekends with that girl from the train platform, those snug swells of hours, those days when you never got dressed except to venture out into the peppermint cold for pizza and six-dollar bottles of red wine.

The next thing you know, you've heard through the grapevine that she has three kids and is living in West Hartford. You imagine that she's in a book club and all her old friends have been displaced by ones she met at her kids' schools. One day in November, a song you hear on your morning run makes you think of that last moment when you let her get onto that train and out of your grasp forever, and you wonder if any of those feelings, those tastes and smells, alive and true as they once felt, ever meant anything at all. You imagine that she thinks of you too every now and again, probably as she's making lunches or gauging the fit of her sweater in her walk-in closet mirror. You'll never see each other again—never—for the rest of your lives. But for one night, twenty-six years after she left, you'll both sleep in the same Marriott in Grand Rapids, Michigan. You'll spend the night four rooms apart and never know it.

The ache you feel, alone on an empty highway after midnight, is the pull of everything forever moving away from you.

There is a danger in pining for people, in pining for things, in confusing who you are with what you want. You lose yourself in it. You lose yourself.

Somewhere deep in Pennsylvania, I sent a text to Sara's phone, knowing that by the time she read it, it would be moot:

"Change of plans. Coming home tonight. Too late to call. Really wanted to hear your voice."

I was surprised to consider those words and realize how true they felt.

In the face of all the changes being hurled in her direction, Sara had not buried her face in her pillow and hidden from the world. She seemed instead to be learning how to move on. I didn't know how far she was capable of moving, or in what direction. But maybe in that singular way, each of us hot and sweaty with the power to change, the will to weigh our anchors and sail on, Sara and I were more alike now than ever.

CHAPTER 18

The next few days were like walking through a low-lying cloud that refused to lift. I was unable to think about music or the band or any of my fellow travelers without seeing it all in stale, washed-out tones. The vibrancy had drained from the music, and I no longer saw the point in any of it. Someone else could do this.

I moped around the condo. I bought a container of Laughing Cow cheese at the convenience store across the street and consumed all eight wedges while watching the second half of *The Shawshank Redemption* on AMC. I tagged along with Sara to a market in North Philly that sold some type of Tunisian olive oil she'd read about. I spackled a hole in the bathroom wall where a towel hook had come loose. I got thirty pages into a John le Carré novel, then realized I'd read it before. I caught the first half of *The Shawshank Redemption* on AMC. I tagged along with Sara to the tailor to have some pants altered. Every time the band seeped into my thoughts, I avoided it by emptying the dishwasher or spraying cleanser on the balcony furniture.

What a profound letdown: to face the realization that someone who had entangled you for so many years and for so many reasons hadn't suffered a moment's entanglement by you.

Finally, I boarded a train for New York.

Coiled in her leather chair and rising over her desk like a cobra, Alaina Farber waited. She waited to hear how I'd gone about conscripting my three old soldiers. She waited for me to hand her another disc with yet more songs that would render her awestruck. She waited to share with me her plan for conquering the world.

"I'm not so sure I want to do this," I told her.

"Not so sure you want to do what?"

"This. This whole thing. Tremble."

"What are you talking about?"

Sinking deeper into my chair, I crossed my legs and took note of a fresh scuff that pushed my shoe past charmingly distressed and into the territory of vagrantly worn. "I might have made a mistake."

"What's going on? The pressures of fame getting to you? Is it all too much? You miss your anonymity, the ability to sit down in a Bertucci's for a nice leisurely pie without being badgered?"

"Knock it off, Alaina."

She turned serious. "I'm not exactly sure what it is you're saying."

"I don't know. I'm just feeling a little lost about this now."

"Meaning?"

"Meaning. . . maybe this isn't what I want after all."

"God, you're a fucking mess!" she exploded. "You're a little lost? I thought you were lost before you started back up with this. I thought this was how you were going to get found!"

"So did I," I said, as baffled as she was. "So did I."

"Theodore, have you really come here to tell me that after your highly public flogging in an art gallery in London, then being introduced to a legion of diehard fans in the fucking Alps, and having that set you off in a burdensome tizzy of songwriting that, against all probability, is actually quite good, and having that earn you the support of the world's best producer and New York's most powerful and seductive agent, and having *that* set you off gathering up your three amigos and convincing them to quit their day jobs—that after all that, upon further reflection, maybe you don't want to play rock star after all?"

I stared back at her. "So, I think maybe you're oversimplifying it, but yeah, that's the gist of it."

Alaina raised her arms to the ceiling. Touchdown! "What am I going to do with you?"

All the charged particles boomeranging around my head lifted me out of the chair and sent me pacing. "I don't know what to say. I think I just had this realization that playing in a band again isn't the answer. Whatever those days were, they're gone and I'm not ever going to be able to find them. I was wrong to go looking."

Alaina was incredulous. "Are you dumb, Teddy? Seriously—like, did you even graduate from college? Have you ever heard a musician say that making music brought them peace and happiness? Because I know an awful lot of musicians, and you know what? They are all miserable human beings. Miserable, tortured souls, suffering for what they've convinced themselves is art—suffering in vain, by the way, because what most of them make doesn't come close to art, but I suppose self-delusion is some kind of Darwinian device that keeps you mental cases alive. Regardless—there is no way you could've reasonably thought that ginning up the band again and diving back into this fucked-up world was going to help you achieve nirvana. Case in point: Nirvana!"

Facing her window, my eyes drifted far over the skyline, past the collective cabin fever that raged through the city, afflicting all, diagnosed by none. And that, I understood at that very moment, was precisely what I'd learned: there really was no escape from any of this.

"What happened?" Alaina's voice was now jarringly gentle.

"I don't know," I said with all the rock star grievousness in the world.

"Did something happen with Mackenzie? Is she out?"

"No, she's in."

"Did she not accept your Facebook friend request or something?"

"She's in," I repeated, fumbling for words. "I just don't know if she's *in*. You know what I mean?"

Alaina's face was a thicket of disbelief. "Not even a little bit."

"She doesn't need this. None of them do. Shit, Jumbo doesn't even need this."

Alaina grabbed an apple off her desk and hurled it at me. It struck me in the chest.

"Ow!" I yelped.

"Of course they don't need this! If they needed this, you would've heard from them at some point in the current millennium. *You* need this because it was your band. It's your heinous mug up in that London gallery looking like a slob. And it's you—and only you—who has the power to change your legacy. To the extent you have one. And to the extent it needs changing."

She paused for an exasperated breath.

"Look. Teddy, my little cheese blintz, I love you. I will always love you. I have a soft spot for you; it's mostly pity, because you have no idea who you are or what you have or, frankly, what to make of anything in this life. But if you walk away from this now, after everything you've done, I'm probably going to skip your funeral."

I stared at her, caressing the apple-sized wound just south of my clavicle.

"That didn't hurt, you big baby," Alaina said. "And pick that up for me, will you? I'm going to eat that."

There was a knock on the door—soft, not convinced it wanted to be heard. It was Marin, Alaina's assistant with the punky 'do.

"Yes, Marin?" Alaina was irritated. "We're a little busy in here."

"Dave Chenier is on the phone."

"Jesus. How often does that guy call you?" I asked.

Alaina rolled her eyes. "You were Dave Chenier once, and I rolled my eyes plenty about you. What does Mr. Fuckface want now, Marin?"

"He's not happy."

"Of course, he's not happy. Nobody's happy! Transfer Mr. Fuckface to the conference room and I'll take him in due course."

"Actually, there's one more thing," the young woman interjected apologetically. "I'm not totally sure, but I think my ex-boyfriend might kill himself."

Alaina glared irksomely. "Do you mean right now or in the general sense that all of us more or less consider suicide at some point?"

The girl gave a cumbrous swallow. "He called me ten minutes ago and said he was going to kill himself now. I guess he meant then." She checked her watch.

"Holy fucking shit, Marin!" Alaina erupted. "Are you serious?"

"Yeah, so I was going to run out for a bit. I should probably check in on him. Do you mind?"

"Are you high? You can't go to a potentially suicidal ex-boyfriend's apartment by yourself."

"Oh."

Alaina was nearing the end of her wits from the many flavors of stupidity presenting themselves this afternoon. All of it finally gave way to a helpless shrug.

"I was fixing to give Teddy here the spanking of his life, but fuck it. Let's go."

Evidently, the *let's* in *let's go* included me, because before I could make my escape, I found myself sandwiched between Alaina and her underling in the back of a taxi, Dave Chenier presumably still on hold.

We zoomed uptown in various states of agitation. When Alaina wasn't barking at the poor Pakistani cabbie for failing to make the traffic vanish, she was consumed with e-mails on her phone. Marin, for her part, seemed far more tense about monopolizing our time than about the health status of her ex-boyfriend. She spent the ride peppering us with apologies.

"By the way," Alaina said without looking up, "do you know who we have the pleasure of riding with today?"

Marin shook her head.

"This is Teddy Tremble." No reaction. "From Tremble. The band."

She suddenly lit up. "Oh yeah. Sure. 'It Feels like a Lie.' Neato. It's an honor, sir."

I groaned and focused on the exotic synth pop dancing out of the dusty dashboard.

We zipped up Third Avenue to the Upper East Side, its endless palette of storefronts and apartment buildings blurring past. I was really hoping a dead body didn't lie at the end of this ride. I was in no mood for grief counseling.

"How long were you with this lad?" Alaina wanted to know.

"Almost three weeks."

"Three weeks and this guy is offing himself over you?" I hooted.

Alaina's eyes glimmered. "You must be a beast in bed."

"This guy's got serious issues," I told Marin. "If he happens not to be dead, I strongly recommend never seeing him again."

"Oh God. I hope he's not dead," Marin panted. "I have a major fear of dead bodies."

"You know what I have a fear of?" Alaina raised her voice toward the driver. "Dying in a taxi with the radio stuck on the Bollywood station."

The cabbie, muttering unintelligible invective, let us out in front of a decaying courtyard behind which a gray brick apartment building rose up about a dozen stories. It was the kind of place that housed the Marins of the world—young professionals rendered borderline insolvent by the city's economic tourniquet.

Marin eyed the front door with palpable trepidation. There was no sign of the police, which meant either false alarm or already-bagged body.

Something drew my attention upward, a slight movement just above my field of vision, a color out of sync. I lifted my eyes three or four stories up, and there it was: a person on the ledge.

It was a jumper, but a jumper with apparent second thoughts, or at least mixed emotions about this whole killing yourself thing. He seemed to be leaning back against the wall as far away from the edge as possible, as if he'd realized that despite the sincerity of his tantrum and the purity of his outrage against life's injustices, at the end of the day—shit—heaving yourself off a building was a far less vivid enterprise in theory than in practice.

I tapped Marin on the shoulder and pointed. "You know that fella?"

Alaina followed my finger and hissed. "Oh Jesus fucking Christ."

I stifled a chuckle. A fall from that height probably wouldn't have even done the trick. It was, in fact, entirely possible that he'd already jumped, dusted himself off, and climbed back up to give it another go.

Marin waved both hands up at the shaggy, yellow-headed figure like a desert island castaway halfheartedly flagging down a propeller plane but just as happy to stick it out on the beach for another couple of years. "Duncan? Duncan, down here!"

"Oh! Look who showed up!" echoed a voice from the ledge. Suicidal, he still had the presence of mind to be snot-nosed about it.

Marin tilted her head. "I thought you said you were going to kill yourself."

"He waited for you to show up," I said. "This isn't suicide; it's vaudeville. If he really wanted to die, he wouldn't be dangling himself over the mezzanine. He jumps from there, at best he twists an ankle."

"Come down from there, Duncan," she implored. "Let's talk."

"There's nothing to talk about!"

"What a mopey little shit," I said. "I'm calling the cops."

I reached into my jacket pocket for my phone.

"Don't even think about it!" the kid yelled down, his back still rigid against the wall. "Marin, tell your dad to put his phone away or I'm jumping! I swear!"

Alaina snorted, relishing the slight.

"I mean it! Same goes for your mom!"

Alaina's hands went fast to her hips. "What did that little puke just say?" Then she eyed both Marin and me. "You clowns just got the compliment of your lives."

Marin stepped forward and began to plead, her voice high-register but too shrill to be an outright squeak. "Okay, okay. Calm down. Nobody's calling the police." This tender young thing hadn't yet learned that when somebody says I mean it, the opposite is typically the case. I dropped my phone back inside my pocket.

"These aren't my parents. These are people who are worried about you, just like I am. This is my boss, Alaina. And this—you'll never believe it—is Freddy Tremble."

"Who?"

"Freddy Tremble. From Tremble. The band."

"I don't know who that is."

"Remember that song? 'It Feels like a Lie?'"

He thought a moment. "No."

"You never saw *Ballad of the Fallen*?"

"No. Why are we talking about this?"

Marin was muttering to herself in rising pique. Duncan had now managed to irritate each of the devoted souls who'd convened to save him. That was bad form.

"Can I come up there?" Marin called.

"No!"

"Come on, Duncan. Why are you doing this?"

"You don't love me," was the bruised response.

Marin turned to us. "He's right. I don't. I've known him for three weeks. Should I just be honest with him?"

Alaina was reading an e-mail.

At that moment, a second-floor window slid open and an old lady with a detonation of white hair poked her head out. "Hey! Why are you people making such a fuss?"

I pointed, and the woman's head twisted upward to see. "Heavens to Betsy!" she screamed. "It's a jumper!" She ducked back into her apartment like a whack-a-mole creature dodging a mallet.

Alaina was grinning at me. "'Heavens to Betsy.' That's what we're dealing with here."

Meanwhile, a pair of older gentlemen was leisurely traversing the street to take in the goings-on. Both were circling seventy and shabbily dressed. One was nibbling at a vanilla cupcake.

The old woman on the second floor was back now, having thrust her head through the window again. "Police are on their way!" she announced. "Firemen too, probably!"

And just like that, Duncan's expo expired. With the authorities on the march, there was now a limit to how long he could perpetrate this gratuitous torture of his ex-girlfriend. He had a problem. However genuine the emotional turmoil that had brought him out here, it was nothing compared to the misery he'd endure by abandoning it like a weenie. He may not have wanted to kill himself, but he certainly didn't want to not die.

So he did the next best thing: he leaned back against the bricks and began to bawl.

Man, was it appalling. Distraught sobbing. Sputtering noises of a grown man's whimper. "My star is fading, man. It's like I'm swerving out of control and there's, like, no chance of release." He paused to snif-fle. "I know no one said it'd be easy. But no one said it'd be this hard."

"Pathetic," Alaina jeered.

"It is pathetic," I agreed. "That's Coldplay."

Alaina and Marin stared at me.

"All that lachrymose drivel—those are Coldplay lyrics."

Alaina looked horrified. "Why do you know that?"

"I'm not proud of myself."

Meanwhile, the two retirees, both clad in paint-spattered overalls, I realized, had made it to the sidewalk and now joined us in the court-yard. The one who hadn't brought a cupcake looked at Alaina. "Do you speak English?" he asked loudly.

She gave him an ice pick stare. "Not a word."

A sudden shriek sent all eyes darting up to Duncan. So absorbed was he in his mortally aggrieved wailing that the dumbass lost his bal-ance. A chorus of gasps rose up from the courtyard as one of Duncan's feet slid clear off the ledge and, with a guttural yelp, he stumbled over the side.

We all braced to follow the doomed beeline of his drop and the inevitable sickening thud. But instead, there was a harsh jerk and the guy stopped falling. He'd somehow managed to slide his hand into the open window and grip the frame. Clutching a corner, he struggled to pull himself up, his legs swinging and kicking over the edge in a desperate and not altogether uncomic search for footing. By some miracle—some unnatural force inimical to the evolutionary process of natural selection—this yo-yo managed to wriggle himself back to safety, and after spasms of twitching and groping for dear life, he collapsed on the ledge. Panting and snorting, but alive.

It was all too much for Marin. She buried her head in her boss's bosom and began to sob.

Alaina held her assistant close and pretended to console her. But I soon noticed that she'd fixed an urgent look on me. Her eyes burned into me with white thermonuclear fire. Alaina seemed to be transmitting some sort of message that I wasn't receiving.

"What?" I finally barked.

"Go up there, Teddy."

"What?"

"Go up there and talk to the mental patient."

Me. The person who had the least business being there. "Fuck. You."

She went stern. "Teddy."

"Why would I go up there?"

"Because of that which swings in your boxers."

"What?"

"That child needs to talk to a man, and laughable as it is, you're the closest thing we have at the moment. He needs a heart-to-heart with someone who can relate to and bond over the cruelty of women. Are you familiar with the cruelty of women, Theodore, or do I have to introduce you?"

"Are you kidding me? If I go up there, it'll be to lift eighty bucks from his wallet as compensation for the train ticket I wasted."

"Go," she insisted.

"You don't want me to go up there. Trust me."

Duncan did not want to be schooled on the harsh truths I was likely to unload on him. He was, to be sure, unprepared for my take on the human condition. Alaina kept on burning me with the death stare while Marin rocked and puffed in her employer's armpit. I was unmoved by any of this, even the crumpled heap of humanity splayed out on the ledge. But we had arrived at an impasse, and impasses meant nothing if not more wasted time.

"I'll go, Farber," I said, wearily. "But only because you guys are all yelleeew."

Naturally, the elevator was out of order, so I had to slog it up three flights in the equatorial swelter of the stairwell. At least the apartment was unlocked.

Inside, a panoramic scan of the room revealed little in the way of furniture, save for the obligatory flat-screen, a device that, with today's programming, was a reliable vehicle for stories and images capable of sending even the sunniest among us into the tar pit of despondency, and ultimately, out onto the ledge.

I ambled through the open room. Upon poking my head out the window, I spied Duncan seated against the wall, the slack embodiment of defeat. He jolted to life at the sight of me, then evaluated through bleary eyes whether my presence foretold good things or bad.

"Why don't you come inside?" I proposed unkindly, shooting for a swift and economical resolution.

"Of course I'm not coming inside. What do you think I'm doing out here?"

"Being ridiculous, for one. You're also humiliating yourself— which is something I happen to know a little bit about."

I suppose the last thing he'd expected was an antagonism. If somebody was going to be dispatched from the ground to try to talk him down, it would logically be the most compassionate of the lot, the one whose eyes would go all soggy when imploring him to choose to live!

Someone who'd say, You don't want to do this, son. Really. I've been there. I, however, seemed to be taking a slightly different approach, that being the hurling of insults. Perhaps Duncan viewed my show of insensitivity as some sort of tough-love tactic. This was just my style. Harsh, but skillfully so. I'd done this a thousand times, never lost a jumper.

"Humiliating myself, am I?" he said distantly. "Well, maybe my pride fell with my fortunes."

"Oh sweet Jesus. If that's more Coldplay, I'm going to get a stick and nudge you over that ledge."

He reddened at having been called out on all that plagiarized heartache. "Shakespeare," he muttered, his eyes cast out to the horizon.

I looked at this afflicted mess, the red face and puffy eyes, and all I could think was, Why wasn't he dead yet? Here's why: because he was an attention-seeking little twerp, oh so much deeper and more complex than the rest of us. A quote always at the ready, one whose relevance eluded you, but you nodded anyway and convinced yourself it was spot-on illuminative. He was the dweeb in college who sat around on the fraternity house sofa flicking a lighter. He didn't smoke, but you never knew when someone might start playing "Every Rose Has Its Thorn."

"Get on up and come in. You can read me passages from the *Norton Anthology of English Literature* inside."

With a sniff, he went groping around in the front pocket of his baggy pants. Then he tossed something in my direction. Reflexively, I caught it. It was a pack of matches with a black and orange logo that read Mimi's Hothouse.

"What the hell is this?"

"It's where we went on our first date," he wailed. "See that Marin gets it."

I tossed it over the ledge. It ruffled toward the ground like an injured sparrow. "You don't fucking need that."

He gaped at me like I was evil incarnate, as if I'd just thrown Marin herself, and not a stupid pack of matches, out the window.

"Duncan—is it Duncan? Listen, I don't know you, I don't know why you think your life is so hopeless, and—I won't lie—I don't care all that much. But you're not as far gone as you think. I know people who are so much more fucked up than you could ever be, and I don't see them throwing themselves off buildings. If you do this, do you know what happens?" I pointed down at Marin. "She moves on. She's bummed for a little while, freaked out more than anything, but she goes to a thera-pist for a few months, or maybe just to her mom's for the weekend, and then she's past it. She's past you, and by Christmas she's giggling and squirming around in someone else's bed. Maybe by Thanksgiving. That's where this is headed. You die for nothing, Shakespeare."

We all die for nothing. That was something Duncan could learn later.

"You're not exactly restoring my will to live," the kid sneered.

"Good, 'cause that's not what I came up here to do. If you really wanted to kill yourself, you would've done it already. This is nothing more than a matinee, a lame one at that. The only reason you're out here is to upset that girl down there. And I can't have that."

I don't know why I said "I can't have that." Sure I could have that. What did I care? I was getting carried away.

"How many relationships do you think go on to flourish after a stunt like this?" I continued. "Do you think Marin—is it Marin?—is down there falling back in love with you? Do you really think this is good for business?"

He looked up at me with washed-out eyes. "You don't know what you're talking about."

At that, I couldn't help but smile. It was a bitter smile. "I'm afraid, my little drip, I know exactly what I'm talking about." I heaved a sigh. "A long time ago, I made a bad decision and fucked over my friends, people I cared about. I know you've never heard of me, but I used to be in a pretty big band. We were no Coldplay, mind you, but we did have our moment."

I scratched the back of my head, considering how far to go with all of this. "My band was offered a huge opportunity. You know the Junction?"

"Yeah, man, they rock."

"That they do. Well, the Junction invited us out on tour with them. That invitation was like winning Powerball. Sold-out stadiums all across North America. Our music being heard by literally hundreds of thousands of people. Radio promotion. T-shirts. And all of this happening at the precise moment that our second album was being released. It was not the kind of opportunity that required a whole lot of consideration."

The kid had parked an expectant gaze on me.

"But you know what I did?" I said. "I turned it down."

Duncan snorted. "Dude, that was stupid."

"That it was. Everybody thought I turned it down because I was an egomaniac. We'd had a monster hit, a platinum-selling album, a song in a movie that won an Oscar—beat out Sting and Randy Newman, I'll have you know—and a phenomenally successful tour of our own. So everybody thought I passed on this golden opportunity because I'd be damned if I was going to be somebody's opening act.

"But here's the thing." I paused. Letting the truth out into the world meant I'd have to face up to it. "I didn't turn down the Junction because I thought we were too big to warm up their stage for them. I turned them down because I knew that Simon Weathers wanted to get his greasy hands all over my bass player."

"So?"

"So. I was in love with that bass player."

I felt Duncan's stare on the roof of my skull.

"It was pure jealousy," I went on. "I nixed the whole thing because I was jealous. I pissed away the band's future and the livelihoods of my friends, people who depended on me, all because I wanted to keep hold of something that was never even mine."

"So, what did you do?" Duncan asked.

"I chose for us a slow, painful death. I insisted we hit the road by ourselves, and just as everyone had predicted, our crowds were disappointing, our record sales were disappointing, and our label soon dropped us—which was disappointing. I'd made a huge misjudgment and it cost all of us our careers."

I stopped talking, ensnared as I was in this miserable memory.

"Do your friends know?" Duncan asked, still looking sluggish and flimsy against the wall.

I shook my head. "I've never admitted it to anyone. So, if you're going to kill yourself, cool. If you're not, I'd appreciate it if you kept it quiet."

"Guys do some stupid shit for chicks," he mused, as if we were now confederates. "Even screwing up their friends' lives."

"The thing is, they're not screwed up. They're all fine, maybe even better off. And who knows? Maybe touring with the Junction wouldn't have been the boon everybody thought. Our second album really was a bit of a snore. Maybe a bigger tour would've just meant putting more people to sleep. Maybe there was just no saving us from us. We were what we were."

"I take it it wasn't happily ever after with the bass player either."

I grunted through the window frame. "I'm not totally sure how she's felt about me all this time," I said, half-truthfully. "I just know it's not the same way I've felt about her."

I'd now talked this out to such an extent that the surest path to redemption was to join Duncan out on the ledge where the thin air really could right all your wrongs. If you just summoned the nerve to tumble into the low sky, all your hard decisions were made for you.

"At least you can do something about it," Duncan said.

I looked at him.

"Just go tell all of them the truth. Apologize."

I noticed I was nodding. Regardless of where Mackenzie stood on the issue of me, at least I knew where she stood on the issue of the band. Everybody was in, not because they needed to be, but because they wanted to be. Maybe I'd never again experience the giddy high of our first trip, but you're only twenty-five once. Why couldn't this be fun at thirty-eight? Wasn't it already?

"So, anyway . . . ," I heard Duncan say. "I don't want to make this all about me, but what was the point of your story? Other than I'm not the only one on this ledge who sucks with girls."

I looked down at him. "Let's go downstairs and talk to Marin. I think it'll help. It might not. Who knows? If after talking to her for five minutes you still want to kill yourself, I will personally walk you back up here and push you out the window." He gauged my sincerity through a raised eyebrow. "I'll do it. Ask anyone."

Fidgeting with the frayed end of one of his shoelaces, he finally seemed on the verge of surrender.

"Things will turn around for you, Duncan. But not unless you stop quoting Coldplay. That's gotta stop now."

No sooner had I helped him through the window than he made for a plate of biscuits on the kitchen counter. They were scabrous things, the color of chewing tobacco and about as appetizing as a urinal puck.

While he snacked, I looked around and noticed that the ramshackle apartment was completely devoid of decoration. Until I started living with an interior designer, I'd never given much thought to what I surrounded myself with, but I wondered if that wasn't part of Duncan's problem. There was nothing to cover up the nothingness. A Heather Locklear pinup, a Che Guevara poster, one of those M.C. Escher mindfucks where the staircases never end—such things could be counted on to supply subtle psychological welfare that a blank wall of chipping paint did not.

I was about to offer some friendly advice on the subject when something over my shoulder caught my eye. Somehow I'd missed a canvas, a stunning oversized painting of a red 1970s convertible Trans Am coasting down an open highway. The view was from the rear, the Pontiac's taillights zooming off into the dry afternoon heat, the car speeding away under a limitless sky toward mountains jutting fiercely in the distance. The artist had awarded the driver an unkempt flow of hair that seemed to be enjoying the ride as much as the driver himself. And in a nod to the bizarre, a nightmare-sized eel was sprawled out across the backseat, sloping over the side of the car. You couldn't help but be drawn into the motion of the painting, the way the convertible was being propelled down the highway by nothing but freedom's wind. Everything about the scene—the mountains, the sky, the driver's hair—suggested the casting off of limits, a point underscored by the fantastically absurd eel, its slimy morphology lazing on the vinyl, along for the ride to a destination gloriously uncertain.

I had no idea what the significance of the eel was. Did it symbolize menace? Did it represent the past? Was it drying up and dying on the backseat? Did the driver even know the eel was back there? I couldn't think of a reason why the answers to any of those questions would enhance or diminish the restless exhilaration that overcame me in the presence of this painting. At that moment, I would have given anything to dive into the passenger's seat.

"*Trans Am with Electric Eel*," Duncan said, watching me study the piece.

I wished I could make music that made people feel the way this painting made me feel.

"My mom was a marine biologist," the young man explained. "Electric eels were her thing. Obsessed with them, man. Spent her life consumed with trying to catch them and figure them out. She was always flying off to the Amazon or some South American river basin to try to harness the power of the electric eel, to solve their mysteries, like how they survive their own shocks." He spoke drily, chewing on the inside of his cheek. "I grew up on stories about how hard it was to catch one of these babies, how she and her team would have to somehow tire the eels out by forcing them to discharge their electric shocks over and over. It sounds pretty stupid, but those critters plagued her.

"Then one day, before she'd answered her own questions, she just gave up. I guess she realized that she was never going to figure them out. She was never going to find what she was looking for."

His voice trailed off, his eyes still fixed on the Trans Am whizzing away like a blissful bullet.

"A few years ago, I saw this painting at a student art festival. I paid twenty-five bucks for it and sent it to my mom with a nice little note about how it reminded me of her. I just thought she'd enjoy it, you know? I even made some sorry joke about how now she would finally have an electric eel in her house." He let out a quick, rueful laugh. "Know what she did? She sent it back to me. She couldn't look at it because it reminded her of her failures, of all she hadn't accomplished in her life. Cold, right? You'd think she'd want to hang it up in her lonely little fucking shack of a house and stare at it from time to time. But no. She couldn't bear the sight of it—a gift from her only son."

He stared down the painting with bereaved wonder.

I asked him, "If it pisses you off so much, why do you have it on your wall?"

"To remind me of what I don't want to become. I don't want anything to ruin me the way those eels ruined her." Duncan then softened, appearing to surrender to the painting's reward. He looked at me and smiled. "I guess I'm not off to a great start, am I?"

He leaned toward the window and peered back down at the courtyard, where Marin, Alaina, and the two overalled spectators were enjoying their intermission at the theater of the absurd. The same thought must have struck Duncan. "Well, 'all the world's indeed a stage and we are merely players, performers, and portrayers.' That one's also Shakespeare. The Bard sure had a handle on reality."

That wasn't Shakespeare. It was "Limelight" by Rush. Something else Duncan could learn later.

We trudged out of the building in a gallows shuffle, Duncan exchanging staccato shots of eye contact with Marin, Alaina standing nearby restlessly gnawing on gum.

"I'm glad you're not lying in a bloody pile of goo," Marin said to him.

With Duncan gathering the remaining shreds of his dignity, the two youths strolled away like octogenarian lovebirds on a country lane. Or like a mental patient and his orderly in the asylum gardens.

Alaina was looking at me. There was the faintest smudge of a taunt on her face, yet at the same time, exploration, as if she were probing for something she hadn't yet discovered wasn't there. "Well, well, well. And in the bastard there beats a heart."

"Who ever said I was a bastard?"

"Who ever said you were anything but? But hey, you just talked a kid out of splatting himself all over the sidewalk, so I guess you weren't as out of your element as you thought."

My element. The word instantly sent me tunneling. Everything seemed to be swirling wider and wider, no two facets of my life touching anymore. I was just as lost as Duncan, with his dreams of suicide, his Pontiac at large somewhere down the road. I watched him and Marin promenade themselves about the courtyard, the very picture of emotional mayhem, the kind that simmered just below the surface until it erupted into the material world like hellfire and you just knew that some god-awful universe was about to be born.

I said, "I don't have the faintest clue what my element is."

"Well, would you mind putting off looking for it until you've found your legacy?" Alaina teased. "One bullshit existential crisis at a time."

I sucked in a hollow of air and said, "If I'm no longer needed at this clambake, I'll be off."

"Off? Off where? I wasn't done chewing you out for being a whiny little schizo and pulling the plug on the reunion that nobody wants to see happen."

"Well, can we finish that little chat some other time? I need to go." I cleared my throat and unearthed the closest thing I had to grace. "I need to go cut a record."

Alaina's face registered horror movie stupor. "A record?" She stepped forward and depressed my toe under her overpriced footwear. "But wait—I'm confused. I thought you'd made a mistake. Music isn't the answer. Those days are gone, they're never coming back. You looked for them, all right; you looked in the pantry, in the garage, in your sock drawer—"

"You can go fuck yourself, you know that?"

"Oh, I know." She tousled my hair, then made a face and wiped her hand on the grass. "Well, I'm glad to hear it, MoonPie. I don't even want to know what nugget of inspiration that suicidal little puke leveled you with up there. Go tell your second-rate novelty acts to dust off their instruments. I'm booking you guys a studio before you throw another hissy fit and change your mind again."

"Probably a good idea. And we'll do our best to come up with some music you can sell."

"Don't worry your pretty little head about it. Whatever you come up with, I'll get you your record contract. I'll get you a tour, concert halls packed with girls in heat, and dressing rooms with craft beer and candy dishes."

"I want M&M's in those dishes."

"Of course you do."

"But just the green ones."

"You shall have only green M&M's, Mr. Tremble."

"Good. But I might change my mind. I might want only the pink ones."

"They don't make those, pumpkin, but we'll get them for you anyway."

"Indeed you will. It is, after all, the little things that matter."

"That's not true, Theodore," she said. "It is very much the big things."

We stared at each other, each of us fighting back a grin as the seconds passed in this one frozen frame of our lives.

One day I'll die, I thought to myself, and this will be one of the things I did with my time.

Just then, the scene was ruptured by a fire truck raising Cain, men with ladders and bullhorns bursting forth with gallant commotion. Alaina chomped her gum with a casual insolence as a hulking man in suspenders and fire-retardant pants strode toward us. Alaina greeted him with an exaggerated glance at her watch.

"You're just in time," she quipped.

CHAPTER 19

I've lost track of how long I've been out here when a lamp in the living room flicks on behind me and the balcony door slides open. Sara, enrobed in a Race for the Cure T-shirt that hangs down over her knees, steps out into the predawn and asks what time I got in. I find myself unable to speak, so she leads me inside into the pale glow of the lamplight. She is staring into my eyes with deep, profound worry.

And then it all comes out. I tell her I'm done, I'm punching out of my useless fantasies for good. The search for lost things has brought me nothing but emptiness. They'll just have to stay lost. I have an almost panicky need to be with Sara, to be safe in our home. I want never to leave again, I tell her. I want to be with her every single day, raise children together, take vacations in SUVs crammed with toys, crumbs, and snack wrappers. I want to pick out Halloween costumes together. I want to do all that and only that and come home every night and close the door behind me. This is what I want for the rest of my life. Nothing else matters.

I say this and then I drop onto the couch. When I look up, I'm startled to the bone at what I see. Sara is an old woman, eighty-five, older even, her features encroached upon by a latticework of wrinkles and wilting skin, her hair shorter and gray. The old woman—it is Sara, I am sure of it—unfurls a tolerant smile at me, my mind having once again gone adrift, and says, "But honey, we've done all that."

I don't understand. And then I catch my own reflection in the glass balcony door and see that I too am old. I've aged a half century in a minute. I am dizzy with the dawning horror that, addled with an old man's dementia, I've forgotten who I am, I've forgotten the life I've lived. Everything I think I've been experiencing these weeks and months already happened long, long ago.

I shake my head, disbelieving, forcing it all away.

I look around our living room and see photographs of our children. They are adults now, surrounded by families of their own— cherubic boys and girls, our grandchildren, distant reverberations of Sara and me in their cheerful faces.

This can happen. It must happen. You live decades upon decades, and the tired and declining mind erases it all and convinces you that you're forty-five or twenty-five or twelve. That your life is still in bloom, still an engine rumbling with promise under the wing of an airplane.

Sara sits down beside me and drapes her hand over mine. "We've had a wonderful life together." She glances up at one particular frame on the wall, and a familiar shadow returns. "Mostly wonderful."

I follow her eyes. The two-year-old boy on a sand dune squints at us from under the glass rectangle.

"We can't be like this now," I plead. "He needs us."

Sara allows her eyes to see the photograph, and for a moment she is with him on the dune in that blue and windy day that we've held on to our entire lives.

She pats my hand tenderly, our purple veins and bony fingers interwoven. The years have slipped away from me like a weightless astronaut on the blue ring of the world. "That was a long time ago, Teddy. Don't think about such things now."

"We can't be old," I insist. "We have to stay. Someone has to stay and remember."

And then I can't breathe. A sheet is being draped over my face and my last breath is a gravelly snore. I claw helplessly at the sheet but only grow more entangled. Time has sped forward again and it is now the end. I am dead; they are burying me. Struggling for breath, I lash against the airless vault into which I'm being caged forever. The end is here. Soon I will feel nothing.

The sheet is yanked back. My lungs swell with air, the room with daylight. I'm lying in my bed, panting.

Sara's hand touches my shoulder and I spin toward her. She is resting on her elbows, jet-black tresses covering the side of her face. "Are you okay?" she asks, then drops back onto her pillow. I edge over onto her side of the bed and fold my face into the hot, moist smell of sleep.

A few moments later, my heart is still throbbing furiously against my ribs. It wants out.

PART THREE

THE MIX

CHAPTER 20

The lead guitar was a little too prominent in the mix, and Warren was pounding the kick drum so hard that my dead Scottish ancestors had a headache. I raised my hand and the disorganized brew of sound stuttered to a halt.

Warren leaned into the microphone that slanted over his kit like a fondue fork. "Sibilance," he enunciated. "Ssssssibilance. Check, check one. My mic is doing something funky. Too much hiss." He frowned and proceeded to tap on the fuzzy black spit guard that cloaked the mic's rounded grill. "And my *p*s are popping. Pop. Pop. Popping."

Jumbo spoke up. "I can't hear me." He cranked up his amp and played a grating blues riff so loud it sent our index fingers into our ears.

"Down! Down!" I howled. "Way too loud!"

Mack seized the chance to suck down a bottle of Evian, then said, "I'm playing a B flat right before we go into the chorus, but I feel as though I'm the only one."

"You are," Jumbo confirmed. "It's an F. But that doesn't mean the bass can't hit B flat there."

Mack contemplated the implications of accenting the fourth note in the F major chord. "I think it does," she decided.

"Anybody think we're playing it too fast?" I queried the group.

As keeper of the time, Warren took the question personally. "I guess I gave it a little bit more giddyup this time through," he allowed, mopping his glistening forehead with a white hand towel. "It felt like it wanted to be played faster."

We were working through "Goodbye to Myself," a straightforward midtempo slice of rock, a species of song that, despite its conventionality, often proved, at least to me, stubborn and tricky. Even nestled in the reliably uninventive verse-verse-chorus-verse-chorus-bridge-chorus composition structure, such songs worked only when the exact pacing was struck, the precise speed that kept the song both from dragging into sluggishness and from hurrying away into some anxious scramble.

"I'm good with playing it a little up-tempo," Jumbo volunteered. "Kind of swings a bit when it's faster." He was holding his '52 Telecaster Reissue away from his body and fanning the front of his shirt, trying to ventilate the drenched black tee that bore the words "This Girl's Got Bieber Fever!" in hot-pink bubble letters—an accidental purchase, he would have us believe.

This was Tremble, a reinstituted band of aging, ailing, sagging, and limping hopefuls grittily readying itself for the world.

Sonny Rivers had called in a favor to Bic, an old friend with a shabby studio in the semigentrified town of Manayunk, a short drive from downtown Philly. Nobody had booked his East Side Studios for the summer months (although I doubt its lack of appeal was seasonal), so Bic turned it over to us for the dog days of July and August. He greeted us on day one in a tank top and white knee-high socks, handed over the keys, and never made an appearance again. And it wasn't that the rotting wood paneling, the mildewing carpet, the murky lighting, the prehistoric stench of drummer sweat, the dusty sound board, and the Weavers-era recording equipment made you feel unwelcome. It just explained why Bic didn't seem terribly overprotective of the place.

The state of the facility was hardly our most daunting obstacle.

Conveniently, the season afforded greater flexibility for those among us who still clung to their day jobs. As for me, I'd crossed the Rubicon with Morris & Roberts. I had emptied my office of my diplomas, my photo of Sara, and my Ron Jaworski autographed football, thereby inking a permanent hiatus.

When Jumbo arrived at the studio, honking his horn with cheery oafishness, Warren looked up from the trunkful of drums he and I were unloading and appeared dispirited, as if up until that point it hadn't dawned on him that he'd actually be working with Jumbo again. When Warren saw Mackenzie, they both slid into laughter—perhaps at the folly of the universe, perhaps out of mutual embarrassment for having shown up. They exchanged tidy digests of the years, Mack scrolling through Warren's phone and gushing over photos of his wife and son. Jumbo swept Mack up in a bear hug and swung her around until Mack nicked her ankle on a table and needed a Band-Aid. While these reunions unfolded, I busied myself plugging cables into the sound board and transferring guitars from cases to stands. But out of the corner of my eye, I witnessed old friends sizing each other up, noticing the changes lurking beneath the familiar faces as they doled out loose compliments and claimed to have missed each other.

Eventually, we got around to what we came there for and started filling the dingy space with music. In the interest of artistic integrity, and to prevent that unseemly college-band-regrouping-at-the-cookout vibe, we spent the first few weeks in rehearsal with no parental supervision. Sonny would show up later to impose discipline and vision. As a foursome, we rediscovered the places where our contours met, and through both harmony and discord, over hot afternoons, we got to know each other again.

Jumbo, instinctively attuned to the flavor of a song, splashed textural seasonings and exhilarating flourishes all over the music, just as he'd done with the demos. The rhythm section locked in tight almost immediately, and Mackenzie and Warren, true professionals, winked and grinned at each other when the groove was just right. I'd forgotten how easy it was to fall in love with the crisp sound of an open chord on a telecaster, or how a rich harmony vocal, kicked up in the mix and riding shotgun on a soaring melody, could make you shake your head and marvel, I didn't know music could sound like that.

I did my best to step out of the way and allow old dynamics to resurrect themselves. I behaved toward Mackenzie in precisely the way I would have had there not been multiple White House occupants and a Von Dutch trucker cap craze since the last time we'd recorded together. Everyone had shown up; the least I could do was not make things weird.

One particularly sweltering day, we flung open the door to take a water break in the parking lot. As we stood there with stains on our shirts that would've made us look like triathletes had we not looked so unlike triathletes, an old woman came ambling down from the porch of her row house. She was moving toward us snail-like but determined, her rigid osteoporotic hunch suggesting peeve, and we prepared ourselves to catch hell for noising up the neighborhood. There was no telling how long this prune had lived across the street from a quasi-professional rehearsal space, how many bands she'd bawled out for disrupting her midmorning siesta. She labored onto the sidewalk and jutted out her wrinkled face to get a good look at the hoodlums who were making such a racket, at which point it crossed my mind that we were a little old to be getting yelled at for being loud. For the longest of moments, she stared at us, and just as I was poised to jump in and preempt her reprimand with an apology and an empty promise to keep it down, the old hag bleated, "You people are pretty fucking good."

We took it as a good omen—Lord knows we were looking for them—and gifted our first new fan with a bottle of water for her long trek home.

We blew through the old songs as if sliding into a loose pair of corduroys, and stumbled through the new stuff like the amateurs we'd allowed ourselves to become. The technical aspects of playing required some modulating on our part. The mix was often hideously out of whack and sometimes a microphone would suddenly emit an explosive shock, nearly searing off my lips. Even standing together in band formation took some adjusting to. For one thing, I found myself squinting down at the frets of my guitar, growing more convinced by the minute that we now needed a band optometrist. For another, I had to reacclimate to Jumbo's bulk. We were roughly the same height, but he just felt bigger. Being Jumbo required more space. There was, I'd learned, a relativity to acceptable workplace girth. For years, I'd been sequestered away at a law firm where, almost as a rule, people kind of let themselves go. (If the folks down the hall were going for a slice of sausage and pepperoni and you declined, it had better be because you were having a colonoscopy in an hour.) Whereas I was a waify little thing among the lawyers, in the bony world of rock, where people didn't eat any healthier but still managed to appear gaunt and strung out, I was Dom DeLuise. Jumbo, however, still made the rest of us look like action figures.

One morning, Warren and I were sipping coffee outside when we overheard acoustic music kicking to life through the studio walls. At first, there was just the sound of Jumbo's easy strumming, killing time during a caffeine interlude. Then Mack's bass glided in, and soon, after a few steady measures, there was singing. An earnest, naked voice: Mack's. The song was "Glad and Sorry" by Faces, a melancholic ballad with a steady, insistent beat that seemed to welcome the unadorned vocals of someone who'd heretofore only sung lead in her shower. I stood mesmerized—at the very sound of her, at the unassuming comfort with which she'd taken the mic. And when the chorus crept around and Jumbo chimed in with effortless harmony—as if this wasn't an impromptu jam, as if they'd actually played this song together at any point before this spare moment had presented itself—I realized I never wanted to hear anyone else sing "Glad and Sorry" ever again.

Warren and I waited until the song ended before stepping through the door. Mack looked over at me with a shy grin, then retreated to the flimsy barstool that she'd positioned next to her amp. I swallowed a sigh and thought to myself, This is how it starts.

A few weeks darted by. One day, a summer shower beating upon the sizzling streets, the door flung open and in strode Sonny. With his hands in the pockets of his charcoal slacks, he nodded around the room at each of us, not necessarily with approval. He eyed the studio, taking in the booth, the upright piano, the vintage control board, and the stained yellow sofa propped up on three legs behind it.

"Bic has really let this place fall to shit," he said by way of greeting. "I've recorded in a lot places, but never in the middle of a rain forest. No matter. Towering genius disdains a beaten path."

Warren winked at him. "Lincoln, right?"

"Our emancipator, motherfucker."

And so it began. I happily readjusted to the creative process as piloted by Sonny Rivers. Although given to occasional fits of speech making, he was generally not a gushy guy. "Let's move on" was high praise. The pursuit of his vision rarely entailed telling you how to play. Instead, he told you what to feel. He spoke up only to motivate. If he was struck ill by a lyric or even an entire verse, he'd merely repeat the offending words, his slow delivery revealing their shittiness: "So, at this point in the song, you want to sing 'I slipped on a banana peel and ended up beside the one I love.' Do I have that right?" That was usually enough to get you redrafting. In the end, you wanted to do it his way because his way worked. Careers were born and reborn under Sonny's sonic guidance.

Considerable pressure for a lawyer, a high school teacher, a sex therapist, and well, whatever the hell Jumbo was.

A studio track is essentially a big lie, an illusion of musicians grabbing their instruments and cruising through a song, each player hitting all the proper notes at all the proper times at all the proper levels. A recording begins as a series of isolated performances extracted from musicians standing tired and alone in a booth over the course of repeated laborious takes—lasting hours, sometimes days—after which they're all slung together and mixed into a seamless, contrived blend. When you hear some hot dish singing her sweaty ass off, utterly depleting herself by song's end, she probably had a kale smoothie and a sushi roll, possibly even a marriage, between the opening line and the final chorus. Your favorite piano track likely took weeks to get right and was put down in fragments. It wasn't even a real piano. Because of the long stretches of tedium, recording an album can often feel like a spectator sport. People take up addictions simply for something to do.

Sonny also happened to be tremoring his way through a smoking cessation program, so he was not looking for a minute of downtime, lest his fingers start fidgeting in the direction of a pack of Newports. He occupied himself by occupying the hell out of us with long hours in the studio. Warren commuted back and forth from Lambertville to maintain a sense of normalcy with Lauren and Patrick; Jumbo crashed with an unnamed childhood friend (I was just happy it wasn't me); Mackenzie sublet an apartment in Old City, taking the opportunity to live in an area of town that had always struck her fancy; and I got to sleep in my own bed every night, which helped me remain somewhat connected to Sara—who seemed somewhat involved in divorcing her husband and somewhat involved in rediscovering him.

One Friday night, as I walked in from a long week in the studio, she greeted me at the door wearing dark jeans, a red silk shirt, and a freshly paved path of lipstick. "Are you up for a movie?" she asked.

Soon, we were sitting at a bar table in a rollicking saloon across the street from the theater, sipping cold lager and eating turkey burgers with sweet potato fries. At the last minute, we sprung over the curb, bought tickets and candy, and dropped into our seats just as the house lights dimmed and a commercial for Stella Artois burst upon the screen with a deafening flash.

Sara had selected a film by an Iranian director with a string of critically lauded dramas. During a heavy scene in which a man forced to leave Tehran during the 1979 revolution is reunited with his family many years later, Sara, without looking at me, placed a Junior Mint into my mouth. As I chewed it, I looked over at her, but she remained fixed on the movie, her eyes flickering with the light that danced off the screen.

When the credits were over, we walked down the block to a coffee shop that served the best vanilla latte in the city, according to Sara. The barista, a young man with hoops in his earlobes and a beard that reached his sternum, smiled with familiarity at Sara and said, "No whipped cream, right?"

Up against the window, on barstools for the second time that night, the soothing tones of Miles Davis's trumpet separating us from the brigades of bar hoppers outside, we sat together and praised the movie. Sara then asked how the record was coming along. I started to tell her how the music was really starting to take flight, what a thrill it was to hear these naked compositions being forged into actual songs. I stopped myself and looked into my cappuccino.

"You don't want to hear about this," I said. "It's boring if you're not actually there."

I also didn't think it fair or wise to amplify the joy I was getting from a venture that didn't involve her but did involve Mackenzie. Mack was still something of an unknown quantity to her. And to me, for that matter.

"It's not boring to me," Sara replied, resting her cheek in her palm. "I've been living with a lawyer all this time. Talk about boring."

So I talked a bit. Sara listened with apparent interest, and stirred another half pack of sweetener into her cup.

The conversation shifted to more mundane topics, and she reminded me that we were low on coffee beans. "They have that Colombian blend you like here," she said, glancing over at the display table that was neatly lined with brown vacuum-sealed bags.

I turned my head. "Nice. I can never find that."

"I know. Let's grab one."

As I stood in line, the beans crunching together in the bag, I looked over at Sara and felt a rush of warmth. She and I really were more than roommates. We had a life together with routines that gave each of us solace. We curled up under blankets in front of movies, she invariably turning to me with some dubious theory about an actor. ("That guy's really British. You can totally tell.") Sometimes under the blanket my hand would slide over her thigh and we'd pause the movie and lead each other into the bedroom. Much later she'd slip out to the bathroom, her long spindly legs unsteady, needing a few steps to reacquaint themselves with the symmetry of walking. On her way back, she'd lift the shade and peer out at the night, checking to see if the snow had started to fall. She'd stand there for a moment too long and I'd wonder what she was looking at, or looking for. Then she'd dive back under the covers into my folded arm, and the next thing I knew, it would be 2:09 a.m., the hall light still on, the movie still paused.

She was nursing the last of her latte now and watching as a gathering of college boys outside the window shoved each other playfully for the benefit of girls standing in poses of affected disengagement. Sara seemed a visitor in a museum, witnessing from the safety of a glass barrier the unfolding of some evolutionarily dictated mating ritual. So this is how the humans behave, her bemused gaze seemed to say.

How many times had I felt that same isolating sense of wonder that I was now reading on her face? That aloneness in the thick of everything.

Having Sara had kept me from drifting off into the shadows, from truly disappearing into myself. Just maybe I'd done the same for her.

Everything came together on the day Jumbo wore a bandana. It appeared out of nowhere, plucked out of his arsenal of inexplicable accessories. It was black and accented with undersea-green paisley swirls that put one in an astrological frame of mind. The way it was draped over his head would have, on anyone else, connoted menace—urban gang, seventeenth-century pirate—but on him looked like a boxed Halloween costume from Walmart.

"What's with the kerchief?" Sonny frowned as Jumbo took a seat in the booth, rested his red Gretsch on his knee, and adjusted the large-banded headphones over his ears. He was preparing to lay down an arpeggio guitar line on "The Warmth of Disease," a song that had awakened me in the middle of the night, demanding to be written, one that I'd managed to quietly cage with a Dictaphone and a nylon-string acoustic.

Once all the fussing over tuning and sound levels had been sorted out, Sonny leaned over the board, pressed the button that allowed communication between the control room and the isolation booth, and spoke: "Don't think of this track as merely texture. This is going to be a part. When somebody describes this song to his friends, he's going to say, 'You know the one with that guitar line? Ba ba ba, ba ba ba, ba ba ba.' You are helping to define this song."

Warren and I were watching from the yellow couch behind Sonny. Warren kept holding his bag of dried mango in front of my face; I kept shaking him off.

"When you play this line," Sonny continued, "I want you to picture your guitar leading the listener through the song, being there for them, something for them to trust when the singer drops out or when the drums get moody or the bass goes a little peripatetic."

I looked at Warren and mouthed "peripatetic." With a resolute nod, he mouthed it right back.

"Dude, I'm all over it," Jumbo declared.

"Let's see," Sonny grumbled. "Ready now. Here it comes."

Then, at the very last second before Sonny hit the record button, Jumbo magically produced a pair of cheap surf-shop sunglasses and slid them on. Warren groaned. Between the headphones, the bandana, and the plastic Ray-Ban knockoffs, the guitar player looked a little like a petty dope hustler and a little like Hulk Hogan. Sonny glanced back at us but decided there were no words. Then he pressed the button.

At first, all that came through the speakers was the pregnant click of Warren's sticks counting off four measures in three-four time. Then the studio flooded with music. The rich tone of Jumbo's broken chords seemed to run like syrup over the crisp hi-hat strikes and rim shots supplied by the drum track. It drifted over Mackenzie's wandering bass and weaved the whole thing into a slow sonic freight car rolling across an open plain. Each one of us was transfixed. It was for moments like this that I put up with everything else that came with that meandering mess of humanity, that avalanche in a china shop.

When the song was finished, Sonny looked up and stated simply, "You're done."

Jumbo grinned with pride at what was often Sonny's most effusive tribute. Consumed with self-congratulation, he forgot that sunglasses tended to impair one's vision when one wore them in a dark recording studio, and standing up, he suddenly found himself tangled in a snake pit of cables. He rocked clumsily, then finally tripped and crashed into the termite-weakened, asbestos-riddled wall.

"Please, man!" Sonny yelled in anguish. "Get out of my booth!"

Lead vocals were next, so I got up.

Mack was smirking at me. "You really want to follow that act?"

I shook my head.

"Listen, Tremble, I love this song," she said.

"Yeah?"

"Yeah. So don't blow it."

I paused. "I'll try not to, but just so I understand, what's the *it* in that sentence?"

"The *it* is the noise that your throat is about to make in that little room right there. You'll only make it for a few minutes, but it will be captured and listened to for all eternity."

"And by eternity, you mean the next six months. A year tops."

"So maybe not eternity, but long after we're all dead, that's for sure," she said, crossing her legs and nestling herself into one of the beanbagesque sofa cushions.

"Thanks. That was kind of you."

"What?" She giggled. "Just trying to help you maintain perspective, to appreciate the weight of the moment. But hey—no pressure."

"Christ, Mackenzie. Whatever happened to 'let's just play the damn thing'?"

She smiled. "Okay. Just play the damn thing."

I started for the recording room.

"But don't blow it," she called after me.

Inside the booth, I cleared my throat while sliding on the headphones and smoothing out the crumpled lyric sheet on the stand. Sonny came in to toy with the microphone boom. "You stand right there," he ordered. "Don't move. And don't touch my mic."

As I ran through a couple of takes, I could feel myself shrinking. The lyrics were the weak link in this song. The imagery was hokey, the metaphors mixed. Pouring cold bottled water down my stupid, thirty-eight-year-old throat, I tried not to notice my bandmates staring at me team-photo-like from the couch.

"Hold up a sec," Sonny commanded from behind the sound board, detaining me in the grip of his stare. "This song, 'The Warmth of Disease'—what's going on here? What do you think about these words you're singing?"

I heaved a sigh. I hated these inquisitions. It was his way of leading me to criticism.

"I don't know. They're a little out there. I guess I liked them originally, but now they're sounding lame." My eyes drifted to the lower half of the lyric sheet. "Now that I look at it, I don't know what's going on in the second verse. I was obviously shooting for a double entendre with the word *infectious*, but maybe that's too clinical. Yeah, you're right. The lyrics need work."

"No, they don't," he said with monastic certitude. He took a sip of his coffee, which he'd been consuming in frightening quantities, having swapped a nicotine addiction for a caffeine one. "You've got some lyrics here that knock the goddamn wind out of me, man, and they're carried upon one of the most natural melodies I've ever heard from you. I've awakened in the middle of the night and heard this song in my head. I feel like I've known this song my whole life. My mother could have rocked me to sleep with this song before I even knew what music was. But I swear on my empty grave, if you sing it the way you did on those practice takes, I'm going to cut it from this record and go to court to get you permanently barred from ever playing it again."

He banged his fist on the table, startling me and sending a tiny brown splash over the brim of his cup. "If we're going to make an awful album, it's going to be boldly awful. We will not make one that limps into awfulness, that isn't even sure if it's awful."

Then he pointed at me, a strong finger jutting out of an autocratic fist. "This song deserves better than what I've been hearing. You're not going after it. Go after it! Deliver this song the way it wants to be delivered. Picture something in your head, something you want more than anything else in this life. Some person. Some dream. Some place. You decide, but think about it, hold it right before your eyes. Then sing as if you're telling that thing how much you want it. You need to convince that thing that you want so bad to give itself to you. You know what that feels like, Teddy, I know you do. There isn't a beating heart out there that doesn't, and it's your job to access that frequency, that cosmic longing that puts all of us in the same leaky goddamn canoe. For the rest of my life—the rest of my life!—I want that desire to drip out of the air every time I hear this song. I'll hear that desire, I'll know you speak my language, and I'll feel a little less alone in this life because of it."

After that, nothing moved but the ceiling fan, its wood-plastic blades clicking over the control room. At that moment, the isolation booth had never felt more isolating.

Then the music began to flow into the headphones. As I waited to sing, my eyes found Mackenzie sitting on the back of the sofa in brown capri pants and a light-blue shirt with a scoop neckline, her bare feet up on the cushion.

I closed my eyes and pondered Sonny's words. What was my dream? No simple question for a man about to begin his fifth decade on the planet, an age by which most people had surrendered or at least downsized their ambitions.

When the faces of my bandmates swept through my head, I found myself wondering if this, right here, was it, if this was the thing I wanted more than anything else the world could offer. And I considered what it was that had brought each of my old friends here to sweat out the summer in this dilapidated room. Why had they allowed me to scare them up out of the afternoon of their lives?

With my eyes tightly shut, my neck craned toward the silver microphone, a look of twisted struggle on my face, a voice unknown to me sailed out of my mouth, and I realized that what I wanted more than anything was the wisdom to know what it was I wanted.

In a split second, the song was over. Red-cheeked and drenched, I hazarded a look out into the control room. Warren and Mack stared back at me inscrutably. Jumbo ruptured the stillness by pumping his fist, pointing a fat finger at me, and mouthing "You!"

Sonny was reclining in his chair, his browning coffee cup held to his mouth, his eyes closed. All at once, he wiped his upper lip and leaned into the mic. "You're done."

CHAPTER 21

Sonny couldn't always sermonize competency out of us. When we took up our instruments and played him "Painless Days," which we all thought was the song most likely to end up under a DJ's needle, Sonny listened with a doubtful scowl and said, "I don't see what all the fuss is about." Decreeing the composition "undercooked," he ordered me to write him a bridge. I took to the piano and attempted to cure it right then and there. I proceeded to improvise, and Sonny proceeded to shout out words of discouragement like "derivative," "uninspired," "beneath you," and "cut that out," until it became abundantly clear that my efforts would not soon produce anything that anyone should have to listen to. "It must not be a song yet," our producer declared, and sent everyone home early.

"Except you," he said, pointing at me. "Stay and fix it. Bic is gonna want this yeast infection of a studio back eventually."

As the people I thought were my friends filed out and abandoned me, I cracked open a Snapple from the mini-fridge and started riffing. I tried everything. A twangy little bounce that got too cozy with Conway Twitty. Analog synths that gave sorry birth to a cheeseball "Uh-oh, it's magic" outtake. Even a jaunty piano that was too much Elton circa '88 and not enough Elton circa '73.

A few futile hours later, I threw in the towel. "Must not be a song yet," I grumbled in my best impression of our leader.

As I locked up, I remembered that Sara had planned on visiting Josie and Wynne's house that night, as friends were gathering there to welcome their new baby. The couple had recently traveled to Ethiopia to claim their eleven-month-old son, and since they'd been back but a week, Sara had only met the kid through e-mailed photos from Addis Ababa. In all the pictures, the new mothers looked disheveled and thrilled, while the little tyke's startlingly wide eyes conveyed how deeply confused, but not altogether uncharmed, he was by all this. I decided to meet Sara out there.

The profusion of cars buffering the house forced me to park down the block in the wooded Mount Airy neighborhood. It was a community where people settled and took up residence for generations, where the wishfully hippie or bohemian middle class could live affordably with a front porch and an undersized lawn and still deflect accusations of having moved to the suburbs.

Wynne opened the door and laid eyes upon the scuzzball of dried sweat that stood before her. "Well, holy fucking shit. Look who it is," she exclaimed.

"Congratulations," I said. "How's motherhood?"

"Great so far," Wynne replied, her flowing fountain of curly blond locks bouncing in step with her head. She was tall and big-boned and seemed to go out of her way to downplay her naturally pretty facial features, as if being conventionally beautiful was somehow sexist— and conventional. "It's real exciting shit, Teddy." She cuffed me on the shoulder and added, "You should try it some time."

As she shuttled me through the house, I spotted decorating choices that betrayed Sara's thumbprint, like the sconce that was a close cousin of the one in our condo, or the slender vase that had become her trademark.

"Teddy!" I heard Josie's raspy croak before I saw her step out of the pack of guests congregating in the living room. She held an almond-skinned baby. "Sara didn't tell me you were coming." She smeared an affectionate kiss onto my cheek, then tilted her head of spiky hair at the baby. "This is Miguel."

Miguel. If there was a reason for that gratuitous conversation piece of a name, I didn't want to hear it. Miguel fixed a serious look on me, the whites of his eyes hypnotically watchful.

I looked at the child. "Good luck, Miguel. You're going to need it."

A cursory scan of the room revealed no trace of Sara.

"He's really cute, Josie," I said. The remark felt hollow without a more human display, so I pinched the kid's cheek.

"He is cute, isn't he?" Josie gushed with a grin that wrapped all the way around her trendy maroon spectacles. "I guess Sara's coming later?"

"I guess," I said, pulling out my phone and thumbing a quick text.

"I'm so glad you're here, Teddy," Josie said, petting my chest to show me just how glad.

The trip, she told me, had been a blissfully exhausting ordeal. Initially, Miguel was less than overjoyed to be handed to this pair of ghosts, and he spent the first couple of days bawling his way from one nap to the next. But holed up in a hotel room for a week with these new mommies of his, he soon got to thinking they weren't half bad, wooing him as they were with Elmo puppets, Cheerios, toy phones, and unreasonable quantities of love. The jet lag, sleep deprivation, and capsized routines could have taken a harsher toll on Josie and Wynne, who were in their late forties and thus somewhat less elastic than most new parents, but what they lacked in youth they made up for in zest. They were the happiest fucking mess you ever did see.

"Sara told me the big news," Josie said. She was smiling at the baby, so much so that I thought maybe Miguel was the one with the news. "The band? The album?"

"Yeah, well, we'll see how it goes."

"That's huge. Huge," Josie affirmed. "I'm so proud of you."

"You are?"

"It takes serious guts to commit to something you love." She slapped my cheek lightly with her one free hand. "You'll never re-gret it."

And yet regret was the emotion that was most prominent in the mix these days.

Wynne sauntered up to me. "Where's Sara?" she asked.

I shrugged. "I thought she'd be here." I consulted the phone in my palm but saw no response to my text.

Ravi, from Sara's office, was there, his connection to the proceed-ings unclear. Next to him, and already as tall, was his twelve-year-old son, Pritham. Despite shuffling with embarrassment at the fact of his father's existence, to say nothing of the unique shade of his old man's sport coat—it was the color of poorly applied spray tan—the kid never ventured away from his dad's side.

"Have you seen Sara?" I asked Ravi.

He shook his head. "By the time I left the office, she was already gone." He touched his son's forearm. "You know, Pritham, this man used to be in a very famous band. In the mideighties, right, Teddy?"

I winced. "Thanks, Ravi."

Pritham bobbed mechanically. "Cool beans." Then, at his dad's prod-ding, he proceeded to regale me with captivating tales of soccer camp.

A little while later, both concerned and suspicious about Sara's whereabouts, I decided to call her. I stood in a quiet corner of the liv-ing room beside a sketch of a bull standing on its hind legs, a lonely lightbulb dangling over the bull's head. The animal stared back at me with wry self-awareness, as if he understood just how out of place he was in this drawing. It struck me that every single human being who took in that arresting little sketch must have felt an instant connec-tion to it, thinking, Okay, tell me again how I ended up here.

Before my phone had reached across the airwaves and rung Sara's, I heard Wynne's voice lilting behind me. "Teddy, look what the cat dragged in."

I spun around and saw Sara. She was elegantly dressed in a long brown leather skirt and a white blouse unbuttoned at the top. Either she'd already been equipped with a glass of white or she'd driven over with it in her hand.

"Teddy." Sara gaped at me like I was an obsessed extramarital one-night stand who'd started showing up at her kid's Little League games. "I had no idea you were coming."

"Apparently," I said.

"Well, ain't this a kick in the ass," Wynne hooted. "It's been a long time since I've seen you two in the same room. I was beginning to think you were the same person, like maybe Sara was Teddy in drag or something."

I pulled back the edges of my mouth. "I'd rather you leave me out of your weird little fantasies, if it's all the same to you."

Sara looked at me and collapsed her forehead into the bridge of her nose. This was code for *What gives?*

"We finished up early at the studio, so I figured I'd surprise you," I explained. "Where were you?"

"At a client's," she said. "You should've told me you were coming."

I eyed her carefully, sussing out clues of deception. Josie and Wynne's studio was obviously unavailable to her as an alibi tonight. The only other place she could've been was with Billy, of whom she spoke only in the most elliptical of terms. My periodic inquiries into the status of the divorce had been met with shallow nonanswers, unremitting evasiveness. Something else that was none of my fucking business.

We were joined by Josie, who was leading her mother over by the wrist. "You met Teddy, Mom, but this," our hostess said grandly, "is Sara. Sara Rome."

Josie's mother, a peppy little dumpling, practically exploded. "Of course! The interior designer. Aren't you adorable!"

"Congratulations," Sara said. "Miguel's beautiful."

The little round woman clutched her heart with great theater. "Is he not the most precious thing you've ever seen?"

Then she proceeded to catalog all her favorite decorative strokes around the house that Sara had authored. Sara modestly accepted the compliments, though she did point to the painting above the fire-place, a blighted wintry street scene, and remarked, "I still think the Vincenzo goes there."

"I know I've said this a zillion times to Josephine, but I'm getting your number tonight. Mel and I haven't updated in thirty years."

When Josie's mother scooted away to attend to her suddenly irritable grandson, I noticed Sara staring at something over my shoulder, something drawing her attention between her increasingly aggressive sips of wine. Finally, when her furtive glances had elevated to the point of obviousness, I turned and followed her eyes, discovering that the object of her absorption was Pritham, Ravi's twelve-year-old. It didn't take long for me to realize why.

"I didn't know Ravi had a son," I said to her carefully.

"Yes, you did. And he has three."

"Anyway. You look really pretty tonight."

She smiled at me as if finally buying into the suitability of my presence there.

Then, a strange look overtook her face, and she snatched my hand and tugged me out of the room. Toward the back of the house we moved hurriedly, past the island in the kitchen where a stack of dirty plates leaned precariously by the sink.

Sara opened a door and flicked on a light. We stood atop a rickety staircase.

"Where are you taking me?" I asked.

A finger to her lips, she pulled the door closed behind us and led me down the steps. The cellar was furnished with a sprawling old mushroom of a sofa, presumably deposited there to live out the end of its life in peace, and was floored with a red Persian rug that fueled the illusion that the entire basement could levitate as if on a magic carpet.

My attention was instantly hooked by a pearly iridescence under track lighting at the back of the room. I looked over and beheld an array of mosaics suspended across the walls. They were gorgeous, mesmerizing creations, some ovoid, some rectangular, one shaped like a starfish, another the female form. Each consisted of hundreds of glass tiles bursting with color, exploding with light.

"Did Josie do all these?" I asked, marveling.

"And Wynne. They were reluctant to hang them, but I insisted."

I watched Sara adore her friends' art, her lips pursed in placid wonder.

"They're amazing," I said.

"Get closer. The detail is staggering. You can really lose yourself in them." She pointed to a large rectangular piece farther down the wall. "I think that one's my favorite."

It was a silhouette of a solitary tree on a hill, the evening sky behind it rendered in swirling layers of orange, yellow, pink, and purple. A circular mirror was positioned high in the right corner to signify the moon.

"This is what you do when you're hanging out at their studio," I said, as much to myself as to her.

Sara nodded weakly. "Sort of. They do it much better, obviously."

It wasn't obvious to me. I'd seen her mosaics and had always felt some kind of power emanating from them. I'd seen my reflection in the tiny mirrors, I'd been swept into the meticulously ordered randomness of the tiles. For someone who'd always had to pretend to love art, it came surprisingly easy to me to love Sara's.

"You're a good artist, Sara. And I really like that I live with one."

A concealed smile glowed just beneath her cheeks. "Me too."

We hung around the party for another half hour or so, and Sara didn't let go of my hand the entire time. As we were leaving, Wynne walked us to the door and said, "I sure hope the rest of these jackasses follow your lead. We're trying to get Miguel on a fucking sleep schedule here."

Having consumed two glasses of wine, Sara declared herself unfit for the wheel and decided to drive home with me. We strolled down the street to where my car sat cradled under a curbside beech tree. Before I could turn the ignition, Sara reached out, gripped my face with two hands, and pulled me into a long kiss. The taste of her mouth, so eager, so present, was almost unrecognizable to me.

Her hands disappeared, and soon I felt the button of my jeans unhook and my zipper being yanked down.

"Whoa," I blurted out. "Here?"

She looked at me, wild and slinky through her mane of black hair.

"We're at a baby shower," I said.

She leaned over and I felt her tongue in my ear. "It's not a baby shower."

As she probed for the fly of my boxers, I peered through the windows. "I don't know about this. Half your office will be coming through that door in five minutes."

"So?" came her defiant reply. And just as I scolded myself—What kind of musician are you?—I realized it was too late to unshame her. With a sigh, she fell back into the passenger seat, a blend of depletion and bewilderment on her face. She was the bull on hind legs in the painting. *Okay, tell me again how I ended up here.*

"I don't know what you want us to be," she said. "Sometimes I don't know *if* you want us to be."

For most of the drive, she sat in silence with her elbow angled against the door. Passing fits of light swept through the car and corrupted the darkness inside. As we exited the highway and glided through the city streets, which were now hissing under us with a smoky sheen of light rain, she spoke quietly to the window. "I got divorced today."

I felt a sudden clenching in my chest.

"Jesus. Are you okay?"

She said nothing and leaned her forehead against the cool glass, oblivious to the high-rises, brownstones, and occasional late-night dog walkers gliding past. As for me, I didn't know exactly what I was feeling. Fear. Relief. The disquiet of a belated revelation.

"You should've told me," I said. "I could've come with you."

I, who in her eyes didn't know what I wanted us to be, didn't know *if* I wanted us to be.

"It's okay," she said, her breath shaky but rising with hopefulness. Her mind was drifting back to the lawyer's office where they'd signed the papers today. Drifting to Billy and away from me.

CHAPTER 22

"Listen—it's not enough to be good. We have an obligation to be interesting, to not be obvious."

That afternoon, Sonny was all up in Jumbo's grill. It was validating whenever another human being reprimanded or otherwise lost his or her patience with our guitar player.

"We know you're technically proficient," Sonny went on, as Jumbo blinked out at him from the recording booth. "Who cares? Technical proficiency does nothing for me. You're in my studio because of your ability to make choices with that there Strat, because of this instinct of yours about what should be done, not just what can be done. I'm not hearing that decision making on this song. You're boring the shit out of me. What you're playing me I can find in any old McDonald's." He pronounced it *MacDonald's*. "Don't bring fast food into my studio. I want a Moroccan market at midnight! Take me to an outdoor churrascaria on the beaches of Rio and serve me something that sizzles!"

Jumbo began to nod, his fleshy face ballooning into a cocksure grin. "I totally get it now. You're looking for a Latin vibe."

Warren and I decided that was a good time for a walk.

"Any word from Mack?" he asked, as we stood at the counter of the coffee shop down the street. Our bass player had traveled back to Pittsburgh for a follow-up visit with her oncologist.

"Not yet," I said. "But she wasn't worried. She says she's been feeling like a million bucks."

I knocked twice on the counter and Warren held up two crossed fingers.

"Look, I can't believe you talked any of us into doing this," Warren said. "But Mack? She had the best reason to pass."

"Or maybe the best reason not to," I suggested.

We dropped into the chrome fifties-era diner chairs and creaked backward from the Formica table. The dull murmurs from the two or three other patrons afforded our eardrums a much-needed respite. We lazed at the table, staring out the window.

"Going well so far, wouldn't you say?" Warren ventured.

"I'm cautiously optimistic," I said tepidly. Confidence was an emotion well out of reach for someone of my particular station.

"You're aware of the irony here, right? Your optimism is always cautious, your enthusiasm always guarded. Yet you're the songwriter, the one we rely on for passion, for fire!"

"I got fired up over my so-called legacy, did I not?"

"A colossal abuse of the word, I admit, but I'm clearly overpaying my penance for that phone call."

He took a slow sip of coffee, then leaned back professorially. "You ever hear of Henri Rousseau?"

"Sure. The French artist. The guy who painted jungles."

"I teach my students about him. We study a lot of his work—*The Dream, Tiger in a Tropical Storm, Eve and the Serpent*—and we talk about primitivism, painting in the naïve style. Rousseau takes you into the forest through a child's eyes. It's dense and exotic, there are wild animals and fleshy naked women, all painted with bold colors, all seductive and fantastical."

I sipped as the art teacher evangelized.

"Here's my question to you," he said. "Do you know which actual jungles he was painting? Which jungles Rousseau visited for inspiration?"

I shook my head.

"Not a one," Warren answered. "Henri never left France. This man, famous for painting the world's lush jungles, never actually saw one. The botanical gardens in Paris were probably the closest he ever got."

"What are you trying to say? What's the big lesson here, teach?"

"I'm just talking, Teddy. I'm not trying to teach you anything," he said with an oblique deadpan. "But sometimes there's a lot of real estate between a man and his legacy—wouldn't you say?"

"That's a terrible example, Square. Rousseau had the opposite problem. His legacy exceeded his experience. He had nothing to correct—wouldn't *you* say?"

"So what's more important—the way you spend your days on this earth or the way posterity views it?" Warren posed. "Your life or your legacy?"

"One of them is around a lot longer."

"They both die, dummy."

I reclined and kicked my heel onto a neighboring chair. "See? You are trying to teach me something."

"I couldn't if I tried."

Then one morning, with an unvarnished lack of ceremony, Sonny brought down the curtain. A prelunch sluggishness had set in. Warren and Mack had just returned from a bakery, and we were all milling about near the mushy banana of a sofa while Sonny frowned under his headphones, listening, concentrating, occasionally adjusting volume levels. Eventually, he stood and faced us.

"That'll do it."

"What's next?" I asked.

"Nothing's next." He broke off a corner of Warren's lemon poppy seed scone. "Pack up. We're done."

We all exchanged uneasy glances. Despite weeks of hard labor, abuse of both the verbal and physical varieties, I hadn't quite arrived at a place where any of this felt complete.

"Done, as in finished?" Warren asked.

"You're happy with it?" I ventured.

The producer shot me a cool look, as if the state of his happiness was any of my goddamn business.

The tracks still needed to be mixed, mastered, and otherwise tamed into something that sounded complete. But now it was Alaina's show. Her long fingers tapping together in a Bond villain power triangle, she'd concoct the ultimate scheme for world domination, which, in this instance, entailed channeling our product into the crowded bay of musical relevancy. She would know the variables that dictated in whose lap to park the tapes—or park herself, if need be. She would know that signing with one record company meant that only the younger demographic would hear about us and that signing with another ensured that they never would. While examining her nails, Alaina would stoke her own fires of cunning invention. She'd first dangle the masterpiece in front of Colin Stone at MCA; he'd earned it, having cohabitated with the bassist. If Colin passed, there was George Glick, the big fat windbag at Interscope who hit on her at Bonnaroo last year and apparently thought her standards dropped whenever she entered Tennessee airspace. If George passed, there was the Weasel, Clay Hapgood, who was still at Capitol, still making mountains of misjudgments, and who would do anything Alaina asked because he still regretted passing on Regina Spektor.

That was for another day. For now, no further instruments or voices were required to realize the dozen or so songs that would become Tremble's comeback album. Our anticlimactic ending was upon us. Mackenzie was the first to start gathering her gear.

"I'm sure going to miss this place," Jumbo said mawkishly.

Sonny stared at him. "Not everything is worthy of sentimentality."

Within a few hours, we'd sleeved our cables, committed our guitars and drums to their cases, and loaded up our cars. The afternoon was thick with all the promise and ambivalence of a college graduation.

Outside, I slammed Mack's trunk shut and dusted off my hands.

She was headed downtown to empty out her Old City sublet and hoped to be heading westward through a turnpike tollbooth by rush hour. As she squinted up at me, I suddenly felt that this was all over too soon.

"The next few months could be quiet, what with Alaina working her tawdry magic," I said. "In the meantime, we'll probably have to start thinking about our live show. I guess that means we'll be seeing more of each other."

Mack smiled down at her blue suede Adidases. "That was the idea, wasn't it?"

"I'm really glad you were here."

"I'm glad you asked me."

I leaned in and hugged her, indulging my senses in the essence of her cheek and neck. The twitch of muscle memory bade me to hold on to her, this thing I'd craved for years of my life, for fear I'd never get close enough again to smell the notes of heather and jasmine in the tangle of her hair. Like the girl on the train station platform. The one who gets away. I didn't know if I was ready.

I hauled my gear back to the condo and dropped it all in the living room. Standing there in the midday vacancy of the apartment, a commotion rose up inside me. My first thought was to call Sara.

"You did it," she said, sounding just as surprised as the band members. "I'm proud of you."

"It's a strange feeling," I said meditatively.

"You made an album. You made a fucking album!" Complications loomed—for me, for the band, for her—but they were not part of this moment, and the purity of Sara's joy in this moment justified the profanity. "I can't wait to hear it. Are you happy?"

I hadn't moved a muscle. My knees were locked, my hand quaking around the phone. Happy hadn't occurred to me. "I don't know."

"Please don't do that Teddy thing you do where you go looking for woe. You know you can always find it. You made an album with Sonny Rivers, and you basically did it all on a dare."

"I wouldn't put it in quite those terms."

"That photographer dared you to do this. He didn't mean to, but he did. Right now, you should feel nothing but satisfaction. Worry about everything that warrants worrying tomorrow. Are you all going out to celebrate?"

Only Jumbo had proposed it, but his suggestion had been roundly ignored, and not just because it was he who had suggested it. The walls of East Side Studios had grown high and imposing, and the bodies and souls that had invaded it for the summer had grown increasingly in need of ventilation.

"I've had enough of them for a while," I said. "You and I are going to celebrate."

She paused, taken aback perhaps at the invitation, probably raking through her Rolodex of excuses; they were never far out of reach, and they seemed to be multiplying of late.

Then she simply said, "Okay." She even sounded pleased.

But later that afternoon, en route to Bristol & Bristol Interior Design, with thoughts of snatching Sara away for happy hour at the rooftop bar of a nearby hotel, I got a call from her. Something had come up.

"I'm so sorry, Teddy. I really can't miss this meeting."

"It's fine. Don't worry about it."

"I'll meet you at home later," she said, and hung up.

Standing downwind of an abrupt ditch, I licked my wounds and re-mobilized. It was still today, the day without worries, the day on which Teddy did not do his Teddy thing where he went looking for woe.

Gripping my phone like a four-seam fastball, I pondered my next pitch. I didn't like where my thoughts were leading me. Market Street foot traffic freewheeled past this once and future musician. Knowing I probably shouldn't, I dialed.

"Have you left town yet?" I asked.

"Still loading up," Mackenzie replied. "As much as I like to consider myself someone who packs light, I might not actually be that person."

I offered to help, and she had no real reason to refuse. Twenty minutes later, I was knocking on an open door on the second story of a row house on Second Street, just north of Arch. There was exactly one piece of furniture in the center of the vast studio apartment—a bed—and Mackenzie was sitting on it, face in hands.

"You all right?" I asked.

She lifted her head and smiled heavily at me. "A little tired, I have to admit."

"Yeah, you look pale. And wan."

"You had to say wan, didn't you? I couldn't just be pale."

Two suitcases sat agape on the floor in front of her. These were no weekend travel bags; they were true pieces of luggage, made from some sort of coated polyester, hardy things with latches and locks, and they were stuffed high with neatly folded clothes.

"You sure you're okay?" I asked. "Does this have something to do with your medication?"

"Strangely queasy," she said. "Not once in that brick oven of a studio the entire summer, and yet the second Sonny sets us free, I go back to being me."

"I could check my glove compartment for more of Jumbo's ganja."

Mack laughed, then swept the hair off her forehead with both hands. "You really didn't need to come over here. I can get these into the car myself."

"If you were just pale, maybe I'd let you. But since you're also wan . . ."

"In that case, I'm going to do something for you that I haven't done for a man in a long time."

"I'm listening."

"I'm going to take you to the store across the street and buy you a grape soda."

"A grape soda."

"Fanta, my friend. When's the last time you had a Fanta grape soda?"

I squinted fondly at a stain up on the ceiling. "It was, I believe, the summer of 'eighty-four."

Insisting she was up to it, we walked over to a tiny, unnamed convenience store wedged between a women's clothing shop and a place that sold candles and stationery. A metal-toothed fan beat down on the Hispanic gentleman sloped over the counter. His graying mustache smiled lifelessly at us as we entered.

The dim and dusty establishment exhibited an air of indifference toward inventory, as there was gum in the front, a refrigerator in the back, and a wasteland in between featuring lonely bottles of mouthwash and aged boxes of cherry Jell-O. Mack found two cans of Fanta in the fridge next to a plastic container of cheesecake, and we drank them outside on a bench beside an ancient church. The color had returned to her cheeks.

"This is such a nice city," she observed. "I really like Philadelphia."

I nodded in agreement, realizing I'd never really lived anywhere else.

"I might have stayed after college if the band hadn't happened," Mack said.

I remembered those days of feeling as though you could live anywhere, that you would live anywhere. As a kid, I accepted it as inevitable that there'd be a chapter in my life where I lived in a small town, some place with a Main Street and a family-run hardware store. There would also be a suburban chapter, a life lived on driveways and garages and lawns, and a European chapter with Vespas and an unaccountable fluency in some other language. I never viewed these episodes as connected to each other or to any kind of ordered path, as in a board game where your piece makes its gradual, inexorable way to an end. These chapters would simply happen. Somehow I'd live in Prague for a while. The world would just carry me there.

"Do you think you're here for good?" Mack asked.

"I don't know. Maybe."

For good sounded so final. But you reached a point in life where you needed a good reason to move, where your wandering blood settled into something that craved familiarity. Mack's question somehow led me to Sara. I would move for her, I supposed, and she for me. At least I thought so. We would follow each other, wouldn't we?

As Mack and I continued to slurp our grape soda and engage in meaningless, comfortable small talk, my thoughts kept returning to Sara. Not so long ago, Sara and I had opened up our high school yearbook for no other purpose than to cringe at the devastation that time had wreaked. I howled in grim amusement at my feathered hair, at the full cheeks that the years had hollowed, at the immaculate cluelessness in my sneer. But for Sara, seeing the brimming optimism of her teenage self, the hope in a young girl's eyes flowing over—it did not strike her as funny, not even ruefully so. There'd been too much road between there and here.

Here I was, deliberately trying to tunnel back into my past with the implied threat of leaving everything behind in my vapor trail of freedom. Meanwhile, Sara struggled daily just to come to grips with her past. Freedom was something Sara would never know—freedom from her memories, freedom from all those cries and whispers that pierced the universe circling around her. They were everywhere. Look, Sara, look at the family playing Uno in a restaurant booth. Look at Josie and Wynne and their new baby. Isn't that wonderful? Everyone could change, move on, escape. Everyone except her.

When Sara looked at that yearbook, her mind saw pictures her eyes would never see. Her son with a girlfriend by the Grand Canyon, with a wife by the Eiffel Tower, in line at Space Mountain with his own peach-faced children. What would he look like in those photographs, standing by the world, gradually growing older? How many times must Sara have found herself walking down a busy street, on her way to some appointment, and been leveled once again by the realization that life really does go on? It had gone on. Here I am, living the ordinary moments of my life, but something awful has happened and there's no one to take my grievance to! Every day those familiar fears sprang up again. The fear of open spaces, the fear of being buried alive, of being swallowed alive, of stray bullets, of everyone being able to read her mind. The fear that every thing and every person in the world exists for no other reason than to certify the darkness. In the end, that's what it all came down to. No matter how many sleepless nights or endless winter Sundays, they all added up to an absence, an unmistakable echo. That echo was the sound of her son telling her that where he'd gone she could not follow.

I found myself wondering why Sara had bailed on me this afternoon, how an unmissable meeting could materialize out of nowhere from one hour to the next. Was this a meeting with Billy? I was letting my suspicions get the better of me. All these thoughts sounded like jealousy, like possessiveness. Sara and Billy were divorced now, at liberty to be with whomever they chose—even each other. The idea of Sara being officially unchained had terrified me before, as I knew it could bear a fresh set of expectations for me at a critical time, a time when I had fresh expectations of myself. But all that changed when I realized that those expectations had been there all along. No one had twisted my arm to move in with Sara or to stay with her all these years. These were expectations I'd willingly submitted to, had had a hand in creating. I must have wanted them there all along. They'd inhabited me, propped me up, defined me when music no longer did—precisely what Sara had been doing for me all this time.

Who was I kidding? We were already married.

When Mack and I had drunk our soda cans clean, I lugged the suitcases down the steps while she pulled her Beetle around and edged it onto the sidewalk. She popped the trunk, then, with the driver-side door open, she kissed me on the cheek and said, "This was fun. Really."

"You know, even if it turns out that we've made a terrible album that nobody wants to release, I'm glad we got to spend all this time together. I hope you have no regrets if that's the way this ends."

She patted me twice on the chest and smiled. "It's a fantastic album," she said, and slid behind the wheel.

I watched the Beetle zip up Second Street. Then I went to hunt down my ever-untraceable girlfriend.

CHAPTER 23

The hostess looked as though she were spitting up on her onesie the last time Tremble rollicked through an evening here, but younger faces aside, the Mirabelle Plum seemed to have been preserved in tree sap since the days of our prime. Jumbo had insisted that this meeting be held here. As he would have it, success was simply a matter of replicating the past, finding our way back to our old selves.

It was an hour past the reservation time, and the three of us who had shown up so far had done no more than order from the bar and victimize the bread basket. Our waitress was nobly masking her ire at our monopolization of her table without running up much of a tab. After checking in with us for the tenth time, she politely suggested we wave her down when we were ready, and then carried her angular features, horselike ponytail, and mirthless smile away from our table.

Warren, Mack, and I were waiting for Alaina, who was off attending a late-afternoon meeting at MCA with Colin Stone and other senior execs, but she hadn't been heard from in hours. Contentious meetings typically lasted longer than harmonious ones, and there was nothing encouraging about the thought of agent and label duking it out in a conference room over us. Alaina had insisted that I stay away. "Go eat gnocchi and let me do my job," she'd said. "Shoo!"

The front door of the restaurant swung open and in sailed our guitar player aboard a big chunky grin.

"I'm with the band," he majestically informed the hostess. In loose-fitting jeans and a navy sweatshirt that zippered up the middle, Jumbo circumnavigated the table and distributed high fives to each of us like he'd just hit a game-winning three-pointer. He was fresh from a birthing workshop in White Plains, some convention needed to maintain his midwifery certification.

Our stress level already in the red zone, Mack was the only one who could bear to make eye contact with him. "How was your seminar?" she asked.

Jumbo winked. "Kobe beef sliders."

That was the sum of his ambition: the convention's hors d'oeuvres.

"No Alaina yet?" he asked the table.

I shook my head.

Unconcerned, Jumbo grabbed the arm of a passing waitress and leaned in with a devious twinkle. "A little SoCo, if I may."

The waitress stiffly regarded the hairy hand on her forearm. "Excuse me?"

"Southern Comfort. Please."

"I'll let your waitress know," she said, and scooted away.

But not even a snappish server could dampen the beam on Jumbo's face. His eyes feasted on every aspect of the room—the dusty light fixtures, the rich red carpeting pockmarked with food smudges, the ceiling stains that looked almost artistically rendered. "I've missed this place," he gushed. Then, jostling me with an elbow, he proclaimed, "You really can go home again."

I had no doubt that Jumbo could go home again, especially if home was synonymous with consuming a half-dozen glasses of hard liquor, then making a late-night snack run to a convenience store where he would mistake a box of tampons for a pack of Charleston Chews. But to his credit, since committing to this enterprise, Jumbo's behavior had exceeded our pathetically low expectations. He hadn't hitchhiked or stumbled through a glass window, and though he did put himself out of commission for one studio day through overuse of Tabasco sauce, he claimed to have recently begun working out again. (Although to Jumbo Jett, exercise could've meant beer pong or Skee-Ball at the local arcade.)

Edgy impatience flooded my limbs. Somewhere in the city the fate of my band was being debated and bargained over, and I was here, watching the focaccia grease twinkle on my drummer's face.

"You're caressing your temples again," Warren informed me.

Mackenzie pointed to the side of my head. "It's leaving a mark."

Jumbo reached over to massage my neck. "Relax, Mingus."

I locked eyes with him. "Don't tell me to relax. And take your hands off me."

"Colin will always do right by us," Mack assured us. "Plus, he's helpless against Alaina."

I'd been trying to access a state of peace over these past weeks, and had occasionally attained it, sometimes even for as long as a quarter hour. But from where I sat, there was no shortage of concerns over which to stew. There was the highly suspect sellability of the band as a commodity. Our image, or lack thereof. The fact that in most circles, the mention of our name prompted distant chuckles. The fact that the new record offered nothing quite as catchy as "It Feels like a Lie," even if, song for song, this was probably the best record of our career. (It was, to be fair, only the third record of our career, so the distinction was akin to being crowned the handsomest member of ZZ Top.)

"Why is Sonny at this meeting with Alaina and not us?" Jumbo wanted to know.

"Politics," I said. "He's Sonny. And Colin basically wants to fellate him."

"Hey!" Mack snapped her napkin at my head. "You're talking about my ex-husband!"

"Maybe that's why he's your ex-husband," Warren suggested.

"Is *fellate* really a verb?" asked Jumbo.

"Ask the sex therapist."

The muscles in Mack's face tensed with sympathy. "Sorry, guys, but for men at your station in life, it's pretty much a past-tense verb."

At about ten fifteen, a pair of violet stilettos carried Alaina into the Plum like a bayonet and deposited her straight onto Mackenzie's lap. She kissed Mack on the cheek and announced that she wouldn't be needing her own chair tonight.

"Thanks for showing up," Warren grunted, sponging up olive oil with yet another rosemary roll.

Alaina surveyed the scene. "You cats ate without me."

By this point, the table was littered with plates: a battlefield of bloody red-sauce stains and chicken bones, ricotta cheese oozing out of sliced lasagna like the innards of the dead.

I was hoping our agent's nonchalance foretold good things.

"So?" I asked impatiently.

Alaina looked past me as Charles, the Plum's manager, appeared at the table and delivered a regal bow. "So nice to see everybody," he said. "Miss Farber, you look radiant as always."

"Sorry, Charlie. I think I'm gay tonight."

"Of course."

"Can you blame me?" Her fingers glided over Mackenzie's cheek. "I hope you got a good look at this before she sat down. It's the stuff of college dorms. The nerve at her age."

Charlie struggled to not look uncomfortable. This was Alaina's new thing around Mack. An over-the-top display of lust was her rather odd way of expressing concern. People go all sorts of crazy when there's a terminal illness in the room. They sit around and speak of weighty themes in dirgelike tones. Hysterical laughter zaps into hysterical crying. Someone puts on the Righteous Brothers until someone else censures them—Really? At a time like this?—so they put on Squeeze and everybody starts telling stories. I'd have understood it if Mack's condition was perilous. But Mack was as close to death as the rest of us—less so, in fact; her cells had just been given the Clorox treatment—which made Alaina's hammy display of sham carnality uncalled-for and, frankly, weird.

"As always, dear friends, my staff and I are at your service." Charlie offered a fussy dip and carried his Greenwich, Connecticut, coif to the next table.

Alaina said, "I know somebody ordered me an appletini."

I looked sharply at her. "I'm going to start beating it out of you in two seconds."

"Ooh. Promise?" She permitted a cruel little smirk to scheme its way over the southern hemisphere of her face, then, at last, she broke down. "Okay, kids, they love it. They came in their tacky houndstooth pants."

"I knew it!" Jumbo hooted, pounding the table. "Did I not call this?"

The rest of us sat there with an idiot's gape.

"Seriously?" I said.

"Are you really doubting me, sugar packet? That's adorable. No lie—they love it."

"Exactly how much do they love it?"

"A lot much. All kinds of ideas in those greedy little heads of theirs. They want to release it, they want to promo the hell out of it, and then they want to send you little boys and girls on a trip to play in all sorts of exotic locations. Like Houston and Cincinnati. You'll bring me back snow globes."

We were all blanketed in bewilderment. I needed the comfort of details. "Say more."

"Here's the deal," Alaina began. "We're reintroducing the world to an old friend. You took a few years off, you grew up, and now you're back with something fresh to say to the world. Like *Tunnel of Love* by Springsteen or . . . pretty much every Springsteen album after that. The point, people, is that this is happening. All questions and sad little insecurities can be directed to Colin. The Dire Wolf himself is on his way over."

"I don't get it," I said. "You just played them the music and they jumped on it? MCA hears our album and immediately signs us?"

"They don't look at it as just getting into bed with you—which would be a tough sell with this band, except as regards the exquisite Miss Highsider. They see it as getting into bed with Sonny too. It just happens to be our stroke of luck that our producer is the guy everyone wants to stroke. Even the CEO, that Maxwell LaRusso guy. Two songs in and his prom dress was already on the floor, and believe me, that's saying a lot. He's an intense fellow for a guy with a ponytail."

"Didn't anybody want to talk about terms?" Mack asked, still pinned under Alaina's ass. "I've been off the grid awhile, but there used to be these little things called record contracts."

Alaina tossed an arm around Mackenzie's neck. "We did talk terms. I don't accept first offers as a matter of reputation, and I'm certain I could get a bidding war going. But we all decided, did we not, that because of his history with the band and having had the world-class pleasure of matrimony with Mack here, Colin is the one we can trust to show this band some love. And I don't know about the rest of you, but I like love."

There fell upon our table a thick moment of mute absorption while the restaurant clamored around us. Despite the long, sordid chain of events that had brought us to that moment—from those heinously defamatory photos all the way up to the summer spent germinating in Bic's petri dish of a studio—success felt sudden. Unearned. Unreal.

"Look, it's precious that you hayseeds are so dismayed by your own victory," Alaina said to our unbendable deadpans. "But this meeting was like good sex: somebody else did all the work, and there was a cookie platter. Honestly, I barely opened my mouth, and you know how hard it is for me to keep it shut. I felt practically ornamental."

Warren stared thoughtfully at her. "I thought we're calling you Asians now."

At that point, Jumbo hoisted his ungainly body out of his chair and, beaming like a cartoon sun, circled the table administering hugs, neck squeezes, slobbery kisses, and other unwelcome currencies of affection. And yet it all seemed so improbable. How could we be the newest entry in a major record company's roster? We who had all the chic edginess of a PTA meeting?

Just as miraculous as the news imparted to us was the fact that, for this one instant in time, I allowed myself to live in the land of the far-fetched.

None of tomorrow's battles bothered me now. Maybe zero copies of our new album would ever leave the shelves. Maybe zero oily teenagers would double-click on our new tracks. We'd finally gotten our legitimacy back, validated by the same music business that had dismissed us. The label seemed intent on showing the world what I'd been pretty sure of all along—that our exile had been premature, unfair, unwarranted. Back then, the industry was wrong, the fans were wrong, my father was wrong. But now, through the punishing miracle of delayed gratification, we'd been taken seriously again.

I wondered if that was all I ever wanted.

Colin's arrival, with a flock of label cohorts in tow, jacked up the noise coefficient by degrees. He announced that the party—it was now officially a party—would be on him, and the floodgates opened. Shameful amounts of food were ordered. Bottles of wine collected at the center of the table like the Hong Kong skyline in miniature. Glasses were hoisted, toasts were proposed, and an unremitting game of musical chairs ensued as each person sought out, or avoided, a few moments in whisper proximity to another. Mackenzie even got her lap back.

As I was about to duck out to call Sara and share the good news, a firm hand gripped my shoulder. It was Colin. He gave my hand a robust shake.

"Thanks for making all this happen," I said. "I'll bet you thought you'd kicked the habit a long time ago."

"I was quite happy to fall off the wagon." He leaned back on the heels of his double monk-strap loafers. "The new material is just great, Teddy."

"Even so, you must've stuck your neck out for us because of our history together, and I just want you to know that I appreciate it."

"It's more than history. You've also stacked your band with ex-wives of mine, an underhanded move but a convincing one." He laughed grandly. "All that aside, I like you guys, always did. Your guitar player's a mess, but whose isn't?"

"I know you haven't kept your job all these years just by signing people you like."

Colin picked up his brandy with one hand and pushed back the jacket of his Armani suit to place his other hand on his hip. "To do what I do, you must understand that people form deeply personal attachments to artists and the songs they sing. I'm probably insulting you with the obviousness of that statement, but let me put it in the starkest of terms. If you asked the average schmuck on the street to imagine a world without his wife and then imagine a world without his favorite five songs, which do you think he'd find it harder to envision? We both know what he would say out loud, but what would he really feel?" His eyebrows leapt at the question. "Perhaps that says something appalling about humanity and perhaps it says something wonderful about art."

"I think it says something wonderful about humanity that we're adept at burying the truth," I interjected.

"But in the end, we always try to find it and dig it up, don't we? Look, I think I've held on to my job for as long as I have because I know who I work for. I work for that twiggy neurotic in junior high who's searching for a rudder to steer her through the channels of emotional imbalance. I work for the forty-three-year-old ninny with thinning hair whose music collection is all he has to animate the myth that deep down where it counts—where it really counts—he's not like everyone else at that drab prison of an office. You see the dichotomy there. Young people choose music that helps them fit in; older people choose music that sets them apart. The entanglement of music and identity is one of the things that makes my job fascinating. I take my responsibilities very seriously, my friend." He flashed a blizzard of a grin, at once mischievous and genial. "Even if I happen to look like I'm only in it for the high-end sushi."

I grunted in reverence. "I'll tell you what, Colin. I know you deliver that speech seven nights a week and a matinee on Sunday, but you still sell it like the dire wolf you are." I tapped his glass with mine.

He chuckled at the invocation of his enduring and rather confounding nickname. The liner notes of countless albums released over the past three decades extolled appreciation upon Colin "Dire Wolf" Stone. Its genesis was anyone's guess; there was nothing even slightly wolfish about the man. When asked, Colin was ever the artful dodger, rolling his eyes with weary joy and saying something elusive like "A question best directed to David Bowie, I'm afraid."

"Something else in your favor, Teddy," he added in a brandy-bathed whisper. "I find your agent deathly sexy. I'll thank you not to tell Mackenzie."

"I'd keep my distance from Alaina," I counseled. "She'll make you do things you don't want to do."

"Oh, but I like that. I want to do things I don't want to do."

I looked over at our agent, anchoring the rotation of the table, each faceless A&R soldier taking a turn to fawn over her when, by all accounts, it should've been the other way around. Colin was then drawn into another conversation, so I seized an empty chair next to her.

"You seem like you're having a good time," I said to her.

She was chewing on a sliver of orange peel that had served as garnish for her martini. "If this were an orgy, it'd be off to a slow start, but all things considered . . ."

"By the way, you do know that Mackenzie is in remission."

"Completely in remission?"

I scratched at the back of my head. "Is it a continuum? I thought remission was like virginity: it's either all there or all gone."

Alaina hoisted her glass and took a sip. "Well, that's the best news of the night."

"I would agree, except it's not news to some of us. We've known she's been out of the woods for a while now."

"Well, Ted, I suppose it's just another act of friendship on your part that you kept that from me."

"It also means that she probably doesn't need you to sit on her lap."

She gave me an Arctic once-over. "I'll sit wherever the fuck I want."

"I'm just saying she's okay. If you were showering her with undue quantities of attention to make her feel better, it's touching but, as it happens, unnecessary."

"When I need advice on how to handle my personal relationships, yours will be the first number I'll lose."

It was a fair point.

"You can go and sit on her lap too if you want," she added, tweaking me with an exaggerated frown.

"Anyway," I said, changing the subject. "Since I have you to myself for the moment, I just want to say that whatever you had to do to make all this happen, I don't want to know about it, but I'm grateful."

She tilted her head. "You don't have to sit in my lap either. We all know who did the heavy lifting here."

"I didn't know you did modesty."

"And I didn't know you did false modesty. There's some great stuff on this record. 'Whereabouts' kicks ass. That could be our single. That 'Warmth of Disease' tune is a soundtrack-ready weepy. I don't know why you felt compelled to write a song called 'The Inevitable Pivot,' but I guess it's never too late to be an English major. It's a winner, my little pound cake, and everyone knows it. Mature but not dated, fresh but not pathetically trend-chasing, tasteful but never overly restrained."

Her compliments were bringing to mind the notion of contours, as if this time out it was our job to walk some sort of line. To be this one thing over here, but not be too much of this other thing over there. That smelled rather unlike art to me.

"Are we really going with *Trans Am with Electric Eel*?" Alaina asked.

I'd managed to talk everyone into naming the album after that painting I'd been introduced to by the semisuicidal Duncan. Nothing I could put my finger on; it was just where my head was at that time. Somewhere out on that highway, in the backseat of that convertible, breezing into the open.

"You don't like it?"

Alaina's face registered indifference. "It meets my criteria: no masturbation references and no roman numerals."

"I doubt it'll matter," I muttered. "It won't be the title that keeps it out of the top ten."

She turned and faced me. "You really are amazing. Can't you just enjoy the moment?"

"I am," I insisted. "Seriously. This is me enjoying the moment. This is how I enjoy moments."

"And yet you still look a little bit like someone peed in your Wheaties. Even on the night you get a fucking record deal. These things happen every day in my world, but this is you. Haggard, old, thirty-six-inch-waist, in-bed-by-eleven-after-*Laverne & Shirley*-reruns you."

"I'm a thirty-four, and during the week I can sometimes make it down to thirty-three." I stared at her, waiting for the innuendo. Something suggestive, vulgar, taboo even. "Nothing? We're talking about my pants here. This is where you insert some seedy proposition that goes way over the line and makes me uncomfortable."

She flipped her bangs and crossed her legs. "Isn't it time you grew up? You've got a girlfriend, for the love of Pete. Go get your dirty talk from her."

The about-face leveled me. Battling her perfunctory come-ons had been a staple of any conversation with Alaina for as long as there'd been an Alaina. She couldn't be going soft. The universe wouldn't stand for it.

Then I realized she wasn't going soft at all. She was looking out for us—for me, for Sara, Mack, the whole ragged lot. Now that I thought about it, there'd never been a time when Alaina Farber wasn't looking out for us.

The respite of fresh air beckoned. I leaned into my agent's ear and whispered, "I'm a whole mess of proud of you."

"Eat me," she said through a schoolyard sneer.

Although it felt like dawn should've been upon us by now, it was somehow still night. Outside the Plum, I kicked gray pebbles off the sidewalk and out into the street, contemplating the aspects of my life that were now going to change, assuming everything went according to Alaina's design—which it usually did. I'd had less to account for and less to lose the first time around. Since then, I'd evolved, or at least changed in ways that now felt immutable. I had no desire to live the wild and turbulent life of Colin Stone; I was too old for that. (So was he.) Nor would I indulge that empty need to be on top. I'd been up there before, and the thin air can mess with your judgment as sure as a bluegrass band can hold off winter.

I called Sara. She didn't pick up, so I left a message. "Hey. Some good news. Give me a call, or I'll see you at home later tonight."

When I looked up, I saw that Mackenzie had joined me. Folding her arms tightly over her breath-mint-green sweater, she complained about one of Colin's young oily-headed cronies who kept overusing her first name. "When somebody says your name too often, you become hyperaware of how it sounds, of what a silly and random combination of syllables it is. Especially a name like mine. Mackenzie, Mackenzie, Mackenzie. Sounds like a hiccup."

Side by side on the curb, our eyes drifted across the medley of apartment windows looming across the street, taking in the lights and silhouettes within. I thought of the beginning.

"Do you remember the first time we played together?" I asked her. "I mean, the first time ever."

A faraway smile bloomed. "You posted a flyer in the campus record store. I was there with a friend. We were each going to buy a different Replacements album and share them. I ripped the number off the flyer and called."

"I remember."

"First of all, can I just say how pretentious it was to make me audition? Who did you think you were?"

"I've never had a convincing answer to that question."

"You had me run through a bunch of Steve Miller Band and Tom Petty tunes. And you had your baseball hat on backwards."

"You were smooth with the Petty, but you absolutely killed it on 'Won't Get Fooled Again.' I do remember being concerned that Jumbo would scare you off. That's why I offered you a Rolling Rock."

"Jumbo did scare me. That's why I drank four of them."

I kicked another rock; it skipped across the dark pavement.

"My parents were pretty pissed that I'd joined a band," Mack said.

"And they were heartened when you moved on to sex therapy?"

"They were both jocks. A musician's life couldn't have been more foreign to them."

"Someday, on a distant shore, all of our parents will go fishing together and bitch about how we let them down. Of course, my dad will say something obnoxious and they'll beat him overboard with an oar."

"You know, my mom found you arrogant. She said you thought too much of yourself."

"Oh yeah? And what did you think?"

"I thought you had the opposite problem."

I chuckled. "Ever the therapist. How do you think your mother would feel about all this now? Our second act?"

Mack raised her eyes and combed the vast black sky for a clue. "I think she'd be okay with it. It was rebellion back then, self-preservation now."

"I like that. I've come to preserve you."

She turned her head halfway in my direction, as if not quite committing to eye contact. "Teddy. It hasn't always been smooth sailing between us, but I know that you've always been my friend."

The remark simultaneously filled me with words and robbed me of them. I wanted to confess. I wanted to tell her that I hadn't always been such a good friend, that my hot mess of feelings about her had long ago caused me to single-handedly bring down the curtain on this band. But that was before I learned the lesson revealed to me in Bic's studio all summer. Before I realized that if our first two albums were about the youthful disturbances of desire, claiming what the universe owed me through the simple act of showing my God-given entitlement to it by slinging a guitar strap around my neck, this third album was about finding my way back, reclaiming myself. It was about looking into familiar faces and being worthy of them. Yes, I'd had feelings for Mack—destructive, consuming feelings, as feelings often are. Feelings that had pitched the band into a ravine on music's highway. But that was before I realized that I loved Mackenzie Highsider the way everybody loves the sight of an old friend—and that that hardly tasted like a letdown.

The door opened behind us and Colin's head of confused gray hair peeked out.

"So this is where the party is," he boomed.

I'd confess to Mack later. If I still needed to make amends.

"I'm going to refresh," I told them, pointing to my only partially depleted beer bottle and yielding them the sidewalk.

The first thing I saw when I was back inside was Jumbo lumbering toward me, a cheeky grin smeared all across his face. He was swaying as if afflicted with some inner ear disorder.

I looked at the fool. Yes, he was a cheese-doodle party yutz who always had some unseemly indiscretion up his sleeve, but he was my cheese-doodle party yutz. Sooner or later, I had to accept that.

He had something important to tell me. He just had that look. It was going to be something irksomely corny, a hackneyed gush about the odds we'd overcome to make history. Perhaps a strained comparison to some monumental rock act (We're basically the Velvet Underground!) or an incoherent military contextualization (It's like the War of 1812 all over again! Wait—who'd we play in that war? The Mexicans?). Whatever it was, it would deftly illustrate how Jumbo always completely missed the point of everything.

He got right up into my face, bearing down on me with a nose packed unevenly with cartilage and nostrils bursting with more hair than anyone could need.

"Mingus, I got news for you: I know how you struggle with me. You want to be repulsed by me, but you're just not."

"I got news for you: I think I am."

"We go too far back. Our paths run deep. It's almost as if we just can't escape each other."

"It sure does feel that way sometimes."

He punched my biceps. "We're the same. Just a couple of Philly boys who live and breathe music, both of us the product of broken homes."

"My parents got divorced when I was in my midtwenties. I had a wife of my own at the time."

"I like to think of it this way," he continued; I noticed a dewy moisture dripping from the tangled undergrowth on his head. "If you and I were riding around in a car and I suddenly suspected that you were an impostor, not the real Teddy Tremble that I know and love, there would be literally hundreds of questions I could ask you to scope out if you were you or not. I could ask you the color of the front door of the house I grew up in. Or the name of the hotel in Madrid where I got food poisoning—the first time, not when we went back and I got gout. Or about the time I got off a plane in Houston and immediately called you to remind me why I'd flown there. And if you didn't know any of those things, I'd know you were a fake." He paused for a slurp of his drink. "That's the kind of history we have, bro."

"Is this something you spend time worrying about? Being stuck in a car with an impostor?"

He nodded resolutely. "Shit, yeah! Ever since I was a kid. I was always afraid that the people in the front seat weren't my real parents, that they were pods or carbon copies of my real parents, and they were kidnapping me to a carbon copy of my home. They'd act like my real parents, but they were really impostors. It terrified me."

"But James"—I don't know why I played along; it was a night for playing along—"if some nice imposter parents brought you home to a nice impostor house and sent you to an impostor school with all your impostor friends, it wouldn't really matter, would it?"

He placed a fatherly hand on my shoulder and massaged it with his beefy paw. "What's real is real, Mingus. You know that better than anyone."

I snagged a fresh Sierra Nevada from a cocktail waitress and took a seat next to Warren. The merriment at the Plum was now on the downswing, each of us detectably wearying of the crowd. Warren was locking horns with the obnoxious little dope from the label, the one who'd annoyed Mackenzie by fetishizing her first name. The drummer making a sport out of disagreeing with him on just about every guitar hero was cliché: Clapton is God, Eddie Van Halen has the fastest fingers in rock, and so forth. Warren wanted to know why nobody ever mentioned Knopfler. Garcia. Prince. How come the best piano pounders were always Elton or Billy Joel, never Ray Charles or Bruce Hornsby?

Through the glass, I watched Mack and Colin out on the sidewalk. They'd melted into a familiar ease, like high school sweethearts who'd run into each other at the twentieth reunion. I could tell they were taking comfort in the grip of each other's eyes, relishing the sound of each other's voices. I started looking forward to the train ride home so I could slide into the crisp sheets and fold into Sara.

My ears continued to bear witness to the puffy-egoed buffoon kicking up a name-dropping hailstorm on Warren: "... but that's just Noel [Gallagher]. He's actually an okay guy, just misunderstood. ... Conor [Oberst] and I disagree on almost everything, but hey, he's a fucking genius, so what are you gonna do? I told him years ago that he'd taken Bright Eyes as far as it could go, but would he listen to me? ... So Ri [Rihanna] was out with us—we were at somebody's place up in the Hills—and she's a little drunk at this point, all over me, and I'm like, 'Ri, babe, you know this can't happen ...'"

Warren was supposed to be impressed by all this, but Warren doesn't do impressed very well. He was reclining with the palms of his hands on the back of his head, a POW on the march.

"... don't get me started on Axl. He tried to fuck me over and nobody fucks me over. I threw him out of the building—literally threw his ass out. I was like, 'You are done, man. You are fucking done! And if you ever pull that shit with me again, I will knock your dick in the dirt!'"

Warren shifted toward me in whispered sidebar. "'Dick in the dirt'? Isn't that what the principal says to Judd Nelson in *The Breakfast Club*?"

"I don't think he was the principal," I corrected. "He was just a teacher."

"*Just* a teacher, huh?"

"... and I've always told Keith that 'Sympathy for the Devil' just doesn't work on *Beggars Banquet*. It's all wrong for that album. He'll never admit it—you know Keith—but he knows I'm right ..."

"I can't listen to this shit anymore," Warren mumbled, and he bolted up out of his chair to hunt down more flan.

That's when Sonny Rivers smuggled himself into the party. He tried not to make a fuss about it, and the man dropped into the chair next to me before I could diagnose the chorus of barks, whoops, and hollers that his arrival had wrought. He slapped my knee and said, "I can't stay."

That sentence was all it took for the din to die down. It was never Sonny's intention to silence a room, but you just knew that he could be in twenty other places more happening than this, and damned if he wasn't here.

A server attempted to take Sonny's drink order, but he declined.

"I was hoping to tip a glass," he said to me, every ear at the party tuning in. "Turns out I don't have time." He needed to make a flight back to LA that left in an hour. He had two meetings tomorrow, one about his possible involvement in the new Wilco record, the other about a long-delayed project with Mavis Staples that was finally getting off the ground.

Even Alaina, stroking the curved stem of her martini glass, fixed her eyes on the legend in the flesh.

"I'm done with this project," he declared, leaning over the table in a gravelly broadcast. "Everybody else here gets to live with it, hopefully for a good long while, but there's nothing left for me to do, so I move on to the next one. That's the game."

He started scratching the top of his head. "Let's talk straight. Nobody in this band writes like Dylan, nobody sings like Otis Redding, and none of you got Jimi Hendrix chops. That's not this band. You don't look like Bon Jovi, you don't move like Jagger, and God help us all if we ever see you in tight pants. In other words, Farber's got her hands full."

Chuckling filled the room, and even Alaina issued a catlike grin. I, however, was hoping Sonny might cut it short. No need to emphasize the deluge of marketing complications we posed to the poor folks saddled with the task of selling us.

"That's why it took some serious balls to do what you did. Serious balls. I know you guys have wet your shorts every step of the way thinking you were going to get laughed at. Laughed at by music fans all over the world. Laughed at by the press. Laughed at by your families, your friends, your neighbors. And laughed at by that old gray-headed motherfucker right there"—his finger found Colin leaning against a mirrored wall—"who still thinks he knows best." Colin adjusted his tie for show.

"I've listened to this record many times," Sonny intoned. "On airplanes, in my car, my living room. Every kick drum, every guitar lick, every harmony vocal. It's not a perfect record, but I can tell you with a straight face that you are most definitely not going to get laughed at." He delivered the palest wink in my direction. "There are people in this room who've heard me say this before, but I'm going to say it again: I've made many records that nobody loved, but I've never made a record that I didn't love."

Sonny's certification was as close to an opiate as I could ask for. My eyes drifted around the table, then around the room, and I experienced something resembling fulfillment.

Sonny gave the table a spirited bang. "I think I know what happens next with this band, but it's your rodeo now, so it doesn't matter what I think."

With that, he stood and issued a clipped, economical nod to his driver, a tall man in a black suit standing stiffly by the door. As Sonny got to his feet, the gathering whirred back to life, chatter flaring up instantaneously as though Sonny had just unpoked the pause button on his stereo.

As I sat there confused, I was darkened by Jumbo's shadow. He was fingering whipped cream off the top of the pie slice he was holding. "Don't listen to him, Mingus. You do write like Dylan and this body of mine was made for tight jeans."

Once breaking free of the herd of industry peeps who'd maneuvered in his path for a handshake, Sonny located me and lifted his chin—code for requesting a word. I negotiated the spasm of tables, chairs, and drunks until I reached him at the entrance.

"Listen, I can't miss this flight, but we need to talk."

I recoiled. "What about?"

"Just something with the record. Something you should know."

"What are you talking about?"

"No time now. We'll talk later."

"Sonny," I began, my mood quickly calcifying. "Life is suspenseful enough."

He grinned. "Isn't it though?"

"Two seconds. Two seconds isn't going to make a difference on the highway this time of night."

"It's funny when you panic for no reason," he said.

"Is it for no reason? Just tell me—good or bad?" Good and bad seemed tidy enough concepts from which to choose.

"Calm yourself. It's not a bad thing, it's not a good thing; it's just a thing." He signaled through the glass to his driver now in the limo. "Tell you what—I'll send you an e-mail from the plane. All will be revealed by the time I land."

"Come on, man. You can't walk out of here with that. You're kicking me when I'm down."

"We're all down and we're all being kicked," he said with a smile. He was looking at me with a blend of patience and tranquility, like a man who could always find peace in the harrowing walls of the tempest. He knew that my life hadn't yet brought me to that place. Worlds of education lay before me.

"You ever hear of a guy called Sidney Bechet?" he asked. "Jazz musician?"

I sighed through my nose. "Aren't you tired of always being the guy with the parable?"

"It comes naturally. Now Sidney Bechet was one of the first jazz soloists, played a lot of instruments—sax, clarinet. He was from New Orleans, so he spent some time with Satchmo. The story goes that one time he was giving a student some advice about the tone and voicing of his instrument. Sidney wanted to push this guy, really see what he had. So he says to his student, 'I'm going to give you one note today. See how many ways you can play that note—growl it, smear it, flat it, sharp it, do anything you want to it. That's how you express your feelings in this music. It's like talking.'"

I nodded restlessly. "Okay."

"Are you hearing that?"

"Yeah, one note," I said, fluttering with impatience.

"Flat it, sharp it, smear it," he repeated.

"I get it. Sounds like a jazz solo to me."

"Sounds like life to me," he said. "One note. Do anything you want with it."

I stared into the vast sweep of his eyes. "You know you could've told me your little secret in the time it took you to tell me this fairy tale."

"Remember what I said to you when you first brought these new songs to me. Be careful of these cunning plans of yours."

Suddenly, and for the life of me I couldn't say why, I was on the verge of tears. "I've been as careful as the game allows."

"I wasn't talking about then. I was talking about now." Then he flashed an easy smile. "Evolution, man, evolution."

Before I could even begin to translate, he draped me in a hug. "I love you, motherfucker."

Then he smuggled himself back out of the restaurant, taking with him a good chunk of the firm ground I'd traveled so far to stand on.

CHAPTER 24

It was after midnight when I slogged off the musty local and onto the platform at 30th Street Station. My leather jacket felt light against the chill that had settled in for the night, but I was too busy brooding over Sonny's words.

Sara surprised me, waiting at the top of the escalator as I ascended from the track. She saw me, both of us amid a smattering of late-night passengers, and smiled feebly.

"What are you doing here?" I asked.

One hand clutched a cup of Dunkin' Donuts coffee while the other bore into the pocket of her stylish navy windbreaker with the slightly off-center zipper. "I wasn't sleeping and I saw your text about training home. I decided to take a walk."

"I don't like you hanging out in an empty train station in the middle of the night."

She shrugged, as if having survived the adventure mooted my complaint. She hooked our arms together and we began to amble out of the desolate concourse.

Then a voice came from behind. "Teddy? Is that you?"

I turned and found myself looking at Marty Kushman, my former colleague at Morris & Roberts. "Marty."

"Hey, Teddy," he said, giving my hand a friendly shake.

Marty was a soft-spoken, perennially sixtyish duck of a man, well liked by peers, clients, and judges. The last conversation I'd had with him was when I gave notice.

"So good to see you, Sara."

Marty remembered people's names. He and Sara had crossed paths at maybe a half-dozen firm events over the years.

"What brings you here this time of night?" he asked me.

"Oh, just coming back from New York," I answered vaguely.

"We must've been on the same train." He held his briefcase down in front of him, gripping the handle with both hands, his pinstripe suit cloaked under a trench coat.

"Late night for you too," I commented.

"A mediation ran over. Took a long time to get nowhere."

I grunted in a collegial, knowing sort of way that I knew one day soon would feel phony.

"So, I've heard whisperings about a career change for you," Marty said.

When I quit, I hadn't supplied a reason, instead offering cloudy mumblings about it being time to move on. I knew nobody would be heartbroken anyway.

"How'd you hear?"

"Oh, I see your old man around town."

"I'm sure Lou had nothing but nice things to say."

Marty dipped his head diplomatically. "I think it's terrific. I wish you all the luck in the world. You think we kept you around because of your legal skills? We were the law firm with a rock star! Just ask my kids."

Sara and Marty shared a knowing wink.

"How's everything at the shop?" I asked.

"Same place it's always been. I imagine you miss it terribly."

I resisted a sarcastic quip. "I think the firm and I will do just fine without each other."

"I take it it's going well then."

"It is. It's going well."

"That's terrific. I look forward to buying the CD." CDs. How quaint.

Suddenly, the cavernous hall vibrated with a voice over the PA system announcing the departure of a southbound train.

"It's late, guys, I'll let you go," Marty said. "But it was great to see both of you." Then he reached out and touched my arm. "And Teddy, good luck with everything, but if you're ever looking to get back into the law, I hope you'll call me." He smiled at Sara and shuffled off toward the taxi line.

I was unexpectedly jarred by the encounter. Coming face-to-face with the firm reminded me of all the people in whose company I'd spent a large, self-contained chunk of my life. For the first time, my separation from that environment felt real. The next time I saw Marty Kushman, we'd probably only wave to each other. Soon, a distant nod of recognition. You can do that. You can walk out of your life and make yourself a stranger to everything you know.

"So is it?" Sara was asking. "Going well?"

"Looks like we're going to get a deal with MCA."

"Are you serious?" I knew she'd bet against it privately. "That's amazing, Teddy. Really."

"Thanks." I looked at her. "So, how do you feel? About this, I mean."

"I'm really happy for you."

"Yeah, but how do you feel about it . . . for you?"

"I'm really happy for you," she repeated, tossing her coffee cup into a nearby trash can.

"You know I'm not going anywhere. Right?"

She smiled and gripped the front of my jacket with both hands. "Aren't you cold?"

I took my hands out of my pockets and rested them on her hips. Her narrow back felt small in my hands. "The last time I did this, I was a lot younger and was married to someone I didn't love. Basically, I had nothing to lose."

She planted her cold lips on my cheek, a look of calm settling on her every feature.

"Sometimes I feel like I'm losing you," I said. It was, of course, an unfair charge, as I was the one upending our lives. "Am I losing you, Sara?"

"You're panicking, Teddy. Change is scary, even when you've been trying to bring it on."

I stared into her. "Am I losing you?"

She threw her hands onto my shoulders. The concourse could've been a high school gym and we a pair of seniors swaying to a Bryan Adams ballad. "Let's not be afraid of each other," she said. "Let's not be afraid of what each of us wants."

"I don't know what that means." This had become the night of evasive responses, of worrisome ambiguities, of nonanswers. Sara, Sonny—everybody was going out of their way to say things that were just shy of what they meant.

But she'd already grabbed my hand and had begun guiding me toward the automatic doors.

Outside the station, the only sound to be heard was the flapping of flags high up on the stately facade. Despite the hour, we decided to walk, and as we made our way down the street, there would be no discussion of the goings-on at the Mirabelle Plum or what scale of havoc the album and a tour would wreak on us. There would be no questions about what Sara was doing awake at this hour, or how it was that she was sufficiently collected to meet me at the train station. Not tonight. Tonight, we would just be two people walking home in the thick, roiling unrest of living our lives.

CHAPTER 25

There was nothing from Sonny in my inbox the next day. Nor did he return the desperation-stenched voice mail I left for him the following afternoon. An e-mail I sent a few days later likewise went unanswered. One would expect more from me. I was on the cusp of accomplishing something unthinkable for someone of my ilk, age, and station in life, and yet Sonny's parting benediction had reduced me to an insomniac.

All day and for vast stretches of the night I'd catch myself poring over the producer's cryptic words with all my bleak imaginings. What was it about the record that he needed to share with me on his way out of the restaurant? One could only speculate, and the sleepless nights provided a near endless canvas upon which to cast those speculations. *MCA only likes it enough to put it out on cassette, but don't worry—most people still have tape decks.* Or, *We're gonna redo the vocals in German, since your only fans seem to reside in the Swiss Alps.* Or, *Those demonic voices you hear when you play the last track backward, that's actually the devil. For real. It's him.*

But as the days came and went, the leviathan eventually loosened its grip around my neck. I tried to rekindle the optimism on display at the Plum and assured myself that if there was something I truly needed to know about this record, I'd know it. Sonny was a lot of things, but shy he was not. Maybe this thing seemed hotly crucial to him at the time, but its importance eroded as the days wore on. The curiosity still hounded me, but the notion that Sonny held some perilous piece of news that was going to derail my life gradually dissipated. Evolution, man, evolution.

The train's four cars were dense with passengers on the midday climb up the Northeast Corridor. I was on my way to New York to convene with the band at Alaina's office on a number of agenda items. Warren boarded in Trenton and met me in my car. In a striped brown sweater—something Charlie Brown might wear if he ever moved to SoHo—he took the seat across from me and tapped a manila folder on his slacks.

"You like any of these?" he asked, frowning.

I opened up my own folder of cover art mock-ups that had trickled down from Colin to Alaina and finally to the lowly band members, whose opinions counted the least. As I sat there on the train and tried to like them better, Warren seemed to grow increasingly disturbed by them, leafing spiritlessly through the dozen or so glossy printouts and muttering, "I mean, you know . . . right?"

"So, tell her," I said. "It's your band too."

Warren's cultured sensibilities as a teacher of art were clearly offended. "Look at this homage to Thomas Kinkade." He held up an oil painting of some Middle Earth meadow with a stone cottage under a tree, windows glowing as dusk settled over a sweet little hamlet. "Fairport Convention must have a new album coming out and we got sent their pile by mistake. Is this what they think of us?"

I sniffed and shrugged.

"And this monstrosity," he said, holding up his next exhibit and trailing off in disaffection. This one was an eighties postcard of the Sunset Strip. On it, a sin-red Pontiac cruised down a palm tree–lined avenue with a neon sign blinking out the words *Electric Eel.* "This kind of thing concerns me."

He bitched a little about another one, a Hokusai-style illustration, then went looking for the café car.

I'd made a play for using the very painting that had inspired the title. The label negged it and instead sent us out on a photo shoot in a sketchy Philadelphia neighborhood. After a thousand clicks in front of cobblestone alleys, bodegas, walls of mad graffiti, gushing fire hydrants, and urban corners that no doubt did double-duty as a crime scene most nights, the photographer hadn't eked out a single snap that didn't highlight our sunken eyes or sagging chins. We radiated the bad kind of mileage (softness, years of comfortable living), not the acceptable, Stonesy kind (heroin, relapse). The only halfway decent shot featured all four of us leaning with relaxed camaraderie against a wooden table in an abandoned row house where we were lucky not to have been capped. Careful inspection of that picture, however, revealed Jumbo's fly to be open. Of course Photoshop could excise all human imperfections and wardrobe malfunctions, but the question had already been begged: Did we really need to be on the album cover? How was that going to help?

Warren returned and slid back into his seat with an energy bar and a Coke. Adjusting himself on the dead springs of his seat cushion, he let the soda fizz to life and resumed complaining. "These suck. I don't know why you're not more pissed off. After all our hard work, we're going to have an album cover that looks like a poster for an English folk festival or an ad for *Footloose Two*."

"They suck, Square. I agree. What do you want from me? We go in there and tell them."

I wanted groovy, arresting artwork as bad as anybody. I just didn't think I was a barometer for what groovy or arresting looked like anymore. And besides, the age of downloading seemed to have pretty much nullified album art. Gone were the days when some breathless kid peeled open a crisp new album or CD and soaked up the photos and liner notes during his virgin voyage through the songs. The cover design now appeared on your MP3 display at one square centimeter. Maybe you squinted at it for fifteen seconds in an elevator, but we probably didn't have to worry about how it would look hung up on a dorm room next to a tapestry.

After a while, Warren set the folder aside and gazed pensively out the window. "I was at school yesterday. Stopped in to see some people."

I didn't say anything.

"Feels weird, man. School's in session and I'm not there. You know, I always figured I'd be there when Patrick was old enough to attend. I'd embarrass the shit out of him in the hall, force him to play drums in the school band so he'd work up some strong resentment toward me—you know, all the good stuff."

I didn't share the ride to wax wistful about my abandoned profession. Law firms had no memory. If you left, you were a nonhacker, disdained by those who stayed behind. Someone else moved into your office and started tagging along at lunch and filling out NCAA tournament brackets in March. Soon all remembrances were wiped away. A year later, you were referred to as, Oh yeah, I remember that guy.

Warren bit absently from his glorified chocolate bar and rocked in his seat, the wheels beneath us rumbling northward.

"So, you miss it," I summarized with mild annoyance. "Is that what you're trying to tell me?"

"I'm not trying to tell you anything."

"You're always trying to tell me something. Everybody's always trying to tell me something."

He gave serious contemplation to the world beyond the window. Some forgotten factory breezed past. "You can be a cold person, you know that?"

"Can I?"

"I'm just not like you," he said, chewing thoughtfully. "I have room in my life for more than one thing at a time."

The moment we stepped off the elevator, I sensed something was wrong. Cataclysmically wrong. The receptionist greeted us with meticulously orchestrated naturalness. He couldn't tell if we'd already heard.

Down the hushed corridor, we filed past Alaina's office and saw her hovering over her desk with her phone against her ear, her expression grim. Warren and I shot each other nervous glances. Something felt gravely off. We continued down the hall toward the conference room, both of us breathing audibly, taking in the strange disquiet.

When I pushed the conference room door open, the first person I saw was Jumbo. He was seated on the far side of the long table, his head buried in his arms like a sleeping student. The only other person in the room was Marin, surely the longest-tenured personal assistant in the history of Alaina's career, sloped against a credenza on the far wall. Jumbo raised his head as Warren and I entered. His eyes were puffy and red. I lost my breath.

"I can't believe it," Jumbo whimpered. He stood and circled the table, blanketing me in a hug.

"What the hell's going on?" I said. Warren stood petrified.

"I don't deal well with death, Mingus," Jumbo sobbed into my shoulder.

I felt a sickening rush in my chest as I noticed Mackenzie wasn't in the room. A wave of nausea surged up from my stomach and I could taste the puke in the back of my throat.

"What is he talking about?" I demanded of Marin.

"You haven't heard."

Alaina was now standing in the doorway. I disentangled myself from Jumbo but was almost too frightened to speak. "Haven't heard what? Alaina—what the fuck is going on?"

"You guys live in caves?"

"Where's Mackenzie?" I croaked.

Alaina shrugged. Jumbo shrugged. All eyes looked to Marin.

"I think the bathroom," she said.

Mack appeared in the door frame behind Alaina. Such intense relief washed over me at the sight of her that my arms went numb.

"Holy fucking shit," I exhaled.

She greeted Warren and me somberly. "Hey guys."

"Jesus Christ, Mack," I said, on the verge of crumbling into a lifeless mass. "I swear to God. I fucking swear to God."

Warren was in a panic. "I'm walking out of here forever if somebody doesn't tell me right now what's going on!"

Without lifting her eyes off the austere gray carpet, Alaina breathed out a leaden sigh. "There was a fire at Sonny's studio last night. And he was in it."

I scoped the room uncomprehendingly.

"Sonny's dead?" Warren ventured, his voice small.

Alaina nodded.

My mouth dropped slack. My brain repeated the words, hoping the echo would lead me to a different meaning.

"Is this for real?" Warren asked.

I slumped into a chair. Warren remained immobile. Routine office noises—ringing phones, subdued conversations of passersby—mixed with Jumbo's sniffling.

"Marin, will you have some coffee sent in?" Alaina softly asked her assistant. The girl nodded and made for the door, brushing past all of us with her eyes cast downward. "Thanks, doll," Alaina added.

Jumbo was rubbing his large red face and occasionally dropping his chin onto the cherrywood table. Mackenzie sat down next to him and glided her open hand over the rolling hills of his back. With searching, childlike eyes, he looked at her and bleated, "I'm really not good with death."

This couldn't have happened. It was against the rules.

After moments spent in a quiet, private absorption of the news, we got up and lumbered into Alaina's office, positioning ourselves around the TV. From her desk chair, Alaina clicked through channels until landing on a young bleach-blond newscaster trying to look grave. With a photo of Sonny's face framed in the corner, she spoke in funereal tones:

"The music world is in mourning today, as legendary record producer Sonny Rivers has died in a fire at his Los Angeles recording studio. The fire is believed to have started late last night and the cause of the incident is still being investigated. At this time, neither foul play nor drugs are believed to have played any role in this tragic event."

You have to lead with the no-drugs thing. A musician dies and people always assume he was found with a needle in his arm.

Details were still unfolding, but the preliminary report from the fire chief was that there had been an electrical problem. The wiring of an old piece of recording equipment had somehow ignited. From the look of things, Sonny was trying to put it out when he lost consciousness from smoke inhalation. The narrative brought a bleak smile to my face. He did love those vintage units, and I could easily picture him resolving to either stomp the guts out of any flames that threatened to swallow his gear or die trying.

On the flat-screen, we watched as impromptu eulogies came sputtering out of the mouths of musicians, executives, and agents when microphones were thrust before their HD faces. Outside their homes and their cars, or calling in to morning radio shows, they expressed grief and shock and sadness, all of it laced with unsurpassed levels of praise.

"This is a tremendous loss for the recording industry," said a well-known elder statesman who looked like Colin Stone with earrings. "As much as we revere his work now, we won't know for years, possibly decades, the profound impact Sonny had on music as we know it."

I sniffed in disdain. This was no time for bogus insight. Is there music as we don't know it?

A clip from London showed an icon of the British invasion looking distraught, fumbling for words: "I can't even begin to express what Sonny's contribution has been . . . He was, you know, a true visionary . . . I can't believe the River man is gone. We'll miss you, old friend."

The faces of the musicians he recorded with and the covers of the albums he produced were flung across the screen in montage format to illustrate the broad sweep of his influence. In the parade of artwork, most of them instantly recognizable classics, some veritable cultural symbols, the cover of our own *The Queen Kills the King* skipped past.

Then the artificially blond anchorwoman transmitted to the world one last obituary item, one that Sonny might've preferred was omitted: "Rivers had just completed work on the would-be comeback album by rock act Tremble, a band he guided to multiplatinum success in the midnineties with the breakout hit 'It Feels like a Lie.'"

And at that moment, amid the intense shock, the anguish, and the wall-shaking unease, another sensation swelled within me just as powerfully.

Gratitude.

Sonny Rivers, on the day of his death, was being heralded as one of the greatest contributors of all time to the world of popular music, and Tremble, a ragtag group of has-beens, was the band to whom he devoted his very last perspiration. I'd been given one note to play, just like everyone else—I'd smeared it, growled it, sharped it, flatted it, done as much as I could with it. And in the end, the humble ruckus I'd managed to raise was just one undeserving man's good fortune.

Alaina spoke up. "We're going to get calls, guys." She swiveled her chair in my direction. "They're going to want to talk to you. You guys are Sonny's swan song. It's going to get attention."

"You can all do whatever you want," I said. "I've got no sound bites for the AP."

Mack came gunning at me. "That's a little selfish. No comment? We don't owe Sonny a few nice words? I've got some if no one else does."

Just then, with a polite knock, Marin appeared with a young man pushing a cart of stainless steel coffeepots and off-white ceramic mugs. The man guided the cart up against the wall, then silently departed. Before showing herself out, Marin craned her neck toward the television, trying to catch a few moments of coverage before being dismissed, but Alaina told her to pour herself a cup and sit down.

"Anybody know how old he was?" Mack asked.

"I'd say early to midsixties," Jumbo postulated. He was on Alaina's sofa, his hair in wild dizzy curls from the constant exploration by his grieving hands. "Sixty-five, sixty-six at most."

"He was forty-nine," I said, staring at the TV. "Forty-nine."

There was a part of me that applauded Sonny for finding himself a nice cinematic demise, an exit worthy of his life. A radiant blaze torching every thought in his head, melting every word in his mouth, consuming every act of genius he hadn't yet perpetrated on the world, leaving it all in a ruin of embers.

And then it struck me. I'd never learn that ominous fact about the new record that Sonny had mentioned at the Plum. That thing he promised to tell me, that thing I needed to know—I'd never know it. I wondered what disadvantage that left me with, this essential piece of information that literally went up in smoke. When there are things out there we should know, it would seem better to know them. And if we end up not knowing them, it would seem better not to know that they're out there.

Jumbo leaned forward. "So, what if he's not really dead?" Nobody said anything. "Come on. Many of the greats have faked their own death. Jim Morrison, Michael Jackson, even McCartney. Think about it, guys."

Alaina rocked in her leather chair. "Okay, Jumbo, that was very helpful, but is it okay if we proceed on the assumption, at least for the time being, that he's not faking? Is that okay with everybody?"

"Listen, there's going to be a firestorm," she continued, then stopped herself. "That was rather the wrong word. But the attention is going to be nuts. Do you have any idea what this is going to do to the public's interest in the album?"

Mackenzie's voice rang out. "Are you serious, Alaina?" She bolted up out of her chair. "If you're saying what I think you're saying, I'm literally going to be sick."

"Mack," I said calmly.

"No. If you guys want to have a marketing meeting to celebrate all the competitive advantages that have been gifted to you because a man's life is over, find yourself another bass player."

Alaina held up her open palms. "Chill, Mackenzie. That's not what I was saying. And believe me, nobody wants another bass player. Sit down. Please. We're all tense right now, we're all shocked, and we're all really fucking sad. All I was saying is that there has to be an official word from the band. I know you guys have been away for a while, but you remember how this works. We need a written statement. I can have someone here knock one out. Jesus, everybody on this floor has a canned eulogy on their laptop. But . . ." Her eyes glided across the room. "But that's not our style, is it?"

"I'll do it," Jumbo blurted out. "I'm feeling so much right now—pain, confusion, a broken heart. Why him? Why now? It's all so unfair! And we all know emotions are best expressed when you're a little out of whack."

"No, they aren't," I interrupted. "I'll do it."

The room went quiet. Nobody spoke up to object.

"Good, get on it," Alaina finally directed. "You stay here. The rest of us will go down to the lounge." She looked at Mackenzie, whose edgy eyes were pointed out the window, her fingernail tapping against her front tooth. "But we're not going anywhere without Mack."

Mack turned to Alaina and sighed. "I'm here."

"Just give me something to write with," I said. "A notepad, a pen, and a half hour on that brown sofa right there. It won't be the unified theory of everything, but . . ." I shrugged. "I'll try to do the man justice."

The fact was, Sonny wouldn't have given a rat's ass about any kind of tribute. A tribute was all about what other people thought. That was never his concern. He made music the way he thought it should sound, music that was true to his own ears, his own soul. That's why he carried himself like he owned the world. Because if you really were true to yourself and to your soul, then you did own the world.

Everyone filed out of the room, absently tipping the coffee pitcher into their cups as they passed. Only Alaina remained, stuck in the doorway, unable to leave.

"For once in your life, Theodore, try to be nice," she said.

I grunted. Look who was talking.

She remained fixed under the door frame, smiling an oddly fragile smile.

"You okay?" I asked.

"No." She pointed at the couch. "That sofa doesn't like being called brown, because it's purple."

I regarded it. "Then why does it look brown?"

"Who the fuck knows?" she replied with a weary flip of her bangs. "Maybe it's exhausted."

I then noticed a new photo on the wall, a recent shot, the frame unmarred by dust. Sonny's arm was slung around Alaina as they posed in front of the mixing board in East Side Studios during the *Trans Am* sessions. It was somewhat underexposed—there was no flash, and the shaft of light beaming down from the ceiling fan just missed them, as if they'd dodged a lightning strike. But as I looked hard at the picture, I could see Sonny's eyes. I felt him staring back at me, holding me in his all-knowing countenance with those eyes that had seen everything. At that, I seized up in panic.

"Alaina," I called out.

She reappeared at the door.

"You know what? I take it back. I don't know if I can do this. I've never written a tribute in my life. Who am I to speak for Sonny Rivers anyway?" I stood there in my agent's office, my head shaking under a stampede of insecurity. "No, I change my mind. I can't do it."

"Teddy," she said matter-of-factly, "it's the artist's job to find beauty, and in beauty, there's hope and optimism, no matter how tragic that beauty. So, for the sake of all of us, do your job. Be the artist you claim to be."

I stared at her hard. "I don't think I know what that means."

"Well." She let out a dark laugh. "You'd better start pretending you do."

And she was gone.

I started adjusting to the aloneness of the room when Jumbo poked his head back in, a warrior's thirst all over his face. "Mingus, I'm right here if you need me, bro!" He was holding up his fist in a show of brotherly solidarity.

I expressed my appreciation by telling him to get out and shut the door.

I sat on the brownish-purple sofa and thought. I put myself in the records Sonny made as a young man. I put myself in his house with his wife and kids as a man full-on in his prime. I set myself on fire. Nothing came that seemed worth saying.

What happens to a man when he dies? Does the physical world take note? What happens to the things he loved when he's no longer in the world to love them? Do his favorite songs play with slightly less radiance because the adoration quotient has diminished? Do the places he always wanted to visit brim with less joy for his never having gotten there? Does his house miss him, the quiet that hangs over its rooms in the afternoon a more somber silence? Do the secrets only he knew find another head in which to conceal themselves?

I gazed up at the photos on Alaina's wall and tried to unbend in the exalted company—the once famous, the overrated, the roadkill. I sent myself into the tunnels of memories I had of Sonny but only found myself becoming more lost.

Sonny was dead. It didn't matter what we did or what we said now. Sonny was gone. Gone forever. Every single person up in those frames, no matter how celebrated or disgraced, was going to die. No matter who heard them sing. No matter what legacy they left behind, or to whom. That's where this was all headed. That's what happens next. That, I decided, was Sonny's unfinished thought.

I reached for my phone and dialed. It went to voice mail. I called back. Again and again—it was the only thing that mattered—until at last Sara picked up.

"It's me," I said, my voice breaking with relief.

Everybody should have someone to whom they're simply *It's me*.

CHAPTER 26

She was typing an e-mail at the desk in our office when I blew into the condo. She spun her chair around and looked at me.

"It's such a horrible thing," she said. "Are you okay?"

I felt my jaw go taut. I wasn't sure I could say it. "Sara. How come you never talk to me about Drew?"

She recoiled.

"All these years together and you've never spoken to me about him. And then Billy comes back and . . . I know Drew is with you, Sara. I know he's with you all the time."

She looked splintered by my bluntness, my crime of violating our long-standing accord to leave this alone. I watched her readying a nimble deflection. She'd tell me that this had nothing to do with him, that I was just thrown by what had happened to Sonny. It would be a thoroughly rehearsed act of self-defense.

But something was different this time. Her expression was changing, going somewhere I'd never been. Her mouth relaxed into a sad, honest smile.

"You're not me," she said. "You could never have known what I was going through. It's not your fault. You've always just been someone else who didn't have an answer."

I lowered myself in front of her. "But I could've been someone you could lean on. And I wasn't."

She reached out and rested her hands on my shoulders. "I've leaned on you, Teddy. But let's face it—you're a person who's constantly caught up in the business of being you."

I looked down. The marine-blue carpet suddenly seemed like an unforgiving ocean that could keep you adrift forever.

"It's okay," she said.

"No. It's not. It's really not. I don't know how you've dealt with it."

"You do know. You were there the whole time. You saw it. I took shelter in you. I attached myself to someone who, even when sharing my bed and sitting at the dinner table, was usually miles away." She heaved a fearless sigh. "I think about him every day, Teddy. Every single day. I hear him calling to me in the park. I see him in those wide shafts of sunlight out the windows of airplanes. Sometimes I could swear he's just up ahead on a crowded block, not even looking for me anymore. I see him everywhere."

Water pooled into the whites of her eyes.

"I used to wander from room to room, praying that for once, just this once, the rules would bend and I'd get him back. Back from where, I didn't know. I just had to believe that my little boy was somewhere. The thought that he was nowhere was much worse. Even if I could never find him again, I had to believe he was out there somewhere. The clouds, the stars, somewhere . . ."

I couldn't even look her in the eye now. For her, all I'd ever been was a branch arching over quicksand. This ramshackle life we'd fused together, each of us clinging to something else, each of us caught up in some squall we hoped might set us down in a better place, a place that was long gone—it was a fiction. A sad clawing for the past was perhaps the thing we had most in common. And hers put mine to shame.

Shame on me. Everything I'd ever done, I'd done for myself. This woman had been cooped up all these years with me, watching as I lugged around this ugly chip on my shoulder all because the world had gypped me out of something I didn't deserve in the first place. Why had she stayed? Why didn't Sara hate me? How can you stomach the folly of melodrama once you've been forced to reckon with actual drama?

Kneeling in a crumpled pile on the floor, I knew there was no apology that wouldn't trivialize everything.

I said, "Do you want to know what I think?"

She waited, as if it had never occurred to her that I thought anything.

"I think wherever he is, he's not in pain. I don't think he's scared and I don't think he's sad."

With a faint look of surprise, she started to nod.

"And," I said carefully, moving closer to her, "I'd really like to go with you next year. On his birthday, to see him."

She rested her face onto the top of my head, her chin burrowed into my hair.

When she sat back up, the tears had been wiped clean. "It's okay, Teddy. I love you almost just the way you are."

I was in no position to ask for more than that.

"But we've got more to talk about," she said, straightening herself. There was something unshakable in her now. It scared me. "All these changes you've made, all these big decisions."

"Yes."

"I've made some decisions too."

"Okay."

"I've made some decisions about us," she said.

Down on the floor, I slid as close to her as I could get. Whatever she wanted to tell me, I'd be right there, hearing her. My heart galloped. I was afraid, but I was ready. I owed her that.

"It's okay, Sara." I held tightly to the bended reeds of her legs. I looked her square in the eye.

She released one last breath, purging herself of any air of doubt caged up inside her.

"It's okay," I assured her. "I want you to tell me these decisions you've made. Whatever they are, I want to hear them. I'm ready."

PART FOUR

EL FAROLITO

CHAPTER 27

It took a long time to get here and the road was, to say the least, circuitous. It's not the Hollywood Bowl, but it's not the Whole Foods parking lot either. Everybody here is happy.

Happy all the fucking time. The first rum cocktail goes down no later than noon, and they chase it with a parade of lime-stuffed Coronas that perspire down the side of the bottle. There are no pissed-off drunks here. And they dress down. The fanciest thing you'd pack for the El Farolito is something you'd wear to the pool.

They set us up nicely. Instead of a room in the main hotel, which would've done just fine, they put us in one of the casitas, soothingly tan villas tucked away under an umbrella of palm trees at the end of a long path. Nestled at the edge of the villas is a forever pool, an amenity that, if you ask me, has never quite gotten its due in the pantheon of opulence. It feels like the edge of the world, like our own private overlook into tranquility.

In the evening, fresh from a shower, I carry my guitar case down the path toward the Flamingo Wing and I actually pass a flamingo.

A man seated at a tall cocktail table calls to me as I walk by, my hair buckling in the sea breeze. He yells out "Goodbye to Myself" and "Well, I'm This Way," titles from the new record, then adds "Free

Bird" just to be a wiseass. He's making requests for the show later. He's no more than thirty and is wearing sunglasses, a yellow tank top, and a wet grin. The grin is due, in no small part, to the gorgeous blonde at his table, whose shorts ride high on the thigh. Honeymooners are untouchable. I smile and wave at them. Look at me—I'm Captain Stubing now.

It's still a bit of an undue thrill that people know the names of the songs on *Trans Am*, which, for a succinct but utterly satisfying spell, put Tremble back on the map. The American youth that bought our music at the mall decades ago apparently tuned in again, this time as they heated up chicken fingers and fries for their kids. "Goodbye to Myself" even broke the top twenty-five and "Well, I'm This Way" made it onto the soundtrack of a popular Showtime series. The album was the most unlikely critics' darling you ever saw, making the year's "best of" list at *Rolling Stone*, Pitchfork, Drowned in Sound, and even the cranky BBC.

Our popularity spiked such that I was interviewed by *Vogue*. They sent a young hipster writer to our condo one afternoon, a hipster photographer in tow, and a month later, there I was in a two-page fluff piece looking intrepid and durable. I signed two copies of the magazine and mailed them to a certain hamlet in Unterseen, enclosing with them autographed copies of the new record. On the one to Heinz-Peter, I wrote, "Isn't this a nice picture of me? Would that really have been so hard?" On the one to Tereza, I wrote, "You were right—I wasn't okay with being someone else, and I did want to play. Thank you."

And because I'm not good at letting things go, I mailed the *Rolling Stone* review to my father. I highlighted the line that read: "Halfway through this vibrant, poignant record from a band wrongly dismissed as time-capsule material, one can't help but wonder why Tremble didn't attempt a comeback years ago." It could very easily be lost on my old man.

Maybe the second coming of our success was just homesickness, a familiar voice stoking pleasant remembrances, blind wistfulness for the past (people even pine for the midnineties now). Or maybe pity: we might have been the dumpy old frau that the bartender cards just to make her night. But who would choose to dwell on that? I was humbled by it all, and proud of myself for feeling that way.

Sonny helped us from the grave. It'd be foolish to deny that he was the reason the spotlight landed on us for a while. But I've given it a lot of thought and have decided I feel no guilt. Even if Alaina and Colin were only taken in by the allure of Tremble redux because of Sonny's involvement, and even if the world took note of our record because our famous producer thefted more than a few headlines in his departure, the truth is that Sonny genuinely dug the way *Trans Am* turned out. He listened to those coarse demos and told us motherfuckers to go make a record. And he showed up at the Plum that night to tell us that we'd accomplished what we'd set out to do. We earned him, so maybe we earned everything that came after. If that's anywhere near the truth, then our royalty checks are not blood money.

Nor does the man's unfinished thought plague me anymore. My contentment with this record, with my choices, with the people in my life—it all testifies to the irrelevance of that secret.

It has only stoked the embers of intrigue that the band broke up before the album ever hit stores. It was the stuff of dazzling tragic mystery: legendary producer and vanished rock outfit meet over the course of a summer to stir up one last farewell, and then one immediately dies and the other vaporizes in a sudden parting of the ways. Mackenzie once said that stories tell themselves. This one ginned up with quite an ending.

"I wasn't all that jazzed about living off a hotel minibar anyway," Warren reflected when I told him I wanted out.

We'd met at a Lambertville bar one afternoon, one where Warren was something of a regular. In the wake of the fire, we'd all retreated to our own corners of the earth to process, to sort through our emotions, to wait for Alaina and the record label to plot our course across the next ten or twelve months. Warren, of course, had gone home to hunker down with his family.

"Being away from Lauren and Patrick for long stretches was kind of making me anxious. I like you, Teddy, but I like them better."

He was taking my decision well, massaging his beard with an aspect of returning peace.

"Stop coming here though, will you?" he said. "Every time you show up, everything changes directions."

Two men floated around the pool table near us, rubbing chalk on the ends of their sticks, sizing up the trajectories of their shots. Over at the bar, a trio of young women ordered drinks and sporadically twisted their necks toward our table.

"You know, I never meant to throw your world into upheaval when I called you about the Tate," Warren confided.

"Now you tell me."

"Had I known it would cause you to flip out and hassle everyone into quitting their jobs, I really would've just kept my mouth shut. I just thought it was funny, that's all. Everything that came after, that's all on you."

I smiled. "You're welcome."

"And you know, the only reason I let you talk me into this was to see if we had one more in us. You're not the only one who's entitled to a midlife crisis."

"So tell me—what did you learn on your midlife crisis?"

He pointed a finger revolver at me and grinned. "That we very much indeed had one more in us."

"At least one," I said.

"At least one."

"It's never the right time to walk away," I said. "It's always either too soon or too late."

"Like dying," Warren mused.

"Like dying."

He rocked back in his chair. "You still think that photograph says something about your legacy?"

"If it says something about mine, it says something about yours," I told him.

"Nah. You're on your own when it comes to those things. My legacy lives in my house. He's got bucked teeth, eats too many Oreos, and is either going to be a centerfielder or an astronaut." He took a swig from his glass. "You speak to Mack and Jumbo yet?"

I shook my head.

He spun his glass on the table between two long fingers. "Mack will be fine, but Jumbo won't be happy," he decided. "He's going to have to go back to doing whatever it was he did before all of this."

"That'll be easy, because it wasn't much of anything."

"He was a stewardess, right?"

"I thought he was a ballerina."

Warren dropped one of his signature cackles. "Isn't that a gender-specific term? What do you call a male ballerina? Ballerino? Balle-roon?"

Jumbo may not go back to living in his ex-wife's basement, but there was no doubt he'd go and do something else equally absurd. That's just what Jumbo did. His whole life was sauntering into the spine center and passing out Hula-Hoops.

I said, "Whatever he is, at least he'll be able to afford his own place."

I got up and started for the bar. "One more, Square."

Warren issued a halfhearted protest, the kind that begs to be ignored.

I leaned toward the bartender. "What do you have in the way of bourbon?"

He winked. "I do have a little something I keep for your friend over there." He was a big guy with pallid Slavic features and a KGB accent. "Special occasions."

Warren was already shaking his head when I set the glasses down on the table, one in front of each of us. He surveyed the gasoline-brown liquid, instantly recognizing the Eagle Rare, the nightmare you go to sleep hoping will return. "Jesus, man. I used to trust you."

I held up my glass. "You'll know better next time."

He threw back a healthy swallow, savoring what tasted to me like jet fuel.

"Not everything goes to hell with age," he concluded, admiring the shimmering glass.

Other than the crack of billiard balls and a Smashing Pumpkins tune playing low on the jukebox, the bar was quiet. I couldn't say what my problem had been all this time, whether it was that the afterparty never died down or that it never really kicked in in the first place. But now, sitting right there in that bar with my old friend, I knew that this was the kind of revelry that suited me best.

Warren looked across the table at me. "I didn't mean it, by the way. When I told you to stop coming here."

That was a while ago now. These days, I'm full-time here at the El Farolito. I've still got the condo in Philly—that's where the royalty checks are sent—but the casita in this island paradise is pretty much home and the Flamingo Wing is the office. With four or five shows a week, I suppose I qualify as the house band, if you call me and my acoustic a band. Artist in residence would be even more of a stretch.

I play "It Feels like a Lie" at every show—you have to dance with the girl who brung you—but I also do plenty of new songs, and no one seems to mind. I toss in covers because the Tremble catalog is neither bounteous nor terribly exciting. And who doesn't welcome the innocent bounce of "Brown-Eyed Girl" or the naked romance of "Wonderful Tonight" while lounging under a palm tree, the sweet aromas of tropical fruit and coconut sunscreen drifting through it all? When I start busting out "Kokomo" and "Don't Worry, Be Happy," the manager will probably stuff me into the ferry for the mainland. But until then, I'm on the website. I look like shit in the picture, but at least I wasn't eating nachos.

There's a nice little town nearby, a crossbreed of a Banana Republic and Palo Alto. Good restaurants thumping with local fare and staffed by tanned young locals who grew up in the neighborhood. The preschool is a quick drive down the main road, little more than a mile. Sometimes I drop Phoebe off, sometimes the three of us go together. Nothing of more importance beckons.

Now I move slowly across the dry sand, Phoebe's tiny fingers enveloped in mine. She looks down at her feet as she steps. It could take an hour for her to cross the beach, what with the constant distraction of seashells, every variety of which seizes her attention. We saw a tiny sand crab four days ago and she hasn't stopped talking about it. Does it like to swim? Does it have a mommy and daddy? What does it like to eat? And I relish the challenge of inventing answers, a task that forces me to recall Alaina's words: it's not the little things that matter, it's the big things. In the life I wake up to these days, I am finding that they are very much one and the same.

Sara is backlit by the late-afternoon sun dipping behind her. She loves the beach at this hour. It's a good time to face the tide, she says; the sea relaxes her at the end of a long day. She has always dreamed of living by the water, and I'm happy for her that she made it, that we made it. It is never hard to pick her out among the languid flock of beachgoers, her long bony legs folded at the knee so they don't dangle over the edge of her chaise. The flow of her body is easily detectable to me even when she's still and reclining by the tide. That's how it is with people who've been together so long. We even know each other's shadows.

Phoebe and I are now fifty or so yards away and I notice Sara checking her watch, then closing her book and sitting up. Spotting us right on time, she waves eagerly, with all the joy and gratitude in the world, like she's been waiting forever to see us. It's the way I imagine Alaina's grandfather waved to her at the airport when she made it back to Shanghai. It's the way I felt the first time Mackenzie showed up at my apartment with her bass, drawing me into a two-decade entanglement during which I confused the way I felt about making music with the way I felt about her. I suppose the world will have to end and kick in again before these moments return and offer everyone a second chance.

With a gleeful shriek, Phoebe detaches herself from my hand and starts sprinting ahead to her mother. Then she breaks her stride and pivots back toward me, interrupting herself with her own scattered thoughts. With a randomness that never fails to delight and enchant me, to make me right, to make me young, she asks how that baby crab from the other day learns to swim. Who teaches a crab to swim? she wants to know.

I'm going to have to go deep on this one. I'll tell her about the things that are inside us, who we're born to be, what we're born to do, and how sometimes we never have a say in the matter, never even understand why. Like the rest of us, she'll find that most of her life will pass before she grasps what I really mean. And I hope that of all the moments I've had, it will be this one—right here with her on this beach, in the irrepressible blush of a sinking sun—that returns to comfort me one day when the end comes.

The singularity of this hour staggers me. One day I'll die, and this will be one of the things I did with my time.

Her question posed, Phoebe is hanging on my answer, her eyes expectant and wide, like the mouth of a river. Open to everything flowing toward her, but like nothing I've ever seen before.

ACKNOWLEDGMENTS

I'm enormously grateful for the efforts of so many people whose contributions to this book cannot be overstated.

My agent, Caryn Karmatz Rudy of DeFiore and Company, for her tireless efforts on the many, many drafts, for her guidance, support, and encouragement for much longer than justified, and for all the terrific ideas that made their way into this book. And also for the Jell-O shots.

Sally Kim, my editor, for her truly amazing insights that made this book infinitely better, for her wells of enthusiasm, and for her guidance throughout this process. Heartfelt thanks to you.

Also to the rest of the team at Touchstone—Etinosa Agbonlahor, Susan Moldow, David Falk, Brian Belfiglio, Meredith Vilarello, Jessica Roth, Wendy Sheanin—thank you for your hard work and creativity.

Simon & Schuster for such tremendous, generous support.

David Small, for his novels that continue to be a source of inspiration, and for his workshop at Franklin & Marshall College, which demystified for me the process of creative writing.

Leslie and Ferne Abramowitz, my parents, two wonderful people whose love of books, music, and all other arts set this project in motion. I'm eternally grateful for that, and for so much more.

I got very lucky in the family department: Michelle (and Mitch) and Jon (and Stacy) (and their kids), siblings of mine that I'm fortunate enough to call friends, and my in-laws, Terry and Elliott.

My friends at Spector Roseman Kodroff & Willis, good lawyers and great people, and a firm that is, fortunately, quite unlike the one depicted in these pages.

Melissa, Jon, Amy, and Rich, for all their support early on, and for their friendship.

Chloe and Chelsea, two of the three most beautiful faces on the planet, and the people who show me every day just how lucky I am.

And most of all, my beautiful wife Caryn, with all my love, admiration, and gratitude. Our stories are my favorites.

ABOUT THE AUTHOR

Andy Abramowitz lives in Philadelphia with his wife and two daughters. He is a lawyer with a past in music, but he has no musical legacy to correct. This is his first novel.